I0607864

Descension
Dial 323 L O V E
Book #2
By: C.M. Arnold

Printed in the United States of America

This is a work of fiction. Names, characters, businesses, places, events and
incidents are either products of the author's imagination or used in a
fictitious manner. Any resemblance to actual persons, living or dead, or
actual events is purely coincidental.

For information about special discounts available for bulk purchases, sales
promotions, and all other inquiries, email cmarnoldwrites@gmail.com

ISBN 978-0-9997132-2-8 (paperback)
ISBN 978-0-9997132-3-5 (eBook)

Chapter 1

It is the nineteenth day of January and they have been in New Orleans for three weeks. It has been three weeks since the police had invaded 360 Hollywood Place, taking them all in for questioning; three weeks since Rafael got deported back to Cuba; three weeks since Garrett got sent to jail, where he would remain for the next two years. It had been three weeks since he'd let Anjanae go. It had been three weeks since he won them their trial. It had been three weeks since he'd had sex, for money or otherwise. It had been three weeks since he'd been on California soil.

Seven months since he'd been home.

AJ awakes in his temporary bed before the sun rises, after only a few hours of fitful sleep. In a fevered dream he had pushed the crisp white sheets down to his ankles, the pale pink afghan discarded on the floor. There are eight bedrooms in the antebellum mansion; his is on the third floor. He knows it had to have been Maggie's childhood room. The walls are painted in pastels and a white lace curtain hangs around the bay window, where antique dolls and stuffed animals that look like they've never been played with sit pristinely on a bench seat. On top of the big oak dresser are numerous trophies and ribbons. He'd studied them once in the wee hours of one morning or another. Among them are awards for the debate team, math club, and several equestrian competitions. They are all for first place. The walls have no traces that anything has ever defiled them; no rock star posters, no taped-on pictures, no sentimental scribbling. There are only three pictures in the entire room, all of them framed. One is of a steely, grey-eyed preteen girl dressed in a school uniform with her blonde hair pulled back in a ponytail, standing front and center with her arms around two other girls in identical outfits, same classically familiar smile on her face. Another picture is a pretty teenager in a cap and gown with a long shawl around her shoulders that suggests she was the valedictorian, a proud looking man dressed to the nines at her side, smiling, who has the same exact eyes as her. Probably the last picture they took together, he had thought one night while staring at it and wondering how trains get so far off track so quickly. Maggie had taken the master suite on the main floor. Theo, Dominique, and Austin each have their own rooms on the second floor. He is in the silent desolation of someone's past, the one controlling his present and future.

He hasn't been sleeping well, but he blames it on the strange bed and new environment. That's not to say he doesn't like his new environment. He can look out his window and take in the ambiance of the long, manicured drive—oak trees lining both sides—when the morning sun cuts through the slants in the limbs. During the evening he can go sit outside on the veranda under the ceiling fan and sip the sweet tea that always seemed to be available. He can take afternoon walks through the sprawling sugar cane fields. And he does all these peaceful activities every day in an attempt to bring some peace to his life while living at Maggie's family's beautiful plantation.

AJ doesn't know how the mansion has managed to stay so well kept when no one has lived there in the five years since Maggie's mother went to a nursing home. Since they'd been staying there, a maid comes every other evening and cleans. She's a very quiet, older white woman with hair the color of snow. Maggie says this woman has been her family's maid since she was a child. AJ thinks Maggie lies. AJ thinks the family maid had been black. AJ had found another silver picture-framed photo—stuffed deep inside a drawer in his room—of a young, pig-tailed Maggie with her cheek pressed against an older black woman's. The woman had on an unmistakable getup and AJ knew instantly what she was. Also, on one of the nights he couldn't sleep, he had been rummaging through the cupboard downstairs for a light snack when he happened upon an old mammy cookie jar purposefully hidden behind an antique toaster. He thinks Maggie is a lot of things, but a racist is not one of them. On second thought, he supposes he can't even be sure about that. But he assumes she was simply trying to portray a different picture of a plantation than the one Dominique and Theo had in their heads. But it is what it was.

As it is, the white maid rarely says anything to them and never asks any questions. Like why Maggie travels with four younger men or what's caused them all to take refuge out of the blue. Supposedly, in its heyday, Southern Cross had a butler, a groundskeeper, and a chef in addition to a maid. But for obvious reasons Maggie didn't want all those extra eyes around forming their own storylines on her life.

AJ usually admitted defeat on the sleep front a little before dawn. He'd roll out of the bed that wasn't his around five thirty, and amble across the hall to one of the five bathrooms in the house. He'd stand under the spray of the shower, attempting to clean the static from his mind till the water grew cool and snapped him out the space he'd stared off into. Afterwards he'd get dressed and make his way downstairs. There was something eerily comforting about the old mansion's quiet in the morning. He'd tiptoe around once he left his third floor solitude, careful not to wake the others. He rarely bothers to turn on the light in the kitchen as he makes a pot of Folgers. While he waits for it to finish, he's gotten into the routine of walking down the long drive to retrieve the morning paper. The southern air is pleasantly cool in the early hour, the sounds of crickets winding down and birds starting up, each adding another layer of tranquility that he tries to soak up. He'll momentarily go back inside to grab his mug, and then he goes out onto the front porch. He sits on one of the white rockers, sipping his coffee and reading the paper as the sun slowly rises from between the oak trees. He'd never been a coffee drinker before moving to Los Angeles, but has been drinking two cups a morning religiously for at least the last five months. Late nights every night will bring on that addiction, and then it's a hard habit to break.

By the time he goes back inside for his second cup, Maggie is usually up and dressed, pouring herself a full thermos of coffee from his pot. She'll smile her smile, occasionally say good morning or ask him how he'd slept. He'll say good morning back and tell her that he slept well, and then she'll leave in the rental car to go get breakfast. Around nine the others will start to wake and make their way downstairs. Maggie will come back with a box of assorted goodies from her favorite bakery, and then they'll all eat pastries in the parlor like one big happy family, never speaking of their collective dysfunction.

The names Ali and Ray haven't left Maggie's lips once since they've been here. She had immediately hired a real estate agent (the irony not lost on AJ) and had already sold 360 Hollywood Place over the phone and bought a new office, sight unseen, on the 57th floor of a 60-floor high-rise in Downtown LA. Actually, she hadn't bought *an* office on the 57th floor; she bought the 57th floor. Austin had asked why she hadn't just bought the top floor. She told him obviously that would be too obvious.

This is how it has been going almost every morning since they'd arrived. But this morning is different, because this afternoon they have a flight out at twelve. AJ feels confliction over this as he stands under the shower's onslaught, the bathroom shades of dark blue with the lights off and the sun still down. Part of him is happy to be returning to reality and leaving the Deep South denial they have all been living in. He'd had a decent enough time in New Orleans. He'd gone to a couple Pelicans games with Nique, gone bar-hopping on Bourbon Street with Austin a time or two, let Maggie show him around the city, taken a river boat ride with Theo, toured multiple haunted mansions and eaten many a beignet. But it was time to face facts and move on. Another part of him dreads the thought of getting on that plane and going back to Los Angeles. What did he have to go back to? What did he have to look forward to? He thinks he may have cloaked that denial around him like a child does with their favorite blanket. He thinks about the four all-too-close walls of his studio in Koreatown. He thinks about how empty the house in Reseda will be now, how he'll have to explain to his neighbors where he went and what happened to the girlfriend they thought he had. He thinks about all the new lies he'll have to tell. All the new women he'll have to seduce. All the old ones he'll have to go back to sleeping with. And all he feels is hollow.

The water has gone from scalding hot to shivering cold. He doesn't know when it happened, but the droplets sear either way as they pelt his skin repetitively.

He turns off the shower. Steps out. Dries off. He looks into the steamed up mirror. There are dark circles under his eyes that he doesn't particularly care for, and his new facial hair still throws him off every time he catches a glimpse of himself. He'd forgotten to pack a razor and had lazily waited a few days before asking Maggie to borrow the car to go into town to the store (the house is supplied with most accouterments and necessities that a guest needs, but no razor). She told him she liked the scruff and thought he should keep it. Of course, she didn't want him to grow a full beard or anything extreme, but a nice five o'clock shadow kept things sexy and swarthy. So he'd started to shave only once or twice a week, taking care to maintain but not erase what she alluded would make him more profitable.

Back in his room he throws on a clean t-shirt and a pair of sweatpants, something comfortable for flying all afternoon. He pads down the three flights of stairs, reaches the bottom, rounds the corner…

"Yo, I've been waiting for you to come down."

AJ startles and turns to see Dominique sitting in the dark living room with his computer on his lap, the glow from the screen illuminating his face.

"Nique. What the hell are you doing? It's six o'clock in the morning."

"I ain't go to sleep. I've been up all night," Nique says excitedly.

A stinging septum. A rush of adrenaline. Lost focus, refocused, hyper-focused. Numbness. Rinse, repeat.

"Doing what?" AJ asks, shaking his head once to rid his mind of the unwanted memory.

"I told TT to release the mixtape last night. He dropped it on DatPiff and SoundCloud at midnight."

"What?" AJ asks. "It didn't even have a name yet."

"Well I named it. Its already got five thousand downloads and two songs already have quadruple digit plays."

"Are you serious?" AJ says, eyes going wide. Granted, five thousand wouldn't be a lot of downloads for an established artist. But for one who has literally no previous catalog or promo of any kind to speak of, it was damn near miraculous.

"I'm dead serious, bruh," Dominique replies with a full-toothed smile. A smile so wide and genuine AJ knows he can't be lying. "Check it out."

AJ can't help but smile too as he goes to join Nique on the couch. He's never seen him so happy, and he's happy for him. Nique turns the screen towards him, and then AJ stares at the Twitter feed of a trending topic, reoccurring tweets with #DominiqueDavisEP incorporated into them flash before his eyes.

"Self-titled?" AJ asks with a sly smile. "How original."

"Gotta let em know who the new prince of R&B is," Dominique replies. "TT's a fool. He started a hashtag out of the title and has been re-tweeting the link to the download like crazy. You know he's got a lot of followers, too. He's puttin' all them rich Brentwood kids on to my music. He's even tagging producers and famous people. Look," he says enthusiastically, pointing at the screen. "He tagged Drake right there. And Timbaland there. Man, I ain't even gonna know how to act if they respond. You think they're gonna respond?"

"I don't know," AJ replies honestly. On one hand, Turner's persistent approach might come off as annoying and get him blocked. On the other hand, after seeing a link so many times, the people he wanted to click on it might just click on it. And AJ knows once someone actually listens to it, they won't regret it. For this he is sure. "Word of mouth is strong," he adds reassuringly. "All it takes is for the right person to hear it and then tell the right person. And it's been getting a decent amount of downloads, and plays, and re-tweets. I think it's only a matter of time."

Dominique stares seriously for a second at his co-worker, co-writer, and confidant, then nods fervently in agreement and goes back to reading the incoming thoughts on his computer screen.

~

Four hours later the living room is filled with light. Everyone is awake and spread out across the room with their suitcases lined up in a row at the front door, waiting for Maggie to finish getting ready and drive them all to the airport. She walks out of her room rolling her Louis Vuitton luggage set behind her. Her eyes land on Dominique, who's sitting in the recliner with his feet kicked up, and a scowl immediately comes to her face

"Take that fucking shirt off."

"Damn you only been without a man three weeks, Miss Hunter," Nique says with a smart-ass grin. "You already that ravenous?"

"You know what I mean," she says, snapping her fingers and then pointing one at his chest. "Change."

He's sporting the t-shirt he got made at the mall that says *Free My Dawg* in big arching letters across the chest with a blown up picture he'd found on Instagram of Garrett in a pink sweater with his blonde hair straightened to perfection underneath. It was done satirically, of course. Nique really never did care for the pretentious little prick, but he had enough money to make a t-shirt just for shits and giggles.

"Come on, I been wearin' it the entire time we've been here," Nique argues.

"Well we're leavin' here," she retorts in a mocking tone. "You can't be seen wearing that when we land in LA. None of us need to be promoting a convicted prostitute that was linked in the press to us."

That was one of us, AJ thinks, but doesn't say.

"Fine," Dominique consents in a whiny voice. He pulls the t-shirt off over his head and folds it up.

"I think someone went to one too many crawfish boils and ate one too many bowls of gumbo," Maggie comments, taking in his shirtless upper half. "You're looking a little pudgy. Gonna need to get on that treadmill when we get back."

"I'm too pretty to be pudgy," Dominique tells her, stuffing the old shirt into his suitcase and pulling out a new one that's not so loudly decorated. "You wish you could be this effortlessly fine."

"Mmhm," she mutters, fishing her keys out of the new Fendi bag she bought in the French Quarter. "Come on. We have a plane to catch."

~

At the airport waiting for their flight to board, AJ peruses one of the duty-free shops for a new novel to read on the plane while the others thumb through magazines at an adjacent kiosk. He picks out a three hundred-page thriller and a travel size bag of Twizzlers, and as he's checking out he hears a set of familiar laughs. Austin and Dominique are both having a good chuckle over a particular tabloid. Theo is paying them no attention as he skims the latest issue of *Vogue*. AJ pays and walks over to them

"Look at this," Austin cackles, flipping the cover back closed so he can see it.

"Shit's pure comedy," Dominique snickers.

AJ sees Garrett's mug shot in one of the bubbles off to the side of the main focus of the cover, which is some smiling pop starlet with supposed love life problems. The words under Garrett's face read, *Soap Star's real torrid life as secret gigolo juicier than his storyline. How daytime's new dreamboat went from sharing a set to sharing a cell in a matter of months.* Dominique and Austin are both still cracking up as they flip pages to show him the inside story. AJ doesn't find it funny. He doesn't find it funny at all. He wonders if they've already forgotten how close they all came to getting locked away. But again, he says nothing.

Suddenly Maggie appears out of nowhere behind them and rips the tabloid out of their hands, returning it to the appointed slot on the rack with a reprimanding look. She walks away from them without another word, Starbucks cup in hand.

They board shortly later, and once they're in the air and at their cruising altitude, Dominique turns his laptop back on. A few online publications are actually reviewing his free EP. Every few minutes he elbows AJ, who's sitting next to him, to show him another new blurb of personal praise.

"Dominique Davis is the younger, more risk taking Maxwell," AJ reads aloud from the screen. "Well that's good," he says, looking back to Nique. "Maxwell's a great singer."

"Look at this one," Dominique says with a shit-eating smirk, changing tabs to another review. "Davis is the sexier Leon Bridges."

"Damn," AJ replies. "That's a little harsh. I mean, good for you, though."

"And this one," Dominique points to another line, still smiling. "He's Trey Songz if Trey Songz could actually sing."

"Don't get on these peoples' bad sides," AJ says.

"They love me. This one says 'Dominique Davis's EP is a solid first effort. His sound is textured, alternative, funky, smooth soul. A fresh new voice in R&B that transcends the genre and will undoubtedly have labels scrambling to scoop him up'." Dominique looks up at AJ. "They're right, too. Look at all the agents in my DMs." He switches tabs again and AJ is face to face with his friends overflowing inbox.

"That's crazy," AJ says in awe, because it is. It is crazy. This is the overnight success thing that people talk and dream about.

"Your boy's bout to blow!" Dominique exclaims.

"We're in a first class cabin full of white people," Maggie says in a lowered voice from across the aisle. "Can we keep the urbanity to a minimum for the people who probably just interpreted your last sentiment as you either about to experience some kind of violent combustion or perform mile-high fellatio."

Dominique rolls his eyes, then says quietly to AJ, "She's just salty cause she's 'bout to lose another employee."

AJ smiles in agreement, even as a wave of abandonment washes over him.

Because he knows he's about to lose someone else. Again.

~

Five hours later AJ is back in LA, driving down La Brea on his way home. It does feel good to be back in his car, the familiar smell of leather and the lingering notes of the cologne he applies before dates welcoming his return to what he's grown used to. The scenery of the city that has become his dwelling passes by through the window, shimmering in the evening sun through the slits in the palm tree leaves. There's a crowd of people gathered at the corner of 8th Street. He wonders why for a moment, but then sees the big purple van and smiles.

He pulls off and parks in a vacant spot along the street. The scent of suitable food is in the air as he walks up to what has become one of the most popular food trucks in LA. He sees from the menu out front that today's theme is soul food, except that the soul is spelled Seoul in honor of the chef's heritage. Korean-infused country fixins, he's not sure what that entails, but he's sure that it is good. There's a long line, so AJ goes around back and peeks his head in the side window. There's a blonde girl in there with him. At first glance AJ assumes its Mackenzie. But then he sees that it's not. She's got long blonde hair like Mackenzie, about the same height as Mackenzie, but much tanner. Her flat orange stomach is on display in a crop-top version of the t-shirts Jae had mass made with his logo on it. She's leaned up against the soft drink machine, texting on an iPhone with press-on nails and blowing a pink Bazooka bubble through her overly glossed lips. She's not paying attention and Jae is busy serving, so he patiently waits. When his friend turns around to grab the next Styrofoam container, his eyes go wide, and AJ can't help but to smile at his excitement.

"The boy is back from the bayou!" Jae exclaims, momentarily disregarding his work and coming over to the side window. He holds out his fist and AJ pounds it.

"I have returned."

Jae nudges the blonde. "Yo, Britt, this is my ace chingu, my brother from another, my main man, the one and only AJ Brooks."

"In the flesh and thankfully not stripes," AJ says cheekily.

When the girl looks up from her phone AJ notices that her eyes are blue like Mackenzie's, too. He smiles to himself while thinking that Jae clearly has a type. She smiles at him, but her face isn't nearly as kind as Mackenzie's.

"Nice to meet you," she says; bubble popping and lips smacking as she sucks the gum back into her mouth. "Jae's told me lots about you."

"Hopefully not too much," AJ says with a secretive smile.

Jae discreetly shakes his head behind her to confirm that he hasn't. "AJ, this is my new girlfriend, Brittany."

AJ wants to ask what happened to Mackenzie, and he will later, but for now he holds out his hand to the new girl and smiles politely. "Nice to meet you, too, Brittany."

She gives his hand a weak shake, and when she lets go, she goes right back to texting on her phone. The crowd outside the truck is growing and starting to sound impatient. Jae looks over his shoulder and then back to AJ.

"Hey, I'll be back around nine tonight," Jae tells him. "I'll stop by?"

"Yeah," AJ says. "That's cool. I'll be in my apartment."

The little lonely studio is just how he left it, minus edible food. He knows he'll have to go to the store in the morning; not much keeps for three weeks and his cupboards are bare. But for the night a bowl of dry cereal will do. He's physically and emotionally depleted from being up since the wee hours of the morning and traveling all day. All he wants to do is settle back in and sleep in his own bed. That's when he remembers that there should be a few beers in the fridge. AJ isn't one of those guys that keeps his place stocked with booze at all times, but he had picked up a case at the supermarket not long before shit hit the fan. And when he takes a look he's happy to find that there are still four left.

An hour later he's on the couch in his pajamas, he's had a healthy helping of cheerios and two Heinekens, and has just made it to page number two hundred in the book he started that morning when there's a knock on his door. He puts a bookmark in his novel and gets up. Jae stands there with a Styrofoam takeout container of food in one hand and a folded up t-shirt in the other.

"Pulled Korean pork barbecue, thick macaroni, baked beans, greens, and a Jae in LA promotional shirt, free of charge for my best friend," Jae proclaims as he walks in and sits the food down on the coffee table. He then turns back around and hands AJ the t-shirt that reads *JAE N LA. Delicious Food To Go. Look For The Ugly Purple Truck & Follow Us On Twitter @JaesTruckLA.* "You don't have to wear it when you go visit your rich lady friends, but you certainly can."

"I'll keep that in mind," AJ laughs, folding the shirt back up nice and then walking into his kitchenette area. "You want a beer?"

"Sure," Jae says, plopping down on the couch.

AJ grabs the last two Heinekens and a fork, and then joins Jae on the couch, handing him one of the green glass bottles.

"Thanks," Jae says, following AJ's lead and popping the lid off on the edge of the table.

"Thank you for the food," AJ tells him, immediately digging into the macaroni. "You didn't have to bring me anything."

"Well I didn't know if that haughty bitch had been feeding you while you were away," Jae says flippantly, taking a sip of his beer. "It was the least I could do."

AJ snorts. "I was well fed." He covers his mouth as he chews, manners garnered from keeping company with wealthy women. "Probably ate too much." He takes a drink and swallows. "So many restaurants, and chefs, and street vendors. Definitely a foodie place, you'd love it down there."

"So N.O. was all that?"

"It was cool," AJ say laxly, scooping some greens onto his fork with a bite of barbecue. "I'm glad to be back, though." He pauses before putting the fork in his mouth. "I guess."

"What was the point of her dragging you all out there, though?" Jae asks him. "I mean you all won your trial...beat your case...evaded charges...whatever." He leans back against the couch cushion. "I don't know *how*," he adds contemplatively. "The evidence was rather glaring. No offense. I'm pumped that you're a free man and all, I'm just saying." He takes a drink and swallows. "I suppose that the British kid technically was the only one caught with his hand in the metaphorical cookie jar. Still. Luck was on your side, brother."

"I slept with the judge," AJ mutters out of the blue in-between bites of food.

Jae snorts and then takes another sip of his beer.

AJ glances up. "You think I'm kidding."

Jae's face goes from a smirk, to a smile, to mouth open in shock. "What..." He sits back up straight and stares at his friend in disbelief. "What...you're serious?"

AJ puts his fork down and sighs. "I was convinced we were all going to go to jail. I was thinking irrationally, though, in hindsight, smartly. I got her home address from a client. Went over there one night." He picks his beer back up and takes a long drink before continuing. "Spent a few hours with her. Convinced her to pin it all on Garrett. Extradite the rest of us. Of course there wasn't anything I could do for Rafael, he was screwed as soon as they ran his name when we got arrested." He shakes his head once. "Anyway. I didn't know if she'd really do what I said. But she did." He takes another sip. "Five walking away is better than none, I guess."

Jae blinks a couple of times. "Wow...that's...that is cray."

"I'm getting to the point where nothing surprises me anymore," AJ replies, closing his food container and pushing it away. "Enough about me, though," he says, settling back against the couch and crossing one leg over the other. "Let's talk about the girl you've got riding around in your van, serving sodas and sporting your name on her chest." He gives Jae good-natured smirk. "Tell me what the hell's up with that."

"I know," Jae laughs self-deprecatingly. "It's moving kind of fast, but I kind of really like her."

"What happened to Mackenzie?"

"We broke up," Jae tells him. "We actually broke up a couple of weeks before you left for New Orleans. I meant to tell you, but you had a lot on your plate. The whole ordeal with Julius. Breaking up with Anjanae. The arrest. I didn't want to burden you with my relationship woes." He takes a sip of beer. "Anyways, she got accepted into the graduate program she wanted in D.C. Huge opportunity, only a few make the cut. We talked about doing the whole long distance thing, but in the end decided we'd just be friends. It was amicable…just simply wasn't meant to be."

"So Brittany."

"Yeah, Brittany." Jae smiles, puppy love expression. "I met her out on Redondo Beach. Had the food truck out there one afternoon during peak lunch time. It was poppin', as they say. Line almost to the ocean. And she comes up out of the water in this little bikini, hair all wet and skin all tan. This old man let her cut in front of him. Everybody waiting started pitching a fit. I stood up for her, and when she paid for her food…she'd slipped her number behind one of the bills." Jae is cheesing proudly. "We've been inseparable ever since."

"What does she do?"

"She works at a surf shop on Tuesdays, but other than that she's usually on the truck with me. She needs a relatively open schedule because she–"

"Wants to be an actress?" AJ guesses knowingly

"Yeah. I know," Jae replies with a timid smile. "But she's realistic. She says if it doesn't happen she'll be ok. She went to dental hygienist school and has a certificate. So she can always do that."

AJ nods, keeping his face neutral as he takes another sip.

"There's just something about her," Jae muses aloud. "She's simple, and cool, and so pretty. We have fun. And I really like having her out there on the road with me." He takes a drink and continues on wistfully. "The food truck business can get lonely. Before I just had some high school kids helping me. Now I've got me a right hand lady, a partner in crime. I don't know, I guess you could say I'm smitten." He looks over at his friend, who is gulping the last little bit of the liquid out of the green glass bottle. "I'm sorry," Jae adds quickly, consciously. "I don't mean to keep rambling on about squishy feelings when you've just gone through a…well when you've lost…I just don't mean to be insensitive."

AJ smiles. "It's cool, Jae. I'm fine," he says, sitting the empty bottle down on the coffee table. "It is what it is."

Chapter 2

Across town in Santa Monica, Austin is warming up a frozen dinner, sporting an Ohio State t-shirt and sweats after showering. He's not expecting any more out of the night other than collapsing on his comfy couch, watching *SportsCenter*, throwing back a few Bud Lights, and chowing down on some fake fettuccini. He's just about to grab a fork from the drawer when there's a knock at his door. He's taken aback; nobody ever comes to visit.

When he opens the door, Hermosa is standing there in her work uniform, looking flushed and flustered. But she's smiling. She's smiling so big.

"Mo…" He says, shocked, but not unhappy to see her. "What are you–"

"I thought you went to jail," she blurts out exasperatedly, unable to hold back the emotion in her voice. "Your phone didn't ring…I didn't know…I didn't know how to get ahold of you. I was about to start calling correctional facilities but I didn't know what I would say or if they would let me…and then I was like…well I'll write him I guess, but do I put the jail's address or…or is it like the county jail or the state or–"

"I didn't go to jail," he says evenly in what he hopes is a calming tone. "We won our case. I don't know how, but we did."

"The last time I talked to you, you told me you thought that you were going to lose. You had court the next morning and then…and then I never heard from you again."

"I changed my number," he tells her apologetically. "Maggie made all of us as a precaution. I'm sorry. I should have called you," he continues sincerely. "We went to New Orleans afterwards to lay low for a while. I just got back a couple of hours ago."

"I just thought…I mean…your truck was gone," she rambles absently. "I go by every day after I leave work. One week, two weeks, it's still not there. And then I go by today and…." She lets out a little relieved laugh. "And it's there…your truck…I came straight up. I thought…I thought I'd never see you again."

"I'm really sorry. I really should ha–"

Suddenly she's kissing him, hands on his face, lips on his. He's surprised at first, but recovers quickly and kisses her back. He moves one hand to gently cup the back of her head, and the other goes to the small of her back to draw her nearer. She's fierce and firm in the way she molds her mouth to his, and it draws the same kind of passion from him. This is what he's wanted, for her to see him as more than a friend, for her to want him like this, like he wants her. This is what he'd hoped for, but as her tongue slips into his mouth and she starts to back him towards the bedroom, he forces himself to stop. He pulls away and has to take a ragged breath before he can speak, because he must have stopped breathing, or he was just breathing her, and God, she smells so good, like vanilla or cinnamon or something. She moves back in before he can get any words out, and he stops her by softly placing two hands high enough on her waist for it not to be misconstrued, stilling her motion. She looks confused now, all big brown eyes and bit lips and brown hair falling in her face...and she's so beautiful. He has to take another breath. And then he looks her in her eyes.

"Are you sure you want to do this?" He asks her, taking a serious yet tender tone with her. "Because I know you said–"

"I want to do this," she replies without hesitation, staring right up into his eyes. "I'm sure."

"Okay." He nods his head, trying to soak up what he's feeling. "Okay."

"Okay?" She reiterates, continuing to stare up at him. "So are you like going to kiss me or..." Her lips start to quirk into a grin at the corners. "Or am I going to have to take the lead and make all the moves? Because I don't want to cross no line and make you feel like I'm taking advanta–"

He silences her by sealing his mouth back to hers and sweeping her feet up off the ground with ease, causing her to squeal with laughter as she wraps her legs around him. He smiles against her mouth and carries her to his bedroom.

Forty-five minutes later they're both on their backs on the bed, staring up at the celling with smiles on their faces as they try to catch their breath.

"It may be distasteful for me to say this," she murmurs when she regains her ability to speak. "But I see now why people pay you."

He chuckles. "Would you believe that a year ago I didn't know how to have sex?"

She turns on her side and eyes him skeptically. "You didn't have sex till a year ago?

He rolls so he's facing her. "I've been havin' sex since I was sixteen. I just didn't learn how to do it right till last year."

She laughs. "Don't worry. I bet there are many men much older than you that still don't know how to *do it right*." She leans in closer to him and strokes his smiling lips with a single finger. "I am glad you learned, though," she says lowly with a grin.

He kisses her fingertip. "I'm glad you're here."

She moves her finger from his lips and kisses him. "Me too."

He threads a hand through her long hair. Their noses rest against each other, mouths less than a millimeter away as they bask in the moment together.

"Where do we go from here?" He asks quietly after a few minutes.

She sighs, retracting her eyes from his. "I don't know." Her hand is smoothing the skin from the base of his throat down over his hard and chiseled chest. "Why do we have to go anywhere? Why can't we just stay here?"

"We can."

"I just…I don't want a complicated relationship…you know?" She says, grappling over heart and mind matters while still stroking his skin. "I want this to feel how it feels right now. I want us not to change. So I think we should just let what happens happen, and not try to make more out of it and ruin it."

"Okay."

"Okay?"

He smiles. "Yeah." Letting her know with a single word that even though he'd like for her to be his girlfriend, he respects what she wants.

She smiles back. They stare at each other in the stillness of the falling night, eyes twinkling in the slowly darkening room.

"You want to go again?" He asks her with his boyish grin.

She raises an eyebrow at him playfully. "Can you go again?"

"Mo…I'm a pro."

This makes her giggle, and she only giggles harder when he rolls her under him and attacks her neck with tickling kisses.

Chapter 3

Theo is outfitted in one of his silk pajama sets, laid back on his white leather couch with his Versace slipper clad feet propped up on the matching ottoman. He's glad to be back in his luxury loft, enjoying a bowl of popcorn and a glass of chardonnay while he goes through the mail he accumulated in his three-week absence. The T.V. is on and playing low in the background as he thumbs the newest Neiman Marcus catalogue.

"In the wake of Troy Langham's big announcement yesterday, Twitter shows their support for the newly out of the closet actor," a reporter's voice says.

Theo's head snaps up.

"Langham surprised fans yesterday by revealing that he is divorcing his wife of twenty years, Patrice Grove, and that he is currently in a relationship with a man. The reveal came yesterday during a sit down interview with Diana Sawyer for her Oscars Special. Langham, who is nominated for two awards at this year's Oscars, was discussing the downfalls to his highly successful career when the interview took a very interesting twist that even seemed to shock Sawyer herself."

A clip plays on the screen.

"I've known I was gay for a long time," Troy says in an intimate studio setting across from the acclaimed journalist. "I've been gay forever. I was gay when my career started. And my career one hundred percent is what kept me in the closet. There was nobody in my ear telling me that I needed to keep this to myself, but there didn't need to be. The type of roles I was always cast in, the ladies man persona, the wordless notion that…if you want to support yourself, you need to be who the world thinks you are. Only a very select few knew the truth."

"What's different now?" Diane had asked.

"I've lived my entire life in fear of being outed," Troy continued. "In the last month I've had moments where that fear has been escalated…and afterwards I thought…why let a reporter or a tabloid have the power to do what you should have done a long time ago? Take control of the story. Take control of your life. I'm forty years old. I'm tired of hiding, of not being happy. I've sacrificed for my success, now it's time to enjoy it. I've met a really great man recently who has helped me accept who I am, and who I want to be able to be publicly with. When you meet someone so special...so worth it...that's what's different."

The clip cuts out and the reporter's voice returns.

"That man is said to be Hollywood stylist Rashad Waverly, whom Langham was pictured with in an Instagram post he shared with followers yesterday following his interview. Capturing the photo with simply one word: Happiness."

That Instagram image is now on the screen. Troy smiling with his arm around a tall, dapperly dressed black man Theo has never seen before.

"Langham told Sawyer that he will always have love for his wife, whom he says at one point he thought made him straight, and that he will always consider her a friend and confidant. When asked if she knew he was gay, he says he doesn't kn–"

Theo can no longer concentrate on what's being said, heat boiling in his veins and steaming his brain over with disbelief. He jumps up off of the couch, sending his bowl of popcorn flying, and snatches his phone off the counter in the kitchen. He dials Maggie's number because he doesn't have Troy's. He's been having sex with Troy for nearly three years and doesn't have the faintest clue what the digits are. A man he's been inside of and had his mouth on, and who's been inside of and had his mouth on him, and he has no idea how to get hold of him.

"Yes, dear?" Maggie answers.

"Have you seen the news?"

"Oh that plane that disappeared over Canada? I know, how horrible, right?"

"Entertainment news," he seethes tersely, no patience for her tonight. "Have you seen any *entertainment* news?"

"I've been home two hours, Theo," she retorts back curtly. "I haven't had the time."

"Troy came out while we were gone," he blurts out.

"Oh...well good for him."

"No," he says in a harsh tone that he wishes he could control because he knows it makes him sound overly emotional. "Not good for him. He has a boyfriend."

"Theo...."

"I need his number," he tells rather than asks her.

"I don't think that's a good idea..."

"*Give* me his number."

She sighs. "Fine. But you *better* not be stupid with it."

He hangs up on her as soon as he gets it and immediately dials the number. But Troy doesn't answer. He's not surprised. He's sure that he's been getting a lot of phone calls in the last few days for statements and questions, and he'd be stupid if he did answer some unknown number. Theo texts him then. Troy replies a few minutes later and agrees to meet. He's been staying at the Beverley Wilshire since splitting with Patrice because it's close to his house and paparazzi aren't allowed on the premises. An hour later Theo's knocking on his hotel room door—not an unfamiliar motion—and Troy lets him in to his penthouse suite.

For a moment the two men just stand there, staring at each other. Even as anger makes the hair on his arms stand, Theo can't help but to be attracted to Troy. He seems at ease—unlike him—a thousand pounds lifted off his shoulders, standing there in a light sweater and cropped jeans, barefoot, pushing his dark blonde hair back with his hand that no longer has a wedding band on it.

"So you're out?" Theo asks rhetorically, dryly, finally breaking the silence.

"I am," Troy replies with an easy smile. He looks happy, and Theo wants to be happy for him, but it's not that easy. It's far from easy. However selfish he may be for feeling the way that he feels, he can't help it.

Theo tilts his head with a serious stare. "How do you go from being in that room when Maggie was telling everybody it all might come out…and you're standing there in the corner scowling and seething and looking downright disgusted by the prospect of the world knowing your preferences…to literally not even a month later coming out as a gay man on national television just as proud as can be?"

Troy sighs, walking over to the dresser where a glass of wine sits. "It wasn't that I was disgusted by you or what we've done; I didn't want my name connected to a brothel, you can't fault me for that." He takes a small sip and turns back around to face him. "Me being forced out under those circumstances would have been totally different than what I did on my own accord yesterday, and you know it."

Theo looks down, smirks, and then looks back up. "So who is this guy that you've fallen into *happiness* with overnight?"

"It wasn't overnight," Troy states calmly, sitting his glass down so he can pour one for Theo. "He styled me for a shoot about a year ago. We hit it off as friends, nothing less nothing more. I knew he was gay, he didn't know I was." He walks to Theo, hands him the glass, and then strides off in the opposite direction with his back to him again. "Anyway, the more we hung out, the more comfortable I got with him. A few months ago I confided in him that I was in the closet. He was really supportive, really relatable. And then one day he asked me if I wanted to be more than friends…and I did."

"How romantic," Theo says, facetiously. He takes one long drink from the glass he was given and then discards it on the nightstand. "You should write a high budget biopic based on it, option it to your director friends, and land your first gay role starring as yourself. Bet you'll get an Oscar for it."

"I don't know why you're being like this," Troy says, shaking his head. "I thought you would be happy for me. I thought– "

"It was supposed to be me!" Theo yells with flailing arms, silencing a shocked Troy in an instance. "I was the person who knew your secrets, I was the first man you were with, I was the one you were yourself with…for *years*. And then you just go…" His thought trails off. He rubs a hand over his face, trying to calm himself down. "And then you just go and come out with another man." He locks eyes with Troy, face screwing up in anger. "How?"

"You never didn't take the money, Theo," Troy tells him plainly.

And it's true.

Theo always took the money.

"What was I supposed to think?" Troy asks him, staring to pace now himself. "Was I supposed to let myself fall for an escort? Let myself think that this would be more than a *paid* exchange someday?"

"You know it was more than a paid exchange," Theo says flatly, standing perfectly still. "You know it wasn't just me coming over, servicing you, and then leaving. We spent *time* together."

"Time that you were royally compensated for," Troy retorts calmly, coming to a stop a few feet away from him. "And that was fine. It was worth it being able to be myself for a few hours when I wasn't ready to be myself in front of the world. I truly enjoyed our time together. I'll never regret it or you, Theo. I won't." He pauses, staring his former lover somberly in the eyes. "But now it's time for me to be with someone who sees me as more than revenue. And that's not you."

The two men hold each other's gaze until Theo looks down. He nods, no longer looking angry, puts his hands in his pockets, and walks to the door. Troy watches him quietly.

"I am happy for you," Theo says at the last minute, looking up before he opens the door. "And I apologize for my selfishness."

Troy gives a small smile and nods.

"I hope you have a great life," Theo tells him definitively, sincerely. And then he lets himself out of Troy's hotel room for the last time.

Chapter 4

The air smells like fresh starts, new renovations, and opulence incarnate when the boys step off the elevator on the 57th floor. It's their first day seeing the new office space from which Maggie will now be running her business. In the same building medical specialists, number crunchers, and other white-collar citizens run their respective businesses. But the 57th floor is strictly devoted to the lucrative profession of sex. Not that an innocent individual with the intentions of remedying their plantar fasciitis, who on their way to their podiatrist accidently gets off on their floor, would see anything suggestively suspicious. The hall is marble paved. The walls are artwork adorned. The different doors are unmarked.

AJ, Theo, Dominique, and Austin round the corner into a large open area. A long white sectional made for lounging is against a large window overlooking Downtown Los Angeles, the light that's let in bouncing off of an enormously majestic chandelier hanging from the ceiling. The couch is flanked by two leather love seats on either side. The bar cart sits in the corner, stocked with top shelf liquor, as always. A zebra skin rug is thrown diagonally across the floor in the middle of the room. A Venetian table sits atop it, housing an array of magazines and a vase of fresh flowers. The billiards table is against the back wall. Maggie's same mahogany desk is off to the side, but not enclosed. She smiles and stands when she sees they've arrived.

"Well. How do you like it?" She asks them. The big, proud, pleased smile on her face says exactly how she feels about it all.

"It's alright," Theo replies indifferently. He briefly glances around, then walks straight to the bar cart, pours himself a drink, and plops down on the couch.

Maggie stares at him for a second, a bit perplexed, and then with half a head shake moves on to the start of the hall.

"I think it's pretty," Austin offers.

"Thank you for noticing, Austin. I think it's quite pretty myself," she replies, turning to face them. "I had the contractors knock down a few walls—eliminate the offices, make more room—strip the floors and redo them, and install the amenities we would need. Got rid of the regular bathroom they had with two sinks and two stalls and created a complete cleansing masterpiece. Seriously, you have to see it. Floor to ceiling mirrors. Spacious vanity. Showers with detachable heads."

"Who's that for?" Dominique asks cheekily.

AJ and Austin grin to themselves.

"I sent the interior decorator a sketch of what I had in mind," Maggie proceeds, paying them no mind. "And she brought together some fabulous art and furniture pieces."

"What chu tell her you do?" Dominique probes, purposefully being pesky.

"Behind door one is the workout room," Maggie says, still ignoring the smart remarks. "Got some new equipment I think you all will like."

"I feel like I'm in a game show," AJ says under his breath as they all follow her down the hall. Nique and Austin snort.

"Behind door two is the washroom," Maggie continues. "Again, I think you all will be really impressed."

They all come to a stop in front of the last door.

"Behind door three...well...there's nothing behind door three," she admits. "Not yet anyway. I've got some free space to figure out what I want to do with."

"Throw some beds in that bitch and it'll be a one stop shop," Dominique offers, stopping to check himself out in one of the many mirrors. He pulls a comb from his back pocket and runs it over his well-kept waves.

Maggie gives him a look. "Who are you getting all pretty for?" She interrogates suspiciously. "You don't have a client scheduled for tonight."

"I got a meeting with a record exec in an hour," he replies, slipping his comb back into his pocket and walking to the bar cart to pour him a brandy.

"The one you texted me about?" AJ asks, following him back out into the main lounge area.

"Yup. The big label." Dominique drops an ice cube in his drink and takes a sip.

"Well don't take the first deal you get offered," Maggie tells him, imparting her self-serving kind of wisdom, coming to take a seat behind her desk.

"If they offer me a good deal...I'm takin' it," he tells her straightly, leaning up against the arm of the couch.

"Dominique, you can't just make rash decisions like that," Maggie says, giving him an exasperated look. "You have to take your time and read over all the fine print, and even if you do, you won't know what half of it means. These companies will try to play you with big words and hidden traps. That's what they do. You have to be careful. Here," she picks her purse up off the floor. "Why don't I go with you."

"Yeah. Let me take my pimp with me up into a business meeting," he remarks sarcastically. "That's a good look. Nice lil first impression."

She sits her purse back down and gives him a look.

"I ain't stupid, Miss Hunter," Dominique tells her seriously. "I know you think cause you swept my ass up off the streets and saved me from a supposed life of gangbanging that I'm a dumb lump of putty forever indebted to you. But I'm not. If they offer me a good deal I'm *going* to take it." He tips his head at her with a smile and raises his glass. "As they say in your hometown, *believe dat*."

AJ smiles to himself as he stares at the floor with his hands in his pockets, proud of Nique for standing up to her and setting her straight.

Maggie puts on her artificially sweet smile. "Don't forget what happened to the last person you knew who was running too fast towards the spotlight."

"And don't you forget that some cops dress like regular folk," Dominique retorts.

She disregards what he's just said to her completely and starts opening the stack of mail on her desk. They all know that she won't speak a word of what happened with her former fling. To do so would be belittling, and she would rather bring literally any and everybody else down before she brings herself down.

"Oh, here's my Oscars invitation finally," she comments idly, opening a rather lavish looking envelope. "Must have got lost. We'll have to go shopping this week for new outfits, Theo."

"You can't be serious right now," Theo says blankly, turning his head to give her an incredulous look from his spot on the couch.

"What?" She asks obliviously, looking up. "You always go with me."

"Troy is going to be there," he states, as if she should naturally know better, and then he looks back away and starts nursing his glass again. "I'm not about to be in the same room as that man."

"Oh my God," Maggie mutters to herself, rolling her eyes as if she thinks he's being dramatic, and then goes back to opening mail.

"What's his issue with the Langham guy?" Austin asks AJ in a lowered voice.

"Troy just came out of the closet and into a relationship with a man…who is not Theo," AJ whispers back, having seen the news.

"Ohh," Austin replies, making a pained face.

"So you lost your favorite client," Dominique says carelessly to Theo. "AJ lost two girlfriends in one day last month. Look at bruh, he's fine."

AJ looks off to the side and shakes his head.

"Time heals all," Nique continues to wax philosophically. "Plus, if new dude don't fuck him right you know he's gonna be callin you." He takes a sip and smirks to himself. "Homie looks like he probably be puttin it down though. Your mans clearly know chocolate the way to go."

Theo flexes his fist and takes a long drink.

"You're being ridiculously childish, Theo," Maggie says, setting her mail aside and looking back up. "It is a huge event in a huge theater. You probably are not even going to run into him."

"I know I'm not going to run into him because I'm not going," he tells her flat out, cutting his eyes to make sure she gets it.

"Fine," she sighs. "Andrew will go with me."

AJ's head shoots up. "Oh…I don't…you should take Nique or Austin."

"I didn't ask Nique or Austin, I asked you. You're going."

"K," he consents quietly, not bothering to tell her that she needs to look up the definition of *asking* next time she has access to a dictionary.

"Two weeks from Sunday night. Mark your calendar. I'll buy you a new tux." She flicks the mouse of her desktop Mac and glances at the screen. "None of you have dates tonight besides Andrew. So go frolic in your freedom. Sing songs, get signed, live the aspirational life you all so desperately cling to."

"You ain't gotta tell me twice," Dominique says, draining his glass, returning it to the cart, and walking towards the elevators. "Y'all pray for me."

"Good luck tonight, Nique," AJ tells him as he passes.

"Good lookin out, bruh. I'll let you know how it goes."

He presses the button, it dings, and he climbs aboard. AJ can't help but to wonder if this was Nique's first and last visit to the new office. For Nique's sake he hopes so. AJ genuinely wants his friend to win.

Austin turns to him then. "You wanna go get a drink before your date? I saw a bar down the street."

"Sure," AJ replies. He glances over at Maggie before he leaves. "Mrs. Kelly, right?" He asks to be sure. It was Monday, after all.

"No, Mrs. Kelly has been bumped off of Mondays to accommodate your knew Monday," she tells him without looking up. "I'll be moving her to another day."

"But Mrs. Kelly has had Monday night forever…Mrs. Kelly is a very well paying regular…"

"Your new client takes precedence over everyone else," Maggie tells him flatly without looking up from the screen.

"Ok…well…text me the address I guess," AJ says, assuming he's not privy to an explanation and accepting it for what it is because what does it matter.

"You already have her address," she says then. "You've seen her once before."

"Oh." Realization hits him. "*Oh*."

Maggie looks up then, smiling with her eyes. "Yes."

Austin looks like he wants to ask, but he doesn't. The two walk to the elevators together. AJ looks back before pressing the down button.

"You wanna come with us, Theo?"

"Nah," Theo replies from the couch. "I'm cool here." He drains his glass. "Thanks for askin, though."

"Ok," AJ says tentatively, pausing and then stepping onto the elevator with Austin when the doors open. He knows how Theo feels. He knows how heartbreak feels. And he knows that he himself doesn't really want to go out to a bar and act happy when he isn't. He doesn't really want to go have sex with Judge Esque later. He doesn't really want to go anywhere anymore. But he has to push through it. He tells himself he's pushing through it, even though he has no idea how to make himself feel any less hollow than he actively feels.

The doors close and they descend.

Chapter 5

The bar is a little brick building with flashing lights that spell out OPEN in the one window, and a faded sign plastered just under the overhang of the roof that reads THE BLUE BAR. It's an unoriginal name, but it suits the little out of place brick building that's crammed between skyscrapers and all but dwarfed by the adjacent high-rises towering over it. A bell chimes when they walk through the door, and the sound is oddly welcoming. The lights are low and there's classic rock playing in the background. There are a few booths against the wall; some girls are having small talk and wine. A few tables in the middle; some guys are having burgers and beers. A pool table and a dartboard in the back; some friends are doing shots and playing games. Then there's of course the bar itself, a high-set countertop that stretches the circumference of the front. There are some loners on stools: an old man with nothing but Southern Comfort for company, a young guy popping peanuts and working on a Budlight, and a middle-aged woman with a vodka spritzer and cheap shoes that suggest she wouldn't be able to afford their time should one of them spark the conversation. Behind the counter are cabinets of glasses and shelves of liquor, anything you could want from the expensive stuff to the cheap stuff and everything in between. The walls are decorated in sports memorabilia; blue Dodgers banners, yellow and purple Lakers jerseys, and Bruins foam fingers.

Austin instantly likes it. It's much less pretentious than many of the other bars, clubs, and hotspots he's visited since moving to LA. It has a homey feel, a relaxed environment that's not trying to be more than what it is. A bar.

He and AJ sidle up to the counter and pull up a stool. The bartender on duty is a young guy of about twenty-six or twenty-seven. His skin is the complexion of someone who more than likely has a mixed ethnicity. His stature is neither short nor tall, his figure somewhat dainty. He's sporting hair that's trimmed neat on the sides, with well-gelled dark curls left to grow naturally on the rest of his head. He possesses the slightest of stubble and wears black coke bottles glasses that suggest he's a hipster, nerd, or both. The short-sleeved pale purple shirt that's tucked into a pair of well-tailored pewter pants says he takes his appearance seriously. His nametag says his name is Calvin. He tops off the old man's drink and then makes his way over to them, smiling genially in the way someone in search of good tips does.

"What can I get you guys?" He asks them, upbeat tone in his voice.

"I'll take a Jack and Coke," Austin says.

"Woodford Reserve on the rocks," AJ replies.

"Alright, I'll be right back with it," the bartender replies, turning from them with a smile and strutting away with a slight switch in his hips.

There are a few steel cans of peanuts lining the bar. AJ and Austin both reach for the nearest one and grab a handful.

"Nice place," AJ comments, looking down at the varnished counter while absently peeling the shell off a peanut. "Quaint."

"Yeah, I like it," Austin replies, plunking a peanut in his mouth.

"And so conveniently located," AJ adds, the dryness in his voice evident no matter how hard he tries to hide it, dropping a peanut into his own mouth.

"I guess it's kinda dumb for us to come over here and pay for drinks when we got a full bar-cart back at the office, huh?"

"I feel like we pay for those, too," AJ tells him sagely. "Just not with money."

Austin smirks as he pops another peanut. "You sayin our bodies built that new office?"

"I'm saying she certainly must have been saving her money," AJ says, sweeping the discarded shells into a neat and manageable little pile.

Austin cracks another one. "It was pretty nice, wasn't it?"

"Better than most pimps' headquarters I'd say."

Austin laughs.

The bartender comes back. He lays down two napkins and places their drinks down on top of them. "There you go, boys. Let me know if you need anything else. My name's Calvin."

"My name's Austin and this here is AJ," Austin introduces himself and his co-worker to the bartender randomly. "You'll probably be seein' a lot of us. Our uh…corporation…just moved in to one of the high-rises next door."

"Oh really. What do you all do?"

"We're in sales," AJ says before Austin can fumble again, smirking off to the side. "Marketing. That type of thing."

"Cool, cool," Calvin says. "I mean…probably boring work for you all. But good money."

"For sure," AJ replies with arid ambiguity, and Austin has to shake his head at his friend's glibness.

"Alright," Calvin says, throwing his towel over his shoulder and turning to go serve the rest of the bar. "Holler when you need a refill."

"Thanks," they both reply.

Austin takes a sip of his drink. He is usually strictly a beer guy, but every once in awhile he treats himself to something different, and on those occasions it is always Jack and Coke. That had been his pops' drink. And taking that first sip, well, it practically conjures his father's image. It's been a couple weeks since he talked to him. His pops had been out of town in some desolate part of Ohio without cell service, laying asphalt for the company when Austin called for their weekly talk. He called the house and got his mom, she told him his father was due back in a few days. She asked him how he was doing and if he was going to church. He wasn't. Since moving to Los Angeles he hadn't seen a single Church of Christ, which was the denomination he'd grown up in. While driving around the city day-to-day he'd passed a few scientology places, a lot of Catholic cathedrals, and some buildings that housed dominations that didn't even exist back where he was from. He was sure if he tried to find a Church of Christ in LA that he could, but being that Saturday nights usually had him working late, sleeping late on Sundays was something he looked forward to too much to lose. He hates to tell his mom that he's too lazy to find a church and actually go, but that's basically what it boils down to. His mom and pops think that he got a promotion at the airport working sixty-hour weeks without Sundays off. If his mom knew what he really did she'd be pressing him even harder to go to church and repent. If his pops knew what he really did, he'd be disowned.

Austin notices that the middle-aged woman a few seats down is ogling the bartender's backside. He's pretty sure she wouldn't have any luck barking up that tree, even if she transformed into a centerfold. But Austin has to give the guy credit; his attire does him favors where it counts. The sight makes him wonder if women stare at his ass when he isn't looking, too. The sight makes him want to ask the bartender where he buys his clothes. Austin didn't used to care much about such things, but living in superficial Santa Monica has made him take more interest in his style, especially with Maggie nagging him to expand his wardrobe while paying him a salary that allows him to do so.

Austin takes note, then, of his co-worker and friend next to him. He'd rarely ever seen AJ drink. They'd gone out for beers a couple of times, but outside of that, never. He doesn't drink at the office. He always orders water anytime they go out to eat as a group. But here he is with a glass of bourbon. No mixer, no chaser.

"So you and that one director's wife split up?" He asks unsurely, taking another sip of his Jack and Coke.

"Yup," AJ says simply, taking a sip of his own drink.

"And your girlfriend back in Tennessee broke up with you?"

"Yup."

"That sucks," Austin concludes, not knowing why he even brought the topic up, other than to lend an ear if he wanted to talk about it, which he obviously doesn't.

"Pretty much," AJ replies, taking a drink that's more a gulp than a sip and grimacing. "You know I don't know why Maggie asked me to go to that awards show with her," he says then, changing the topic on a dime. "You should go. You're the one who wants to be an actor. I'm just going to tell her I'm not going and to take you."

"No, you should go," Austin tells him, cracking open another peanut. "Being an actor was never a big dream of mine or nothin'. It was just somethin' I thought I could do, and I needed to do somethin'."

AJ turns his head towards him, an ungrasping look in his eyes. Austin knows that to someone like AJ, his lack of ambition is probably unfortunate; the fact that there's no place he needs to reach to feel fulfilled probably enviable.

"Plus," Austin adds. "The dudes that wrote all them movies they're givin' awards to will be there, too. You can network and shit."

AJ smiles slightly, looking back away. "With Ms. Hunter on my arm?" He gives Austin a side-eye as he raises his glass to back to his lips. "As Nique would say, 'that's a nice little first impression'."

Austin smirks as he takes a drink. "She does have a tendency to get in the way, don't she?"

"So bad," AJ says almost comically, tilting his glass back to drain the last drop.

"How'd she even get an invitation to the Oscars?" Austin wonders aloud.

"That's what I want to know."

Austin shakes his head. "Her iron is in so many fires."

AJ laughs. Then he laughs. Then they order another round. For a while they just sip their second drinks in silence, occasionally reaching into the tin for a peanut.

"Do you ever miss Memphis?" Austin asks after a few minutes.

AJ stares ahead, face never faltering. "I try not to think about it."

Austin supposes he tries not to think about Ohio, too.

But sometimes he does. And when he does, the nostalgia is strong.

Chapter 6

The next night AJ is back in Mrs. Kelly's bedroom after a three-week pardon. The familiar scent of Chanel is thick in the air as he strips off his clothes and she drinks her champagne out of a glass with a skinny little stem and a big round bowl.

"I thought I was simply going to lose my mind before you got back," she says in a distressed accent that wants desperately to be British. "And then Maggie calls and tells me I can't have you on Mondays anymore." She drains her goblet and immediately refills it. "I had to restrain myself in order to not curse the woman out."

She's got a new negligee on, something from a luxury boutique that sells slips and little scraps of lace for upwards of four digits. He knows she'll keep it on for the first half hour, until the drugs kick in. He knows she's self-conscious of her varicose veins, sagging skin, and wrinkles, despite all the elective surgeries, and injections, and rejuvenations. Every time he sees her naked there's a new scar accompanying a firmer this or smoother that. He knows around the thirty-minute mark her mind will begin to be freed. She'll pull her negligée off over her head, push him on his back, and put on a show. Her silicon breasts don't move much when she bounces atop him, and her tight face can't alter a lot when she comes, and none of it really does anything for him. But the more eager she is for more, the more money he makes. He gets the feeling tonight will be particularly lucrative.

"Yeah, I don't know why she moved you off of Mondays," AJ lies as he folds his pants and shirt up and places them on the edge of the bed for when it's over. "Miss Hunter doesn't really fill me in on things."

Mrs. Kelly pours herself a little coke out onto the vanity, and then holds the vial of powder out to him.

AJ just stares at it there in her hand for a second. "Oh. No. I don't want any," he stammers awkwardly. "That was just a one-time thing."

Mrs. Kelly smiles slyly. "You did it more than one time that night. If I remember correctly…you went back for seconds *and* thirds. We used all of what I had."

He gives her a placating smile. "I was having a bad week. I had court in the morning. I thought I was going to jail."

"I just assumed that you liked it and would want more…I mean…you seemed to enjoy yourself on it." She gives him a naughty look. "We had fun that night, didn't we?"

"It was fine, but I'd rather not do it again," he tells her.

"Suit yourself," she says simply, not really caring one way or the other. She then turns back around, bends down, and snorts her line up off the vanity.

~

Hollywood & Highland gets a reprieve from its typical tourist traffic one night out of the year when a sea of movie stars transforms it into a scene of glamour. AJ has never been to an awards show before, why would he have? He's an unknown twenty-three-old without an acting, production, or writing credit to his name—aside from the UofM school paper, Dominique's mixtape, and a couple poetry contest wins, but those small triumphs don't count for anything here. He is merely in attendance because Maggie didn't want to go alone, and how her name got on the invitation list he will probably never know. Still, the Oscars are a place many aspire to be. And even though he'd prefer to be there under different circumstances —like for recognition of his own aspirations—he'll still relish the privilege to be in the presence of such elite talent.

The driver she hired drops them off at the entrance of the red carpet. AJ's wearing the brand new tux she bought him. She's wearing a red couture gown. The press is congregating. Cameras are flashing. Reporters are screaming actors' names to get their attention. He's trying not to stare at the stars he sees, because the more he looks at them the more he feels like a zoo-goer with his face pressed up to the glass. Except there is no glass separating them, he's in the exhibit. No one is paying them any mind because they are nobody, so they can move about the carpet relatively undisturbed. A few non-famous people stop along the way to say something to Maggie, recognizing his boss from the high rolling circles she runs in and the ornate events she attends—not by her shadowy profession. No one actually famous speaks to her. Of course, that doesn't mean some famous people don't know her, it merely means they don't want to be seen fraternizing with their sex provider while under the spotlight of the world.

About halfway down the carpet foot traffic becomes congested. All of the photographers are suddenly scrambling, the onlookers in the roped off outdoor stands are losing their minds, and everyone collectively begins to scream a word the begins with K. Maggie cranes her head, trying to see around the crowd.

"Ugh," Maggie sighs in annoyance. "It's that Kadence Jane. What is she even doing here?" She ponders aloud. "She's a singer, not an actress."

There's a part in the sea of people, and AJ gets a glimpse at the tall, thin blonde causing all the commotion. She's got the pose down pat; one hand on her hip, one leg cocked out, a perfect smile, and a piercing stare right into the lens.

Kadence Jane is a young pop starlet who had put out two highly successful albums since she broke onto the scene a few years back. The first was country pop and the second was mainstream pop. AJ had never willfully chosen to listen to her music—wasn't really his style—but it was hard to turn on the radio and not hear her. It seemed she had multiple hit singles in rotation at all times, her face gracing the TV talk shows and mainstream magazines as she quickly became America's sweetheart. The always smiling, never cursing, blue-eyed, blonde haired, downhome, girl-next-door. The crowd is going wild.

"She must be dating that guy," Maggie says, motioning with her eyes to the smartly dressed, dark blonde actor whose arm she's on. AJ recognizes him from a few movies. "I think he's a nominee," Maggie adds. "He was in that one crime-thriller that took place in Berlin." And then under her breath, "She was with a politician's son the last time I read a tabloid, but that must have been last month." She takes AJ's arm. "Let's see if we can cut around this mess and get to the entrance another way."

They manage to get out of the swarm of people and finally make it to the prestigious steps leading up to the Dolby. AJ gentlemanly offers Maggie his arm, and she takes it as they begin to ascend. When he looks back up his heart stops.

He had considered the possibility that she might be here. But he couldn't have called and asked her. He could no longer check on her. He lost her by no fault other than his own. He gave her up, gave her away, and in doing so relinquished his rights to her life. He didn't know when he'd see her again, if ever.

But there she stands at the top of the stairs.

She has her side to him, engaged in conversation with a well-known actor's wife. The apples of her cheeks rise as she laughs at something said to her, the corners of her eyes crinkling, a desired side effect of her bright smile that he misses more than anything. The actor is talking to her husband, who up until now AJ has never been in the same room with. But he can't bring himself to care about that man. Not when she's fifteen or so steps away from him, and getting closer with every step.

She's got on a beautiful burgundy gown the color of wine. The fabric hugs her delicate form without constricting, flowing out when it hits the floor. There's no bells, whistles, glitter, or excessive embellishment to distract the eye. And she looks better than anything and anyone he's ever laid eyes on, in that elegant, effortless style of hers that puts to shame all those people back on the red carpet who try too hard. Her hair is up, her delectable neck is on display, and only a slender strap of material covers her covetous shoulders. When she finally turns her head and her brown eyes meet his green ones, everything outside of the moment falls away.

The briefest glimmer of pure shock passes across her face, and for a second she has to work to control her expression. He can tell. But then she's turning back around, putting a genial smile back on, and refocusing on her husband and the other couple's conversation.

The sound of Maggie clearing her throat brings him back to reality. He becomes aware again that his boss is on his arm, and that he's not supposed to be staring at the woman he's staring at. He diverts his eyes and pretends he doesn't know the people before him as they reach the top of the stairs, and he doesn't have to look at Maggie to know she's doing the same. Out of the corner of his eye he catches Julius's gaze straying to him as his actor friend continues to talk. He and Maggie enter the theater, leaving the uncomfortable moment outside.

Their seats are a good thirty rows back from the stage. But AJ doesn't care. He doesn't care if the biggest star in the world walks up to him right now and introduces themselves to him. He doesn't care about meeting important people. There's only one person he wants to talk to, and he'd have to mentally maneuver out of the thick fog of emotion that's fallen over his mind, find a way to silence the pounding sound of his heart in his ears, in order to make conversation with anyone else. His eyes are trained on the entrance where actors and actresses and screenwriters and producers and their spouses are trickling in off the carpet. He's waiting for her to walk in while consciously trying to not let Maggie catch him watching. He's only vaguely aware that some guy has come over to where they're at to say hello to her. His boss and the stranger that she seems to know make small chit-chat, and he takes the opportunity to unabashedly stare at the door.

"What are you doing now?" Maggie asks the man.

"I work A&R for Epic," the little be-speckled, plain-suited man says. "I'm here with the Kadence Jane team tonight."

"Oh yes," Maggie replies in her pleasant voice. "I saw her out there a little earlier." She then turns to her date and touches his arm. "This is one of my clients," she tells the man who is clearly under the popular guise that she's a talent agent. "Andrew Brooks. He's a songwriter."

AJ would have ordinarily been pleasantly surprised to hear her introduce him as a writer to someone in the industry, but he's barely paying attention now. Anjanae and Julius have just entered the building and he doesn't want to lose track of where they sit.

"Oh," the man says, acting intrigued. "Anything I know?"

"He recently did a mixtape for Dominique Davis," Maggie replies, and for once it's not a lie. "Young up and coming R&B guy," she explains, not expecting for her friend to know who Dominique Davis is. But he surprises her.

"Yes, I've heard of him," he says. "Kay loved the tape. Thinks he's the next big singer up."

The two chitchat for a moment more about this and that, and then the A&R guy moves on.

"Do you think Dominique is really that big already?" Maggie asks AJ idly after a beat. "Or do you think he was just amusing me?"

AJ can't hear the question because his ex-girlfriend's husband has his hand resting possessively on her thigh, and AJ could swear Julius just looked back at him and scowled. Or was it a smirk? He swears he's losing his mind.

"Andrew…"

"Huh," he finally says, snapping out of it and facing her. "What?"

Maggie is giving him a knowingly scolding look. "If one of these innocent bystanders passes in front of your line of visions right now while you're staring down that woman from across the auditorium their eggs are liable to become fertilized." She rolls her eyes and re-crosses her legs. "Knock it off. Cool down. You're putting off the body heat of a furnace powered by the coals of hell."

He can't help it. And the moment Maggie looks away he looks back.

He racks his mind for an idea of how to get her alone. He wants to tell her what a mistake he made. He wants to tell her how bad he knows he messed up. He wants to tell her that she is still everything to him. But he doesn't know if he were to get her by herself, if he were able to say these things to her, if she'd even want to hear them. He doesn't know if she's glad to see him here like he's so glad to see her. He doesn't know if her flesh is broken out in goose bumps right now like his is. He doesn't know if her stomach is in knots at the sight of him next to the person who brought them together and tore them apart, like his is over the sight of her next to her husband. He doesn't know if she still feels for him what he will always feel for her. For all he knows he might have made her hate him, and he wouldn't blame her one bit if she did, because he honestly kind of hates himself.

She glances back at the last minute, and his eyes are wide open and waiting to connect with hers. They meet and hold for the count of three breaths. Then the lights dim and he loses sight of her.

The ceremony lasts for what seems like forever. And just when he thinks he can't endure another restless second more, it finally comes to an end. The sun had gone down in the time they were inside, and he can't find her again in the frantic sea of famous people and black limousines.

There's some kind of after party thing at the hotel that's conjoined to the theater. Maggie wants to go, and what choice does he have. She promises him they'll only stay for an hour or so, and then he can go home. Music is playing and champagne is flowing. Maggie immediately grabs a flute and starts to mingle. AJ has never been one for pointless small talk, especially not in a room full of people who are on a completely different level of wealth, success, and notoriety than him. He attempts to awkwardly blend in to the back wall while he waits for Maggie to get her fill of importance for the night and put him out of his misery.

And then his eyes land on Julius Collins. The renowned director is in the middle of the room with his back to him, surrounded by three other recognizable directors. Out of all the after parties currently taking place around town, Julius would choose for him and his wife to attend the same one as them. Except his wife is not next to him right now. It feels very much like fate to AJ, and every second of the arduous night now seems suddenly worth it. His eyes dart around the room, trying to spot her before Julius can spot him. He finds her standing along the wall on the other side. She's respectfully smiling as she makes conversation that he can tell is tedious with an older woman in a tacky cotton-candy pink taffeta ball gown. The woman momentarily stops talking to take a drink of her champagne, and Anjanae glances off in his direction. Their gazes find each other. He motions to the exit with his eyes. She makes no gesture that she's understood his request. But when the other woman resumes babbling, Anjanae faces forward, says something with a polite smile, and then excuses herself. She doesn't look back at him again as she discreetly walks to the doors and slips out. He waits five seconds, and then follows.

There's a set of bathrooms right outside the party but she continues past them, out into an open space and then on down a hall. AJ follows her to a more desolate part of the hotel, making sure to stay at least twenty steps behind her. The music from the ballroom fades the further they get from the festivities. They come up on an empty lounge area on a landing between one floor and another. There's another set of bathrooms. She goes into the women's. AJ briefly glances around to make sure there's no one around, and then he goes in after her.

The second they're alone together the world slows down. His lungs fill with air, his chest untightens. Every little feature, blemish, and beauty mark on her face comes into focus. Her arms are crossed. She doesn't look happy. And he wants so much to change that.

"Well," she says, glancing away from him when she speaks. "You've been staring at me all night. I assume you want something. So what do you want?"

She makes herself look at him then. She makes her stare stark and cold. But he can see past it, he can still see her even when she doesn't want him to.

"I…" he stutters for a second, she makes him lose his words sometimes. "I wanted to talk," he tells her softly. "I thought maybe we could talk."

"You want to *talk*?" Anjanae repeats, and she shakes her head with a snort like she finds what he's just said funny. But he knows she doesn't, because a dead serious look is right back on her face a second later. "I don't want to *talk* to you."

AJ's mouth opens and closes. He can't make her talk to him. Despite the fact that it pains him, he respects her wish to not hear him out. And he's just about to turn around and walk back out of the bathroom when she flings herself at him. He catches her in his arms as her mouth lands harshly on his, teeth hitting from the forcefulness of it. He doesn't stop her. Doesn't stop her from grabbing him up by the collar of his suit jacket. Doesn't stop her from pushing her tongue into his mouth. She loses herself in it, kissing him with abandon, pressing her lithe body against his and pulling at his hair with both hands. But then she stops herself.

Anjanae backs up two steps, looking shocked by her own actions. She's won't look at him now. He's breathless. It all happened so fast, and his senses are ablaze. The taste of her mouth. The smell of her skin. He waits for her to look up. She does. And then it's the look in her eyes, and the unspoken things, and everything.

He abruptly picks her up and pins her to the nearest wall, lifting her over him and settling her on his shoulders.

"AJ!" She gasps in surprise.

He pushes her gown up around her waist and pulls her lace underwear far enough down for him to reach his intended goal.

"Some…someone might…"

He silences her concerns by burying his face between her thighs. Any doubt he had that she might not still want him is quickly extinguished. She squirms, hips jerking and rocking against his mouth for more as she tries to contain the needy little noises that slip out of her mouth. So wet. He can tell instantly that she needs this as much as he does. It doesn't take long at all. She comes faster than ever before. Afterwards he gently lowers her back down to the ground. He watches her trembling legs with awe and adoration as she steps out of her underwear. When he looks back up, he sees her eyes on him. The darkness of them is something he has seen so many times and it still didn't cease to send a shiver down his spine. She is not quite smiling, assured and wanting, but never breaking eye contact as she quickly undoes his belt and opens his pants. His hands go to her face, bringing her mouth right back to his. As soon as his tongue slips into her mouth she's sucking on it. Biting lips. Hands in his hair. Emotions high. Every move they make spells out desperation and the hunger to have the other once more. Two separated soul mates sidestepping and stumbling towards the vanity of an empty bathroom.

He considers turning her around so he can watch her in the mirror as he reunites with her. But he wants to feel her legs around his waist and her nails digging into skin. He wants to be face to face and breathing her air. Most of all, AJ doesn't want to stop kissing her. So he picks her up again and sits her down on the counter. He wonders, as she spreads her legs and simultaneously shifts his pants and briefs down, if she sees the similarity in this and their first time together. But the way she keens when he enters her makes him lose track of this thought and all others. He moans into her open mouth, her familiar silky walls enveloping him tightly. She's already panting. Then again, he is too. He pulls away just enough to hold her gaze in the moment, for a moment, and then he's grabbing her ass up, pulling her further onto him. He swallows the scream that escapes her.

It all works out, because he can see the expressions she makes over his shoulder in the reflection of the other mirror directly across the bathroom. It's an incredibly erotic sight to behold; mouth open and eyes squeezed shut, the straps of her expensive gown sliding down her arms wantonly, the light catching the diamonds in her ears and the one on her finger. She bites down hard on his cloth-covered shoulder to stifle the scream that wants to happen; a long, low, muffled moan caresses his ears instead. He can tell she's fighting to contain the pleasure she feels. The feeling is mutual, building at the base of his spine and threatening to make him lose what little control he has left. What she does to him is damned near unbearable in the best way. As it is, he manages to hold off his impending peak, even as their movements become more and more frantic, each thrust bouncing her a bit off the edge of the vanity. He has to try to prolong it. For her. For them. Because he doesn't know when he'll see her next. And he knows there are words that need to be said and conversations that need to be had and apologies that he needs to make and so much more, but *need* wins out.

In the back of his mind he's aware that what they're doing and where they're doing it at is precarious, potentially detrimental to them both. Anyone could walk in at any moment while he's in another man's wife. He doesn't want to think about that, though. He can't think about that. Not when her lips are on his earlobe and her nails are grazing his neck and she's squeezing around him the way that she is. The way that lets him know she's close again. He slips a hand between them, rubbing her in time with the motion of his hips. Seconds later her entire body starts to shake violently, head falling back in bliss. He blazes her throat with his mouth as she contracts around him, eventually burying his face in the crook of her neck as her orgasm pulls him over with her. He strokes once, twice more, and then releases inside her with hoarse groan.

They're trying to catch their breath, neither making a move. The air is fragile in the aftermath of raw emotion; reality slowly reabsorbing in their snared subconscious. He looks at her and she looks at him. One breath. Two.

"I love you," he tells her.

And then the look that was previously on her face is gone. Now she's looking at him like he's crazy, anger refilling her eyes in the absence of pleasure. Like how dare he tell her that after he chose money and that woman over them. How dare he think he still has the right to say those words to her after he left her when he promised he wouldn't. She pushes him away, pushes her gown back down, and climbs off the counter. He focuses on the floor as he tucks himself back in and pulls up his zipper, hearing her grab a few tissues from the dispenser as she quickly cleans up.

And then listens dejectedly to the door open and shut a moment later with a definitive thud.

He waits a full minute before leaving the bathroom, and he's almost back to the ballroom when Maggie seems to appear out of thin air, startling him.

"Where were you?" She asks in a shrill voice. "I've been looking all over. I thought you'd be ready to leave…"

"I um…I just got bored. Thought I'd…take a look around the hotel," AJ tells her, barely able to speak evenly after what just happened. "It's really nice."

There's a second where he's sure she doesn't believe him. But then a little smirk comes to her face and she nods. "I know. They have a really nice panoramic suite. That's the room Garrett got arrested in." She nonchalantly turns and heads off towards the lobby. "Come on," she says over her shoulder. "I've already called the driver. He said he'd be out front."

AJ lets her lead the way, not knowing how he got to where he's at or how to find his way out of it.

Chapter 7

AJ has never *worked* out of state before.

He and Theo are having lunch at a Manhattan pub Theo claims has the best pastrami sandwiches in the city, though from the way he tells it there are many establishments vying for the title. Earlier in the week a Park Avenue housewife Maggie used to cater to regularly called and asked for Theo to be put on a plane. The way Maggie sees it, if she's going to go to all the trouble of booking flights and rooms, she might as well send two guys to make twice the money. AJ knows she'd probably rather send him to any other city besides New York, but being that Dominique formally quit the Monday after the Oscars, and seeing as how she never seems to give Austin the big opportunities, he was her only option.

They had taken the red eye and got in around nine that morning. After dropping their bags off at the Waldorf, Theo had taken him around the Upper Eastside and shown him some of the sights. While strolling down Fifth Avenue, AJ had looked up at all the luxury apartments towering above. He knows Anjanae lives in one of them. Julius probably wasn't home, he never was. He could've probably gone straight up to their penthouse, helped her pack a bag. They could've caught a cab to the airport, picked a plane, and been on their way to anywhere in the world in a matter of moments.

He'd talked himself out of that thought, of course

Now he's forcing down bites of toasted rye and melted Swiss and slimy cold cuts with too much flavor for his lost appetite, washing it down his dry throat with swigs of draft beer. A couple of Saks bags sit under the table from their previous perusing, and few Cartier boxes in the booth next to him. Theo is sitting across from him, looking more at ease than he has in the last couple of weeks as he digs into his sandwich with both hands and a wide mouth, momentarily allowing himself to relinquish the properness he usually exudes.

"So Dominique really did it?" Theo muses, taking a vigorous bite that sends some of the mustard dropping out the back of the bread.

"He really did," AJ replies, picking the pickle off his plate and nibbling on it. "He hired a lawyer to go over the paperwork with him. It was all legit, so he officially signed the deal on Tuesday."

"How much?"

"Two mill," AJ says.

"Woo!" Theo exclaims like he just touched something hot. He puts down his sandwich and wipes off his ring-clad hands with a napkin. "That boy did that."

AJ takes a sip of beer and smiles, happy for his friend. "I know."

"Well good for him," Theo adds, picking his sandwich back up. "I always believed he had the blessing. Beautiful voice. Too talented to not use it."

For some reason that last sentiment has AJ growing pensive. They eat in silence until a man comes up to them, fidgeting a bit, not quite smiling but definitely not frowning.

"Theo Lewis?" The man asks. He has a timidly kind smile, a nice suit, and an accent that reminds AJ of the Jewish characters he's seen on T.V.

Theo turns his head to look at the random man standing by their booth and gives him an aloofly quizzical eyebrow raise and a nonchalant, "Yes?"

"Phillip...Phillip Stowers," he stammers with a smile. "We went to Public School back in Queens together. Class of '93."

Queens, AJ thinks then, *he has Queens accent.*

Theo stares at the man a moment more, then recognition hits him. "Phil Stowers!" He exclaims, face softening with a smile. "Yes, of course." He's quickly grabbing his napkin and giving his mouth and hands a quick wipe, suddenly concerned about his appearance again. "Mrs. Bernard's fifth period sophomore geometry, you sat behind me." He faces Phil and holds out his hand with a brightly charming smile. "Long time no see."

"I know, right?" Phil chuckles, giving his hand a shake. "It's crazy that we haven't ran into each other in two decades."

"It's a big city," Theo replies, insinuating that he never left it for LA.

"What are you up to these days? What do you do?"

"Oh you know..." Theo muses in order to buy himself some time to come up with a lie. "Workin' for the man, doing marketing for one of these big companies," he says, gesturing with his eyes in the general direction of Wall Street and not bothering to elaborate. "Thinking about getting out of it and doing something else," he adds, and then quickly changes the subject. "What about you? What do you do?"

"I sell insurance," Philip confesses with a bit of an embarrassed shrug. "I know. It's a rather bland, ho-hum career, but it pays the bills."

"Oh. Well that's all right."

Phillip stares, mystified smile and look of intrigue on his face. "I always wondered what happened to you."

Theo grins bashfully, taking a sip of his spritzer. "Please."

"No, really," Phillip says. "You know you were the most confident kid at that school. You were different, but never afraid to be yourself." He grins bashfully now, too, and then adds, "I was envious."

Theo smiles to himself. "Thank you for saying that, but I definitely didn't feel enviable back then. I got picked on more than I got praised."

"You just knew who you were already. Everybody else was still figuring it out." Phillip gives comical little shrug. "Plus we went to school with a lot of losers."

"That is true," Theo chuckles.

There's a second of silence where both men are just staring at each other appreciatively. And then Phillip breaks it, reddening a bit around his cheeks.

"Well it was nice running into you, Theo," he tells him. "You look good." Then nervously adds. "You look like you're doing good."

"You, too," Theo replies with an honest smile. "You too."

Phillip hesitates briefly. "Look…I'm…I'm not really good at this," he stumbles shyly, taking his billfold out of his pocket and opening it. "But if you'd ever like to go out for a drink or to dinner sometime…well…here's my number." He hands Theo his card. "Give me a call. You know. If you want."

Theo takes it and nods politely. "Okay."

Phil gives a final smile, nods, and then walks away.

Theo takes another sip of his spritzer. AJ just stares at him with a shit eating smirk on his face.

"What?" Theo asks him.

"Nothing," AJ replies innocently, taking a drink of his beer. "I just can't take you anywhere without somebody coming on to you, that's all."

Theo laughs. "Phil was always a nice guy. He never gave me shit like some of the other guys I went to school with. I never knew he was gay, though."

"Well he probably didn't know he was gay. You all were teenagers."

"I always knew I was," Theo says, draining his glass and sitting it back on the table. "Gay looks good on him, though."

AJ shakes his head with a snort.

Theo stares down at the card he was given, the number on the back making him feel more like a person than he has in awhile.

~

Being that he doesn't have a prescheduled client like Theo, AJ decides to go to the Regency Hotel down the street, making the conscious choice to not do business where he's staying. It's a little after nine when he takes a seat at the elaborate lobby bar. He could have gone to any of the many nightclubs in the city, worked his charm in a dark and vibrating room, taken a chance on a party girl with the hopes she wouldn't balk when hit with a price tag. But AJ knows better. Hotels are full of transients from other places in route to another, many minus a mate and traveling alone, often with less inhibition wherever they're at than wherever they're from, freed from the fear of being seen by liable eyes. And, if the hotel is of the luxury variety, the lobby bars are often filled with those who have a little extra money to spend. It's the perfect combination and setting for picking up a client in a pinch.

Shortly after he arrives, a woman sits down two stools down from him. Without looking at her, he can tell she's looking at him. Only for a second. Then she's ordering a glass of white wine and focusing on that. While she's nursing her poison of choice, he steals a peek or two at her. Forty-something. Bare ring finger. Burberry bag. Marc Jacob reading glasses. Demure diamond studs he determines are real. Sporting the chicly short haircut stylish middle-aged women get. Respectable black dress and medium height black heels that suggest she just got out of a meeting of some sort, tired expression to match. AJ orders a bourbon, biding his time while she works her way to tipsy town, and then he makes his move to the stool that's separating them.

"I'm AJ," he tells her. No *can I sit here, can I buy you a drink, can I ask your name?* He doesn't need to do that.

He watches her give him a once over with her eyes, even though he secretly knows this is technically the twice over.

Her eyes move back up and meet his. "What, did you have issues with your mother as a child? You know you're young enough to be my son, right?"

She wasn't an out-of-towner. She was a New Yorker.

He grins. "Only if you were promiscuous in your teen years."

She fights a smile. "Do you want to buy me a drink?"

"No," AJ replies, smirking at her over the rim of his glass.

"You're a little smartass. That's fine." She turns to the bartender and snaps her fingers. "I can buy my own drinks. I'm an independent woman." Her glass gets refilled and she takes a sip. "Probably not even old enough to buy me a drink. How old are you anyway?"

He takes a sip. "I'll tell you if you tell me your story first."

"You really want to know?"

"I wouldn't have asked if I didn't," he tells her suavely.

"Ok. Well. I was born and raised in Manhattan. Married my college sweetheart because he was smart and driven and I knew we would make a lot of money and live a very plush life together. However, with power and pay raises he developed a secretary addiction. Six mistresses and twenty years later I finally came to my senses and filed for divorce." She pauses to take a long drink before continuing. "That was eight fucking months ago; the papers just got finalized this week. I got the Hamptons house in the settlement and he got our 57th street apartment. Don't get me wrong, I like the extra square feet and the land. But when I have to drive an hour or take the damn Jitney anytime I want to go to the city, I start getting homicidal ideations towards my ex, who can just pop out the door and be within walking distance of all my favorite places, know what I mean? The company's been letting me do most of my work from home, thank God, but I still have to come out here for the big stuff. It's such a hassle. I just stay at hotels when I have more than one meeting in a week. I can't do all that back forth on the highway without a Valium. And I can't drive on drugs. So therein lies the problem."

AJ grins as he takes a drink. "What do you do?"

"Bank specialist for Goldman Sachs. What about you? What do you do? I bet you're a trust fund baby, aren't you? Hanging out at expensive bars for kicks."

He can tell she has a good sense of humor, meaning he can press a little after his reveal without the fear of her taking out her phone, calling the police, and telling them there's a prostitute in the Loewe's lobby. He knows she won't punch back at his flirtations with empty threats and evil eyes. She'll punch back with snarky jabs and easy mockery. He knows if she doesn't want to become his client for the night, she'll simply say no, not catch an offended attitude and start speaking loudly to make a spectacle of him and his secret profession. He can tell she's cool. He can also tell she's open minded, and open minds can easily be changed minds.

"Listen," he says. "I know this is going to sound a bit dubious..."

"Not dubious," she smirks.

"Yes," he replies with a light chuckle and a perfectly executed, pearly-toothed smile. "Are you familiar with the term escort?"

She stares at him. Blinks once, twice. Then looks away as she takes a sip. "Is that what you are?"

"If it is, would I be able to make a sale tonight?"

After a moment she locks eyes with him again. "You know you could really make a woman question her appearance," she says with a quizzical smirk, then lowers her voice. "Do you think I need to pay a gigolo to get laid? Look at the man at the end of the bar eying me up and down." She points with her eyes. "You don't think he'd screw me for free right now?"

AJ smirks as he holds her gaze. "One: I prefer the term professional lover. Two: that man at the end of the bar is a bored businessman with a wedding band and hair plugs. Yes, I think he'd love nothing more than to screw you right here and now for free. His wife probably stopped putting out twelve years ago and it's probably been since the last time his corporation sent him to a convention that he's had any. Three: Would you rather have two minutes of your life you'll never get back or two hours you'll never forget?"

She's staring at him again, fighting a smile again. "I think it's probably wisest for me to head up to my room alone."

"You sure?"

"I think," she says as she stands, but it stills sound like there's some self-convincing going on. "I appreciate your offer, though."

"How about I give you a preview in the elevator. Free of charge. And when we get to your floor, if you decide you want to pay for the whole episode, I'll follow you to your room. If not," he shrugs simply with a little smile. "I'll go back down."

Her eyes stay on his for the count of at least three breaths before she breaks contact. She reaches down to pick her glass back up, drains it of the last few drops of liquor, returns it to the table, and turns to leave. He stays on the barstool. She walks six or seven steps, and then shoots him a look over her shoulder as if to say *are you coming?* He drains his owns glass and gets up.

There are four elevators on either side of the hall, and one other person besides them waiting to go up. They let the little white-haired lady get on the first one that arrives; she holds the door expecting them to get on with her. They pretend to be distracted by the dispenser of fresh fruit flavored water on the end table against the wall until the old lady gets tired of waiting and lets the doors close. The second the next elevator dings, they're both right there. The doors open, they quickly jump in, and hold their breath as the doors slowly shut, hoping nobody else rushes on at the last minute. They don't. The numbers start ticking up.

"What floor are you on," he whispers in her ear, one hand already in her hair and the other on her lower back, holding her flush against him.

"63rd," she breathes out.

His lips brush against hers. "Mm. Perfect," he grins against her mouth.

And then her back is against the glass wall, and the hand that was on her lower back is now skimming over her ass and down her thigh, hitching one leg up and holding it at the knee. With his other hand, he glides a single finger over her lips, off her chin, down her throat and to her chest. He touches her breasts with the faintest touch, and when he drags that hand down her abdomen, he feels her stomach pull taught. He looks her in her eyes when he snakes it under the skirt of her dress. His thumb starts to press circles while his middle and index delve. Her breath hitches and she tries to kiss him, but his mouth has moved to her neck. His tongue teases the skin behind her ear, his teeth briefly nipping at a lobe before his head dips, sucking at the junction of her shoulder. She groans. He lets her now trembling leg go, his fingers sill working as he starts to descend her body. Open mouthed kisses to her chest, her cloth covered belly, her pelvis. The elevator dings. He pulls her dress back down and stands up. The doors open. No one is waiting on the other side. They both just stand there for a second; she is breathing heavily and he's perfectly cool. That's when she grabs his hand, leading him out of the elevator, down the hall, and to her room where the do-not-disturb sign is promptly put on the door.

~

The next morning AJ meets Theo in the Waldorf's restaurant for breakfast. Theo has already ordered and there's plates of bacon and eggs and French toast on the table; flutes filled with mimosa, water glasses and coffee mugs on the side. AJ actually has an appetite this morning, having worked one up last night, and immediately grabs a piece of bacon.

"How did it go with Park Avenue lady last night?" He asks, pouring syrup over his toast as he chews.

"I didn't go to her last night. I went out with the guy from the deli. Phillip."

"Moved quick on that," AJ mumbles between forkfuls of scrambled eggs. "He give you more than she would have you think?"

"No, I went to dinner," Theo corrects. "I paid. And nothing else happened. Well." He takes a final bite of his French toast and wipes his mouth. "I kissed him at the end of the night. But that was it."

AJ looks up mid-bite. "Maggie's not going to be happy when we get back and you don't have the money."

"I'm not going back."

AJ puts down his silverware. "What do you mean you're not going back?"

"I'm quitting and staying here in New York." He smiles dreamily, a smile he rarely smiles. "Phillip and I are going to the symphony tonight."

"But...you can't...I don't..." AJ's thoughts stumble around as he tries to wrap his mind around the prospect of Theo not working for Maggie anymore. "You're willing to give up your life back in Los Angles and a good paying job on a whim with a guy you've only gone on one date with? What if it doesn't work out with him?"

"What life back in Los Angeles?" Theo asks, briefly glancing over at his co-worker with a wry smirk as he pours himself a little more water.

AJ is unable to elaborate. He looks down at the table.

"Look, I'm realistic," Theo says, sitting the pitcher back down. "I know it might not work out with Phillip. That's not the point, though. The point is I'm done living my life for her. You know I've never had a real boyfriend?" He pauses and AJ looks up again and meets his eyes. "I've slept with a ton of guys," Theo continues. "A ton of women for that matter. I couldn't even begin to count them. But I've never had a relationship. I'm over thirty years old and have never shared my life with anybody. I want to go on dates where *I* pay. I want to go on dates with someone *I* like. I want emotional and mental with the physical. I want commitment, and honesty, and love without motive." He takes a drink of water and then pushes his glass and plate away. "So even if Phil and me go out one more time and then never see each other again, at least I'll always have the experience of going out with someone who never knew me as a prostitute, and who never saw me as one. And as long as I don't work for her, I'll always have the ability to have more of those experiences."

"I get it," AJ says after a beat. "I respect it. But you haven't worked a normal job in over a decade. What are you going to do? What are you going to put on résumés?"

"I don't know," Theo says honestly, sitting back in the booth and looking unconcerned. "Fortunately, New York City is full of people who don't know what they're going to do. Fortunately for me, I've saved my money. Fortunately for me I've been here before. I'll figure it out. Honestly, a normal job working in a restaurant forty hours a week sounds pretty good right about now. Normal is underrated."

AJ nods. He can't argue that point.

"Will you tell her for me?" Theo asks him.

"I guess I'll have to."

~

Eight hours later AJ is stepping off the elevator on the 57th floor. He came straight from the airport. Maggie is sitting at her big mahogany desk.

"Well hello, Andrew," she says, looking up with her patent smile that he knows soon will fade. "How was New York?"

"Good," AJ replies, taking the wad of money out of his Saint Laurent wallet and handing it to her.

"Was your co-worker too tired from flying first-class all day to come in?" She asks sardonically as she starts to count the hundreds he just gave her. "You know, he stood up the woman I sent him out there for. Probably to fuck some upmarket Manhattan businessman out of a chunk of their high salary. Old habits die hard. I'm going to have to have a word with him when I see him."

"You're not going to see him"

She snorts derisively as she recounts the money. "What do you mean I'm not going to see him?"

"He didn't come back."

Her fingers stop flipping bills.

"He decided to stay in New York," AJ tells her.

"He quit?" She asks to be sure. No hurt in her voice, no surprise in her eyes. She's as nonchalant as ever, masking emotions that she may or may not even have.

"Yes."

"Very well then," she says as she turns her chair away from him to face her computer screen. "You and Austin will have to take some of his women until I can hire some new help. I hope you're okay with having a slightly fuller schedule."

"Sure," he says, heading back for the elevators.

She embraced the loss without much ado. But AJ gets the feeling she'll be in the Courvoisier just as soon as he leaves her to it. Then again she might not actually care. He might actually miss the man that's been her confidant for years more than she will. AJ had almost looked at Theo like an older brother. An uncle. A wiser man that he could look up to and go to with questions. Someone who had longevity in the field and was still so together. An example of it all turning out okay.

Gone.

Chapter 8

Maggie is sitting at her desk in deep thought. It's early in the afternoon and the California sun is streaming into the glass-enclosed office without invitation. She stares off into space at the skyscrapers outside the window. The entire 57th floor is empty; the only sound is that of her nails hitting the mahogany wood. She has barely seen AJ and Austin in the last two weeks since Theo quit. They've been taking on extra work and she's been stressing, scouring the city for handsome young men with bad judgment and empty pockets for her to coerce with easy currency. She currently doesn't have anyone to service her male clients, nor can she add any new male clients on without a gay worker or a straight worker willing to go gay for the right pay. She had broached the subject with AJ when he came to pick up his check a few days ago. She thought she had made an enticing argument, the promise that male money was even better than female money, the promise that biting a pillow for a few uncomfortable minutes and pretending that your taste buds are geared towards a different, slightly saltier flavor a couple of times a week would be totally worth the raise in pay. But alas, Andrew had turned down her offer. He told her he had to draw the line somewhere. And she understands, but that doesn't make the money she's losing any easier to swallow. She hasn't had the chance to ask Austin yet, and she doubts he'll take the bait either, but she has to try.

As it is, she has found two new guys who are coming in for an interview later. She's prayed to God twice that they're bisexual. One is a blue-eyed blonde and the other is a light-skinned black guy. The fact that she will probably hire both of them is good, but not good enough. In a little over a month's time she has lost four guys. Four. So while two may help out, it won't make up. And training them will be a whole other story, because easy on the eyes doesn't always equate good in bed.

She has just pulled up one of her future employee's Instagram pages to check out the goods one more time before he comes in for an interview when her phone rings. It's the white phone, her personal line. The number flashing on her screen looks familiar, but she can't place it instantly. And then realization writes itself across her face, and she picks up with a stoic expression.

"Yes?" She asks disinterestedly.

She begins to organize her penholder as whoever has called her starts to talk.

"I'm not sure why you felt the need to call and tell me this," she says as she turns all the Papermates in the right direction and separates the blue ink from the black ink, keeping with the same bored tone. "But congratulations. Your life seems to be on the up and–"

The person on the other line cuts her off, and her hands immediately still their task. Maggie's face slowly changes as she listens to the voice in her ear; disinterest turning into tempered shock, turning into collected denial.

"And why would you think that?" She asks. "They haven't–"

The person cuts her off again. As she listens, she minimizes the Internet tab and pulls up the calendar on her computer.

"Well what exactly do you want me to do about it?" She asks aloofly, an unreadable expression on her face as she fixates on the dates on her desktop's screen. She waits for the answer, and when she gets it she shakes her head. "No, I'm not increasing it," she replies absolutely, rolling her chair away from her desk and standing up. "Is there anything else you want to ask me?"

She walks to the window while the nameless person makes another plea.

"I certainly won't if you don't want me to," Maggie says, slightly more compliant to whatever the last request was than to the previous. Through the crystal clear glass, she stares down at the bustling city fifty-six floors below. "No, I don't see a reason why he needs to know either," she adds. She nods her head definitively. "All right. Best of luck, then."

Maggie ends the call with an eye roll, slipping her phone back into her pants pocket. She continues to stare out the window, perhaps still trying to wrap her mind around the conversation she just had. But the ding of the elevator out in the hall brings her mind back to the matters at hand.

"Are you here, Ms. Hunter?" Austin calls.

"I am," she calls out, starting to turn. "And I was actually wanting to talk–"

That's when she sees that he is not alone. There is a pretty, young Hispanic woman in a sundress trailing behind him.

"I thought I saw your Mercedes in the parking garage," Austin says, coming to a stop a few feet away from her. "There are a lot of Mercedes in the parking garage, course. I think a lot of doctors work in this building. But yours is the only one with the red leather seats." He gives her his typical boyish grin. "Sets ya apart."

"Austin," she says in her artificially sweet voice with her artificially sweet smile. "Who is this?" Her eyes fall upon the girl standing there, who now appears guarded.

"Oh," Austin stammers, growing nervous as he picks up on his boss's displeasure. "This is my…friend…Hermosa." He looks lovingly back at Hermosa, and then to Maggie again. "Hermosa, this is my boss, Miss Hunter."

Maggie stands silent as she stares, accessing the situation and this strange girl that's been let into her office without her permission. Unlike her boyfriend—fuck buddy, whatever Austin is to her—the girl only grows tougher under Maggie's scrutinizing gaze. She's got her chin up and her arms crossed and she's staring back like it's a contest that she's not going to back down from. This makes Maggie smirk, but still she doesn't break her eye contact with the girl. Maggie thinks of her as a girl because she couldn't be older than twenty-one, twenty-two. Too young to be a client. Attractive but not wealthy. She wears her clothes well, but they are by no means designer labels. That dress she has on is more than likely from Target, maybe H&M. The sandals are probably Old Navy. Not any of her jewelry is real gold or silver. Her thick dark hair is pulled back in a loose ponytail and she's done some kind of cheap looking design with her eyeliner, but she's cute nonetheless. Austin has himself a looker. Maggie just can't help but to hope that she doesn't make him any stupider than he already is.

"We've just been runnin' around town. In the neighborhood," Austin starts to ramble, the awkward silence making him antsy. "Gonna go to an opera later tonight and I left my best suit here." He laughs nervously. "Anyway I told Mo she could come up with me to get it so she didn't have to sit in the truck."

Maggie's face is completely deadpanned.

"It's cool," Austin reassures her, grabbing his suit and taking Hermosa's hand and walking back toward the elevator. "She knows about everything."

"Is that supposed to make me feel better?" She calls after him, shaking her head in disbelief once he's gone.

Later, the elevator dings. She's already given the two new boys their physical inspections; they've redressed and are sitting on the couch while she goes over the rules. AJ steps off the elevator, sees there's a meeting going, and goes over to the window to wait.

"One moment," she says to newbies, going over to him.

"I didn't want to be a bother," he says, handing her a thick rubber band roll of cash. "Just wanted to drop off my week's earnings."

"Oh, you're not a bother," she says in a lowered voice, taking the money. "You know what's a bother? Austin bringing his fuck buddy here so she can get a good look around."

"Hermosa?" AJ asks. "He introduced me to her last week, she's cool."

"I'm sure she is," Maggie replies dismissively, looking over her shoulder at the couch and then back to AJ. "So…" She says, wicked little smile on her face "What do you think?"

"How old are they?" AJ asks, giving his boss a look of both skepticism and concern.

"They're both nineteen," she retorts, giving him a pompous look right back. "And yes, I checked their ID's. I'm not stupid."

"Ok," he says simply, staring out the window.

She looks at him, thinks once about saying something, thinks twice, and decides against it. He catches her staring at him and gives her a look.

"What?"

"Nothing," she says quickly, diverting her gaze.

"Alright," he says then, turning to leave. "I got a strange call from Kadence Jane's people last night. They want me to come to this studio and talk to someone about maybe writing a song for her. Said they knew I was credited with a lot of the writing and production on Nique's tape and wanted to see what I can do."

"Cool," she says dismissively.

He's almost to the elevators, stops, and looks back over his shoulder. "You sure there's nothing you want to tell me?"

"I'm sure," Maggie says.

And so he leaves for his meeting.

Chapter 9

AJ arrives at the address given to him a little after eight. The studio is a one story, ranch-style, inconspicuous building that looks more like a modest home than it does a place where some of the best musical artists record. It's plainly painted, no signs anywhere, and only a couple of cars in the lot. He gets out and goes inside.

Security is right on the other side of the door. Two men dressed in all black ask him his name. He tells them. They ask to see his I.D. He shows it to them. They ask to see his phone. He hesitates briefly, but hands it to them. They tell him he'll get it back when he leaves. And then they let him pass by.

As nice as Turner's little studio had been, this one is three times as nice. The front room lounge area looks like it belongs in a top-floor office suite in New York, a vast interior contrast from the exterior first impression. There are five recording rooms, but the first four are empty. No one has told him this directly, but he gets the impression that no one else is allowed to record while Kadence is recording. He can hear the bass of a beat that's a lot harder than the typical pop songs he's heard from her seeping through the supposedly sound proof walls. It's that loud. He knocks on the door, but no one hears. He walks in, but no one notices. A heavyset black man with a thick gold chain around his neck and a Laker's flat bill on his head sits at the switchboard, nodding his head to the music. AJ recognizes him from something Nique had showed him online once, but he can't place his name at the moment; he's pretty sure he's a producer. A skinny white guy with long hair that's pulled back into a ponytail sits next to him, nodding his head in unison as well, occasionally turning a nob to adjust something. Kadence and two other girls he feels like he's seen somewhere —like in a magazine or on a movie screen—are dancing un-rhythmically in the background, lost in the music. Kadence has on a white crop-top tank top and skintight black leather leggings. She's stable in her strappy stilettos, and the array of gold bangles on her arms clink while she gyrates. Her thin arms are raised over her head, toned muscles noticeable there, as well as in her flat abdominals that flex as she undulates. Her eyes are closed, and he knows she's in her zone, her element. A place very few people probably get to see her in. The bohemian pony-tailed guy looks up and sees him.

"Kay, you got company, doll," he says while simultaneously cutting the music.

Everybody snaps out of it and suddenly all eyes are on him. The two girls that were dancing with her only stare at him briefly before going over to sit at an oval-shaped table; red Solo cups and a bowl of de-shelled nuts and dried fruit sit on the table. They stick their manicured hands into the snacks and drop cashews into their mouth. Kadence smiles radiantly, not seeming at all embarrassed that he caught her in a moment, and walks straight to him.

"You must be AJ Brooks," she says, extending her hand to him.

He suddenly becomes very aware that he's in the presence of a very big star. Sure, he's used to being around women with clout, women with money. But he's never been this close to someone this famous. There's some anxiety, even though he's read that she's a very nice person. Visits cancer-stricken kids at hospitals, holds extra-long meet and greets for her fans, regularly stops to take pictures while she's out and about. And her bright baby blue eyes and kind face are telling him the same thing. So he shoves his star-struckness down and shakes her hand while confidently meeting her eyes.

"I am."

"Very nice to meet you," she replies, still smiling. "I'm Kadence Jane."

"Yes," he grins bashfully, moving his hand back once she lets go. "I know."

"Well, you never know if someone has heard your music or not," she says modestly. "I try not to assume that everybody knows who I am."

"Trust me," he tells her with a good-hearted smile. "I'm pretty sure that everybody in the world knows who you are."

She laughs. "That may be." She grabs a bottle of Fiji water off the console next to her, unscrews the lid, takes a small sip, and then sets it back down. "So I see that you have many writing credits on Dominique Davis's EP."

"Yes, I worked very closely with him on it."

"I absolutely loved the tape," she says, staring him right in the eyes.

"That was all Dominique. He's insanely talented."

"But you wrote the words."

"Yes, some of them."

"And played instruments."

"I did the Sax and the piano, a little guitar on a track or two."

"The style was everything," she compliments. "Very unique."

"Turner Tevenot produced it. He's really the one who put all the sounds together. I'm sure he'd love to work with you. I have his number if–"

"I don't want Turner Tevenot, I want you," she states matter-of-factly.

The pot-bellied producer chuckles. The pretty girls at the table smirk. Kadence's red-painted lips are curling at the corners, too, as she crosses her arms, amusedly waiting for him to accede.

"Ok," he replies with fluster, feeling his cheeks flush a bit. "Yeah, I mean…I'd love to work with you, too. Of course."

She smiles, pearly white teeth all perfectly aligned. "Great."

He watches her turn around, the small of her back sashaying away from him. She walks to the table and moves to perch upon on it, picking a single piece of fruit out of the bowl and plunking it into her mouth. The other two girls are no longer paying attention, engrossed in their phones that they got to keep.

"So um…" he starts tentatively. "Are you wanting to me to add an instrument to something or to collaborate with you on a song or…"

"I want you to write on my new album," she says simply, reaching her hand back into the bowl.

"Gonna be her biggest one yet," the gold-chained producer says.

"We just started sessions about two weeks ago," the pony-tailed engineer fills him in. "Right now we're figuring out production, going through beats—that's why Red's here," he says, nodding to the man next to him.

"Hell yeah," gold-chained Red replies.

"We're trying to find what we can jam to, make waves with, create hits on," Ponytail continues to elaborate. "We're trying to build an entire vibe, you dig what I'm saying, man?"

"No, yeah, totally," AJ replies unsurely. "Beginning stages."

"Play him that song we did yesterday, Eddie," Kadence tells Ponytail, dropping a few cashews into her mouth. "The one with the hook and nothing else. See if he's got any ideas of where to go with it."

"Alrighty," Eddie replies, looking it up on his laptop.

"We're going to go, Kay," one of the pretty girls says, standing up.

"Yeah," the other one says. "We've gotta go get changed for the club. That new place in WeHo is having its grand opening tonight. Invite only. You should come. We can dance. Chill. Drink Rosé."

"I'm going to stay here and get some work done," she tells them. "You girls go and have fun, though. We'll catch up later."

"Ok. We'll miss you," one of them says in a sentimental voice.

"I'll miss you hooches, too," she returns in an equally sentimental tone.

AJ watches as all three of them kiss each other on the cheeks with resounding *mwahs*, and then the two girls walk past him out of the room. He doesn't realize he's still staring at the table where they'd all been until he feels a set of eyes upon him. He turns around and sees the engineer staring.

"You got a pen and some paper, buddy?" Eddie asks him. "Or are you one of these new-age 'it all lives in my mind' kind of guys?"

"No, I write stuff down still," AJ says nervously. "I have a notebook that I usually bring everywhere but I didn't know that I was going to be–"

"You need to be prepared, man," Eddie reprimands him. "This kind of opportunity comes once in a life time. You can't be slipping on a job that might get your ass a Grammy, dude."

"Be nice, Eddie," Kadence scolds, but her eyes are on AJ, and they're shimmering with a smile. "We've got paper here, get him a sheet."

"Sure, sure," Eddie says submissively, getting up and disappearing into another room.

Kadence pats the back of the chair next to her. "Come. Sit."

AJ leaves his post by the door and does as he's told, taking a seat at the table she sits upon. Her long, leather clad leg is resting right in his line of vision. Eddie comes back with a sheet of paper and a pen. He lays it on the table, then sits back down at the switchboard and puts the music back on. AJ listens diligently to the melody that fills his ears, paying close attention to all the empty spaces between perfectly sung choruses that he's there to fill. And then he picks up the pen.

Chapter 10

It's eleven o'clock on a Friday night. Austin just spent the last four hours at an upscale soiree in the hills with an elegant sixty-something on his arm. His date told him to keep his mouth shut going in, not wanting the other rich attendants to hear his country twang and become unimpressed. For his hourly price he was okay with being the silent, sexy, smiling stud she wanted. He let her do all the talking and tell whatever story she wanted to tell about him and how they met, supportively nodding and caressing her hand. After faking a relationship all night he was finally off the clock. And after sipping champagne all night, he was ready for some whiskey.

He texts AJ and asks if he wants to meet for drinks at the Blue Bar.

Austin's still got his Armani tux on, complete with the little bowtie and the pocket square. When AJ walks through the door Austin chuckles, because his coworker is sporting a Tom Ford tux of his own.

"Where you comin' from?" Austin asks as AJ plops down on the barstool next to him.

"The theater," AJ answers in a fake aristocratic voice, smiling. "You?"

"Mansion party," Austin says.

"Are we talking *Eyes Wide Shut* mansion party, or just a house party with butlers and hors d'oeuvres and gold diggers?" AJ asks, only half sarcastic.

"Somebody on the private drive adopted a new Ethiopian baby," Austin tells him. "It was like a 'welcome home' thing, except I never saw the first kid, let alone baby. Seemed like just another fancy excuse for rich folks to get drunk. My client was a recent divorcee. You know how that goes. Gotta have a new boy-toy for the shindigs so your friends won't think you've become a spinstress."

"Well at least all we had to do tonight was be arm candy," AJ says, grabbing a couple peanuts from the can on the counter. "No second tier folder shit."

"Well…"

"Hey now," AJ says with a randy smirk.

"I wasn't really expectin' it to go that far," Austin admits as he toys with a peanut shell. "She was actin' kinda shitty towards me the whole night, but then when we was leavin' she pulled me into the back of the limo and started rippin' my clothes off."

"Make that money, "AJ tells him.

Calvin finally makes his way to their end of the bar, typical good-natured smile on his face. The first few buttons of his floral printed shirt are unbuttoned, and a single, dainty chain hangs on his smooth chest. Austin looks up and then away.

"Well look at you two dapper dons," Calvin kids when he takes in their appearance and attire. "What can I do you for?"

"Funny you should ask," AJ kids jokingly.

"Jack and Coke," Austin says quickly, looking instantly flustered.

"Bourbon," AJ says.

"I'll be back in a flash," Calvin tells them.

Austin relaxes on his stool a bit and shrugs his suit jacket off. "So," he says to AJ, grabbing a handful of peanuts. "Is it true that you're gonna be writin' for Kadence Jane?"

"Our boss has a big mouth," AJ says stoically, though he doesn't sound mad.

"I ain't gonna tell nobody," Austin assures him.

"Yeah," AJ relents after a beat, trying to keep the smile off his face, but Austin can tell how excited he is. "I'm going to be working with her on her upcoming album."

Calvin drops their drinks off and then gets back to work; the bar is bustling.

"Man, that's crazy," Austin says, taking a sip of his whiskey. "All the girls back in Ohio idolize her."

"She's a pretty big deal," AJ admits, keeping his enthusiasm collected while taking a cool sip of his own drink.

There's a shout from the other end of the room, and they both turn to look. There's a table full of obvious out-of-towners, by the looks of it probably there for the Pacers and Lakers game later that week. They are clearly very drunk, and acting obnoxious and rowdy as they try to holler at a group of girls across the bar who clearly aren't interested in their advances. The loudest one is wearing a yellow and blue jersey with Wrangler jeans that are tucked into a pair of cowboy boots. He's got a camouflage Cabela's hat with a fishing hook stuck on the bill, and a tattoo of a deer head on his pale upper arm. His two friends are dressed similarly. Austin is very familiar with the getup.

"What state are the Pacers from?" AJ asks him, eyeing the idiots judgmentally out of the corner of his eye.

"Indiana," Austin tells him. "They're playin' us tomorrow night."

"Hm," AJ replies uninterestedly, focusing back on his bourbon.

One of the rednecks drops a glass, and they all cuss and laugh as it shatters on the floor.

"Hey, bartender!" A guy with a rebel flag belt buckle yells. "We got a mess over here! You better prance your little ass over here and clean it up 'fore one of us gets cut and we sue y'all!"

Calvin immediately stops what he's doing and goes behind the bar to grab a broom and a dustpan.

"Hurry up, dude!" One of the other guys yells. "I gotta piss and all the glass is blockin' my way to the john. I'll take a piss right here on the floor if you don't get it cleaned up fast, and then your ass will have to clean that up, too."

Calvin silently and quickly gets all the glass swept into the bin, trying his best to ignore them, but before he can walk away they stop him.

"Hey, where you goin'?" The ringleader asks him with a crazed look. "I need me another Jim Beam, I'm talkin' pronto."

"I think you've had enough," Calvin tells him neutrally.

The deer-tatted ringleader looks at his friends and then stands. "You hear this little nigger trying to tell *me* what *my* limit is?"

Austin watches as Calvin's head immediately drops and he takes two steps back from the table, clearly threatened and scared. In the same second, out of the corner of his eye, Austin sees his co-worker's head snap around.

"Hey!" AJ shouts in terse yet controlled voice. "Watch your mouth. You're not in the sticks anymore and we don't talk like that around here."

Austin sits quietly and stares at the counter, even as his own blood begins to boil, while AJ reprimands the out-of-towners with his words and his eyes. He glances over, and can tell instantly that AJ has struck a nerve with the hicks. Their focus has moved from Calvin, and now they're glaring across the room at them.

"Shut the fuck up, pretty boy!" The ringleader yells at AJ. The look in the redneck's empty eyes is menacing. He leers as he leans and points his thick finger. "I ain't takin no damn orders from you. I'll talk however the hell I wanna talk, ya hear me?"

"It's fine, AJ," Calvin says quietly, passing by them as he goes back behind the bar to empty the dustbin. "They're not worth it."

But AJ can't be deterred. He's still glaring right back at the racists.

"Try picking up a book sometime or stepping outside the lines of your miniscule, underworked, closed-off little minds," AJ tells them dryly, taking sip of bourbon. "Because you sound ignorant as hell."

"Oh yeah?" Says the ringleader. He gets a dumb smirk on his face, and then he turns his hateful eyes back on Calvin. "At least I don't sound like a fruity ass faggot like your little bartender friend."

The two backup bigots start to laugh.

And that's when Austin's control snaps.

He may not have shrewd comebacks like AJ, but he has hands.

He jumps up, sending his stool flying backwards to the floor with a thud. He gets to where the hillbilly is standing in two strides and punches him right in the face, knocking him straight to the floor in a single throw. One of the big mouth's buddies charges at him, but Austin gets him in a headlock and has flipped him to the floor before he can do anything. The third guy doesn't even try, and instead takes off out the back like a dog with its tail between its legs. Patrons gasp and then the bar goes silent. AJ and Calvin's eyes are wide and their jaws are on the floor, the surprising turn of events shocking them both into a stupor. The rednecks are on the ground moaning in pain and cursing under their breath. The kitchen door swings open and the owner rushes out from the back, having heard the commotion.

"What the hell is going on?" The older man asks, scanning the room with his hands in his hair. His eyes land on the two Pacers fans who are trying to pick themselves up off the floor, and Austin who's standing a few feet away holding his hand. "Do you all want to go to jail tonight?"

"That fuckin' idiot in the dress shirt attacked us," the bleeding ringleader whines as he moves into a sitting position. "We ain't do nothin'"

The older man turns to Austin. "You," he says, snapping his fingers. "Out."

Without saying anything, Austin opens his wallet, throws some money on the bar to cover his drink, and calmly heads for the exit. AJ jumps up and follows him.

"Do these idiots need a medic, ya think?" He hears the owner ask someone right before he pushes the backdoor open.

"Remind me to never mess with you," AJ jokes once their outside.

The cool air soothes Austin's hot cheeks. "Yeah," he says, sticking his hands in his pockets and looking bashful for someone who just laid two grown men out on the floor like it was nothing. "I ain't a violent person like that, but I just felt like I needed to defend him against them assholes."

"It was pretty badass," AJ tells him. "I'd buy you a drink at another bar, but I have an early client in the morning."

"Yeah, I got an early client, too," Austin replies.

"Is your hand going to be okay?" AJ asks, taking out his keys and unlocking his GTO.

"It'll be fine I think."

"Alright," AJ says, opening the car door and getting in. "I'll see ya."

The vintage sports car comes to life with a growl and then peels out of the parking lot. Austin unlocks his truck and is just about to get in when he hears a voice behind him.

"Hey, Austin, wait up!"

Austin turns around and sees Calvin sprinting towards him.

"Here," the bartender says breathlessly when he catches up. He holds out a bag of frozen vegetable to him. "Pees for your hand."

Austin grins boyishly. "Thanks," he says, taking the cold bag and putting it on the back of his sore hand.

"You know you didn't have to do what you did," Calvin tells him

"They shouldn't have been sayin that stuff," Austin replies simply.

"Yeah," Calvin utters.

They both just stand there outside of his truck for a moment, looking at each other and not saying anything. Austin can tell that Calvin is genuinely grateful for him sticking up for him, and Austin is genuinely glad that he did.

"Well," Calvin says after a while, looking down at the ground bashfully and sticking his hands in the pockets of his bright green pants. "I better get back to work."

"Okay," Austin says.

Calvin turns to leave, and then stops. "Thank you."

"No problem," Austin replies.

He watches him walk the rest of the way back to the bar, and then he gets in his truck and leaves.

Chapter 11

The second time AJ goes to the studio to meet Kadence, the sun is down and the parking lot is empty. He walks in, and there's the burly man in all black.

"He can keep his phone this time."

AJ turns around and sees her strutting down the hall towards them. She's smiling like she was last time, wearing a white lace top, dark wash skinny jeans, and brown cowboy boots. A throwback to her Nashville roots, he thinks.

"If you wish, Ms. Jane," the man says.

"I think I can trust him," she tells the security guard in a playful tone, and then she suddenly locks eyes with him. "I can trust you, right, AJ?"

"Yes. Yes, of course."

The corners of her mouth curl into a smile. "Good." She stares at him a second more, then looks way. "This is Bill, by the way. The other guy you might have seen last time is Mike. They've both been with me since the beginning."

AJ nods his head at Bill and Bill nods back. And then Kadence leads him back down the hall from where she came.

"What's up with the phone thing, anyway?" He asks as he walks into the empty and quiet recording room, a vast difference from the last time.

"It's just a precaution, something we do with people who aren't in my immediate circle. Don't want someone recording snippets of a new song that I don't want to release yet, or leaking pictures of people I'm working with, things that I want to keep a surprise for my fans. Also, as I'm sure you know, privacy is something a person like me has to really strive to maintain, being in the center of the public eye and everything. Discretion is important to me and a bunch of extra phones in the room really endanger that."

"I can respect that," he says sincerely, then grins. "And I'm very discreet. I promise, I won't even so much as look at my phone. Even if it's going off like crazy. Even if it's my mom."

"It's cool," she says with a smile, sitting down on a chair. "You give me a very trustworthy vibe."

"I'm glad," he replies, taking a seat in a chair a few feet from hers. "So where is everyone else at?"

"It's just us. Is that okay?"

"Yeah, of course. I just thought we'd need Red and…what's his name…Eddie here to make music."

She snorts derisively. "No. Red isn't even one of my regular producers. We've never done anything together. Don't get me wrong; he's a hot producer, maybe even the hottest producer right now as far as hip-hop goes. Anytime we're at events together he's always talking *let's do a song, let's do a song*. So when he heard through the grapevine that I was starting work on a new album, he naturally wanted in on it. Or, should I say, he wanted a production credit on it. Not to toot my own horn, but I'm pretty much a sure thing when it comes to awards. That's just a fact of life. People want to ride my wave to the Grammys. And that's fine, I get it, but Red makes rap records. I like to listen to it, but do I really look like I'm about to spit some slick shit about slinging grams, and throwing signs, and whipping Wraiths?"

"Not in those boots," AJ tells her, grinning.

She rolls her eyes with a smirk. "Anyway. I just wanted to work on writing today. And Eddie will just get in the way of that. He's great at what he does as an engineer, but he's not the deepest guy, if you know what I mean. He isn't gonna come up with the words or concepts I need. So until it's time to press the buttons and turn the knobs, he can stay home as far as I'm concerned."

"Ok," AJ consents with a smile. He sits down on the piano bench and pats the spot next to him for her to do the same. And she does. "So I guess the first step to help you help me know what kind of songs to write, is for you to tell me what kind of album you want to make? Do you want to stick to pop? Do you want to go back to country?"

"I never wanted to be a country singer," she admits easily. "But country fans are loyal. You win them over once and they're with you for life. They buy CDs. They buy concert tickets. They come to see you anytime you're in their town, and if you don't come to their town they drive to see you. Country fans are the definition of ride or die. They make pop fans look fickle and hip-hop fans look downright cheap. I knew I wanted to build my base around a country core. All I had to do was give them one album, give them a Dolly or a Reba rendition whenever I'm in Tulsa or Tupelo, and they'll support me for the duration. In their mind I might be a sellout, but like it or not they're still buying what I'm selling. So with the funds from my first album—which went platinum in a month, might I add—I made the mainstream album that would get me the kids, the radio stations, and the number ones. Now I've got everybody."

"So what you're saying is…you pandered to the people of country to get your start," he sasses her a bit, still giving her a good-natured smile just so she knows he means no harm by it.

"I didn't pander. I just gave them something I knew they'd want."

He nods with a small smile, accepting what she says but not necessarily believing it. "Still," he says. "Coming from Memphis, for example, blues and jazz is always going to find its way into some of the stuff I write, whether it's for an R&B guy, or a rocker, or whatever. I can't imagine that you weren't at least somewhat influenced by country music growing up in Nashville."

"Well…" she starts, hesitating a moment, like she doesn't know how much she really wants to divulge. "I'm actually not from Nashville. I was born and raised in La Folette."

"Oh," he replies, thrown off a bit because he doesn't remember reading anything about that when he did his Google search of her. "Is that like a suburb of Nashville, or…"

"It's like three hours away. Poor little Tennessee town that nobody has heard of. It's just easier to say I'm from Nashville. Plus, when the world first met me I was living in Nashville. I moved there as soon as I got discovered, like fifteen or sixteen. So I basically did kind of grow up there."

"Going back to my first question," he says, pushing past the mystifying fact that the Inter-web doesn't know her actual birthplace or that she's not a native Nashvillian. "Now that you've got everybody, as you say," he quirks his head cutely at her and she smiles. "Now that you've got the entire world's attention…what do you want to say on this third album? What is the tone you want to set?"

She thinks about it a second, then looks at him. "Raw. Strong. Serious," she says with conviction. "I want to be taken seriously. I want the world to see me as more than just some teenybopper pop star. I want to be seen as a legend."

"Okay."

"Think Barbara. Mariah. Whitney. I want to transcend demographics and genres; I want them to see me as a vocalist and not just a hit-turner-outer. I mean I still want hits. I still want at least six singles, don't get me wrong."

"Right, right."

"With this album I just want there to be no question who the person at the helm of this here music thing really is. I want it to immortalize me."

"You want it to be timeless," he says.

"Exactly," she agrees.

"You want it to say 'I don't really need to rely on the gimmicks and the auto-tune and the catchy hooks. I was just doing all of that for fun, here's the real talent.'"

"Yes."

"The stripped down sound."

"Yes."

"So maybe we don't use overly produced beats they send by the CD-full," he suggests. "At least not for every song. Maybe we use a little guitar."

He picks his up and starts to play a few cords, settling into a nice rhythmic pattern of strumming in no time.

She smiles and nods her head like she likes it.

"Sing over it," he tells her.

She hesitates. Looking a little like a dear in the headlights without any words.

"Say 'I want you to see me'," he helps start her off, never ceasing what he's doing with the strings.

She nods, listens for a few more seconds, then sings, "I want you to see me. See me."

AJ nods, continuing to play as she harmonizes wordlessly, her voice bare and beautiful.

"What it takes to be me, you wouldn't want to be me," she continues singing, coming up with her own words now. "No this isn't easy. Easy."

"Perfect, AJ says quietly, smiling now as he strums.

"But I won't let it beat me. Beat me."

AJ takes one hand off of his guitar to hit a few keys on the piano, leading her into the first verse.

"Sometimes I shut the whole world out. So many critics full of doubt. So many faces whose smiles are fake, so many people who don't know me full of hate. No, I can't change their minds or make them see–"

"My will, my ways, this is destiny," AJ contributes as it comes to him, though he knows he sounds like shit because he can't sing.

"They could never comprehend what this world has tried to take from me," she follows.

"My heart, my art, the most important parts of me," AJ adds, coming up with words easily. He stops strumming.

"But I want you to see me. See me," she sings, finishing the stanza off a-capella.

They both just stare at each other when it's over, grinning from ear-to-ear.

"That was a really good start," she tells him excitedly. "The music. The words. That felt really natural."

"Yeah," he agrees, still grinning.

And then the next thing he knows his guitar has slipped to the floor and their mouths are fused together. After a heated moment they both realize what's happening, and quickly pull apart. Her mouth is agape and she looks just as shocked by the kiss as he feels. He's not sure who initiated it, whose lips got to whose first, but he suddenly feels the need to apologize.

"I'm sorry, I–"

"No," she says, meeting his eyes. "I want you to. I want you."

With that omission, he picks her up and locks his lips back on hers. Their tongues fight for dominance as he walks them backwards. He deposits her down on the couch and watches her watch him with her blazing blue eyes as he unbuttons his shirt and shrugs it off. The second he's over her, her hands are everywhere. He peels her clothes off piece-by-piece, teeth nipping and mouth plundering each part of her as it's exposed, reveling in the way she writhes under him. Her own fingers are making quick work of his belt and zipper, her own mouth sucking and teeth biting on the skin of his neck in a way that will surely break blood vessels and leave a mark. But he doesn't care. Once he has her completely naked, he runs his hands over every inch of her body, then his tongue, and then when she's shaking and quivering all over he moves inside of her. They move through different positions on different surfaces: couch to floor, floor to table, table to piano, piano to wall and then back down to the floor where they collapse when it's over.

"That was…that was like…" She's stuttering breathlessly, trying to find her words when her mind hasn't reconnected with her body just yet.

"Like what?" He asks with a coy smile.

"Like the best. The best ever," she says with a big smile, turning her head to look at him, blue eyes sparkling.

"Thank you," he replies, consciously trying not to sound too smug. They're both on their backs on the throw rug covering the floor. There's no sheets or blankets to cover them, nothing but air between them, both completely exposed. He's just about to reach out and pull her to him when she starts to stand.

"Thank *you*," she says back lowly, voice still husky and hoarse. She picks her panties up off the floor and slides them back up her slender legs, then grabs her bra off the arm of the couch and puts it back on, clasping it behind her back.

AJ follows her lead. "My pleasure," he says modestly, finding his boxers and jeans and pulling them back on. They're both quiet for a while as they get redressed.

"Listen," she finally says, sitting down on the couch to pull her boots on. She's got her jeans back on, but she's still topless save for her light pink bra. The skin of her pale chest is speckled with the red flush of recent sex. "I'd really appreciate it if we could keep this between us. Not that I think you'd run and tell a gossip site that you slept with me or anything like that. But even if you tell a friend, they can tell a friend, and…well…you know."

"I won't tell anyone," he tells her, tugging his undershirt down. He retrieves his flannel from the floor and returns it to his body.

"It's just something I always have to worry about." She rolls up her lace-embroidered shirt and pulls it on over her head. "Male celebrities and ball players, they have their liaisons sign confidentiality agreements, they have those papers on deck because they do it so often. Us female celebrities, we don't have random encounters like that all the time. At least I don't. But God forbid I slip up, front page news. Yanno?" She pulls a compact out of her Birkin bag and checks herself in the glass. "We women, we don't have the privilege of not being scrutinized for our sexuality. It's just –"

"Kadence," he cuts her off with a comforting look, sitting down on the piano bench to tie his shoes. "You have nothing to worry about with me. I get it. I understand. And I promise I won't say anything to anyone. I would never do anything to jeopardize your wellbeing or your career."

"Thank you." She snaps the little mirror shut and stares at him. "That…that means a lot."

"Now," he says, taking a playful tone with her as he laces his sneakers. "Am I offended that you referred to me as both a random encounter and a slip up in one breath? Yes." He looks up and flashes her a smile. "But I suppose I can get over it."

She laughs out loud. "You know I didn't mean it like that."

"Made me feel a little like a cheap gigolo, if I'm being completely honest."

"And what does a cheap gigolo feel like?" She asks flirtatiously, playing along.

"No idea." His eyes sparkle with innuendo she'll never know.

She giggles again and shakes her head. "Well I would never want to make you feel like that." And then she gives him a serious look. "You're special."

"Pshh," he says, crossing his legs and looking down at his notebook. "You're just saying that cause you feel bad now."

"No. Really," her voice comes sincerely. "And I hope…I hope that what happened here today won't affect what we're doing with these songs. At least not negatively. I don't want you to think I called you over here to…trust me, I had no idea that was going to happen…we just have such a strong energy and chemistry and it briefly lapsed into something other than music. But I still very much want for you to work with me on my album."

"I still very much want to work with you on your album," he replies, meeting her eyes.

She smiles. "Good."

They finish the first song and start writing another, although they don't get all the way through. He doesn't hear from her for three days after he leaves the studio that night. Then on the fourth day she calls and asks him to come over so they can complete the second song. He assumes she means the studio. But she means her house, and texts him the address he knows many probably wish they had.

The evening sun is burning low as he pulls up to her sprawling Tarzana mansion. He gets buzzed in at the gate—something he's used to by now when visiting women, though he's sure she probably thinks it's new for him—and heads up the winding private drive. The house is built into an incline, the first floor only visible from one side. It's a four-story stucco mix of contemporary and Spanish with a lot of glass. The acreage goes on as far as the eye can see, no neighbors in sight, and every manicured blade of grass is perfectly green, despite the San Fernando heat. There's three luxury vehicles parked out front: a red Porsche 911, a white Mercedes G-Wagon, and a mat-black Rang Rover. Off to the side of the house in a separate cobblestone lot, a few other nice—but not as nice—cars are parked; he gets the feeling they belong to other people.

He gets out and strolls up the walkway to the door with his notebook in hand, pressing a finger to the bell and listening to it echo grandiosely on the other side. A second or two later a middle-aged maid opens the door. She smiles but doesn't step aside, staring at him with a questioning gaze.

"I'm here to see Kadence," he tells her politely, returning her smile. "AJ Brooks."

She still says nothing.

"Thank you, Consuelo," he hears a familiar voice say somewhere in the house, and then Kadence appears behind the woman. "I'll take it from here. Gracias." She smiles sweetly with her red lipstick-covered mouth as she puts her hands on the older woman's shoulders and ushers her out of the way.

AJ takes in the young pop star. She's still in full makeup, but she's dressed very casually in a baggy, black zip-up hoodie that has a red heart with angry eyes in the upper right hand corner, a plain white t-shirt underneath, little denim shorts, and a pair of Adidas Original Superstars on her feet.

"Sorry about that," she says, turning and walking away from him. "The language barrier makes her self-conscience, I think, so she just chooses not to speak. Did you find it okay?"

"Uh…yeah," he says, closing the door behind him and following her into the house. "Biggest house on the street. Only house on the street, really."

"Yeah," she replies with a nonchalant laugh. "Gotta do it big when you're this far out to compensate for not living in the city. I had a condo in West Hollywood when I first moved to LA. It was fine at the time, but privacy became a huge issue." She leads him past a high-ceilinged living room with wood floors, white rugs, new age furniture, and an ornamental fireplace. "And then I was looking at a place in Malibu before I got this one. But paparazzi stays parked at the bottom of all those hills."

"Well it's certainly nice. And three cars to boot, too," he playfully chides her.

"Four. There's a Bentley in the garage," she smiles over her shoulder.

He's heard other people talking ever since he walked in the door, but he didn't know where the voices were coming from until they get to the kitchen. A thirty-something woman in a pants suit with a stylish bob is sitting on one of the barstools, furiously typing away at a laptop. A forty-something man in a blazer and slacks is pacing the expanse of the kitchen, phone pressed to his ear as he argues with the person on the other end, eventually coming to a stop at the table to type something on his own laptop. And then there's a twenty-something girl with a nervous face and a ponytail, doctoring up a drink in a Starbuck's cup, the discarded Styrofoam carrier sitting a few feet or so away on the countertop.

"This is my publicist, Bridget. My manager, Ken. And my assistant, Shelley," she explains, pointing to each person. "Guys, this is AJ Brooks."

"Hey," they all say in unamused unison, none looking up from their respective tasks.

"There's been a bit of a social media shit storm today," she tells him. "Another artist from a less popular genre of music felt personally offended that I racked in more nominations for the upcoming music awards than her, and decided to channel her pangs of rejection and inadequateness by stirring the pot on Twitter." She shrugs. "I'm letting them handle it."

The three people in her kitchen continue to work without speaking.

"Gummy bear?" Kadence offers, lifting the lid off one of three glass canisters sitting on her island. The other two have perfectly arranged cupcakes and multicolored macaroons in them. The gummy bear jar seems to be the only one that gets eaten out of, as it's half empty.

"No thank you," he declines, watching her pop a green bear and a red bear into her mouth.

"Here you go, Kay," the ponytailed girl says as she puts the lid back on the Starbucks cup and hands it to Kadence.

"Thanks, Shell," Kadence replies graciously, taking the cup and taking a sip.

The mousy girl nods meekly and then retreats back into the kitchen. Kadence takes him by the hand and pulls him forward. The somewhat intimate gesture of her holding hands with him takes him by surprise, seeing as they are currently in the presence of three other people, but he doesn't refute it.

"C'mon," she says, "I'll show you the upstairs."

He lets her lead him past the white winding staircase, and down the hall. The walls are covered with eccentric artwork and bright paintings.

"Is that a Delaney?" He asks, pointing at a particular painting he recognizes, the style reminding him of an art exhibit he went to with Anjanae.

"Oh I don't know," she says. "I'm not really into art."

This statement sounds strange to him, especially coming from a musical artist. But then he supposes the different expressions aren't all fluent, and a singer doesn't necessarily have to have appreciation for a painter and vice versa.

"I just wanted something crazy and cool to hang on the walls, they looked so plain," she explains. "My interior decorator picked out the pieces."

They come to a stop in front of the elevator. She presses the button, and it's instantly there. They bypass floors 2 and 3 altogether and the doors reopen at 4.

"This way," she says, sashaying off the elevator down the sunlight-lit hall.

"So are we going to work on the song?" He asks, skeptical of her agenda. If she wants to have sex with him again, he's fine with that, he just wants to know what his mind should be focusing on

"Yeah," she says, disappearing into a room. "I just need to grab something real quick. I thought we'd go up on the rooftop terrace and work on it while there's still some daylight left."

He comes to lean up against the open door she went in, peering into what appears to be her bedroom. It's a wide-open space with an entire glass-enclosed wall, walk-off balcony, the works. Her bed sits up high with a canopy over it. There's a long dresser flanked by a gigantic mirror on one side, the entrance to an elaborate walk-in closet on the other side, and a circular glass table with a single vase of pink peonies smack dap in the middle. The color scheme of the room is blush with gold accents, floored with rich Brazilian walnut boards.

She takes a sip of her drink, grimaces, and pitches it in the wastebasket.

"That bad?"

"I don't know if I'm not annunciating clearly or if the girl doesn't understand what I mean when I say a plain Chai Tea, bring it home, add two teaspoons of honey and half a packet of Stevia, because that clearly had Starbuck's Sweet-and-Low in it."

"Well shame on her," he ribs her.

"I love Shelley, I'm sure it was an honest mistake." She grabs something that looks like a sunglasses case off her dresser, smiles as she walks past him back out of the room, and then leads the way up a small staircase and out onto the roof.

He immediately has to squint. Even though the sun is setting, it is still bright. But once his eyes adjust, his breath is taken away. He walks from one end of the roof to the other, taking it all in. One side looks down onto her backyard: a huge in-ground pool with mixed stone steps, an attached hot tub in a romantic alcove, four fire pits, five cabanas, six palm trees, and an array of exotic looking flowers. Her gardener is roaming around below, clipping and spraying plants so everything keeps a healthy glow. The other side looks out over a hillside that rolls out into the valley, spurts of grass and trees that stretch to the end of the horizon, the sparkling lights of the city visible way out in the distance.

"Wow," AJ utters in awe. "What a beautiful view."

"It's pretty nice," she replies coolly, sitting down on one of the lawn chairs.

He walks over and takes a seat in the lawn chair closest to her, laying his notebook on the table between them. She pops open the sunglasses case and takes out a Bic lighter and some rolling papers. He eyes her curiously, a smirk forming on his face. She grins at him, wagging her eyebrows mischievously as she reaches into her hoodie pocket and pulls out a bag of marijuana. He watches her lay out a paper, placing a filter at one end, and then start to break down the leaves and arrange them in a nice even layer.

"I didn't peg you as a smoker," he comments.

"A girl's got a lot of stress, gotta take the edge off occasionally."

"I don't blame you. Your life is crazy."

"You ain't seen anything yet. This is my calm season, when I'm working on an album. Wait till release time when I have to do promo twelve hours a day in twelve cities a week, in between shooting videos for the singles and shooting covers for magazines and signing CDs in fifty different Targets," she explains as she expertly rolls the joint between her fingers to compact it. "And then after the album drops and having to plan a tour, rehearsing dance routines for hours on end, taking it on the road for six months straight, meet and greets, eighteen hour flights, sending guest verses from foreign countries, talk show appearances, award show performances. Shit gets crazy, this is just the calm."

"I can't even imagine," he says honestly. "I don't know how you do it."

She licks the edge, twists it up, and packs it down. "Light me," she says to him, placing the filtered end between her red lips.

He grabs the Bic and sparks it, holding the flame to her handy work until it catches. She inhales deeply, holding that first hit in for some time. The thick aroma is already filling his nose. He's always found the scent atrocious, but he's certainly not going to stop her from indulging and unwinding. She exhales a huge plume of smoke without coughing.

"It comes with the territory, you learn to deal with it," she says, her voice strained and altered, eyes already reddening. "I had my first single at seventeen and it went to number one in two weeks. Instant fame. Didn't have a clue what to do."

She puts the joint between his lips, and he doesn't refuse it. He inhales and hopes to God he doesn't choke. He does. Coughing and hacking for a good ten seconds before he gets his breath back. She doesn't say anything, though; just smiles and takes the joint back from him, taking another easy drag off it.

"Luckily for me," she continues, after blowing a sexy string of smoke through her pursed lips. "I had a great team and got through it unscathed. None of those ugly pitfalls that other teen stars fall victim to."

She holds it out to him and he takes it again. This time he doesn't cough, though he still has to fight it.

"Yeah, your career has pretty much been straight up," he replies hoarsely. "No dips or nose dives or scandals." He takes another hit before passing it back to her. "That's pretty..." he searches for a word in his mind but can't find it. "Good."

"Yup," she says, voice cracking. She coughs once. "Now I'm twenty-two. Two albums in. Fifty singles later." She leans off the lawn chair and grins at him, her already small eyes looking exceptionally squinty. "Imma pro, baby."

He's grinning, too. "Fifty singles...you think you might be exaggerating there a bit, Miss Jane?"

He reaches for it this time. She takes another hit and then hands it over.

"Close enough," she tells him, shrugging her hoodie off and sitting back.

"I want to ask you something," he says after a moment. "There's something I want to know...something I've wondered about my whole life." He inhales deeply, holds it, and then exhales. "That's a lie. I've wondered about it for...mm...maybe a week. Coulda been day." He's about to take another hit but then stops for a second, scrunches his eyebrows up, and looks over at her. "What was I saying?"

She takes the joint from him. "You wanted to ask me a question."

"Right, right." He pauses again, still a little foggy on what that question was. "Oh yeah, I got it now." He presents it to her in a very serious tone. "Okay. Is Kadence with a K your real name?"

"Nope," she croaks.

"Cadence with a C?"

"Nope." She takes another hit.

"Well what is it then? The suspense is killing me."

"Here," she says, retuning the quickly diminishing joint to him. "You can't tell nobody, okay?"

"Pinky," he says, wagging his little finger as he returns the joint to his mouth.

She hesitates for a few seconds more, then relents.

"Caroline."

"No it's not," he laughs, hearing the inebriation in his own voice, and then chuckling again out how silly he sounds. "Caroline what?"

"Caroline Janie Sanders."

"So neither your first nor middle...middle...middle last name is accurate?" He shakes his head. "Such a deceiver, you are," he jokes, starting to hold the joint a little more naturally as he takes yet another drag. "Tell me one more thing. And I promise...I swear I won't tell a soul if you are. But I have to know. Are you related to the Colonel?"

She gives him a confused look.

"The Kentucky fried Colonel. Colonel G Sanders."

"No," she laughs with a snort.

He nods his head reflectively. "My real name is Andrew. People just call me AJ, but that's not what the birth certificate says. I don't correct them. I let them speculate what the A and the J stands for. Could be anything." He holds it back to his lips, inhales, exhales. "I like to keep with the mys*tique*."

She's staring at him with a shit-eating grin on her face.

"What?" He asks with obliviousness, passing the little stub to her.

"You are so lit right now," she informs him, taking a final hit, putting it out on the table, and then tossing the roach to the floor for her hired help to clean up later.

"I think it might have been good weed," he remarks, sitting back.

"Do you think I'd have bad weed?" She asks sarcastically.

He just smiles.

She gets up off her lawn chair and climbs onto his. "You're cute stoned," she tells him, running her fingers through his hair as she stares into his low eyes.

"Thank you," he replies, pulling her face down to his so he can kiss her.

"Have you ever had sex on a roof?" She asks against his mouth, moving one slender leg on either side of his body to straddle him.

"I might have, but honestly I can't remember much right now," he tells her, knotting one hand in her blonde hair.

She just laughs and pulls her shirt over her head.

The next morning AJ is making his way back down the private drive in his GTO with the windows rolled down. He hadn't intended on spending the night when he arrived the evening before, but he wound up sleeping in her big California King canopy bed with her anyway, and he wasn't complaining. The sun is bright as he reaches the bottom and pulls out onto the residential street, a ray reflecting off the glass of a plain silver Prius parked along the side of the road. He thinks nothing of it as he drives on, but a second or two later he looks up into his rearview mirror and sees that the little silver car is right behind him now, tailing him dangerously close. At first AJ thinks undercover cop, but he's never known a cop to drive that type of vehicle, and when he checks his speed, he sees that he's not going over. The car looks like it's trying to sideline him. *Someone with road rage who's pissed they can't pass yet*, he figures. AJ decides to be a good sport and pulls over so they can go on by. But as the silver Prius pulls even with him, flashing lights blind him. Camera flashes. Multiple. Bursts in quick succession like shots from a silent sniper rifle. He instinctively moves his hand to cover his face. And then he can *hear* the shots, *snap snap snap*, because his window is down, and now theirs is, too, and they're not moving on. He hears someone say *What's your name, kid? You Kadence's friend? Kind of early, you spend the night?*

AJ's foot hits the gas hard, cutting the wheel with one hand and rolling up the window with the other. He roughly maneuvers his car through someone's yard and then jerks it back onto the road; swerving as he briefly loses traction and before quickly straightening it back out again. He hits eighty in no time, then ninety. Once he makes it to the highway he passes the first two cars he comes upon in order to put them between him and the Prius. He makes a left turn, then a right turn, and then once he's satisfied that he's thrown them off his track, he takes out his phone and calls Kadence.

"I must have left some impression on you last night," she answers seductively, smile in her voice.

"I'm so sorry, Kadence," he blurts out. "They were parked at the end of the street and it was an unmarked car and I didn't think...I wasn't thinking...if I had known I would have went another way or waited or sped by before they could...I'm so sorry. I didn't say anything to them and I got away but they–"

"AJ, calm down, I don't know what you're trying to tell me," she says calmly. "Now take a deep breath and explain slowly."

"The paparazzi. They saw me leaving your house and I think they might have got some pictures of my face. And they definitely got pictures of my car."

"It's okay, AJ," she tells him, sounding surprisingly unbothered by what he's just told her. "They're vultures just circling, it's only a matter of time before they swoop down and try to pick something up. Anything. Anything to sell a story."

"You're not mad?"

"No. It'll probably never make paper, but if my people get pressed for a statement we'll just say you're a songwriter and you were over here working on my album. We'll say other people were here, too. It was a late session. Hell, you might have been over here to see Shelly…who knows. They sure as hell don't."

"It's that simple?"

"Sure. Or I just won't make a statement at all. They don't have to know who you are."

"Ok," he says, breathing out a sigh of relief that he hadn't just inadvertently put a major snag in her day.

"Ok?" She reiterates, just to make sure he's ok.

"Yeah."

"Good. Now…I have a photo-shoot to get ready for, and somebody kept me up half the night, meaning it's going to take some extra time in the makeup chair to have me cover ready," she says with trouble in her voice. "So I'm going to hop off here and I'll call you later. Alright?"

He chuckles lightly. "Ok. That's fine. Have fun."

He hangs up feeling pleasantly light, but tangentially off kilter.

~

Jae comes over with food later, and AJ breaks his promise. But he has to tell someone, and he trusts Jae probably more than anyone else in the world.

"So you know how I told you I was writing some songs for Kadence Jane," he says, scooping some fried rice onto his fork out of the handmade carton with Jae's food truck logo on it.

"Yeah," Jae says, taking a sip of beer.

"Well…I've kind of been spending time with her outside of the music. I'm uh…well…I'm sleeping with her."

Jae glances up. "For money?"

"No, for sport, "AJ replies. He rolls his eyes with a smile and takes a drink. "I like her. I like spending time with her."

"Oh," Jae says simply.

"What?"

"She just doesn't really seem like your type," Jae tells him. "That's all."

"And what's my type?" AJ asks curiously.

"I don't know…someone a little more two dimensional and deep."

AJ smirks at him. "Are you saying she's one dimensional and shallow?"

"Hey…I don't know how she is," Jae says, putting his hand up. "I don't know the girl personally. I'm just going off of the teenybopper songs I hear on the radio. And when I see her face on TV or on a magazine I get a petty mean girl vibe from her. But that's probably just me. I'm predisposed to judgmental-ness."

"No, Kay's nice," AJ tells him. "And she can be deep. And smart. And cool. Plus, she doesn't need to be my type. It's not like I'm going to date her or anything. We're just…having fun. That's all."

"That's fine then," Jae says with a supportive smile. "You deserve some fun. Just don't get too attached to Little Miss Country Sunshine Sellout. She seems fickle as fuck."

AJ laughs, not worried at all.

Chapter 12

Austin goes over to the bar after he drops a large sum of money off at the office; he'd just seen one of Rafael's old clients, a woman who brought a new meaning to the word demanding. She was incorrigible. He's dead tired, freshly showered, ready for bed, but in need of a drink. Hermosa has a late class. AJ is still out working. And he's all alone. But bars are made for loners.

It's an hour before closing on a Tuesday night and there aren't many people there. He crosses the empty dining room and pulls up a stool.

Calvin walks out of the back, their eyes meet, and they both smile.

"Look who they let back in," Calvin jokes as he makes his way over. "The white Mayweather live in person."

Austin smiles coyly. "Your boss wasn't too mad about it, was he?"

"Nah. I told him what went down. He said those jerkoffs deserved it."

"You have a cool boss."

"Rough day at the office?" Calvin ascertains.

Austin smirks. "Somethin' like that."

"You smell good," Calvin tells him. "Paco Rabanne?"

Austin laughs, amused. "How'd you know that?"

"I know my shit," Calvin replies sassily with a smirk, then turns on his heels and sashays over to where all the liquor bottles are. "Your usual?"

"Yup."

Austin doesn't think he's ever heard him cuss before. The fact that it's a slow night and that there aren't many patrons around has him a little more unguarded than usual. He looks comfortable in his skin as he mixes the drink with his back to Austin, shimmying his hips a bit as he does his thing. When he's done he turns back around and brings the glass of brown liquid to him, sitting it down with a smile.

"What's this?" Austin asks with a smirk in his voice as he looks down at his usual drink that has a random cherry floating atop it.

"I thought you might want to try something different," Calvin offers, leaning over the counter. "Cherry coke is better than plain coke, isn't it?"

"I spose," Austin replies genially. He takes a sip and, admittedly, the sweet tang of cherry syrup did add a nice layer of flavor.

Calvin watches him with a slight smile. "It's not too fufu for you, is it?"

"Not when three fourths of it is whiskey," Austin remarks. He takes another drink and grimaces a bit at the strength of it. "You're the right kind of bartender."

"I know," Calvin says with a cocky smile. He leaves his post against the bar then and walks over to the nearby sink to wash up all the discarded glasses from the night.

Austin sips his drink, maybe a little faster than usual because it does really taste better tonight, and surveys the bar. The last patron throws some change down on the counter next to his empty glass and gets up. The door chimes with his departure a moment later. Calvin has started drying the glasses with his bar mop.

"So are you like Dominican or Mediterranean or…." Austin wonders aloud, the liquor making his tongue a bit loose and his words a tad obtuse.

Calvin gives him a little judgmental eyebrow raise, and then softens it with a smile because he knows he's merely curious. "I'm afraid I'm just high yellow."

Austin smiles impishly. "I don't know what that means."

"My dad's black. My mom's white," he explains. "Both born and raised in Chicago. I'm just a regular old American chocolate vanilla swirl."

Austin smiles a bit. "So you're from Chicago?"

"That I am."

"So what's your story? Why did you leave *The Chi* for LA? That's what the people call it, right? The Chi?"

"You're late. Our new nickname the non-natives like to use is Chiraq," he jokes. "Fashion, though. I came out here to pursue a career in fashion. I want to be a designer."

"Why didn't you go to New York then? Ain't that like the fashion capital of the world?"

"Actually, it's Paris. And I did go to New York. I lived there my first year out of high school. Went to school on the Upper Eastside, lived in an exorbitantly priced efficiency in Brushwick with two other guys, worked an unpaid sweat shop style internship in The Meat Packing District for a C-list designer with an A-list attitude, and bussed tables at two different bistros to barely make ends meet. Shit was bout to make me lose my mind," he laughs. "Plus I was broke all the time. So I transferred to the Fashion Institute over here sophomore year. LA is so much more chill, and West Coast livin' is so much more my style. The beach, the sun, the simplicity. Plus, the men are better lookin. All tan and ripped and shit.

Mm. Or in your case, the girls. I'm sure you've noticed it's a breeding ground for pretty people."

He smirks. "I live in Santa Monica. I've definitely noticed."

"You live in Santa Monica? I love Santa Monica!" Calvin exclaims, putting the last glass up and throwing his towel over his shoulder. "I go to the beach at least twice a week."

"Well if you ever see me while you're down there, holler. We can go grab lunch or margaritas or something. You know," Austin smiles "Have a drink for once instead of serving them."

"I could go for a margarita sometime," Calvin replies.

Chapter 13

The third time AJ goes to the studio it's late at night and they're alone once more. He's starting to think it's intentional, and while he doesn't mind being her muse or fuck buddy or whatever she wants him to be, he tries to keep the train of thought on track. She does have an album to make, after all.

"Do you have any idea what you'd like to call the album?" He asks her. They're sitting side by side on the piano bench again, no music playing yet. He likes to pick her mind first, ask her the questions that maybe the others won't.

"Hell, I don't know," she replies, not really seeming worried about it. "My first album was *Tennessee Dreams*. Horrible title, but I was eighteen and from Tennessee and my dreams were being fulfilled. It felt fitting at the time. Second album was called *K*. Sweet and simple, I liked it. Being that this is going to be the third, I was thinking maybe it's time for a self-titled. *Kadence Jane*. Or maybe just *Kadence*."

"What about *Caroline*?" He offers.

"No," she says, sounding utterly disgusted. "God, no."

"Why?" He probes slightly. "You said you wanted to make a more serious album, a more intimate album. What's more intimate than self-titling it with your real name? Let your fans get a glimpse at the more personal side of yourself, let them get to know the real you."

"Maybe I don't want them to know me *that* well."

"But–"

"Caroline is not a title option," she cuts him off, voice cold and stern. "Ok, AJ?"

"Ok," he submits, feeling bad that he pressed too far.

"We'll figure it out," she says then, taking a gentler tone. "We've got time." She gets up and walks towards the door. "You know…once we start making more songs…maybe the title will just present itself to us."

"Yeah," he replies optimistically. "I'm sure it will."

She opens the door slightly. "Mike, will you bring me my clutch please," she calls out down the hall. AJ thinks nothing of it, despite her pink Birkin bag being just a few feet away, and despite not knowing why her security guard would have her clutch. She sits back down on the piano bench with him. Mike walks in a moment later with a silver sequined clutch in his hand. He passes it to her. "Thank you, doll."

Mike nods and walks back out of the room, closing the door behind him.

He glances over and sees her laying a credit card…or maybe it's her license…on the piano, and before he can process what's going through his head she removes a little twisted up baggie. What's in it looks like a clump of flour, but he knows that's not the case. He wants to believe it is, because this is Kadence Jane, America's sweetheart, dumping a small pile of white powder onto a black Yamaha grand piano and surely to God it's not what he thinks it is. But he knows it is, and who knows, maybe cocaine is just the mark of great musicians. The Stones did it. Zeppelin did it. Etta James did. Hell, all the greats did it. Of course, those people weren't making songs for young impressionable pre-teen girls who hadn't even outgrown retainers and training bras. They hadn't made songs like her, songs that made you think the singer never cussed or had an overly impure thought, let alone tote a bag of pure cocaine in a designer clutch that she makes her security carry. He tries not to overthink it.

"You do that?" He asks, trying to sound casual.

"You don't?" She asks semi-sarcastically, with a curious lift of an eyebrow.

"Maybe like once," he admits sheepishly with an innocent smile.

"Maybe like once?" She mocks with a grin, arranging a line with her black Amex and a sheet of his songwriting paper. "Did you like it?"

"It was alright."

"Well maybe you need to do it again," she suggests, starting to make another line that he assumes is for him. "Maybe you didn't do enough. Cause it's more than alright."

He thinks back to that depressing night in early December, and he's pretty sure he did enough. He'd felt ten thousand feet off the ground. It wasn't a feeling one could easily forget, and if he's being honest with himself, he'd thought about it more than once in the weeks and months since then. How he'd gone from despondent to giddy in a matter of minutes, how every neuron in his brain had felt like it was firing on the highest level and how every cell in his body had felt attuned to his whims.

"It's not addictive like heroin and meth and all that junk," she says, taking out a hundred-dollar bill just like Mrs. Kelly, if not just to flaunt. "People will tell you that it is, but it isn't," she continues, rolling the bill up till it's skinny and hollow. "I know a ton of people who do it and have done it for years and they're all functioning just fine. It's just something fun." She's about to put it to her nose when she stops and looks over at him. "Plus, it boosts creativity. You'll be amazed at what you can accomplish while on it."

He watches her as she bends down over the piano and snorts the line up through Ben Franklin. When she gets to the end she lifts up a little, sniffing slightly and swallowing. Then she switches nostrils, puts her nose right back down on the tip of the bill, places it at the start of the next line, and snorts straight to the other side. *Ok*, he thinks, *maybe that one wasn't for me after all.*

She takes a recomposing breath when she's done, wiping at her nose and sniffling a bit as she sits back up straight. "Ok, your turn," she says then, dumping a little more white powder onto the glossy black paint.

He stares at it for a second, then tentatively reaches for her credit card. With the piece of plastic and the folded up edge of his parchment, he shifts and shapes a line until it looks right. She passes him the rolled up hundred and he sticks it to his right nostril. He hesitates before laying it on the line, his heart is racing and he hasn't even done it yet, not sure that he even wants to. That night in Mrs. Kelly's bedroom had been a rare occurrence, something he wrote off as a misstep that would never happen again. He'd been in a dark place. Not unlike the place he's in now, because what had changed? Nothing. And it had made him feel good. It made him feel like he could write a million brilliant words a minute. But he had wasted the high screwing and then sitting in court, and by the time he had got home, it had worn off. What was the harm in doing it just one more time, if not just to give it one good proper try?

He starts to snort it up, even though he's scared. It burns a bit, and he's relieved when he gets to the end. But then he sits up and swallows, and tastes it dripping down the back of his throat. He momentarily panics. *Was the line too long? Would his throat go numb?*

"Why do you look so distressed," she laughs, putting everything back in the clutch. "You said you did it before, right?"

"Yeah, but it was a while ago," he says, subconsciously touching his nose. "And just once."

"Loosen up," she tells him. "Let it move through you. In a couple minutes you're not even going to care."

He sits there on the bench for a while, trying to take her advice and not panic over the numbness that's spreading from his nose across his entire face and the adrenaline that's steadily starting to ramp up. He begins to play the piano to get his mind off it, a wordless melody that he just made up, that he *is* making up as he goes. His fingers float over the keys with ease, creating a simple string of sounds without much thought, a string of sounds that stretches for seconds and then minutes without them saying anything. She's swaying on the bench next to him, eyes closed.

"Progression in C," he says out of the blue.

"What?" She asks, eyes still closed, upper body still moving.

"The title of the album."

"Yes!" She exclaims, eyes flying open. She's suddenly standing up, moving across the room, grabbing his notebook off the table, and then grabbing a sharpie.

"Play on the word progression, which is a harmonic *cadence*, emphasis on your artistic name, *and* also what you are actively doing as an artist with this album—progressing," he explains. "C representing the key, obviously, but also the first letter of your real name, subliminally."

"Yes!" She exclaims again. She's writing *Progression in C* in permanent ink across the moleskin notebook Anjanae gave him for his birthday. He wants to be upset about it, but he can't be. He literally cannot channel the offended emotion because he's too busy channeling genius thoughts coming at a breakneck speed out of the left field inside his brain. Or maybe it's the right. He doesn't know and it doesn't matter. The light has been switched on.

"We can name certain songs—like one at the beginning, one in the middle, and one at the end—after the different types of cadences. Perfect authentic, and we can call the song *Perfectly Authentic*. And then *Imperfectly Authentic*. And then for the evaded cadence we can just call the song *Evaded*. It can have an eerily dark sound, full of obscurity, and you can be singing with inflicction about all the things you've *evaded* for fame and your career."

"I fucking love where you're going with this, I swear," she says,

His fingers have been playing this whole time, but he suddenly changes the keys he's hitting, slowing down the rhythm and creating a descending sound, reminiscent of rain falling to the ground or an angel falling from the sky.

"How about this for an intro," he says, continuing with what he's playing. "Call it *A Falling*, which is what cadentia means, which is Latin for cadence."

"That's it. That's it right there. That's the beginning of the first track." She's pointing her finger wildly, and then she throws his notebook at him as she races across the room. He catches it with one hand, smiling from ear-to-ear at her enthusiasm. "I'm getting in the booth," she tells him, already slipping behind the glass. "Put a mike on that piano, do what you just did, and record me. I'm about to lay down the vocals. Track one, take one. Let's go."

"I don't know how to work this equipment," AJ admits honestly. "Don't we need an engineer?"

"We don't have time to get someone in here. We gotta get it down while it's still raw and fresh. You'll figure it out, babe. You're smart, I got faith in you."

He dismisses the fact that she just called him babe—even though, if he's being honest, he kind of liked it—and starts messing with wires and buttons.

"Do you have any words to sing," he asks semi-sarcastically, briefly glancing up from setting stuff up to look at her through the glass. She's holding her hands over her big headphone as she sidesteps, shuffles, and shimmies with pent up energy, waiting on him to tell her to go.

"I'm just going to harmonize with the piano for now," she tells him. "If the words come to you before they come to me, write them bad boys down."

"Ok."

And just like that, they fall into sync.

~

A few nights later they're back in the studio. This time Eddie and another production guy named Salar are there. She plays them the intro she and AJ recorded, then fills them in on the working album title and consequent concept. Eddie and Salar both love it. AJ thinks Eddie is starting to warm up to him, starting to see that he's more than some little no-name writer Kadence picked at near random. The four of them start at six, writing and recording in a harmonious zone, and by the time they realize they've been holed up for hours and are hungry, it's almost three o'clock in the morning. The suggestion is made that they go to a little all-night diner down the road in Hollywood for a late supper early breakfast. They're all down for it because they've all been drinking, besides Kadence who was on her best behavior in the presence of the producers. But she's down for it, too, because the hopes are that the papz won't be out at this hour.

The four of them make it into the establishment unnoticed. Kadence threw on a low-brimmed baseball cap for good measure, and AJ is finding it hard not to find it cute. They all pile into a booth and order plates of greasy goodness; besides Kadence, who asks for a fried egg white and a bowl of fruit. While they're waiting on their food, Salar's phone buzzes.

"Ah, it's wifey wondering where I'm at," Salar says with an impish grin, taking a look at the screen of his iPhone.

"One of the many pitfalls of livin' a life committed to a single human of the opposite gender," Eddie comments, adding three creamers to his coffee. "You always gotta check in. One of the main reasons I split with my old lady."

"Emma divorced you, Ed," Salar reminds him as he picks up the call.

Kadence snickers and AJ smiles.

"Only cause the little biddy beat me to it." Eddie tears open two sugars packets at once and sprinkles them generously over the steaming mug. "You ain't got a special somebody waiting up for you, do ya, AJ?"

"Sure don't," AJ replies, raising his un-doctored mug of black coffee to his lips and taking a sip.

"You're a free bird, aye," Eddie muses idly, taking a gulp, grimacing, and grabbing another creamer.

Salar tells his wife where he's at, who he's with, and when he'll be back in his native tongue. The others pay no attention to his lapse into another language.

He hangs up with a sigh. "I'm good to go. Got another hour before she completely loses it."

AJ smiles and looks over at Kadence. "Do you know that Salar just told his wife that he was with you, your engineer, and your boyfriend?"

Kadence seems confused, looking between him and Salar.

Eddie leans back and laughs out loud. "You're gonna have to watch what you say around this one, Sal."

Salar's eyes are wide with surprise. "You speak Farsi?"

"Some," AJ replies, hoping nobody asks him where he learned because he could never tell them that he picked it up between the sheets with his older Iranian lover who pays him by the hour, and it's too late and he's too tired to formulate an alternate story for his bilingual abilities.

"Isn't he *so* smart?" Kadence remarks, clearly impressed.

"Mmhm," Salar mutters knowingly with a smirk on his face.

"Salar," Kadence says seriously with a smile, leaning on the table to look him in the eye. "AJ is my writer."

"I know he is a writer. But I get the impression that he is more than a writer." He takes a sip of coffee and shrugs with a smirk. "At least to you. To me and Eddie he is still just a writer."

"Whatever, Salar," she says with a playful eye roll as she squeezes a lemon wedge into her glass of water. "You think you know everything."

Salar chuckles. "I think no such thing," he tells her innocently, taking another sip of coffee. "I am merely a good observer."

"Mmhm," she mutters as she sips her water.

"You two just got some crazy good chemistry, that's all my dude Salar's sayin," Eddie chimes in with his two cents, looking between Kay and AJ. "You finish her lyrics. She matches the tune your playin on the piano with her voice." He takes a drink of coffee and nods his head sagely. "It's all very Lindsay Buckingham Stevie Nicks. Minus all the coke and resentment, of course."

AJ briefly glances at her out of the corner of his eye to peg her reaction, unable to stop from smirking as he does so.

She just smiles, looks down, and twirls her straw. "I think you just want me to make a one woman *Rumors*, Eddie."

"That'd be nice, Kay," Eddie tells her facetiously, emptying out another sugar packet into his beige coffee. "That'd be real nice."

They all have a good laugh.

After they finish their meal, they pay and exit back out onto the street. Thirty minutes of normalcy over bacon and eggs has their guards down, and out of nowhere a small flock of paparazzi swoop in. AJ keeps his head down and puts one foot in front of the other as they make their way to the parking lot. Kadence keeps her head up and her gaze straight ahead, cutting through them like she's Moses and they're the Red Sea. Of course Bill is there—though AJ has no idea how he got there, when her got there, or where he came from—and he keeps the circling vultures at a safe distance. They still rattle off their questions in rapid, never ceasing succession.

How are you tonight, Kadence? Have you been out clubbing? How was your meal? Is Salar producing the new album? Salar, are you producing Kadence's new album alongside Eddie? When's the single coming out? Kadence, what do you think about what T-Sheikh said on Twitter? Do you think you're favored? Do you think she's jealous? Are you gonna put it in a song? Those shoes you got on look really good, Kay. Who's the guy in the blue shirt with you tonight?

And then she stops.

And suddenly AJ's heart is in his throat, because from the smile on her lips and the gleam in hers eyes he just knows what's going to happen next.

She turns around and looks dead into the camera closest to her face.

"He's my boyfriend."

A second suspends...and then the cameras are flashing at twice the speed.

What's his name? How long have you two been dating? How did you meet?

Salar and Eddie get into Eddie's truck, and AJ gets into Kadence's Porsche with her. Bill slams the door shut for him from the outside, and the crazy people scramble to press their faces and cameras up against the window. Kadence coolly starts the engine, puts it into drive, and expertly navigates out of the throng. Once in the clear she hits the gas so she can lose them before they can get into their cars. AJ sits back against the leather seat and takes a deep breath, trying to wrap his mind around the last minute and a half of his life. He looks over at her after a second. She's got it going about eighty, calm as can be, eyes straight ahead on the road like nothing happened.

"I thought I was your writer," he says tentatively, playfully as to not make her think he's mad about the little announcement she just made.

"You are my writer," she says, eyes still on the road. "But Salar and Eddie were right. You're way more than that." After a few seconds of silence she becomes self-conscious and apologetic. "I'm sorry, I probably should have talked to you about it first. It just flew out of my mouth and for some reason I thought you would be okay with it. You just make me...I don't know...I just get so caught up in the moment when I'm with you. And I thought I was reading signs...and I made a grand assumption that you wanted to be more than friends with me. But I completely and totally understand if you don't want to be in a relationship with me. I know my life is a lot. Next time I get asked about you I can just say that we broke up. They think I go through them quick anyway, so it's not like anything I haven't heard before will be said about me."

"Kadence, are you kidding me?" AJ says, looking right at her. "I never suggested that we be more than friends because I never thought you'd want to be with someone like me. I'm just a regular person, and you're...*you*."

She glances over at him briefly, then back to the road. "Maybe I need a regular person."

"Maybe you do."

"So you're okay with being my boyfriend?" She asks definitively, the unmistakable hint of success in her voice.

"Yeah," he says after a slight pause, even though inside he feels like he might be making a huge mistake. "I'm okay with it."

She takes her eyes off the road to smile at him. "Good."

~

From that point gossip bloggers, cheap magazine writers, and Kadence's every fan make it their business and personal mission to find out everything they can out about him. What songs he's wrote. Where he's from. What his parents do. His relationship with Grace from old Facebook posts they dig up. Where he went to college and what he majored in. They find out pretty much everything about him in a matter of hours, besides Maggie, which would have been the real juice amongst his otherwise bland life. Names hadn't been released in the initial story that broke when the office raid happened in December, and since the case got thrown out in quick order, there was no printed evidence or paper trail connecting him to any illegal activity or otherwise suspicious behavior. His occupation remains thoroughly swept under the rug.

But still...

"I don't like this," Maggie says instantly the second he steps off the elevator on the 57th floor the next morning. She's holding a tabloid in her hand and pacing the floor. "I don't like this one bit."

"They already have it in print?" He asks, somewhat surprised. "I thought it was only circulating the Internet. Damn, that was quick."

"America's Sweetheart just looked straight in camera one and said she was dating you. No, actually, she skipped courtship and went right into commitment. She called you her *boyfriend*."

"I really had no idea she was going to do that," he replies neutrally.

"You had no idea that Grace or Mercy or whatever her name is was flying in to visit, or that Julius's wife had stashed your sex tape under a thin layer of socks. You seem to be rather in the dark when it comes to the women you fuck for free."

"I'm not fucking Kay." He pauses. "I mean...I am...but it's more than just that. Well, I don't have to tell you. You've seen the news, you know," he adds almost flippantly.

"Andrew, you are aware that the paparazzi follow *Kay* everywhere, right? So, by penis preference proxy, the paparazzi is going to follow *you* everywhere."

"I know how to keep a low profile."

"They are excavating every layer of your life past and present as we speak..."

"They're not going to find anything worth finding," he tells her evenly. "I haven't posted on my Facebook…or for that mattered even logged in to it…in over a year. I assumed it had been deactivated. I don't have a Twitter or Instagram or whatever else there is to have. And the only people in the world who know about you and what I do is Jae, Anjanae, and–"

"Your ex. You told me that she found out, right?"

"Yes but she's not going to say anything."

"Even if they fly out to Memphis and offer her a check with more zeros at the end than she's ever seen? She's a scorned woman, Andrew; you had one emotional affair and copious paid sexual encounters on her. You don't think she'll talk?"

"Stop freaking out. We've got a judge on speed dial and I can probably seduce an attorney, too, should we need one."

Maggie looks like she doesn't find him funny.

"You told me that I could have one girlfriend, special friend, whatever, who wasn't a client. Remember that?" He asks her. "You didn't make any other specifications."

"Yes but I didn't think you'd go out and bag the biggest pop star in the world."

He winks as he walks over to her Mac. "Always underestimating."

"Please break up with her. I'm asking nicely."

"Listen to this," he tells her. He presses some buttons on her keyboard, scrolls the mouse, and then starts to read. "*No offense to him, I'm sure he's a nice guy, but he seems so straight laced.* Re-tweeted twenty-nine times. *She's dated the bad boys; she needs someone simple like him. Plus, he's from the South so you know he knows how to treat a woman with respect.* Favorited forty-two times. *Aww he's cute, but he's not going to know what to do with a straight dime like Kay, look at his exes.* Shared seventy-eight times."

Maggie comes to look over his shoulder as he clicks on a link.

"These are the only two girls they think I've been with besides Kay," he says, turning the screen towards Maggie so she can see the side-by-side pictures Media Takeout had posted for their story. One is of him and Grace embraced under a Christmas tree in matching holiday sweaters three years ago. The other is of him and his high school girlfriend standing next to each other, him holding a saxophone and her holding a flute. The bloggers had acquired both photos by digging way back into his tagged Facebook photos.

"God you looked like you got shoved in lockers and wet-willied regularly."

"It's hard to look cool in a band uniform." He turns to look at her then. "The point is…you have nothing to worry about."

Maggie stares at him for a long parade of seconds. "I'm highly doubtful."

"If you're doubtful, limit my first folder duties."

She raises an eyebrow quizzically.

"The less dates I go on, the less likely I am to get caught with a client," he elaborates. "I can get in and out of houses and hotels without being seen, I'm confident in my sneaking and lying abilities. But if I'm sitting at a table out in the open across from a woman I can't control who sees me."

"So you want to be a strictly sex escort?" She questions.

"Let's be honest, most of them aren't paying top-price for the way I eat my food. Dinner is an unnecessary prelude to the main show that can easily be cut in most cases."

There's a pause, then with a humored look she nods. "Ok. Well. Let's hope your clients will be okay with this."

"They will be," AJ assures with a smile.

~

The limo picks him up first at his apartment, then heads to Beverley Hills to get Kadence from the hotel where she is getting her hair and makeup done. AJ twiddles his thumbs anxiously as he waits outside the limo for her to come out. Tonight is the first night of his life that the world will have their eyes on him. His heart is beating out of his chest and he's praying he doesn't sweat through his Tom Ford tux. It's one of the ones Maggie bought him for business but Kadence has never seen him in it, so she'll think it's new. Kadence has never seen him all spiffed up; this will be their first event together. He had the tux dry-cleaned and steam pressed in advance, laid it out on his bed and stared at it for days. He had considered spicing it up with a red bowtie, maybe blue, a coordinating pocket square, pop of color. But in the end he decided to stick to classic black and white, that way he wouldn't accidently clash with her or draw extra attention to himself.

When the door opens and she emerges, his breath is stolen. She is everything she should be, and he knows in an instant she will dominate all the fashion blogs tomorrow. Her gown is a pale taupe-colored fabric that hugs her body closely. The neckline is a deep v-cut, the visible skin of her chest covered in an elegant mesh that's embroidered in something that sparkles—crystals, maybe sequins. The train of the gown drags the floor, her matching beige Jimmy Choos only visible when she walks. Her lips are red, her makeup is immaculate, and her blonde hair is slicked back in sophisticated way he's never seen it before. She smiles when she sees him.

"You look gorgeous," he tells her as he holds the limo door open for her.

"You look pretty handsome yourself," she murmurs lowly, sliding in.

He slides in next to her and pulls the door closed behind him. The short little balding driver with tufts of white hair behind his ears turns around and looks at her.

"Are we ready, Miss Jane?" He asks her in a distinguished voice.

"Yes, we are ready, Earl," she replies, flashing him her radiant smile. "To the Staples Center."

Earl returns her smile and then turns around. "As you wish."

They start to move and she looks over at him. "Are you nervous?"

"A little," he admits with a sheepish smile, even though he's way more than just a little bit nervous.

"Me too," she says.

"Why are you nervous?" AJ asks, surprised by this omission. He shifts on the leather bench seat so he's face to face with her, and then gives her a reassuring look. "You're Kadence Jane. You've done this a hundred times. You've performed on this stage how many times?"

"I'm not performing tonight, though," she replies. "I'm presenting. A *huge* award. A lifetime achievement award. Performing is fine," she adds, looking away as she starts to wring her hands. "I'm in my element when I'm putting on a show and singing. But public speaking...*ugh*...I hate it. What if I forget what I practiced? What if the teleprompter quits working or I can't see it?"

Her vulnerability does something to him, makes him want to make it better. He stares at her until she lifts her chin and meets his eyes again.

"You want me to take your mind off of it?" He asks her seriously, keeping his eyes on hers as realization, then shock, and then trouble takes form on her face.

"I can't mess up my hair or dress..." She tells him simply, the corners of her mouth betraying her tone.

"I promise I won't touch your hair or dress."

"We're only like fifteen minutes from the venue…" Her voice has dropped and her blue eyes have started to darken. She's scooting towards him on the seat, inching her gown up ever so slightly.

"That's plenty of time," he replies lowly, hand moving to rest on the knee she's bared to him.

She smiles wickedly and then looks over her shoulder. "Earl," she says, getting the old man's attention. The driver looks up into the rearview mirror and Kadence makes an upward gesture with her finger.

"Yes, ma'am," he replies, immediately pressing a button and then training his eyes back on the road obediently.

As the dark window slowly slides up, she attaches her mouth to his. As he kisses her, he slides his hand from her knee, to the inside of her thigh, and then up under her dress. She's not wearing any underwear, and he smiles against her mouth. Behind the protection of the partition, she parts her legs wantonly for him, and he skims a single finger down her slit. Her breath catches. He gathers the moisture between her thighs his suggestion alone created, and moves his slickened thumb to her clit. Firm and sure circles wind her up, little aroused sounds leaving her mouth. She's got her hands in his hair; sharp fake nails digging into the base of his neck. He keeps his promise not to ruffle her gown or hair, holding on to her bare ass with his other hand. Her plundering mouth prompts him to open his, and she sucks his tongue into her mouth, grinding against him. He eases two fingers inside; she bites his bottom lip. Breathless little gasps are escaping her in quiet emissions as she tries to keep kissing him, but she's losing focus. He pulls away enough to watch her face as he presses his fingers upwards and then curls them, caressing her interior walls. Her head goes back when he hits the right spot, an audible sound somewhere between a moan and a scream leaves her mouth. AJ's sure the driver heard it through the glass, being that there's no music playing to muffle her noises. But she seems not to care, so he doesn't care. He just redoubles his efforts, drawing more of those sounds out of her, drawing more dampness around his fingers. She clenches around his fingers, rocks her hips, riding his hand. He lets her do what feels good, stilling his stroking. Her mouth is all over his neck, breath against his ear.

"AJ…do it," she moans.

He returns his thumb to her clit and resumes circling. His middle and pointer curve once, twice more…and then she's tumbling over. A rush of wetness accompanies her sharp cry. Her forehead falls against his shoulder as she rides it out, and he doesn't withdraw his hand until the final pulses subside.

"Fuck," she murmurs, lifting her face back up and meeting his eyes. A slow smirk takes form on her lips, and it's contagious because he's soon smirking, too.

He holds her troublesome gaze and is just about to lick her essence off his fingers when she grabs his wrist. He watches her, enrapt with lust, as she guides his two fingers that were inside her into her mouth. She sucks them clean, twirling her tongue suggestively before letting them go with a wet pop. He stares a second more, feeling himself redden and harden even more than he was before, seeing how pleased she looks to be wreaking havoc on him, and then he has to look away.

"Mm," he mumbles, shaking his head with a smirk.

"Are you going to be okay?" She asks mischievously, eyes falling upon the noticeable protrusion in his well-tailored pants.

"I'll be fine. Just let me think about something else for a minute."

"Ok," she laughs, scooting away from him and taking a tube of lipstick, a mirror, a can of hairspray, and an emergency packet of tissues out of the backseat console. She reapplies her red lip in the handheld mirror, looking herself over with a slightly worried look. "I've got to get rid of this red blush all over my face and neck. Earl!" She taps on the window. A second later it starts to roll back down. "Earl, can you turn the air all the way up? Please and thank you."

"Yes, ma'am," her driver replies, eyes never once diverting from the road.

"What's the ETA?" She asks, spraying her hair.

"We're about three minutes out, ma'am," Earl says.

That's enough to cool AJ down. "Oh boy," he mutters absently.

"You'll do fine," she tells him, leaning over to wipe her lipstick marks off his neck with a tissue. "It's just a red carpet and a bunch of reporters."

"Right," he replies, unconvinced but glad that she feels better about the night. He stares out the window as they creep along the last few miles. Traffic has started to clog as they progress through Downtown, some streets totally shut down. People line the streets screaming and other limos and black SUVs with heavily tinted windows are ushered through the masses, lining up to the entrance of the red carpet, the Staples Center looming in the background. Earl hangs back until the prime spot is cleared. AJ watches as girls in gowns emerge from luxury vehicles, adjusting their boobs behind their handlers before proceeding into the craziness. There's a woman standing on the curb waiting for the limo to stop. AJ recognizes her as one of the people in Kadence's kitchen the time he went over to her house. Earl stops the car and Kadence looks over at him.

"Ok," she says, taking a breath. "Go on."

AJ opens the door and steps out. Loud. That's all there is to describe it. A million people screaming a million different things. He turns around and offers Kadence his hand. As she slides out of the car all the screams become clear, all the screams condense down to one word. The people down the street, the people in the outdoor stands, the people with the cameras waiting for her to step onto the carpet so they can take her picture. They're all screaming her name and her name alone.

"AJ, you've met my publicist, Bridget," she says, getting his attention back.

"Nice to see you again," AJ says to the woman, smiling politely.

"Yes," Bridget replies, giving him a curt nod and then turning to face Kay. "Now. I know you don't like any questions about your love life, and you'd prefer they not ask you about the whole T-Sheikh Twitter thing where she suggested other deserving artists get snubbed in favor for you. Is there anything else that I need to advise them as off limits?"

"They can ask me about AJ," Kadence tells Bridget. "He's my boyfriend," she says as plain as day, turning to look at him. He exchanges meaningful smiles with her and then she looks back to Bridget. "I already confirmed it. There's nothing to hide."

"Ok," Bridget says in a tone that suggests she's surprised, and perhaps just a bit disapproving of the decision. But she looks down at her phone and types something to someone, adding in an agreeable voice. "I'll tell them that's okay then."

"Great," Kadence replies through her smile.

"Next," Bridget continues, looking back up. "Remember Bryan wants you to keep your responses about the new album coy. You want them to know that you are working without giving too much away. Cast intrigue with your answers. Elaborate little, and insinuate big. We want to build excitement, anticipation, and speculation. What will it be about? When will it drop? Tease them just enough to leave them writhing for more."

"Blue-ball the world, got it," she replies flippantly.

"And also," Bridget says seriously, lowering her voice just a bit. "Don't forget what we discussed the other day. If the opportunity presents…and there's people around to see it…"

"I know," she says with boredom in her voice, no longer looking at Bridget as she cranes her neck to see who else is arriving. AJ no longer has any idea what they're talking about.

"You want the flashcards I made when we practiced what you'd say?"

"I think I remember how the convo is spose to go," she tells her publicist tersely, waving with a smile at an approaching limo.

"Do you have your acceptance speeches memorized, too?" Bridget asks just to be sure.

"Yup." The limo she just waved over opens. "Over here, guys!" Kay yells.

Two more middle-aged women emerge from the limo. They are both dressed demurely in black as to not distract from the artist. They seem very comfortable and in their element as they draw near. Kadence smiles when she sees them.

"It feels like minutes," Kay jokes with them.

"Twenty to be exact," one of them says with a smirk. "I hope nothing came out of place in the car ride over."

Kay blushes a bit, giving him a naughty look out of the side of her eye. "AJ, this is Trish and this is Catharine," she tells him. "They're here to make sure I don't have a wardrobe malfunction or a hair emergency." She gleams as she looks between the two women. "They made this all possible," she adds, waving a hand down her body theatrically. "Without them I wouldn't be beautiful."

"Oh stop," the two women say in unison.

"You're always beautiful," he tells her in her ear.

She smiles. Another limo pulls up and two middle-aged men get out this time. AJ recognizes one as her agent and the other as the man he'd seen at the Oscars. Kadence is asking Catherine for a mirror when the two men approach.

"AJ," Bridget says. "This is Bryan Schilling. He's an A&R rep for the label. Bryan, this is AJ Brooks, Kadence's ne–" She stops midway through the word when she hears how it sounds, deciding to drop the adjective. "Kadence's boyfriend."

"Ahh, yes," Bryan says in recognition, holding out his hand. "I believe I saw you at the Oscars. You were with your agent Maggie."

"Mmhm," AJ mutters in reply, shaking the man's hand and putting on a smile, but hoping the conversation ends there. He glances over his shoulder as he gets his hand back, seeing that Kay's preoccupied with Trish slicking a fly away down. Thankfully Kay's agent is quickly whisking Bryan away before another word can be said, rambling on about some other artist they are both involved with. AJ takes the opportunity to retreat to his girlfriend. Catharine and Trish add their final touches to her and then turn her loose.

"Ready?" She asks him

"Ready as I'll ever be."

And with that they head off down the red carpet.

The spectators' screams rise in decibel once they see her. He stands off to the side any time they encounter a swath of flashing cameras, letting her have the spotlight and attempting to stay out of the way as best he can. The first two reporters act like they don't even see him standing there in the background, and forgo questions about her love life in order to interrogate her about when to expect a new album instead. He's totally fine with this, and hopes the night continues on this note, but then the third reporter throws a wrench into that wish.

"First and foremost, congratulations on the four nominations tonight. I get the feelings it's going to be another sweep for you," a bespoke man with a microphone and a bright suit says once he's got her in his corner.

"Oh, well thank you," Kadence beams graciously. "It would certainly be wonderful to win, but so much great music has been made this year by so many different people. The competition is so real. It's so strong. Especially in the best female category. I am literally in awe of all those women. I listen to and love all their stuff, and them, and regardless of who wins I'm just honored to be nominated alongside such immensely talented individuals."

"Can I just say…you are truly a class act," the reporter tells her. "The way you always uplift and support other artists, that's why you're such a good role model. I know you know some people choose to throw shade or salt or whatever the kids are calling it, but you never engage in the negativity. You stay cool headed and calm, and that is to be commended. Your modestly speaks volumes and your ability to stay grounded is admirable."

"Aww," Kadence replies in a touched tone of humbleness, both hands going to her heart. "You're too kind."

"And might I just add, for those who don't know…those four nominations are for songs from *last* year's album. Four nominations without even putting an album out this year. I can't imagine what next year's Grammys will look like after the world has your third album, which

I'm sure will be yet another masterpiece. Not to put any pressure on
you. I'm sure you've got something planned, though."

She winks. "I've always got something planned."

"I can't wait." His eyes momentarily flick away from her and then
back again. "Switching gears, I have to ask, is that new mysterious boo
back there?"

She grins girlishly and nods. "Yeess. That's AJ." She looks back at
him and gestures with her hand for him to join her in the limelight.

AJ hesitates, only momentarily, then walks over.

"Jason Thomas," the reporter says, though AJ knows his name
from other interviews he's seen on T.V. A hand is outstretched.

AJ shakes it with a smile. "AJ Brooks."

"Nice to meet you, man." He lets go of AJ's hand and looks back
over to Kadence, and then between the two. "So how did you guys meet?"

"Well he's a songwriter," Kadence starts.

"A songwriter, really?" The reporter sounds intrigued.

"Yes. He is an *amazing* writer," she says, and suddenly her fingers
are threading through his. "So I saw him on the credits of a song I liked,
and I had my people reach out to him because I wanted to work with him.
But when we met we just instantly clicked on multiple levels.
And…well…here we are," she concludes with a bright smile for the
cameras.

"And here you are," the reporter reiterates, then looks to AJ. "Well
you must be some amazing writer to garner the attention of this one. I
know we in the media tend to overlook the people behind the scenes that
make possible the music we love to listen to, but you're going straight to
the top of my list of ones to watch."

AJ nods with a smile, realizing he's ok with this, too. Really ok.
Because it actually feels really good. It feels good to be recognized for his
intellectual skills, and to be at an event, holding the hand of someone he's
actually with.

"How does it feel to be here at the Grammys tonight supporting
this girl?" The reporter asks him.

"It feels like an honor," AJ answers, looking at his date. "I feel
honored to be by her side tonight."

"Spoken like a true gentleman," the reporter closes. "You all have
a great night, guys."

There are a few more similar interviews. She introduces him to
famous artists along the way and he almost doesn't know how to act,
shaking hands with people he's been a fan of forever. Halfway down the

carpet they run into her best friend, Sailor. The young woman's long brunette hair hangs down her backless, emerald, curve hugging dress. She has a slightly fuller figure (by Hollywood standards, anyway; a size 4 to Kay's 0). AJ had already done his research on her. She's from the Midwest, started out singing in the church choir and county fair circuit, got discovered at fifteen, and had her first hit single around the same time Kadence had hers. He knows their friendship is lauded and applauded by the media. Their always supportive, never competitive, utterly uplifting, undying love for each other was the heartbeat of the home viewers. The two besties shriek when they see each other, immediately going into a bear hug. The cameras flash crazily. The three of them have a brief conversation while everyone watches. Sailor says she approves of him with a smile. He feels like she's a genuinely nice girl, and he's glad Kay has a friend like her who can understand everything she goes through.

After a while they are all ushered into the auditorium. Unlike when he had accompanied Maggie to the Oscars and they had to watch the show from damn near the back of the theater, he and Kadence are dead center in the front row. The best seats in the house. The most panned to seats on T.V. The seats that see everything and get seen by everyone. He doesn't care who's at home watching. He doesn't care if it's making Maggie a nervous wreck. He doesn't care if it's making his clients jealous. Because it's amazing.

And the night only gets more amazing.

Kadence wins three out of her four nominations. He lets her have her space, smiling supportively from his seat each and every time she goes up. She does great, killing all her acceptance speeches and the introduction she had been worried about. The performances and tributes are great, and he's so close to the stage that he feels like a part of each one, the energy electric. Immediately afterwards, Trish and Catharine are waiting outside, whisking her into the back of a heavily tinted SUV. She reemerges minutes later, sporting a fun pink mini dress and professionally tousled hair. He then accompanies her to the after party down the street.

There are, of course, multiple after parties, all of which she was invited to, but naturally she chose to attend the biggest. Once inside the darkly lit building he notices that even more famous people are in attendance here than were at the actual show. There are musicians taking pictures with actors, millionaires snapping selfies with models. Celebrities acting oh so casual in their natural habitat with the paparazzi and peeping toms getting checked at the door, only a few reporters getting a pass. The hottest acts in the world are there, including the curvy, caramel complexioned, pink haired head turner who's currently the center of attention in the middle of the room. Her gold chains, long nails, and bright attire make her hard to miss. She's an artist who juggles both R&B and rap, while turning out hip-hop hits with ease, making huge business moves, and always staying true to her Detroit roots. She doesn't shy away from speaking her mind, doesn't alter her voice as to not sound too *hood*, and never backs away from controversy. She had actually taken to Twitter to share a few choice words about Kadence recently.

Which is why AJ is surprised when Kadence excuses herself from him and makes a beeline for the female rapper. He watches from the sidelines, close enough to overhear. That's when he realizes everybody else is watching, too.

"T?" Kay says sweetly as she approaches.

T-Sheikh looks surprised when she turns around and sees the blonde pop star behind her. Her sculpted eyebrow arches. Her plump, hot pink painted lips purse.

"I wondered if we could have a word?" Kay asks politely, gingerly.

T-Sheikh looks behind her, then back to his girlfriend. "Yeah sure," she says, glancing over her shoulder again. "I'll be back in a second, aight babe?" She says to her date, and then steps off to the side with Kadence. "So what's up?" She asks aloofly, crossing arms semi-defensively.

"I just wanted to clear the air," Kadence starts, sounding sincere. "I would never want you to think that I have a problem with you. Words get put in my mouth when I don't say anything, and I don't want myself to be misconstrued. I didn't respond on social media because I wanted to have a face-to-face conversation, because I think it's important that we as a collective of musical artists have these conversations. But I heard you. I hear you. And I feel you. It is unfair that so much greatness gets glanced over. But I just want you to know my views don't reflect that of the voters. I respect you so much as a woman. I respect you so much as an artist. You've shattered so many glass ceilings, and you deserve every accolade that there is for what you've done for an entire generation and the generations to come. So I hope we can find some common ground, because at the end of the day we're both extremely hard working women with intense passion for what we do, and I'd love nothing more in the world than to work with you."

T-Sheikh stares, but then, sure enough, a smile softens her face. "Girl, that was just me in my feelings," she says in an easygoing voice now. "It didn't have nothin ta do with you fa real. I know you ain't the one out here pickin' the noms and shit. It's them money grabbing little old men on the board with they're outdated ears havin asses."

Kadence lets out a big belly laugh that sounds real and nods, though she doesn't add any commentary on the old men who always vote for her.

"We cool," T-Sheikh tells her. "My nieces and nephews love your stuff. Hell, I be gettin' my cardio and Pilates in to that second CD of yours, too."

Kadence smiles. "Listen, I'm having a fundraising concert at Fox Theater in May. I'd be honored if you'd be my surprise guest."

"Ok," T-Sheikh says after a moment. "I'll be there, I'll be there. Have Kenny send me the date, okay?"

"Great," Kay replies with another picture perfect smile, and then she holds out her arms. The two girls embrace in a heartfelt hug.

AJ notices many have captured the moment with their phones.

She's got a V.I.P. table for them in the back of the venue. Sailor and her eighteen-year-old brother—who she brought as her date and who is being served liquor without issue—join them. Also joining them is a young actress friend who Kay refers to as Char. This actress friend has brought her older actor boyfriend, who AJ immediately recognizes as a bigtime movie star. A longhaired, tattooed-covered drummer from a mainstream punk rock band comes and goes out of their section as well. He's Sailor's on-again-off-again beaux, who looks like he wants to be on tonight by the way he crowds up to next to her and whispers in her ear just long enough to make her smile before returning to the rougher rock table across the room, obviously not wanting to be seen seated with the pop stars for too long. Last but not least at the table are the two newcomer artists who had opened for Kadence's previous two tours. They'd each had their moment during the show tonight, and Kadence had cheered for them like they were her own children. AJ had noticed how any time either of them had a microphone in their face they praised her to the heavens, forever grateful to her for giving them their starts. If he's being honest, neither are attractive enough to become superstars off their looks alone, and he's not sure that there's enough raw talent between the two to make up for it either. The boy is on the tubby side and already balding at twenty-two. The girl, on the other hand, is pear-shaped with a pronounced chin. The girl had one smash single and the boy had a mildly successful album full of radio friendly love ballads. While their success was minimal compared to Kay's, they are both ecstatic to be here, and AJ feeds off of their enthusiasm, deciding right then and there that he likes them.

There's a bucket of ice with a bottle of Rosé in it. Movie Star Man pops the top, and everyone reacts theatrically like they're supposed to as pink foam sprays out and runs down the side. One Hit Wonder asks what they should toast to. Balding Ballad Guy suggests Kay. Sailor and Miss Actress Thing concur. *To Kay*, they all say. Glasses clink harmoniously. They hob-knob, rub shoulders, and talk with braggadocio while sipping on champagne. Some time later someone brings their table a round of shots. Grey Goose. They must have known it was Kay's favorite, but everyone drinks it like it's theirs. Eight hands throw back eight little glasses of clear liquor in unison. He throws back his too, grimacing briefly at the burn. He hates vodka, but he loves life. The DJ plays one of Dominique's songs. Kadence tells everyone in earshot that he wrote it. Someone tells him that it's their jam, somebody else tells him he's brilliant. Another person calls him and Kay a power couple, songwriter and songstress, and he thinks he agrees. When the next bottle of Rosé is delivered, and the lid is popped, and the glasses are re-filled, he is the one they all toast to this time.

"I gotta pee," Sailor says a few moments later. It would have sounded a little tacky if they weren't all trashed and if the person who said it wasn't famous. But in context it sounds exactly like something a tipsy twenty-something would announce aloud. "Will you please come with me, Kay?" She pouts. "I don't want to go alone."

"Of course, lova," Kay replies in a faux accent of sorts, standing up.

The two girls start to leave the table, and then he feels a hand grasping his wrist. Kadence is pulling him to his feet, too, smiling wickedly. He laughs, not sure what's happening and too drunk to care. They make their way through the swelling throng of intoxicated celebrities and friends of celebrities. The crowd thins out as they move down a hall. He sees the bathrooms looming ahead. He's about to swerve towards the men's when she yanks him towards the women's. That's when he sees Mike, or maybe it's Bill, blocking others from getting through the lavatory door. AJ wasn't aware that she even had a guard on duty tonight. But there one stands, carefully sliding something silver out of his all black ensemble. It's the clutch. He discreetly passes it to her the exact second her hand pushes the door open.

The bathroom is bright in contrast to the dark club. It's also premeditatedly empty. With Bill or Mike outside she obviously doesn't feel like they have to go in a stall. AJ slowly becomes aware that he's grinning as he watches her make lines on the long vanity. An image flashes in his mind then, a memory made in another mirror at another after party, and suddenly he's not smiling anymore. Now he's stepping up to the counter, unfolding a bill out of his wallet, and crouching down.

"We have to be quick," Kadence tells him, drawing her own Benjamin out of the little bag. "Don't want to raise suspicion."

Sailor is already snorting her line up.

Kadence made four. There are only three people.

So AJ does one and splits the other with his girlfriend.

The two besties check each other's noses, check his, briefly touch up their makeup in the mirror, and then they all leave the scene.

Back inside the party things only get better. The music seems louder. His confidence seems stronger. Kadence introduces him to more people, some he's long admired. Artists inquire about the instruments he plays, ask for his number, allude that they want lyrics.

Not sex.

And he talks to these people with the professionalism of someone who has been in the songwriting business way longer than a few months. Their interest is piqued. And he feels like he's at his peak, body weightless and brain supercharged.

He downs another glass of champagne and joins Kadence on the dance floor. She had previously been bumping and grinding on Sailor and some other girl whose name he doesn't know, but he politely interrupts and steals her away. They're both all smiles as she slides her arms around his neck and he takes her waist into his hands. They do slow songs, they do fast songs, they do all the songs. There's another quick trip to the bathroom, and then it's immediately back to the floor. He dips and twirls her; she spins and twists. He moves his hips in a way that he usually only does in the bedroom and she backs it up on him like she's in some kind of rap video. They dance until everything is a kaleidoscope of skin and sweat and visible sound, the room turning into one big beautiful blur of beautiful people.

It's after three when they make their grand exit out of the party and into an awaiting limo. She's still not what he would call sloppy drunk, and he's trying his hardest not to act as high as he feels. Just in case the cameras are on them, which he's sure that they are. He can tell she's aware, she's always aware of her surroundings, and she handles her liquor and uppers exceptionally well. But once the car door is shut and they're behind the privacy of the tinted glass, she falls over on him in a fit of giggles. He laughs, too, though at what he doesn't know. She licks a slobbery trail up his neck.

"Ugh," she groans, biting his ear. "I so don't want to ride in this backseat all the way back to Tarzana. Anything more than ten miles and I think I'll vomit."

"Well we certainly don't want that. You want to get a room?"

"What about your place? Didn't you say you have an apartment Downtown?"

"Koreatown…"

"Let's just go there."

"Are you sure? I mean…it's really not much. Really not what you're used to."

"Babe, I can barely see straight. I'm in no shape to be taking critical inventory of anything. Maybe in the morning I'll care, but right now I just wanna crash."

"Ok," he chuckles, pushing a stray hair out of her face as she rests her head on his shoulder.

They stop at In-And-Out Burger on their way, even though a mile before she mentioned potentially puking, and even though he's really never seen her eat anything besides gummy bears and the dried fruit and cashew mix she keeps in the recording room. She insists that it's a "thing," and she's not one to break trend. So he orders what she orders and watches as she attacks the greasy burger with vigor and gulps down a Diet Coke like a deprived person. And by the time they pull up to his building, everything is gone.

They stumble out of the limo and onto the sidewalk. A few papz have followed them, but not many. Once the front door locks the cameras out, she kicks off her heels, suddenly realizing she's in a restaurant, and looking highly confused. He tries to explain it to her, and also that there's no elevator and he lives on the fourth floor, but she seems not to be comprehending too well. So he sweeps her up off her feet like a damsel in distress and starts to carry her up the stairs. She laughs loudly at this, prompting him to laugh too. It's all just enough commotion to bring a few of the Koreans and college kids who live there out into the hall.

"Is that Kadence Jane?" Someone says.

She ignores the oglers, burying her face in his shoulder in case someone has their phone out. She's still giggling, though, and he's still smiling, even though he's winded and can't really feel his arms by the time he gets to his door. He struggles to get his hand in his pocket so he can retrieve his keys without putting her down. His struggle only serves to make himself and her laugh harder. He hears a door crack.

"AJ?"

He turns around to see Jae standing in the doorway across the hall. AJ's sure it all probably looks very comical, him standing outside his six-hundred-dollar a month apartment with America's sweetheart slung over his shoulder in her six figure attire, acting like a couple of drunkards. But he doesn't care how it looks, because he's still buzzing and everything in the moment feels just right.

"Jae!" He exclaims with a beaming smile. "I'd like for you to meet somebody special." He turns back around and backs up so Kadence's face is facing Jae's. "Kay, this is my good friend, Jae. Jae, this is my bad girlfriend, Kadence Jane." He gives her ass a smack when he say's it. "You might have heard of her."

"Yes, but I never knew she was immobile," Jae replies jokingly with a kind smile that covers his skepticism. He holds his hand out to her. "Nice to meet you."

Kadence giggles some more. "Nice to meet you too, darlin," she says, country accent slipping out just a little under the influence. She takes his hand and gives it an exaggerated shake. "I hope we didn't wake you."

"No worries," he tells her once he gets his hand back, immediately giving it a wipe on his pajama bottoms to get rid of the grease from the burger she had. "I have a lot to get accomplished today, really probably needed the early start."

"We've been out celebrating," AJ says with his back still awkwardly to Jae, not realizing that it's awkward, and not thinking to put his girlfriend down.

"Oh," Jae says with a look of realization. "Right. Tonight was the Grammys wasn't it?" He looks up at the inebriated starlet hanging off of his best friend. "Did you win?"

"Oh honey I always win," she tells him with a blatant simplicity that she keeps tucked in on camera. She gives her nose a frantic little rub, then adds, "Don't have enough room on the mantle as it is."

"Well...congratulations," Jae tells her, forcing a convincing smile. "I'm glad you had a good night."

"Aww thank you," she says girlishly, grinning in such a way that her little blue eyes all but disappear. "You're so sweet." She pat's AJ's back and tries to turn her head all the way around. "Babe, your friend is a sweetie pie."

Jae tries his hardest to keep smiling and not grimace.

"Yeah, he's the best," AJ replies with whimsy as he gets his finger around his key. "They don't come no better than Jae Reeh."

"Thanks, man, "Jae replies semi-sarcastically. "I think I'm gonna go back inside, put the coffee on, and start getting ready for the day. Serving breakfast in Venice this morning."

"Oh, are you a waiter?" Kadence asks while AJ works the lock on the door, still clinging to him even though he's technically let go of her.

"I'm a business owner," Jae corrects her.

"Huh," she says.

AJ finally gets the door unlocked.

"You all enjoy the rest of your...night slash morning," Jae tells them, stepping back into his apartment. "I'll holler at you later, AJ."

"Aight, bud," AJ replies.

Jae's door closes. AJ kicks his open, carries her over the threshold, and kicks it back closed. He playfully throws her down on the bed and she bounces with a giggle, falling flat against the sheets and fanning herself out like an inebriated starfish. AJ starts undoing the buttons of his dress shirt, realizing then that he must have discarded his suit jacket at some point in time during the night and forgot it somewhere. An ordinary person would be aghast at losing a five-thousand-dollar article clothing, but being that he can make five thousand dollars in a night, and being that he technically didn't even buy it, he's unconcerned. He pulls the shirt from his pants, shrugs it off his shoulders, and tosses it to the floor carelessly.

"He's a business owner and lives in this scuzzy place?" Kadence muses from the bed with a snort. "That doesn't seem likely. Are you sure you know what he *really* does?"

AJ smiles to himself. "He has a food truck. I've really seen it," he tells her, walking over to his dresser. "And I thought you were going to hold off on passing judgment on my scuzzy building until you sobered up enough to fully appreciate it in all its scuzziness."

"You're a struggling artist. You're spose to be livin in a place like this," she says, sitting up and starting to work on the zipper at the back of her gown.

He opens a drawer and grabs one of his t-shirts for her to put on, purposefully picking one Anjanae had never slept in.

"But," she continues, nimbly getting the dress all the way unzipped on her own. "Now that you're with me..." She begins to peel it from her body until she gets his green eyes on her, then she smiles. "You'll have all kinds of big breaks. I promise."

He stares at her bared upper body a moment, then walks to the bed. "What kind of big breaks are we talking about?" He asks, handing her the t-shirt with a smirk on his lips. "Mental or monetary?"

"Ha," she retorts dryly, snatching the shirt from his hand with an eye roll. "Funny."

He smiles, and then watches the expensive gown pool at her feet when she stands. She steps out of it and pulls the sleep shirt that was given to her on over her head. Her blue eyes are bleary in the late hour and her slicked back hair is starting to lose some of its sculpt, the mess and the elegance somewhere between a younger Charlize Theron and a slightly tighter-wrapped Courtney Love.

"Do you have a spare toothbrush?" She asks, strutting away from him and towards the open bathroom in her Manolo heels and his high school band t-shirt. "I need to scrub the guilty reminder of that burger out of my mouth. That's another ten thousand calories I'll have to burn off tomorrow in the spare time that I don't have."

"Yeah there should be one in the second drawer."

He strips down to his boxer-briefs and then sits down on the edge of the bed. A wave of something akin to anxiety and mimicking nausea is starting to hit him, it was shallow feeling at first but has quickly escalated into a tidal wave of worked nerves. He holds his head down and listens to the water run in the bathroom, concentrating on his breathing, trying to mentally calm himself down. He hears her exit the bathroom, and then shortly after feels the bed dip.

"I'm not feeling so good anymore," he tells her.

"What do you feel like?" She asks.

"Like I'll never sleep again."

She laughs. "You will."

"It's like…the rush wore off but the jitters didn't." He holds his trembling hands out to her. "Do you see my hands?"

"Yes, that's normal."

"I feel like I did too much. Like tonight was just too much. I mean…tonight was amazing, crazy amazing…but now it's like…wow. Do you think I shouldn't have drank with the…you know…the *other* stuff? Do you think I did too much?"

"You didn't do too much," she reassures, unconcerned. "You just did enough for the first time to feel sucky after the fun's over."

"Ok."

"If you want to sleep I brought my pills. I always pack them when I plan to sleep away from home. I don't adjust well to beds that aren't my own."

She gets up and grabs her clutch (the gold one, not the sequined one) off the floor where she tossed it. She unzips it and dumps the contents out on the bed. There's makeup, her phone, a thing of Tic-Tacs, and a prescription bottle filled with pills. The latter of which she picks up and passes to him.

He holds the little orange bottle in his hand and looks it over. It's a prescription for Ambien 10 mg. Made out to Caroline Sanders—which is his first time seeing her real name in print, anywhere—and filled at a pharmacy in Beverley Hills. Says *take one at night as needed for sleep.*

"Nothing bad is going to happen, is it?" He asks her.

"No," she chuckles. "My doc gave them to me to take on long flights so I can just sleep through it. He says all his patients in the industry have a script for them. They're good for adjusting to different time zones, or for when I'm at work all night in the studio and want to sleep during the day." She pauses, and then smirks slyly before adding, "Or for when I want to skip the come down after a night of partying."

He shakes his head at her, even though he's smirking, too.

"He's been doctoring for over forty years," she explains in attempt to assuage his fears. "He wouldn't prescribe them to everyone if they were bad. They're totally safe as long as you don't try to drive or do something stupid like that."

He knows he's read articles to the contrary but he pops one anyway, and then watches as she does the same. They undress the rest of the way and then crawl under the covers. They start sex, but he doesn't think that they finished it. He wakes up late in the afternoon, having slept a full eight hours for the first time in God knows when. He vaguely remembers the feel of cold air on him at some point in the night, like he might have been out on the fire escape, but he doesn't ask her if he got up, and she doesn't tell him that he did.

And all is well.

Chapter 14

Austin has the night off for once, so he's going to take Hermosa out for dinner when she gets off. She's been keeping a busy schedule—school, two jobs—and Austin thinks she deserves some steak, maybe a lobster, and a bottle of good wine. He made reservations for seven at a new place nearby. Hermosa recently got transferred to the library Downtown, which is less than a block away from the office. So he told her she could wait for him there when she got off, take a shower, and change clothes if she wanted to, and he'd pick her up at six-thirty.

He steps off the elevator on the fifty-seventh floor. Hermosa looks up from the couch with a smile. Maggie looks up from her desk with the evil eye. He ignores it.

"Ready to go, baby?" He asks Hermosa.

"Yup," she says, standing with a smile and returning the magazine she was reading to the table. He takes her hand in his, and they head towards the elevators.

"Can I talk to Austin alone for a moment?" Maggie asks out of the blue.

Hermosa looks hesitant.

"I'll be down in a minute, okay, Mo?" He tells her gently. "Wait in the lobby, don't go out to the parking garage by yourself."

Hermosa gives him a nod, a quick kiss, and then gets on without him.

"What?" He asks Maggie when the doors close.

"Why do you have this random girl hanging out here all the time? Eyes soaking up secrets, mind cataloguing every minute detail, ears hearing how we do business. *Mouth* that can repeat it all."

"She ain't a random girl," Austin tells her matter-of-factly. "She also ain't Ali or Anjanae," he adds, getting a little ballsy. "So please, I know you think I'm dumb, but give me the benefit of the doubt that I actually know the person I love. She's not working for the LAPD. She's not married. She's not a risk."

Maggie stares at him but says nothing.

He turns for the elevator. "Stop stressin'," he calls to her over his shoulder.

~

Later that night, after sex, Hermosa is draped over his body like a sheet. She hadn't bothered to move from where she'd fallen after the final throws. He wasn't going to protest, enjoying the gentle weight of her atop him and the warmth of her skin. She hums contentedly every once in a while as he runs his fingers through her hair, but she's otherwise silent.

"Hey," he says quietly after a beat. "What are you thinkin'?"

"Who said I was thinkin' anything," she mumbles softly.

"I can hear your mind goin'," he chides playfully.

"Oh really," she says, smile in her voice.

"I think you're thinkin…maybe he is boyfriend material after all."

She laughs against his chest, but says nothing else.

Chapter 15

Kadence wants to introduce AJ to the girls she calls her close friends. So she has a small get-together for those privileged enough to be part of her posse, and invites him over to join in on the middle school-esque slumber party shenanigans.

The living room is filled with a bunch of white girls (save for the two who have foreign mothers, but their skin is also white) watching some chick flick on the huge, fancy flat screen television. There's an array of Sprinkles cupcakes laid out on the table in front of them and the Pinot Grigio is flowing freely. They are spread out all over the room, laid across couches with their feet propped up on the armrests, or stomach down on the floor, not concerned about getting their spray tans on the white carpet—clearly very comfortable in her home.

Two are models (Fryderyka and Katrina), two are actresses (Charlotte and Christine), one is a friend from her hometown who is clinging desperately to the dream of being somebody herself (Susie), three are rich Beverley Hills' kids who do absolutely nothing (Lillian, Notalya, and Lauren). And her best friend, Sailor.

All of these girls have money, some have success, but the fact of the matter is none of their stars shine as bright as Kay's. Not even close. Their bank accounts aren't even close. Their fan base nowhere near. Kadence Jane is the sun their planets revolve around. And AJ can see it instantly.

They welcome him into their fold happily, made amiable by the abundance of their favorite liquid. So he joins the ten of them as they eat and drink and gossip themselves into a comatose state over the course of the night while *Breakfast at Tiffany's* plays on the television under a glistening Waterford chandelier.

The next morning he wakes up with the kind of hangover one gets from spending all night listening to girls giggle in high pitch and drinking white wine you don't even like; on an empty stomach, no less. The air smells like vanilla frosting, incense, and self-tanner, bringing about a wave of nausea that makes his throat constrict. His head is pounding; he slept on the corner of a couch in an unpleasant position that has his neck out of whack. The sun is pouring in from every angle. Too much glass, there is too much glass in her house. Everything is bright, and he has to squint, and it just makes his head hurt worse. He glances down at his watch, a quarter past nine. He has to be at Fereshteh's house by eleven for his Tuesday morning appointment, and he still needs to go home and shower and brush his teeth and get dressed. And he's running on just barely four hours of sleep. He stretches his muscles and swings his legs over the side of the couch. All the girls are still sound asleep—some even snoring—having drunk themselves into a sugar coma. Their once perfect hair is in shambles, the makeup they didn't take the time to wash off surely staining Kadence's pillows.

He doesn't see Kadence.

Perhaps she had retreated in the night to the comfort of her own bed. He stands stiffly and quietly makes his way out of the living room, shielding his face from all the light with his hand. He passes the staircase and can hear the hum of the vacuum running from the floor above, letting him know Consuelo has already arrived for work. He takes the elevator up to the fourth floor. Her bedroom door is cracked. He pushes it the rest of the way open and, sure enough, there she is. She's wrapped up in the thick duvet, her head just barely visible. The floor length blinds are pulled shut across the balcony exit, and she's got a sleep mask pulled down over her eyes. A glass of unfinished Pinot with a bendy straw in it sits on her nightstand next to the Ambien bottle.

"Hey," he says quietly, gently nudging her. She doesn't budge at first, so he gives her a second nudge. She pulls the blankets up further and buries her head down into them with a grunt. "Kadence," he repeats, sitting on the edge of the bed.

"Hm?" She mumbles, finally beginning to return to consciousness, slowly at first, and then with a start. "What?" She lifts her head and simultaneously pulls down her mask, her eyes landing on him. "Oh. Hey." She blinks a few times. "What time is it?" She asks groggily.

"A little after nine," he tells her, still keeping his voice soft. "I've gotta leave in a bit, I didn't want to just disappear without telling you."

"Aww," she whines in a disappointed voice, sitting the rest of the way up, silk strap slipping off her boney shoulder. "What for?"

"I've got a meeting with an HBO showrunner's assistant," he lies on the spot, surprising himself at how good he's got at it. "He's a friend of a friend who told me there's going to be an open spot in the writer's room come fall. I'm trying to weasel my way in. At least maybe get an interview or something."

"Oh. Cool," she replies apathetically with a yawn and a stretch, buying it without him having to explain any further.

There are dark circles under her eyes that he's never noticed before. And then he realizes she doesn't have makeup on, that this is the first time he's seen her without makeup. There are some zits on her chin, not many. A few weathered lines that betray her young age; a couple slivered scars and dull blemishes on her cheeks.

"Do you want anything before you go?" She asks him. "My chef is off today, but I'm sure Consuelo can whip up some eggs ranchero or something. I think I have eggs. I don't know. There's definitely some pressed juice in the fridge. Papaya and Acai. Beets and Apple. Raw aloe and cucumber. Chai seed and activated charcoal. There might be a wheat grass and ginger shot in there, too. That'll get you right."

"I need coffee," he tells her with a kind smile, and then as an afterthought furrows his brow and ponders aloud, "Chai seed and activated *charcoal?*"

"I don't keep coffee in the house," she informs him.

"What do you mean you don't keep coffee in the house?"

"I'm a sweet tea girl, you know this."

"Well...do you have any caffeinated tea anywhere in this humongous house?"

"No. I only like it fresh from Starbucks." She pushes the sheets away and pulls her pink sleep shorts back on over her polka dot panties, getting up. "The stuff they sell in the stores isn't the same. Hold on." She makes her way over to her dresser. She opens a drawer, roots around, and retrieves a little fuchsia bullet shaped thing that at first glance he thinks is a vibrator. "Here," she says, unscrewing the bottom off, walking to the middle of the room, and shaking a little white powder out onto the glass table.

He raises an eyebrow at her skeptically. "At nine o'clock in the morning?"

"Better than waiting in a long drive-thru line for coffee and then having to pee nonstop for the next three hours," she replies stoically, pulling the straw out her wine glass and handing it to him.

He stares at her for a moment more. "I suppose that's true," he relents, kneeling on the floor in front of the glass table. He shapes it up and then takes it up through the straw. It was a very little amount, probably not even equivalent to a large cup of Colombian roast.

They ride back downstairs together.

Shelley is in the kitchen unloading multiple boxes of fresh pastries out of a bag. She's got her stringy hair pulled back in her patent ponytail, sporting her typically plain wardrobe. She spins around spritely when she senses them behind her, smiling jovially from ear-to-ear.

"Hey, guys!" She beams. "You two are up early. I was hoping to get back before everyone awoke. I've got bagels, croissants, scones. And I asked that everything be only the freshest, most straight out of the oven stuff. So excellence is guaranteed." She grabs a lidded cup off the counter. "Here's your tea, Kay, I already doctored it up."

Kadence takes the cup from her without a word and sits down on one of the barstools in front of the island.

"Here, AJ," Shelley says, opening up the first box. "Pick you out a goodie."

"I'm not really hungry. Thank you, though."

Kadence is about to reach her hand into the glass canister of gummy bears when she freezes. Her lips purse into too tight of a smile to be taken kindly, and she cuts her eyes across the room at her assistant.

"Shelley," she says in a voice that is disconcertingly collected. "Why are there yellow and clear bears in this fucking jar?"

"Oh," Shelley utters, full of nerves. She turns around timidly and her eyes are as big and as apologetic as a puppy that just knows its nose is about to be rubbed into some piss. "I must've–"

"You must've *what*?" Kadence cuts her off, tone now hinging on unhinged. "Forgot that I specifically asked that you pick out all the orange, yellow, and clear bears because I only like the green and red ones?" And then she snaps. "Can you not see colors? Can you not follow basic instructions? Are you incompetent? I mean…I have only been eating gummy bears my whole entire life. I was eating them when you came into my life, I was eating them before you came into my life, and I'll still be eating them when your unemployed ass is filling out job applications at Burger King and Wendy's. This was rule one from day one and you've been working here for over two fucking years. Did you have a damn aneurysm? A stroke? Do I need to be rushing you to the hospital for a head CT? How many fingers am I holding up? I mean God, Shelley, how fucking hard of a job is it to sort candy? The people at Haribo do it for a fraction of the generous fucking salary I give you. I tell you, I think you've gotten too comfortable. You've become complacent. I think I need to put a little fear in your heart. A little fire under your ass. So here it is; if I so much as see one wrong colored bear in this house, you're gone. Understood?"

"Yes, Kadence," Shelley replies submissively, face and neck totally red. "Would you like a pastry?" She asks in a voice so quiet it can barely be heard.

"Oh yeah let me shove my face with some carb loaded bread," Kadence retorts with an eye roll. "Get me my breakfast juice out of the fridge and act like you have some sense."

Shelley does as she's told. AJ just stands there, baffled by what's just happened. He's never seen Kadence act like that before. Of course he's only known her on a personal level for a month or so. He watches her unscrew the lid off the bottle of pressed juice Shelley just handed her. It's filled with deep burgundy liquid; she holds it to her mouth and takes a drink. He wants to ask her if she's okay, but he's suddenly afraid to say the wrong thing. He hears sheets rustle and furniture creak somewhere behind him. He turns around and sees a few of the girls in the living room have started to stir awake, stretching and yawning.

"I'm going to go ahead and head out," he tells her.

"Ok, babe," she replies, her voice reverting back to sweetness after her brief outburst. She looks up and smiles at him. "Call me later, ok?"

"Ok," he says, returning her smile. She puckers her lips and he places a kiss on them, a routine gesture that sings of regularity. Then he walks out the door and drives home to get ready for his morning rendezvous, writing his girlfriend's behavior off as a fluke, blaming it on a lack of sleep and a mild hangover.

~

The next week Kadence goes to Milan for fashion week. Kat and Freddie are both walking in multiple shows, and his girlfriend intends to spend all seven days. AJ wanted to take off and go with her, but Maggie wouldn't let him. He makes up some excuse that Kay believes, rides in the limo to the airport, and kisses her goodbye.

Two days later, AJ starts to feel weird.

Uneasiness that turns into emptiness that turns into yearning.

On the third day he decides it must be some kind of separation anxiety. They'd spent almost every free minute he had of the prior week together. At the studio recording, in Tarzana messing around, at the big send-off shindig for the models at somebody's mansion partying. He must just miss her.

On the third night he lays awake in the throes of anxiety. His body aches and his stomach feels as though it will reject even the mildest food. He becomes super aware of just how little his apartment is, and how close the walls are. He turns on the television, but can't focus on the screen. He tries to write, but can't focus on the words. He's too tired. Yet he's only able to fall asleep for about an hour before his racing mind and restless body wakes him up again.

The fourth morning he considers the prospect that it's not her that he misses.

The yearning inside him is profound and foreign. It's not for a body, or for affection. It's for a feeling. A feeling of catapulting adrenaline and wondrous creativity. In its absence he's a malfunctioning machine, rendered utterly useless.

He can't eat.

He can't sleep.

He can't write.

All he can do is pick at his skin and try not to puke.

However, there are still rich women that need tending to, and he has to peel himself off his bed, shower, dress, and leave his apartment every evening to do so despite feeling like a walking wreck.

On the fifth day he sees that Mrs. Kelly is on his schedule, having lost track of what day it is, and his spirits rise ever so slightly. He drives up to the hills with high hopes. She's left the front door unlocked, which he hopes speaks of the state of inebriation she's already in, and he lets himself in. He passes through the parlor, noting the empty space she still hasn't filled where the piano she gifted him used to be, and heads up the stairs. Her bedroom door is ajar, and he pushes it the rest of the way open. The smell of Channel is thick in the air, making his already unhappy stomach twist tighter.

"Well hello, darling," she says when she notices he's there. She sits her glass of chardonnay down and comes over to him, kissing both his cheeks and then planting her lips on his. They make a smacking sound when they separate. "How lovely to see you."

"You know the front door downstairs is unlocked," AJ tells her.

"Oh, it's no biggie," she replies, walking back over to her dresser to reclaim her glass of wine. "This is hardly the inner-city. If some hoodlum wants to risk his life jumping over a thirty-foot fence after getting by the attendant at the front gate then by all means he can take my televisions. Though I won't hesitate to shoot any crook for my pearls. I keep a Smith and Wesson under the bed."

"Oh," he says, because he doesn't really know what else to say. He starts unbuttoning his shirt. Pulls it free, shrugs it off.

"You can lock up when you leave if you're worried about me, but I rarely get concerned anymore," she says definitively. Mrs. Kelly drains her glass and discards it on the vanity. And then she walks straight to him and starts to undo his belt, skipping a pivotal part of her usual routine. "Let's get these off of you," she murmurs with a naughty smile, getting his pants open and pulling down his zipper.

"I thought...I don't know...that we could do a little line before we get started," AJ says hesitantly.

"Oh," Mrs. Kelly says, hands stilling and pulling back a bit to look at him. "I didn't see my friend this week who supplies me with it."

All hope is extinguished.

AJ wants to ask her who this friend is. If maybe he can get a phone number. But instead he masks his disappointment. "Oh. Ok. That's fine."

"I thought you didn't like it?" She asks with an eyebrow raise.

"I just thought it might spice things up tonight, that's all."

"I'll have some next week."

"It's cool," he says coolly, though his palms are sweating, because the wave of disappointment that's washed over him has left him limp in every sense of the word. And for a moment he's quite sure he won't be able to get it up.

However, Mrs. Kelly is patient. And handsy. And eventually he does get an erection. They fuck for an hour, and it momentarily gets his mind off the uneasy feeling that's been plaguing him, but as he gets redressed it all comes crashing back. The fact that another sleepless night filled with the white noise of another generation's sitcoms looms ahead of him makes his anxiety triple tenfold. He can already see himself staring at a blank piece of paper, trying to compose something smart but coming up short. He can already feel the hunger pangs disguised as nausea returning, the claustrophobia his little living space induces resurfacing.

"I've been having trouble sleeping lately," he says, sitting down on the rumpled bed to put his shoes on. "You wouldn't happen to have anything for that would you?"

"I've got a prescription for Valium," Mrs. Kelly offers graciously, pulling her slip back on and slipping out from the sheets. "You think that will do it?"

"Probably," he replies, not really knowing if it will or not.

She gives him two.

Once home he takes one of the little blue pills and saves the other. He washes it down with a glass of water, climbs into bed, and flips the television on. Twenty minutes later the uneasy feeling is almost completely gone, and AJ actually feels comfortable for the first time in a long time. The next thing he knows he's opening his eyes and seeing that nine hours have elapsed. He gets out of bed feeling refreshed, well rested, and ready for the day. He sits down at his desk and over the course of the afternoon writes a poignant new song that he can't wait to show Kadence, immediately writing the bad week off as a fluke

Chapter 16

"It's like…I know she's in love with me but she's afraid to commit," Austin says in between breaths, one Nike-clad foot hitting the sand after the other, water bottle in his right hand like a baton. "That's spose to be a man's problem, right?" He turns his head to look at his running partner.

Austin and Calvin are jogging along the Santa Monica shoreline midafternoon, Austin in basketball shorts and an old t-shirt with the sleeves cut off, and Calvin in a fashion forward tank top and brightly colored board shorts. They'd met up earlier for margaritas at a place on the pier like they'd talked about doing, and then Austin had cutely coerced Calvin into going for a run with him. Austin doesn't have very many friends in LA. He's grown apart from the guys he'd befriended during his brief stint as a TSA agent at the airport, and all his buddies back home are living a completely different life than him and he only talks to them intermittently anymore. Aside from Hermosa and AJ, he isn't really close to anyone else. Hermosa is in class today. AJ doesn't get to hangout anymore because a pop star is prioritizing all his free time. Austin works out alone almost everyday, and he has gone out for more meals by himself in one year than he ever did in Ohio. He craves company. Plus, Calvin is cool. He likes Calvin.

"How do you know she loves you?" Calvin pants, out of breath and clearly struggling to keep up.

"I guess I don't," Austin replies, consciously slowing his speed. "I guess that's part of the problem." He looks unusually reflective as he fills his lungs with a deep breath of ocean air. "That shit makes me self-conscious, yanno?" He confides in Calvin. "All the other girlfriends I had back in the day, back before I knew better, back before I knew what love was… they was the ones who chased me and wanted commitment." Austin swipes the back of his hand over his slick brow as they continue to jog. "Now I can't even get the girl I'm with to let me call her my girlfriend. It's like I put myself all the way out there and I don't even know if she feels the same."

"Should we have drunk before we went on a run in the sun?" Calvin asks raggedly, using his arm to collect the condensation off his own dripping brow. "I feel like this is a dehydration risk. Alcohol is dehydrating. And I'm sweating. I *hate* sweating. You know you're a real crafty motherfucker. Luring innocent bystanders in with half-priced margaritas and then convincing them to exercise afterwards. Got me out here with my chicken legs struggle sprintin' like a track and field reject."

"Hey, I made sure you bought that bottle of Dasani before we left the boardwalk, didn't I?" Austin says with a smile in his voice. "I was lookin' out for ya. Plus, it was just a little bit of alcohol in that margarita. Mainly fruity juice and ice. Tequila in moderation is good for you."

"You're one of those guys who throws raw eggs in the blender with some...I don't know...some of that whey shit, hot sauce...and just tosses it back for breakfast like salmonella ain't a thing, aren't you?"

Austin grins. "Maybe."

"I knew it," Calvin replies knowingly, and then sighs deeply. "Shit. Can we take a break? I know I'm skinny but I'm so out of shape. And you're like...professional athlete status over there."

"Yeah," Austin chuckles. "Let's take a break."

They both come to a stop about a half a mile down the shore from where they started. Austin typically does three to five miles without stopping, but he doesn't mind because it's been a lot less lonely today. Calvin is leaned over with his hands on his knees, huffing and puffing theatrically, trying to catch his breath. Austin thinks he's a bit dramatic most of the time, but funny; he makes it hard not to laugh or smile. Austin pops the cap on his sports bottle and takes a long drink. Calvin unscrews the lid off his water bottle once he gets his breath back and does the same.

"She feels the same," Calvin says after he swallows, wiping his lips and resting the lid back on the mouth of the plastic bottle.

"Huh?" Austin asks, stripping his sweat soaked t-shirt off over his head. He catches Calvin's eyes on his body before Calvin catches himself and looks back away. Austin smiles to himself, but pretends he didn't notice as to not embarrass him.

"Your girl," Calvin replies, staring out at the waves crashing onto the sand. "I think she probably does love you, and that's probably why she closes herself off to commitment. To protect herself. You know, like a defense mechanism. She's afraid to get too close"

"You think?"

"Sure. And that's not necessarily a bad thing. That says she has values and respect for herself and her heart. You don't want someone who makes it easy, who's just blindly throwing themselves at you, over-optimistically hoping you'll catch them when you might not. I'm not saying you're a bad guy or anything like that, but maybe there's something about you that makes her think you're a flight risk."

"Well I don't know why she just can't tell me this instead of sending me mixed signals. One day she's kissing on me out in public and letting me pay for dinner, then the next day she's telling me to back off on the boyfriend behavior."

"That's why I don't fuck with the female gender. Fickle as hell."

"Yeah that's why," Austin kids with a smirk.

"Do you think it's because of what you do that she acts that way?"

"What do I do?" Austin asks as he raises his water bottle back to his mouth to take a drink, genuinely not knowing what Calvin means.

"Well you and AJ are escorts, aren't you?"

Austin chokes on his water, sending some of it out his nose. "What?" He asks when he recovers, feigning obliviousness as he dabs his mouth and nose.

"Don't play," Calvin tells him, smirking as he takes a sip of his own water. "The last time you all were at the bar together there were two busty blonde college girls two stools down from you and you both only had eyes for the sixty something widow across the room with the immaculate hairpiece and the Hermes bag. Either you both ironically have some serious mommy issues and were looking for some suga, or you were both pacing the car lot with the intention of only offering the keys to someone who could afford more than a test drive."

Austin wipes his damp forehead with his discarded t-shirt, saying nothing but looking guilty.

"Plus, I saw the outfits you all had on," Calvin continues knowingly. "Tom Forde and Armani. Rolex watches. Balenciaga shoes. I'm a fashion fanatic; I know how much threads like that cost to the dollar. Even if you two were really in *sales…*" He accentuates the word and gives his running partner a look. "You couldn't be more than mid-twenties. Someone only a couple years out of business school might make good money for their age, but not *that* good."

Austin glances over at him for just a second and can't help the smile the starts to curl his lips. He looks back away and shakes his head as he raises his water bottle to his lips again.

"Come on," Calvin prods with a smile. "I'm your bartender. Which is basically the same thing as a therapist. You're supposed to tell me all your deep dark secrets."

Austin flips the lid back down on his bottle and takes off jogging again.

"Well wait up!" Calvin calls out to him, running to catch up and then falling back into step with him. They jog side by side in silence for a few seconds.

"I didn't go to business college," Austin admits after a while. "I didn't go to college period." He pauses after thinking about it. "Well...I did for like three months before I fucked it up. But I don't have no degree or nothin'."

Calvin nods. They jog a few more yards before he speaks. "So women really pay for sex?"

Austin tries not to smile. "These women out here are a different breed, buddy. They got the money so they're gonna buy what they want. Designer duds, diamonds, dick, you name it."

Calvin busts out laughing, and soon Austin is laughing out loud, too.

"Look," Austin says seriously after a beat, breathless from the physical exertion and the laughter. "You can't tell anybody, though. My boss gets all paranoid about people knowin' her business title and I think it's startin' to rub off on me."

Calvin meets his eyes as they jog in the sun. "Bartender's promise. What's said between me and you stays between me and you."

Austin holds his gaze for a moment more, then faces forward again so he doesn't fall, focusing his eyes on down the beach, smiling to himself yet again.

Chapter 17

The night before Kadence is due back from Milan, AJ has a date at a Beverley Hills restaurant with Vera. He breaks his new "sex only" rule for Vera because he likes her as a person, and because he hasn't seen the paparazzi all week, he assumes that they don't see him. After all, to them the only interesting thing about him is her, and she is currently abroad.

It's the third Thursday of the month, meaning dinner will be followed with a nightcap, meaning he'll make extra cash tonight. Conversation is always better with Vera than with his other clients, and he can now almost hold an entire conversation in French, though Vera dumbs it down to English for him when his mind is too tired to formulate foreign sentences. He can now also pronounce all the wines on the menu, and has finally developed a taste for the best ones. In fact, he's on his third glass of the night.

He gets up to go pee between the main course and dessert. After he leaves the bathroom, he's making his way back to the main dining room, and is about ten feet from his table when he is stopped in his tracks by a familiar voice that sounds way more menacing than it usually does.

"Well, well, well. Look what we have here."

He looks up and there stands Kadence. She's wearing a slinky dress with a slit up the side; hands on her hips and head cocked at him in an amusedly accusatory way that suggests she's pleased to catch him slipping. Charlotte and Christine are standing next to her with a similar pose. His girlfriend is smiling, but not in a safe way. In fact, the look she's giving him looks damn near dangerous.

"Kadence," he says, unable to hide the shock in his voice, and quickly attempting a smile that he hopes errs on pleasantly surprised. "I thought you weren't getting back in till tomorrow?"

"Surprise," she says lowly, keeping that smile plastered on her face as she walks to him. She pretends to adjust his collar so that the spectators at their tables who undoubtedly have their eyes on her won't hear what she says to him. "You taking another girl out in my absence?"

"What?" He utters, trying his best to sound appalled that she would think such a thing. "No. Kadence, no," he says quickly, hoping she believes him. "I –"

"Suspicious stutter, shocked expression," she cuts him off, speaking with the same eerily calm and coolly even tone as she runs her hands through his hair. "Full suit, fancy shoes, five-star restaurant…" She pulls back enough to look him in his eyes. "Sure looks like you're on a date to me."

But before he can say any more, another voice comes out of left field.

"What happened to ya, honey bun, you get lost?" Someone says behind him.

AJ spins around and sees Vera coming up behind him. His heart is hammering away in his chest as she rests her hand lovingly on his shoulder. He doesn't know what the hell is happening and he's too flabbergasted to form a verbal response, eyes nervously darting between his Thursday night client and his girlfriend.

"Can't be leavin' me by myself like that in a strange place. You know all these fancy LA folk make your granny nervous," Vera continues, talking in a strong Southern drawl that he'd never expect to come out of her mouth. A convincing Southern drawl at that, not even a hint of her real accent in it. "I flew all the way out to this here dag-nab dirty city to spend time with my grand baby, not sit at a table all by my lonesome."

"My bad, grandma," AJ replies after a second, going along with the alibi provided to him, and thanking God that Vera's quick on her feet. "You see, I ran into someone special on my way back from the bathroom." He looks back over to Kadence then, whose face has softened completely in the last thirty seconds. She is clearly buying what is being sold to her, her fears extinguished by the sight of a dramatically older woman instead of the seductive young trollop she expected to see. Because for what other reason would he be with someone near seventy if she wasn't his grandmother? "Nana, I'd like for you to meet my girlfriend, Kadence Jane. Kay, I'd like for you to meet my Nana..." He scrambles for a fake name in his mind. "Norma...Jean...Brooks."

"Ugh!" Vera exclaims with a dramatic, toothy smile. "She looks even prettier in person than she does on the T.V.!"

Kadence has the mile-wide smile on, embracing Vera in big bear hug. "So nice to meet you," she says in an overly chipper voice to his client.

"I feel downright honored to have got ta meetcha before the rest of the family," Vera says when they separate.

"I feel so silly," Kadence giggles girlishly. "Here I was thinking he was out on a date with another girl."

"Oh heavens no, honey. All he does is talk about you. He's helplessly smitten. You ain't gotta worry bout this one strayin," Vera assures her.

"Aww. Well thank you for sayin that," Kadence says graciously, looking down at the floor bashfully even though AJ knows she's not. "I'll let you all get back to your dinner." She turns and kisses AJ on his cheek. "I'll call you later, ok, babe?"

"Ok," he smiles back.

Her and her girlfriends are taken back to their private room, roped off just for them, and AJ and Vera return to their table.

"Tres impressionnant," he compliments discreetly, sitting down and raising his glass to his lips with a coy smirk.

"Je vous remercie," Vera replies coquettishly, taking a sip of her wine. "You have been so eager to pick up French from me, I thought I could exercise a little Tennessee twang on your behalf."

"Well you didn't pick up that Tennessee twang from me," he replies, sitting back in his chair with his glass in his hand. "I don't sound like that." There's a pause where she doesn't correct him, and he leans back forward with a concerned expression. "I don't sound like that, do I?"

She laughs out loud and shakes her head. "No mon cher, you do not."

"Dieu merci," he sighs, taking another drink. "I was starting to panic."

She smiles. "I learned from the American sitcoms and old westerns on the channel with the re-airings. I watch it when I cannot sleep at night."

"Me too," he replies with a grin. He takes a final bite of his cheesecake and then pushes the plate away, seeing that she's done with hers too. "So...back to your place?"

"I think I will pass tonight," she replies. "No offense, but I am not feeling prodigiously sexy after playing the role of your grandmother."

"Right. Totally understandable," AJ says gently, trying to mask the disappointment for all the money he just lost himself. "Sorry."

"Do not be sorry. She had her hands critically close to your throat. I did what I had to do."

AJ chuckles. "Thank you."

"Just be glad you have a gullible girlfriend," she tells him. "Norma Jean? *Please.*"

They both share a good laugh.

~

AJ arrives at the studio the next afternoon a little after two. When he walks into the last recording room, she's alone, sitting in the swivel chair with her heeled boots propped up on the console, smoking a cigarette. At first he thinks it's a joint, but it's not, and he can't imagine that tobacco is good for her vocals. Though it's not like he's going to tell her that. There's a glass of clear liquid sitting on the table next to her. She looks up and gives him a brilliant smile when she realizes he's there, rests her cigarette on the ashtray, stands up and walks over to him.

"Hey, baby," she says, throwing her arms around him and kissing him on the cheek. "I missed you *soo* much."

It's like last night never happened. Like she didn't run into him at the fancy restaurant and accuse him of cheating on her. He supposes he's okay with her glossing over it. After all, he had actually been the one in the wrong, she just didn't know it.

"I missed you, too," AJ tells her, leaving out the part about how without her and her unending stash of coke he thinks he might have went through a case of moderate withdrawal.

"I've got big news for you," Kadence says, the cheer in her voice sounding both girlish and also mysteriously motivated. She takes him by the hand and leads him over to the table.

"Oh yeah?" He asks, sitting down in one of the chairs and placing his notebook on the table.

"Oh yes." She plops back down in the swivel chair and immediately picks up her cigarette; she ashes it before returning it to her lips. He waits patiently while she takes a long drag and exhales a plume of smoke. For a second she just stares at him smiling, like she just knows the news she's about to deliver is going to make his week, and then she sits forward and cocks her head. "I talked to Bryan this morning. The label wants to offer you a publishing deal." She reclines in her chair and grabs her glass of vodka. "You know, before we start dropping singles."

"So they can reap what I've wrote?"

She stops smiling, looks away, and takes a drink. "No, because their job is to build the best team in the business," she articulates plainly. She puts the drink back down, returns the smile to her face, and turns her eyes upon him once more. "And you're talented, so naturally they want you on the team."

"Maybe I want to be able to move around," he says without attitude. "Maybe I don't want to be stuck on one team." He looks at her and gives a little shrug. "I kind of want to be like a free agent."

Kadence takes another drag, blows it out. "Well who else do you want to work with?"

"I mean…I don't know," he stammers, looking down at the hole in the knee of his jeans. He starts to toy with the frays. "This is all new to me. But I do know my writing is all I have. I want to stay in control of it."

"Your loss," she says simply, putting her cigarette out on the glass tray. "They probably would have given you six, maybe seven figures to sign."

"I don't need the money."

She stares at him, looking him up and down in a way that makes him feel oddly self-conscious. He tries to read her, gauge her mood, but he can't and it's disconcerting. She almost looks like she might be offended that he didn't want to take the deal. A deal that has very little to do with her, other than the fact that it would chain him to her contractually. And he wonders briefly if she wanted him to sign more for herself than for him. He looks away first, because she refuses to.

"Anyway," he says. "I wrote a song for the album while you were away. I can't wait for you to lay the vocals to it. It feels really special. Honest. Raw."

She takes a sip of vodka. "You only got one song wrote while I was gone?"

"I mean…yeah…" AJ stammers again self-consciously. "It was an intricate song." He flips through his notebook looking for it. "Why?"

Kadence shrugs. "For some reason I thought you would have gotten more accomplished." She takes another sip. "Maybe I was overshooting your work ethic."

The comment is rude and takes him aback. He glances up at her, but of course she's not looking at him now. She's engrossed in the task of picking red gummy bears out of the bag in her purse. AJ goes back to thumbing through his notebook. He finds the song. He entitled it *Interrupted (deceptive)*, keeping with the cadence theme. It's a song about someone who lives her life under a microscope, but who still manages to hide enough of herself to be elusive. It's a song about personal transformation due to new elements of power and environment changes. It's a song about a regular life that gets interrupted at a young age, forcing said girl into a life of endless facades. It's a song that subtly speaks of the secret parts of a person that the average eye can't pick up on. He's extremely happy with the song, and secretly considers it his best work.

"Here," he says, placing his notebook in front of her. "Tell me what you think"

She reads expressionlessly as she chews a gummy bear. "I hate it," she says in monotone voice after just a couple of seconds. She flips his notebook closed and pushes it back across the table to him. "Do you understand what I'm saying?"

AJ looks up at her. The staid look she's giving him would be hard for even a blind man to misconstrue, because the disdain can be felt. She *hates* it. He doesn't know why she hates it. He doesn't know if it's too raw, or too honest, or too personal. He doesn't know if it struck a nerve. That wasn't his intention. He didn't intend for his song to hurt her. But her blatant, dismissive assessment of his song admittedly does sting a bit.

He doesn't tell her that, though.

He doesn't tell her that for a good portion of the time she was gone he couldn't come up with anything for wanting to pull his hair out or put his head through a wall. He doesn't tell her about how when he had felt better, he had sat down with his pen and paper, slowly and thoughtfully composing an entire song. He doesn't tell her that she just crushed his pride and put a dent in his ego. He doesn't tell her that this was the first sober-written, conscious-thinking song he's composed in a few weeks, and what her hate for it makes him feel like and think.

"Message received," he tells her instead, looking down dejectedly at last year's best birthday present with the words *Progression in C* now written sloppily across it. "I'll try to do better with the next one."

~

The next day she's in a better mood, and he takes her to his house in Reseda.

He's apprehensive to introduce her to his neighbors but surely by now they know he's dating her, so it only seems respectful. As much as they loved Anjanae, they'll want to meet his new girlfriend, even if it's a bit of a conundrum to them on how he went from a normal girl to this. Not that they have any reason to dislike Kay. In fact, he knows Rebecca is a fan. He heard Kadence's music being blasted from the young girl's backyard radio way before he ever knew the singer personally.

It boils down to a free, private meet-and-greet for the people in his community.

Everyone on the street comes outside the second he pulls up to his neglected second residence with her in the car. She treats his neighbors like she treats her fans: kindly continuous smile, heartfelt handshakes, and generous selfies. His middleclass neighbors are expectedly smitten. Nancy and Fred gift her with homemade banana bread. Miranda and Jack thank her graciously while she signs Rebecca's CDs. Carla and Antonio almost weep when she signs their son Ricky's music sheet and congratulates him on his accomplishments as a young pianist. Jesse doesn't have his daughter this week, but has a concert t-shirt for Kadence to sign for her, and gushes in a star struck way as she does so. Almost all of his neighbors invite her to their homes for dinner sometime, and she acts like she'll happily hold all of them to their offers. But AJ knows it will be a long while before she accompanies him to regular old Reseda again. And even though she's still smiling convincingly, he knows she's ready to go inside.

So he takes her inside and shows her around his house that he knows doesn't impress her at all. And then lets her have her way with him on the staircase, then the bed.

He can see her from the little window in his office now. She's sitting out on the deck where Anjanae used to do her paintings. There used to be an easel set up in the middle with a canvas on it, a paint splattered toolbox underneath it filled with her supplies, and a little barstool with wheels that she used to sit on. Now there's a pop star on a lawn chair, thumbing through last month's Cosmo for the third time while smoking a joint and drinking Grey Goose mixed with pineapple juice.

He can't help but to compare her to Anjie, and he catches himself involuntarily doing so often. Kadence's skin doesn't feel the same. The nape of her neck doesn't smell the same. She doesn't *taste* the same. Not that these differences are bad, just…different. Not the same. Not what he had grown accustomed to, fell in love with, and then gave up. The two women actually have very little in common. Their similarities end with them both being slim with delicate arcs and bends, however Anjanae had been on the healthier side of thin, around 115 or 120 pounds if he had to guess. Kadence was maybe 100 and somewhat scant. Anjanae was of a petite stature, no more than 5'3" without heels. Kadence was at least 5'7" or 5'8", and stilettos put her over 6'. Despite Anjanae's smallness, she had a nice, high sitting ass. He remembers how her jeans hugged the subtle curves of her backside, the swell of it in a sundress. How it looked when she was on her stomach and he was behind her. Kadence's butt was courtesy of specialized padding that she wore under her clothes. The outside world thought she had a decent derrière, but being that he was intimately acquainted with it, he knew the truth. Like all the other truths he knew, and that they would never *ever* know.

Those were just aesthetic things, though, things he could easily get over. What he genuinely misses is the sound of Anjanae's laugh, her little giggle he'd have to work to get out of her. He misses her making him artwork. He misses making love with her. He misses the bright-multicolored splashes of acrylic that got on his shirts that she loved to wear, red and blue and yellow stains that were now fading away. He misses the brushstroke softness of her fingertips on his skin. He misses their debates, the intellectual conversation, and the back and forth banter that served as the foreplay before the foreplay before the sex that was always more than sex. He misses the way she stared, during and after; the warmth he felt in the embrace of her brown eyes, because he sometimes feels cold in the clutch of Kadence's baby blues.

He forces himself to stop comparing the two, to stop trying to find fault in this girl that the world perceives as flawless. He has to work on ebbing the envious feeling he has of the world's ignorant bliss when it comes to her. He has to teach himself to ignore the pangs of doubt pertaining to this person that he's with, to ignore the pining he wants to do for a person he's let go, and focus on the now.

Focus on Kay.

Because he's in something with her—not love, but a passionate thing nonetheless. Something chemical, concoctive, and coarse.

She looks up, sees him, and smiles.

He smiles back.

Chapter 18

Austin is sitting at the bar late at night, a half-empty glass of Jack and Cherry Coke sitting in the circle of his hands. He's thinking about the conversation he had with Maggie a few days ago. And what an emotionally conflicting conversation it had been. At first he had dismissed the proposition she posed to him. However, over the course of the last seventy-two hours, he's found himself multiple times mulling over her suggestion. He'd made a scale in his mind, and had been mentally weighing the pros and cons.

Money. Morals.

Dividends. Dignity.

Sex and sacrifice.

AJ pulls up the stool next to him and breaks his train of thought. Austin turns to take in his co-worker's appearance. He's got bags under his eyes, but from the size of his pupils he's wide awake, and dressed to the nines in his work attire.

"Comin' back from a date?" Austin asks, taking a sip of his drink.

"Nope. On my way to a date," AJ replies, reaching his hand into the peanut tin. "Need a bourbon before I go." He snaps his fingers. "Yo, Calvin! Can I get my usual?"

Calvin looks up from down the bar and nods.

"It's almost two in the morning, though," Austin muses, watching the bartender walk away to get his friend's drink.

"I know," AJ sighs theatrically, peeling the shell off his peanut. "But you know she's got us taking extra clients. There's not enough hours in the night."

"About that," Austin says in a lowered voice. He diverts his eyes and drains his glass before continuing. "Has she um…has she asked you 'bout taking male clients?"

"Mmhm," AJ mumbles as he chews. "I told her that was a no-go. I told her I'll do anything a woman wants me to do, but I'm not doing things with men. I told her I had to draw the line somewhere. As it is, I'm sleeping with women I'm not attracted to, and I'm not about to pretend I'm attracted to men. Sorry, not happening. It's not my fault I'm not gay. It's not my fault that she hasn't been able to replace Theo. It's not my fault she keeps hiring idiots who can barely fuck a woman much less a man. Do you know she asked me the other day to teach one of them how to eat pussy? I'm like…I didn't sign up for this to be a fucking Sex Ed teacher. Told her if you want them to learn you teach them, you have the type of equipment to practice on anyway. I didn't actually tell her that, but I wanted to. But no, she's too busy signing herself up for dating apps. Did you know that? She forgot to close down the tab on her computer and I might have scrolled through it. She's on Plenty of Fish and Tinder. She's got *herself* on there, not us. She's afraid to date in real life. She's got dating-related PTSD. And all of the guys she *likes* or *swipes* or whatever, they're from other places, not in LA. She also had another window open for a timeshare in South Beach. I asked her about that one and she said, 'yeah, she was thinking about getting a condo down there for when she needs to *get away*'." AJ rolls his eyes and pops another peanut. "What the hell does she need to get away from?"

Austin thinks it's a bit odd that AJ hasn't even had a drink, but yet he's talking much more blatantly than he usually does, not taking breaths between sentences. Calvin sits the bourbon down in front of him and then gets back to work. Austin watches as his friend takes a big gulp and grimaces through pursed teeth.

"She's a trip," AJ continues. "She ought to take one for the team and service the male clients herself. But hey, more power to you if you think you can do it. Theo always did say men were willing to give you more money than women."

"No," Austin says quickly, turning a bit red. "No."

AJ glances down at his Rolex. "Gotta go make someone's night," he says dismally, draining the rest of his glass in one tilt.

"See ya," Austin replies.

But he's already gone.

And that's when Austin realizes everybody is gone. The clock is five minutes from closing. Calvin is putting chairs on top of tables. He wipes a bead of sweat off his forehead, rolls his sleeves further up his forearms, and then lifts another chair. A couple of the waitresses clock out and say their goodbyes to him. When he's finished clearing the dining room, he comes back to the bar to count the drawer.

"Do you think I'm attractive?" Austin asks out of nowhere

Calvin flushes with a nervous smile. "Come on, man," he laughs without looking up from the cash register.

"Maggie wants me to take male clients," Austin says, absently running his hand around the rim of his glass.

"You shouldn't do something you're not comfortable with," Calvin replies neutrally, locking up the drawer and filling out the deposit.

"Maybe I am comfortable with it. I don't know."

"That's something you should know before you do it," Calvin says, smirking slightly as he comes over and takes Austin's glass from him and puts it in the sink.

"You didn't answer my question," Austin says, his voice low.

Calvin has his back to him at the sink and lets out a sigh. "And what was that?"

"As a man who likes men, do you find me attractive?"

Calvin turns around and puts his bar mop down. "I mean…yeah," he admits timidly, cheeks going rosy. "Look at you…you're…you're clearly attractive." He puts his back to him again after he says it, flips the sink on, and washes up the last glass.

"Can I come over?" Austin asks once he's tuned the sink back off.

Calvin's head snaps around, surprised. "What?"

"Can I come over?" Austin repeats.

"I mean…I…"

"You said you live just across the street, right?"

"Yeah," Calvin replies holding his gaze, mystified. "Yeah, I live just across the street." He nods his head assuredly. "Let's go. Let's get out of here."

Calvin clocks out, locks up, and they cross the street together. In the elevator ride up to his floor, the air is statically charged but silent, and they realize they haven't said anything to each other since they left the bar.

"Look," Calvin says seriously. "I learned the hard way a long time ago not to make even the tamest pass on straight men or men who might be straight, so if you want–"

"I want you to make a pass," Austin says.

Calvin stares into his eyes a second more, and then he closes the distance and takes Austin's face in his hands, puts his mouth on his, and kisses him hard. At first Austin doesn't know how to react. He'd asked for it, but that first touch has him frozen to the spot. Calvin continues to press his lips to his, gentle brushes of delicate flesh, keeping it slow as he skims one hand down Austin's neck to rest on a broad shoulder, his other hand still cupping his jaw. Austin starts to kiss him back. He doesn't know how long it takes because time seems to have suspended, but soon Calvin's tongue is parting his lips and slipping into his mouth. This stills Austin again, though he doesn't pull away. He lets Calvin plunder his mouth, lick and suck and bite. And when he finally allows his tongue to tangle with his, Calvin reacts instantly, pulling him flush against him as they make out more heatedly. For a second Austin is still in his own head, telling himself that kissing a man is really no different than kissing a woman, and that if he closes his eyes maybe he can pretend that he *is* kissing a woman. If he can pretend he's kissing a woman, maybe he can do it. But he *is* doing it, and the fact of the matter is that Calvin's a good kisser, and he's steadily forgetting his preinstalled fear that kissing a man and not being disgusted by it means he's gay. The uneasiness dissolves; everything slows down, comes into focus. Calvin smells like fading cologne, male musk, and deeply permeating aftershave. It's different, but not undesirable. His lithe form feels hard against Austin's hard body, and their silhouettes mold together sensually despite the absence of the familiar press of breasts against his chest, and the unfamiliar hint of something else against his thigh. The elevator dings and the doors open.

They step off, and Austin follows him down the hall to his apartment. He feels like he's in some kind of drug-induced state from the sheer disbelief of what he's about to do, watching as Calvin unlocks the door and throws back the deadbolt. Then they're inside, and the door closes, and Calvin is shrugging off his jacket and then turning back towards him, looking happy to have him there.

"I've never done this before," Austin utters before he can stop himself.

The smile on Calvin's face softens to a more neutral expression. "Are you sure you want to do this now?" He asks him, looking into his eyes. "Because if you're rethinking it that's fine, we don't have–"

"I wanna know how…I wanna know what it's like," Austin interrupts him.

His eyes travel around the little room bathed in the soft light of the lamp Calvin just turned on. It's nothing more than a studio, but it's neat, just as he expected it to be. The full-size bed is perfectly made, but there are a few sheets of sketch paper strewn across the comforter, charcoal grey led outlines of both male and female bodies covered in colored penciled clothing. There's a yoga mat on the floor across from an old-fashioned record player. A milk crate full of vinyl by a coffee table with a few magazines on it—*Men's Health*, *Vogue*, and *Essence*. In the corner there's a little wooden desk with a bright blue sewing machine on it, a small pile of multicolored fabric off to the side. Hanging on one of the walls is a blown-up city map of Chicago, and on another is a framed picture of the Versace medusa head. It's all very eclectic, just like the person it belongs to. Austin forces his eyes back on Calvin's.

"I'm comfortable with you," he admits to him with vulnerability. "I like…I trust you," he stutters unsurely, ready but scared. "So just show me…show me how."

Calvin looks like he's trying to comprehend. "*Show* you," he repeats more to himself than to Austin. "How to…" he takes a step closer to Austin, maintaining eye contact. And then the previously perplexed look in his eyes is replaced with one of mischief. "Do this?" He asks at last, hands resting on Austin's belt. He starts to undo the buckle as he lowers to the ground. But then Austin stops him.

"I know what I like," Austin says, slight smirk in his voice as he pulls him back up so that he's eye to eye with him. "I want you to show me what you like. How to *do*…what you like," he adds lowly as he slowly drops to his knees before Calvin.

Calvin is speechless, shocked by the turn of events that has Austin kneeling down in front of him, unbuttoning his pants and pulling down his zipper. All he can say is, "Okay."

Chapter 19

It's a little after eight when a black limo rolls up to his building to pick him up. No fancy dinners with older women or paid romps with other men's wives are in the cards for tonight. No, AJ has the night off. Because tonight is Kadence's twenty-third birthday. There will be a fancy dinner, though, at her favorite restaurant on Melrose that will be closed to the public. A fancy dinner with him, her, and her posse of girls. Immediately following her birthday dinner will be her extra extravagant birthday party at a club in West Hollywood. He knows there will be a lavish open bar, a bottle of Rosé for every table, and a cake with at least five tiers. He knows she's had people up since the crack of dawn decorating it just how she wants it. He knows it will be perfect. She's asked one of her favorite groups—an all-girl Canadian punk rock band—to play. He knows they'll perform for free. She's invited upwards of three hundred people. He knows they'll all come.

Because she's Kadence Jane.

He opens the door and slides in. She's sitting there on the long leather seat, wearing a regal red gown that screams Old Hollywood glamour. Flawless makeup, perfectly straight, face-framing hair, and a classic red lip. She embodies everything it means to be a star. And she is. She so is.

"You look gorgeous," he tells her.

She smiles. "Well thank you, babe. You look quite handsome yourself."

He's wearing a new Tom Ford suite jacket, opened, with the deep red shirt that Maggie says makes him look exceptionally dashing underneath. Dark charcoal pants that match the jacket. Pocket square that matches the shirt. Patent leather shoes. He could make a killing in this ensemble, but he isn't after money tonight.

He leans in to kiss her, but before he can get there, she turns her face.

"On the cheek," she says. "I don't want to mess up my lipstick."

He agreeably kisses her cheek, not disputing the fact that a month ago she'd let him make her come in the same limo, in the presence of the same driver, right before she walked out in front of the entire world. Sure, she'd told him to be careful not to mess anything up then, too, but at least she'd kissed him.

She takes out her phone and starts texting. "I told them to seat Lillian furthest down the table from us," she says, glancing up to give him a teasing look. "You know she likes to stare at you."

"What?" He says innocently, acting oblivious when he's fully aware, when he wants to tell her that Lillian is not the only one who likes to look at him; he's caught Charlotte and Sailor staring, too. Batting their eyes. Giving subtle glances. But he says nothing. Her jealously is cute now; he doesn't want to enhance it too much.

"You might not know this," she says, sending out a final text and then putting her phone down. She stares at him as she slowly rakes her fingers through his hair. "But you're sort of a catch."

He smiles.

The dinner goes just as he imagined it would with a table of ten girls: white wine, Filet Mignon, and tawdry gossip. The Beverley Hills girls give her furs and pearls that they bought with their parents' money. The models give her next season's designer wear straight off the runway in Europe that they acquired through their connections and probably a little persuasion. The actresses get her a rose gold MacBook and a Tiffany chandelier for the last room in her house that doesn't have one. Her bestie from back home gives her a first edition book of Sylvia Plath poems that he knows she'll never read and that he will ultimately probably ask her if he can have. Sailor hands her an envelope; inside is a ticket to Turks and Cacaos, a receipt for two rooms at a five-star resort, and a written promise that they will both carve out a week in their schedules come summer to take a bestie vacay together. This makes Kadence fan her eyes like she's crying.

He gives her his gift last, a little box. She holds her breath when she opens it. Inside is a pair of demure ruby studs. Once she'd told him to wear red, he knew she'd be wearing red, and what better than to give her something she could wear tonight? He gives her a card, too. Inside is a picture of the telescope he's having installed on her roof while they're out, and a little poem about stars, and how they'll lay up there and look at them later, and how for as beautiful as the ones in the sky may be, she's still the brightest one in his eyes. He'd bought the telescope first, but he didn't want to err on the sentimental side and leave her disappointed like Susie, so he went back out and bought the earrings. The rubies cost him three checks. But by the way she's taking big breaths and fanning at her eyes again, he can tell he's impressed her. Tears may not be really coming out, but she does take out her diamond studs to put the red ones in.

On the ride to the club she changes out of the red gown and into a gold bodycon dress that's made out of some kind of metallic material and doesn't look the least bit breathable. His earrings get shucked in the wardrobe change, thrown back in the box and tossed somewhere on the limousine floor. This new dress is so tight it looks like it's been painted on her; more glitz than glam this time, but still very much a head turner. The gold glitter covered red bottoms she slips on add to this affect.

Cameras are flashing when they get out, paparazzi that were privy to her plans. Strangers are yelling out happy birthday, and she's smiling at each and every one of them. A pink carpet has been rolled out, where all her guests walk down it to the door where a bouncer is checking names off a list. They're fashionably late; the party is packed. Everything stops when she walks in, salutations are screamed, and then the action resumes with five times the electricity. The band is playing on the stage; the rich and famous are mingling on the floor. She unloops her arm from his and kindly asks him to get her a drink. He turns her loose to the crowd and goes to the bar.

He orders her a Grey Goose cosmopolitan and himself bourbon on the rocks. He thanks the bartender and turns back around. She's out there greeting her guests. Some of the biggest names in Hollywood and the music industry are in attendance.

Including a well-known actor with wavy hair. Tall stature, troublesome face. Mid-thirties. Endearingly awkward with the media, smoothly cool with the ladies. He's got this aura about him that says everything is effortless when it's really purposeful. Oscar nominated. Emmy winning. Lead role garnering. People Magazine's sexiest man alive once or twice. His name is Darren Alderson. A known womanizer. A notorious playboy who runs through models, singers, and actresses like it's a sport. AJ knows his name had been tied to Kadence's a few years back. There was a short time when every tabloid cover had a blurry picture of them getting in and out of each other's cars, or eating at outside bistros together, or standing in a ten-mile proximity of each other at parties and events.

Everybody has a past, though. AJ had a past before her. She had a past before him. And who's to say this guy was even a romantic part of it? Just the gossip rags.

Except the charismatic actor in mention is currently looking at his girlfriend like she is the crowning jewel in his bedpost, the apple of his eye, the one that got away. That's after he touched his hand to her back to get her attention. And after she turned around and smiled with theatrical gusto, gasping happily in surprise like she hadn't expected to see him when she so obviously invited him. After they hugged and the person she was previously chatting with moved on.

Now they're engaged in a conversation he can't hear.

AJ watches with his back against the bar, nursing his bourbon as she leans in and laughs at something the actor says. Her eyes twinkle with transparent charm as she talks. Darren nods as he listens, working his own charm with a white toothed-smile. Some guy comes up and taps the actor on the shoulder. It's obviously someone he knows well; hands interlocking, more movie star smiles. Kay says hi to this new person, and then finally looks up.

Their eyes immediately meet across the room. AJ holds up the glass of vodka and fruit juice he got her. She smiles and struts towards him.

"Thanks, babe," she says, taking the glass from him and immediately taking a sip. "What do you think?" She asks, eyes twinkling for him now. "Pretty big turnout, huh?"

"You're Kadence Jane," he says simply.

She takes another drink. "That I am."

"So." He takes another ginger sip, grimacing briefly at the burn. "That's Darren Alderson." He motions with his eyes to where she just came from.

She takes another drink. "Yup."

He clears his throat a bit, sitting his drink down behind him. "You all used to date." It's not so much a question as a statement.

"We hung out for like a month when I first moved to LA," she replies nonchalantly. "I was like eighteen."

"Did you have sex?"

Her silence answers his question. Then she huffs. "Does it matter? That was years ago."

AJ crosses his arms. "Why is he here?"

"We're friends."

He raises an eyebrow at her. "Friends?"

She's crossing her arms now. "Yes, Andrew, I have a lot of friends."

"So just how many of your friends in here have seen you naked?"

"Ok," she says airily, smiling as she glances over at her guests on the dance floor. "You're feeling possessive." Then she focuses her eyes back on him. "Maybe on another night that would turn me on. But tonight is my birthday. I want to have fun. So feel free to stand over here and stew as long as you want." She throws back the rest of her drink in a single tilt and then hands him the empty glass with a pleased smile. "I'm going to dance."

He watches her rejoin the party, shaking her hips and moving her arms as she goes. Her girlfriends at the front of the crowd cheer when they see her coming. She smacks Lillian and Lauren's butts and the three of them start moving to the up-tempo song that's playing. But it ends quickly, and then a slower song starts. Darren Alderson is still standing nearby. AJ sees her ask him if he wants to dance. Of course he does. Her former lover's hands go to her waist, hers arms lock naturally around his neck. They're pressed close, too close for his comfort, as they move in small steps around the room. She stares over the actor's shoulder right at him, her smile still pleased and the look on her face unquestionably taunting. AJ holds her gaze for a moment, finishes the rest of his drink, then goes outside for some air.

Her engineer, Eddie, is standing at the back entrance of the club, puffing a cigarette through the crack of the door he's propping ajar with his foot so he doesn't actually have to go outside. It's a chilly night by LA standards, just barely fifty.

"Can I bum one of those?" AJ asks, surprising himself a bit.

"Sure, man," the bohemian switchboard worker replies, reaching into the pocket of his skinny jeans and retrieving the protruding Marlboro box. AJ is a bit surprised he smokes a name brand, half expecting him to roll his own tobacco. "Here you go," Eddie says, handing him one.

"Thanks," AJ replies dismally. Then looking at it for a second. "Um. Sorry. You got a lighter?" Eddie hands him a Bic. He sparks it, then hands it back. "Thanks."

"No problem, brother. You better bundle up, though. It's nippy out there."

AJ nods and then goes out the door, not worried at all about the weather. The chill in their air feels good on his hot face. There were too many people inside; too much heat, too much noise. And it's not fun when you're the only one who seems not to be enjoying it. He'd let her get to him.

AJ has never smoked a cigarette in his life, but surprisingly he doesn't cough when he inhales, and even more surprisingly, the aftertaste isn't as disgusting as he thought it would be. He lingers outside, enjoying the silence, though he can still hear the bass bumping from inside the building. He takes his time smoking the Marlboro down to his fingertips, and then flicks the butt into the street. Ten minutes pass, maybe fifteen. Begrudgingly he goes back inside.

Upon reentering, he sees that Darren is dancing with another girl now. He scans the crowd for Kadence, finding her thrashing up against the front of the stage as the band plays. She's with Sailor. They're moving manically to the music, jumping up and down, gyrating every which way, and screaming lyrics at the top of their lungs. He studies her for a second. There's a freeness to her that he knows doesn't come naturally, her blonde hair flying around her face as she headbangs next to her bestie. And then her hands are going up over her head and she's swaying like a ship on a rough sea, switching through different dance moves at a warp speed. AJ leaves his spot against the wall and makes his way through the throng of moving bodies.

"Give me some," he says in her ear, coming up behind her and wrapping his arms around her waist even though he isn't feeling at all romantic.

"Some of what?" She yells over her shoulder, over the loud music.

"You know what," he seethes in her ear, starting to pat down the fabric of her dress like a TSA agent. "Where is it?"

She roughly grabs his hands and throws them off her. "Not in there, idiot," she seethes back, spinning around to face him. "Do you really think I'd try to conceal contraband in a skin tight dress? God you're so fucking stupid."

"I don't know what you'd do."

"Fryderyka has it. Go find her." With that she turns back around and resumes dancing.

He conveniently finds the model near the bathroom. Some sharp-dressed, grey haired fellow is chatting her up; AJ doesn't know who he is and doesn't care. He motions her over to him as politely as he can, smiling genially and waving. She excuses herself from the old man trying to get in her trendy, sample size, probably personally gifted from the designer panties.

"Hey, AJ," she says in her accent with a smile, her pupils three times the normal size. "You wish to speak to me?"

"Uh. Yeah," he starts unsurely, noticing for the first time how sunken her features are and sallow her skin is. "Do you have any...um." He glances over his shoulder in a paranoid manner. When he looks back, her empty eyes are wide and ogling him in a confused fashion. "Kay said you had the..." He runs his finger under his nose subtly. "You know."

She stares at him blankly for a moment more, and then it clicks. "Ooohhh. Kokaina?"

"Yes. Yes, I think," he says with a relived smile and a nod.

"Come." She takes him by the arm and pulls him into the nearby bathroom.

It's empty, and he thinks they're alone, but then a bleach blonde head pokes out of the second stall. It's Lillian. She's got the evidence of what she was doing on her left nostril.

"Oh, it's just you guys," she says, a hint of relief in her voice.

"Who?" Another voice comes from the same stall. He thinks its Katrina.

"Freddie and AJ," Lillian tells her as she goes back in.

He hears some heaving sniffling and some deep breaths. Fryderyka goes to join them in the stall. He follows her.

Lillian is leaned against the cubicle wall, wiping at her nose. Katrina is still on the floor, hunched over the back of the toilet. She looks up when they enter.

"You got more?"

"Yup. In here," Frederyka replies, reaching into the top of her dress and retrieving a little vial from her bra. Because she obviously doesn't have the privilege or power to make other people like her paid help walk around with her drugs so she doesn't have to put herself at risk.

She empties the powder onto the porcelain. Kat makes the lines: one more for her, one for Freddie, and one for him. He hears Lillian lock the stall door. He gets down on the ground and Kat hands him the dollar she was using. He doesn't think about how unsanitary it is as he does it. How close people have shit to where his nose is right now. How dirty the floor he's currently kneeling on is. Or how he ended up doing drugs with the models and the rich kids. All he can feel is the thrill that precedes the actual thrill that will undoubtedly be amazing because it always is.

"You know you can't do this around all of Kay's friends, right?" Lillian says in her stuck-up voice. "Because Kay doesn't do this around everyone," she informs him. "Just a certain few."

"I know," he says, standing back up and taking one last recomposing sniff.

"God, you especially can't mention it around Lauren and Charlotte," Katrina says in her nasally voice that is now even more nasally. She tears off a piece of toilet paper and dabs her nose. "They're such goodie two shoes. They'd freak the fuck out."

"Charlotte drinks lot, though, yes?" Fryderyka asks.

"She's pretty much an alcoholic, but the bitch has been acting holier than thou ever since she started getting the big movie roles," Kat tells her, tossing her toilet paper in the commode. "And you definitely can't tell little Susie-Q. She still likes to think of Kay as the girl she used to play hop-scotch with on public school playgrounds *back in Tennessee* when they were *besties*." Kat rolls her eyes.

"Sailor's pretty chill about things," Lillian muses aloud.

"She goes through phases," Kat adds. "One day she wants to act like a Disney character and the next day she wants to act like Brittany Spears."

Fryderyka busts out giggling.

"But Brittany *was* a Disney character, wasn't she?" Lillian asks, laughing stupidly.

"She was a Disney *actor*, not a *character*," Kat corrects her with a chuckle. "You sloshed trollop."

AJ leaves the bathroom while they're still cracking jokes and touching up their noses in their compacts.

He finds Kadence where he left her, rotating at the front of the floor. He takes her hand if not just to fill the obligation he knows he has to be a good boyfriend, if not just to show those surrounding them that they are the *it* couple. She lets him pull her to him. They dance together for a few songs, and then Charlotte is coming up and whispering something in her ear about another party.

Kay pulls back to look at him. "Char just got a text from her co-star who's at the grand opening of that new nightclub on 5th. She said it's lit, everybody who's anybody who's not here is there." She grabs his hand and starts pulling him. "Come on, I'm going to tell the DJ to announce that we're continuing the party down the road."

"I'm tired of partying," he tells her.

"Come on, it will be fun," she says, continuing to drag him across the dance floor.

"It's like two o'clock in the morning already." He digs his heels in enough that she can't pull him anymore and has to stop.

"That's early!" She exclaims exasperatedly as she turns around to look at him.

His face softens as he stares at her. "Can we just go home?" He asks, giving her a small smile. "End the night together, just me and you."

She stares at him for a parade of seconds. And then she speaks. "I'm going to the next stop of the party. And so is everyone else here," she states matter-of-factly. "You can go home if you want to." She turns on her heels. "Up to you," she adds over her shoulder as she sashays away.

He goes outside and catches a cab to Koreatown.

Back in his apartment he shrugs off his jacket and kicks off his shoes. The coke he did back at the club hasn't completely worn off yet. He knows he won't be able to sleep, despite the bone tiredness deep in his being, so he doesn't even attempt it. Instead, he strips off his clothes and gets in the shower, wanting to wash away the smoky, sweaty scent of yet another bad night. It takes him awhile to get clean, his mind flitting from one thought to another, wired, wrestling with the idea of leaving her. Eventually the water goes cold and he is forced to get out, cursing Mr. Rae for not supplying the complex with an adequate amount of hot water. As he towels off he notices he is shivering. Whether it's from standing under the freezing spray for too long or just him coming down—a mess of worked nerves and plummeting adrenaline—he doesn't know. He doesn't care. He just throws on a thermal shirt and flannel pants and moves onto the couch. There's a heap of beer bottles, candy wrappers, marijuana roaches, and crumpled up pieces of paper containing lyrics that will never be littering the coffee table in front of him. He hasn't had time to clean; he's only ever there to crash. Pushing past the untidiness, he grabs the remote from its hiding place under a discarded fast food sack, flipping on the television. He settles in to focus on calming down.

Two hours later there's a knock at his door. He was just starting to drift off. The laugh track from the seventies sitcom that's playing slowly brings him back. And then there's another knock, this time more demanding and less patient. He picks up his watch off the table and blinks his bleary eyes until the numbers come into focus. A quarter after five. She had some nerve. He begrudgingly drags himself off the couch and makes his way to the door, opening it even though he doesn't want to. But he knows she won't leave until she gets what she wants.

There she stands in the third dress of the night, a little black and silver number that barely covers her, smiling from ear-to-ear with the type of candy-coated happiness he envies. Of course it's all emulation, but she emulates so well.

"What are you doing here?" He asks her dryly.

"I wanted to spend my birthday with my boyfriend," she says simply, moving past him into the apartment without invitation.

"It ceased being your birthday five hours and fifteen minutes ago," he tells her, closing the door and re-locking it. "And I was asleep."

"You were a party pooper and left hours ago." She opens his fridge and takes one of his bottled waters. "You've had plenty of time to recharge."

He watches her unscrew the lid and take a long swig, probably dehydrated from dancing and drinking for hours on end. He can't tell if she's higher, lower, or more sober than when he last saw her. It really doesn't matter.

"What do you want, Kay?" He asks, crossing his arms and looking at the floor.

"What do you think I want?"

The question is redundant and void of care for what he wants. She switches her slim hips with each of the three steps it takes for her to get across the room and right in front of him. She strokes his face with a softness that feels far from authentic, palm cupping his jawline and thumb caressing the corner of his mouth.

"Don't," he says, even though he doesn't stop her.

"Don't what?" She asks with cunning lowness, her other hand pressing over his cloth-covered crotch, rubbing up and down until she feels him respond.

"You should go home," he tells her with the same lowness in his voice.

She separates herself from him, walking backwards till there's a good distance between them. And then she stops; hand on her zipper. The sound of it being drug down cuts the silence. Her eyes bore into his as she slowly steps out of her dress. The look she's giving him lets him know that she can see the weakness in him—his inability to walk away, his crumbling self-worth—and she revels in it. His Achilles heel serves as an aphrodisiac for her, and he knows it. She unclasps her bra behind her back and slides her thong down her skinny legs without breaking eye contact. She's nude now, save for the little smile that's near sinister, the smile she wears even with nothing else on. He tells her to put her heels back on, and she does. He tells her to get on the bed, and she does.

After that there are no more words.

She lays on her back with her legs spread just enough for him to see everything. He stands at the end of the bed, taking in the porcelain skin, the pert nipples, the bones straining against their flesh barriers, long limbs stretching across the expanse of his sheets. Her hand treks between her thighs, two fingers stopping to strum her clit before dipping down and disappearing inside. He watches her now as she writhes, as she breathes out and throws her head back, sliding a slick finger back out and through her folds. Eventually he pulls his shirt over his head, pushes his pants off, and climbs onto the bed.

He moves over her, replacing her hand with his. She raises her head and takes his bottom lip between her teeth, biting hard before soothing the sting with a kiss. He doesn't kiss her back, but he does do something with his fingers that sends her bowing back against the bed. He leans down and licks the course of her collarbone, the salt of dried sweat and the sour of faded designer fragrance coating the back of his tongue. His trailing mouth moves over her smooth chest, biting the side of her left breast with enough strength to inflict pain and leave an imprint. The fingernails in his hair scrape their approval over his scalp. Sinewy legs slither up his back with suggestion, the point of her expensive heels pressing into his skin idyllically. AJ pulls back a bit and looks down at her, and for a split second he sees something he doesn't want to see. He doesn't know if it's the way the moon hits her at an angle through the fire escape window, illuminating the immoral in her. He doesn't know if it's the way her ice blue irises turn a shade of grey in the pale opaqueness of predawn, or her blonde hair, or the condescending way she stares. But right in that moment...she looks an awful lot like Maggie Hunter.

He flips her onto her stomach without warning, eliciting a surprised shriek from her. And then he presses on her back until she puts an arch in it.

PART TWO

Chapter 20

AJ and Kadence are sitting across from each other in silence at the hottest new restaurant in West Hollywood. It's the type of place that is packed every night and has a two-week waiting list to get in, but tonight they are the only patrons, with a wait staff in full strength catering to their every wish. Two dirty martinis specifically requested with significantly more vodka then vermouth, and four pre-pitted olives for her. Three fingers of bourbon with exactly two ice cubes for him. Calamari as a shared starter, and an Heirloom Tomato salad minus everything on it including the tomatoes and the dressing, with only *the most perfect* strawberries in the kitchen and *a few* candied walnuts on the side for her. For the main course, a bottle of Pinot—*no, not from Napa Valley, take it back; I want one from Italy*—chilled for thirty minutes beforehand, but not a minute more. A thirty-five day dry aged New York strip steak done medium rare with a strictly pink center, absolutely no red, and a side of potato puree and broccoli heads for him. And wild sea scallops for her (that she sent back twice because she was convinced the cook had broiled them instead of seared them, not that there's a real difference) with a side of skinned baby squash and a small bowl of baked fettuccine with no breadcrumb topping.

They have excessive needs and little else.

Tonight is their six-month anniversary. Neither one of them is saying a word to the other. He knows if he opens his mouth something hateful will come out, so he's been keeping it closed. Despite the steady ascension of animosity over the last six months, he still rented out the best restaurant in the city, bought her an expensive present, and has a surprise private concert planned for afterwards at the Hollywood Bowl. Because she's Kadence Jane. And he's her boyfriend.

He sits there and stares at her as she pushes her food around her plate with her fork, taking annoyingly small bites but not really eating, because God forbid she gains a pound. He is also acutely aware that she can't sit still, one Manolo clad foot moving in a constant jostling motion, occasionally knocking him in the knee under the table. She doesn't apologize. She'll play with her hair, touch her face, shoot him pompous looks, and pour glass after glass of wine; but she won't speak to him or finish her food. She acts no more mature than a petulant nine-year-old. A petulant nine-year-old with a penchant for problems, zero morals, and five hundred million dollars.

"So how did you manage to get this place cleared out and secured on a Friday night?" She finally speaks, and it sounds just as airy and arrogant as any and everything that comes out of her mouth. She crosses her arms and cocks her head.

"I called a month out and told them I was your boyfriend and–"

"So I got myself my anniversary diner," she cuts him off cattily.

He crosses his arms now. "I'm paying for it."

"Well that's nice of you," she replies dismissively, picking up her fork and flicking a baby squash away from her scallops because it got too close.

"I thought so seeing as it's going to be upwards of three thousand dollars with that bottle of wine you had to have."

"Oh three thousand dollars," she sneers. "How ever will you get out of that massive debt?"

"I'm sorry I don't have half a billion chilling on ice like you," he retorts.

She shakes her head with an eye roll. "I've never dated a guy that loved to pinch pennies as much as you do."

"Out of the last two guys you dated before me, one was an Academy Award nominated actor and one was a trust fund baby. You don't know what it's like to live in the real world where not everyone is rich." He sits back and crosses his legs, picking up his wine glass. "But hey, all your other guys only lasted a month or two at the most. Here I am six months later. Must be doin' somethin right, hm? Most be doin' somethin that they couldn't do…" He lets his voice trail off briefly, and then with a wink adds, "As well." He takes a sip. "At least that's what you tell me when I have your legs by your ears and my hand around your throat."

"Are you high?" She asks him, irritated.

"Are you?" He asks her back with a smug smirk.

"No."

They arrived separately, and haven't seen each other in four days, but he knows for a fact what they both did before coming to dinner.

"Why did you feel like you should wear a purple shirt?" She asks him, choosing to nit-pick his clothes to incite a fight. "It clashes with your eyes and everything else. You should never wear purple."

"And you should never wear a strapless dress without a bra until you buy some breasts to hold it up because you've almost flashed your flat chest to our waiter five times now."

"Also the pinstripes on your jacket are blue," she says, ignoring his comment and continuing to go at him. "Which would have been a much better color to...I don't know...match your fucking shirt with. I can't decide if you simply lack fashion sense, if you suffer from color blindness, or if you just willfully want to look like a lavender loving faggot."

"Oh that's a nice derogatory term, really reflects your uneducated back roots upbringing," he leers. "You can take the girl away from the rebel flag but you can't take the bigot out of the bitch. I wonder how all your gay fans would feel about you using that word."

"I love my fans," she exclaims with an exaggerated hand gesture to her heart.

"You love yourself," he snaps back, staring at her vehemently while shaking his head. "That's it. That's all."

"You know what," she says, picking up her napkin just to throw it down dramatically. "I don't have to take this shit. I'm leaving."

"The evening is not over..."

"Oh I know it's not," she tells him, starting to stand. "I'm going to pop up at 1 Oak with Sailor and the girls and surprise the people. Let them see a star, buy the whole club bottles, hell, maybe even perform a song or two for free. Because I'm *that* nice of a person. Because I love my fans *that* much." She slings her purse over her shoulder. He sees her security guards heading towards the back entrance.

"Do you really think that's a wise idea?" He asks her. "To just show up at a shifty club with no forewarning?"

"I've already cleared it with my team, you just weren't privy to knowing. You're not invited by the way; you've done pissed me off." She picks up the almost empty bottle of Pinot and takes a final chug, sitting it back down hard on the table. "There. Hope you're happy. Happy anniversary."

And she leaves.

He gets into his Pontiac and lights a cigarette, another new habit he's picked up along the way. He puts it into gear and maneuvers the skinny vintage leather wheel with one hand, dialing Maggie's number with the other. He knows he should call the band he's got waiting at the Hollywood Bowl. He had after all arranged for one of Kadence's favorite underground, indie rock bands to be there. They flew in all the way from Montreal. He should let them know the surprise is off. But truthfully he doesn't give a fuck. They'll figure it out when no one shows up.

"Hello, dear," Maggie answers on the sixth or seventh ring.

"I need to make up the money I just threw away," he tells her, taking a drag.

"I thought tonight was your big anniversary?" She inquires coyly.

"Yup," he says without further explanation

She takes a breath and sighs. "Well I already gave Carter your client for the night, and Nick took the new lady who called yesterday."

He blows a plume of smoke out his mouth. "In that case they'll both be calling for a do over."

She snorts derisively. "I'm sorry that other plans were made to accommodate your plans."

"So you don't have anybody for me?"

"I don't have anybody for you."

"Cool," he says, hanging up on her without another word.

He notices that the pinstripes on his suit jacket are in fact blue. In his defense he thought they were purple, that's why he wore a purple shirt. He always tried to match and prided himself on his ability to pick pieces that suited him well. He'd had a touch of double vision before he left the house—it happens sometimes when he does too much too quick—perhaps that had impaired his ability to pair a shirt with a suit. Oh well.

He had spent eighty dollars on an eighth of an ounce from a pricey pusher on Highland the day before. And from what he tried of it earlier, it wasn't even worth what he gave. Probably cut with B vitamins and shit. Tonight cost him two thousand dollars and some change. He has a mortgage and a rent payment due by the end of next week, and God only knows how much his credit card is going to be when it comes due. He had to buy a new Tom Ford suit at the beginning of the month in order to attend some kind of gala with her. She'd insisted that he not embarrass her by wearing something old. Even though all his old suits were in superb condition, dry-cleaned after every other paid date, then stored in an airtight bag in his closet. She had no idea how much she cost him, how much money she made him lose by missing work to be with her. Fuck her for accusing him of being spendthrift; she has no idea what the real world is like. She has no idea the things he does for his money. He wonders, really wonders sometimes, how exactly she thinks he makes ends meet. Sure he gets publishing checks for the songs he writes for her. He tells her he's written a few songs for other people, and he has, but they've been much less successful of artists and the payouts have been much less plentiful. He's also told her that he's sold two screenplays that may or may not ever get made, and that's a blatant lie. He hasn't written a word for his own cause since that one failed attempt. Kadence believes that he's written multiple scripts, though. He can get away with pretending that he hasn't given up on his dream because she never asks to see what he's working on or to read what he's written unless it pertains to her. Because she doesn't care.

Of course, she would care if she knew what he really did, so for that he guesses he is thankful for her ignorance.

He had written one screenplay that he'd had high hopes for, but those hopes were crushed in a way that felt inhumane. One night with a fresh bag of powder in his possession, he put all his half-finished scripts to the side, sat down, and wrote the rough draft of something he considered a rare gem. He edited it for six weeks until he felt it was perfect, and then sent it to an assistant who was a client's sister's son. The assistant absolutely loved it, passed it on to the producer, and AJ had a sit-down meeting with the man a week later. Over two whiskey sours in a Culver City bar AJ was told that his writing was of high quality, but that he should seek employment in a different industry because he probably wasn't going to get much play in the movie making business. When AJ expressed his confusion, the sharp dressed filmmaker across from him informed him that Hollywood was a bit like a cult, a small tightknit circle operating off of hierarchy and who you know. And if one of the higher-ups had something against you, your margins of making it where marginal.

It was in that moment that AJ realized he had been blackballed by Julius.

He hadn't written a script since.

Now he was solely writing for someone else. Kadence had pushed the album back two times now. She keeps changing her mind, keeps taking things off and adding things on, continuously wanting more or less. It had to be perfect. It wasn't coming out till it was perfect, and he doesn't know when that will actually be. *Soon* is what she said on one of late night shows last week. The label is getting impatient, but he knows they will wait however long she wants, anything for their biggest little star. AJ missed a week's worth of work to go with her while she promoted her new single on the New York talk show circuit. She had at least released two singles off the album, both of which he had written and both of which were doing extremely well on the charts.

Last month they went to Tennessee. It was the first time he'd seen his mom in over a year. He almost wishes now that he hadn't gone, because now he can't get the picture of her worried face she tried to hide out of his mind. He can't shake the smell of his childhood home—fresh laundry detergent and southern food—or the sights of a simpler life. The visit was too short-lived to be comforting and only served as a painful reminder of what once was.

Out of their weeklong stay in the state, they spent all of one afternoon in Memphis. She met his mom, who acted like she liked her, but he couldn't be for sure. He *could* tell she was concerned. Concerned about how quickly her son had gone from simplicity to the spotlight. Of course, she should have been concerned way before now, but she could only fear what she knew. Kay met his father as well, who acted like a damn schoolgirl with a crush, chatting her ear off and laughing loudly and smiling giddily at everything she said, acting more personable than AJ had even seen him. Acting like he does when he's trying to close a big truck deal, or in this case schmooze big money in the form of a pretty blonde. And Kay was putting on the airs, too. Putting on the airs like always. Telling his dad that she liked his tie, and laughing at all his bad jokes, and acting impressed when he gave her a tour of their little house that he told her he personally designed. She complimented his mom on her cooking, telling her it was the best meatloaf she'd ever had in her life, the unsaid secret being that it was probably one of the only meatloaves she'd had in her life. Kay rarely ate meat, never ate carbs, and rebuked starch. But she cleaned her plate, scarfing down every bit of ketchup covered ground chuck and butter-smothered mashed potatoes, even going as far as to mop up his mom's brown gravy with a piece of white bread. The unsaid secret being that her finger would probably be half way down her throat the second she was alone with a toilet, and that she'd probably then proceed to go clean off a plate of something else to jump start her metabolism again.

Before they left, while Kadence was in the bathroom, his mom told him that Grace had bought the little red brick house on Rose Street with her new fiancé. She told him that he's a night nurse at the hospital, too. AJ could tell that his mom likes his ex-girlfriend's new boyfriend. AJ could tell that she's met him. That she still sees Grace. And that's fine with him. He tells her he's glad for Grace.

And that's the truth; he does want Grace to be happy. But he doesn't think about Grace lying under the sheets with her male RN, shrouded by white picket fences, a dog at the foot of the bed. When he thinks against his will, the setting is almost always a 5th Avenue high-rise penthouse bedroom. Blankets and beautiful brown skin and an immensely rich, unfortunately inappreciative man who he hopes is treating her right. Treating her better.

He hopes she's happy, too.

And then his mom asked him if he was happy. And he lied and told her that he was. And then he lied again and told her that he loved Kay. And she nodded and gave him a small smile like she might have believed him. And then Kay had radiantly reemerged, and they said their goodbyes and headed on down the road to Nashville.

The trip to Tennessee was made because Kay wanted to record a couple of songs at the studio in Nashville where she made all her first songs, for nostalgia's sake. For her fans, he thinks, because he doesn't see her being sentimental over such things. While in town they stayed at her Nashville estate. It was at least three times the size of her California home. Her parents reside in the west wing, where they had been leading the pampered life for the last four years ever since she sprang them out of poverty. Her daddy had been a coal miner, her momma a gas station attendant. Now they're both spoiled. Mr. Sanders, with his sandy complexion and tobacco-stained teeth, came down to meet him in a Javiar Cotton robe and Louis Vuitton slippers. Mrs. Sanders had been out shopping when they arrived. She came back a few hours later in a Mercedes, arms full of shopping bags, mink stole thrown over her shoulders, hair as big as hair comes. She couldn't hide her twang if she tried, as she oohed and awed over him, coming close to almost pinching his cheeks. He thinks her parents liked him, but again, as with his, he can't be for sure. They invited him for bible study at the huge congregation they'd passed on the interstate on the way in, the biggest church in the city that they both back monetarily and attend when they feel so inclined. Kadence told them they didn't have time for that. Then she led him to her side of the mansion, and they didn't see her parents for the rest of the trip. It only took one meeting for him to understand why she keeps them hidden and never brings them out to award shows.

As he cruises down Vermont, about a half a mile from his apartment, he contemplates pushing back to a more well-to-do neighborhood. Maggie wasn't supplying him with a sufficient stream of women; he had every right to freelance for the money. He could pick any random bar or hotel lobby. Order himself a bourbon, or better yet, wait for someone else to do the honors. Make eyes at the unhappily married and drunk out-of-towners. Reel in whichever lucky lady approaches first, take her to a bedroom, fuck her for a few hours, and get back what he paid for that bottle of wine he only got one glass of.

But then he remembers that eight ball he's got back at home, and for the first time in a long time, something outweighs income.

~

He makes up the money he lost on his anniversary two nights later. Mrs. Tevenot calls Ms. Hunter; Mr. Tevenot is out of town on business. AJ gets to her house at eight sharp to handle business. Tracy is still dressed when she lets him in. Sometimes she answers the door in her expensive lingerie. He prefers when she's half-naked because that's less work for him, though she could never say he slacked on the job. As he makes his way into the house she's droning on about Dominique, and about how much work Turner has gotten since the mixtape. She asks him if he's talked to her son recently, if he knows that he's in Atlanta producing for some rapper. AJ says no, stops in the kitchen to fill a glass with ice, then heads for the staircase. She asks what it's for, and he tells her not to worry about it. She hounds him about Kadence as she follows him up the three flights of stairs to her bedroom. *What face cream does she use? Who does her hair? What juice cleanse is she on? Does she have to pay for her clothes or do designers just give them to her? When's the new album coming out? Can he get her an advance copy?* Like any self-respecting fifty-something should be listening to Kadence Jane.

As soon as he gets to her room he steps out his shoes and starts unbuttoning his shirt. She hadn't even bothered to move Francis' monogramed bathrobe he'd left on the bed, or hide the plastic case with his dentures in them that he must have forgotten. AJ simply casts the robe aside as she rants about the drama she has with some of the other bored women in Brentwood with too much time on their hands and nothing better to do but scheme on each other, rich people problems along the lines of a Bravo show storyline. He takes off his belt but leaves on his pants. He picks her up, puts her on the bed, and she shuts up. With his belt around her wrists and a Versace scarf over her eyes she is happy to receive and not contribute. She finds out what the ice is for, stomach convulsing and skin trembling for reasons other than the coldness. She comes twice before he enters her, and once inside, he makes her go twice more before she taps out.

Tracy falls asleep almost instantly afterwards; she's like a man that way. AJ quietly redresses and then tiptoes into the conjoined master bathroom. He opens her medicine cabinet and scans the contents, his eyes falling on the sixty-count prescription bottle of Xanax. He opens it and is happy to find she's probably only used four or five since the last time he took some from her. He mentally calculates how many he can get away with taking without it looking suspicious, not that she would even blame him if the entire bottle came up missing; she was more strung out on him than the little blue bars he's currently eying with intense adoration. It had been two weeks since he ran out of the small stash of benzos he had last obtained. Last time it had been the Valium from Mrs. Elliot's medicine cabinet. And in the last two weeks he had gone to grab one multiple times in the midst of sweat soaked, sleepless, predawn mornings. Every time he reached in the bottle and came up empty, a new wave of panic washed over him. Being without them makes him feel like a pilot who has been flying a plane for six nights straight through a storm with barely any gas left in the tank, who is then told through static radio reception that he can't land yet. And then he convinces himself that he'll never sleep again, that he'll end up clawing at his skin till he can crawl out of it, that he'll have a seizure because maybe just maybe he'd taken too many and then went too long without, because he's read that can happen. And then he just sits in the corner and cycles through every worst-case scenario until the sun comes up again. The Valium keeps him calm longer, but the Xanax hits faster and harder, practically washing away his worries in an instant, leaving him in a pleasantly subdued stupor…or so it had the first few times he took them. Now he finds nothing really quiets his mind completely. Half the time he stills feels higher-functioning sedated than the general public is sober. Still, they're nice things to have on hand.

He shakes out six into his hand.

He tells himself he'll ration them this time, only take one when he really needs one, save them for when he's coming down. He finds an almost empty Advil bottle that she'll never miss, drops the six pills he's philtered in it, and then shoves the bottle deep inside his pocket. He grabs the money off the nightstand as she snores, lets himself out, and heads straight for the studio.

He pulls into the discrete parking lot twenty minutes later. It's empty, save for her little red 911 that's parked in the prime spot right by the door, and her security detail's black Suburban parked in the back. He can't remember if it's Mike's or Bill's night on duty. Either way it doesn't matter, because for as big as both guys are, they're both super quiet and always stay out of the way. They're both nice guys; he feels sorry for them for what boring jobs they have, trailing a high-maintenance bitch around all day and night so she doesn't get bopped. He parks his car next to hers and gets out. Bill's outside the building smoking a cigarette, AJ tips his head to him as he goes inside. He makes his way through the vestibule and past the lounge area, noting how quiet it is. Too quiet; she's not working. He mentally prepares himself for the verbal onslaught before he pushes into the recording room.

"Where have you been?" She asks as soon as he walks through the door, in a tone that's both irritatingly calm and highly accusatory. "You told me you'd be here by eleven, why did you feel the need to lie to me?"

"It's eleven twenty-five, chill," he says, closing the door behind him.

"The label wants my album by the end of September. I'm on a deadline. I told you I wanted to make a Whitney type of album, a Streisand type of album, and all you've done is write me little sing-along jingles for people to lip-sync in their vine videos, set as their ringtones, and play at pep rallies. You need to be here when you say you're going to be here, you need to sit down, and you need to get this shit done."

"You don't have the talent to make that kind of album," he tells her, shrugging his leather jacket off. "I'm just writing for what I've got, babe, and I ain't got Whitney."

She scrunches her face up at him. "What is that supposed to mean?"

"The only thing that you and Whitney Houston have in common is that you both have an affinity for blow."

"Fuck you."

"Don't have to," he says with a snide smile, hanging his jacket on the coat rack. "Got em lined up around the corner waiting to do it for me."

"What is that supposed to mean?"

"God, you're like a broken record."

She crosses her arms and gives him a snide smile of her own. "You think you're cute because you come up with lyrics in your spare time, the whole unassuming, misunderstood, it's just me and my guitar and these inexpensive looking clothes that cost a few grand vibe. You think you're hot because you've written a couple songs for a superstar. You think you're special because you're sleeping with a superstar. Why do you think anybody knows who you are? Why do you think anybody knows your fucking name? Because of *me*. Because you are dating *me*. Because you are writing songs for *me*. You think you got people lined up to get to you after I'm done with you? Check the line outside my door, baby. It stretches across the world and wraps around six continents."

"Do you really want to play this game?" He asks her seriously, crossing his own arms. "Do you really want me to tell you about yourself?"

"You can't tell me anything. I've got eight Grammys, what the hell have you got? You have *nothing* to be proud of. Literally *nothing*."

He glares at her but says nothing. After a moment of her not breaking his stare like he'd hoped she would, he looks away. He grabs the opened beer on the console beside him, not caring whose it is, and takes a long drink.

"You know I will know if you fuck someone else, right?" She asks, but more so tells him. "So don't try to be slick and get something over on me," she adds, getting up and walking towards the booth. "I'm *highly* aware and I know you and I'll be able to tell instantly."

AJ smirks to himself and shakes his head. "You're so damn stupid," he mutters under his breath, sitting the beer back down.

"What was that?" She asks, turning back around and cutting her eyes at him.

"Get on your knees," he tells her, pulling his shirt free from his pants and unbuckling his belt. He didn't get off when he was with Mrs. Tevenot earlier, and he could use the release. Plus, she may not be the smartest person in the literal sense, but in the metaphorical sense she certainly knew how to put her mind to good use. It was about the only scenario anymore where he actually liked her, where he could actually tolerate being in the same room as her. Probably because she couldn't talk with her mouth preoccupied, and he didn't have to hear that voice that grated on his nerves worse than anything he'd ever encountered.

But the way she rolls her lips and bobs her head and tests her gag reflex repeatedly is the best thing he's ever encountered. Or so it feels in those moments when she's on the ground and he has his hands in her hair. Like he's about to now.

She smiles slyly like he knew she would, because as much as she portrays herself as a good girl in public, in private she's the farthest thing from it. She saunters towards him slowly. There's a stagger in her step and he wonders if she's been drinking. It wouldn't surprise him. She makes a move to kiss him and he pushes her away, pushes her down. And she slides down willingly. Always so willing. Always with that devilish gleam in her eyes that he's sure many before him have seen. Governors' sons. Actors. Musicians. Probably record execs and promoters back in the beginning, how else could she explain how far she's got? She pulls him out and takes him into her mouth. His fingers find their way into her hair as she experiments with speeds and skills. Licking around the tip, grazing him with her teeth, tracing a vein with her tongue, and then going as far down as she can. With her right hand she firmly grips and strokes what her mouth can't reach. She'll go fast for a while, hollowing out her cheeks on each upward motion. Then she'll go slow, loose suction, lots of spit, leisurely twists and twirls of her tongue as her eyes flick up to his. He watches her with a smirk while perversely wondering if she *can tell* that he fucked someone else not even an hour ago. She thinks she's so smart.

"All of it," he instructs, no adoration in his voice.

She comes up for air for a second—face red and splotchy, stray string of saliva sticking to her lips—and then she goes for it. She bobs up and down twice, and then takes him all the way to the base. He feels her throat constrict around him, he hears her choke briefly. She comes back up slowly until her lips only cover the tip. And then she repeats the process, going down as quick as she can, gagging when he hits the back of her throat, and then deliberately dragging her lips as slow as she can back up his length, tongue purposefully pressing along the underside. She does this a few more times; his fist tightens its purchase on her hair. He has always believed in the common courtesy of a warning, but he's been with her enough times by now to know that she doesn't care. And by the way she locks eyes with him right then, he knows she's been with him enough times to know what's coming without being told. Two more up and downs and he climaxes, coming into her mouth with gratified grunt, watching her with hooded eyes as she swallows every bit of it. Once he's gone flaccid she lets him go, wipes her mouth with the sleeve of her shirt, and quickly stands back up.

He zips up his pants and watches as she walks away from him without a word, over to the bar cart where she grabs a bottle of her expensive vodka. She unscrews the lid and holds it to her lips. She swishes the first swig around in her mouth, and then takes two more gulps for good measure. Finally, she looks at him, contempt in her little baby blue eyes.

"Get your guitar, get your pen, and go over there and listen to the beat Devin sent me yesterday," she says. "Forget all the other songs we were working on, I want you to write to this one, and I want it to be big. Not song of the year big, song of the century big." She grabs a glass out of the cabinet now, like class is suddenly a thing, and pours vodka until it's three fourths full. "We're starting and finishing tonight, so I hope you weren't thinking that you were going to go home and sleep. Cause you're not."

He chuckles as he buckles his belt back up, shaking his head at her ridiculousness.

She takes a carton of lemonade out of the fridge and adds it to her drink so she won't seem like the lush that she is, drinking hard liquor straight.

"Is someone coming over?" He observes knowingly, condescendingly.

"Bryan said he might stop by. He wants to hear what I've got so far. He probably won't be out this late, but he might be."

Bryan doesn't show. The second glass and the third glass don't have any lemonade in them. Around one she makes a call, and at one thirty someone shows up with a bag of coke. They both do a line and then promptly get back to work. They finish the new song and four old ones, come up with six different concepts, do two more lines, lay vocals and instrumentals without the producer present, make edits without the engineer's permission, and don't emerge till nine in the morning.

Chapter 21

Calvin walks into Austin's bedroom in his white Calvin Klein
briefs, carrying two glasses of water he got from the kitchen. He sits one
down on the nightstand and hands the other to his lover. Austin is laying
naked under the sheets of his king-sized bed, looking content. The two
have become quite comfortable in each other's company over the
progression of months. Calvin struts over to the dresser in search of the
remote, and Austin snorts in amusement as he watches him.

"You better not be laughing at me," Calvin says slyly with his back
to him.

"Did you know your underwear has your name on it?"

"*No*. I had no idea. Totally never sat up late at night as a child
contemplating what my pseudonym would be when I became successful
and renowned seeing as one of the biggest fashion icons of all time shares
the same first name as me."

"Cause that's what most little kids think about," Austin kids.

"Well I've always been far from the ordinary, baby," Calvin
replies coolly, finding the remote and crawling back under the covers with
him.

"You can spend the night if you want," Austin says, taking a final
drink before sitting his glass on the nightstand. "We'll just have to get up
early though cause I…I have a thing…planned…scheduled…in the
morning."

"It's cool. You don't have to stutter around the subject. I've been
in open relationships before," Calvin tells him, easy-going about it all.
"They're kind of a thing in the gay community. I hooked up with someone
else just last week."

"You did?" Austin asks, a little taken aback, but trying not to
sound so.

"Yeah, but it wasn't very good," Calvin says nonchalantly as he
scrolls through channels on the T.V. Guide. "The whole ginger-bearded
hipster thing was doing something to me in the darkness of the club with
three drinks in me. But in the light of my bedroom I was rather
disappointed by the performance."

Austin doesn't know how he feels about this. It evokes a pang of
something in the pit of his stomach, not exactly jealousy, but certainly not
elatedness. In the back of his mind he supposes he thought that Calvin
wasn't sleeping with anyone else. Somewhere in his mind he might have
even thought that Calvin was so into him, so ecstatic to have bagged a

good looking straight dude that his eyes wouldn't even want to look elsewhere. Of course, he knows he has no right to think these things, nor does he have any ground to act hurt by Calvin's admission to having had a one night stand last week. So Austin works at keeping his expression neutral.

"It's all even," Calvin says then, as if he read his thoughts. "You have your clients and your girlfriend. And I'll have my occasional, sporadically satisfactory, typically substandard trysts." He looks over at Austin and smiles. But Austin isn't smiling.

"She's not my girlfriend," he says plainly.

"Only because she won't let you call her that," Calvin retorts.

Austin heard it, the fault in his voice where the tonally coded emotion slipped through. The hurt. The truth. And the truth was they were both in something that ran just a little bit deeper than the physicality of it all.

"I don't want you to be unhappy," Austin tells him in a soft, even voice. "I don't want you to feel like you're some secret…what was that word you used the other day?"

Calvin raises an eyebrow. "Sidepiece?"

"Yeah. I don't want you feelin' like you're the sidepiece to my work and to my…and to Hermosa. Because I don't feel that way. But if you do, and you're unhappy…"

"Hey, I'm cool. I don't expect you to change anything about your life for me. I knew everything going into this. Can't be mad, so I gotta be realistic."

Austin nods to himself, but says nothing.

"You don't make me pay. I know I'm special. You don't have to tell me," Calvin adds in a lighthearted tone. Then he leans in a little and lowers his voice. "Of course, I know I'm pretty talented in bed myself, so technically I could make you pay."

A smirk slowly comes to Austin's face. "You would never."

Calvin playfully places a kiss to his chest, and then they start again.

~

Austin has been taking on male clients for six months now, while still working over women, too. Some of his original clients disappeared in the wake of their very brief scandal back in December. But the ones he lost he quickly made up for with new, taking on extras in the absence of

Theo, Garrett, and Rafael. The newcomers Maggie had hired weren't
up to the standards the others had set, and more often than not he picked
up their slack as well. Some days Maggie even had him double up, taking
one woman on a date and taking another to bed before he clocked out.

On Mondays he sees Hermosa's old boss, Mrs. Vernon. The once
closed-off, mildly crotchety older woman was coming around to new
ideas. He had persuaded her into letting him take her out on the town a
few Monday nights out of the month, reigniting the spark within her she'd
lost with age by wining and dining her at some of her favorite restaurants
she hadn't been to in years. By spending more time he earned himself
more money, and her spirits were so lifted by the attention he paid her that
she didn't mind paying him extra.

Every Tuesday Austin drives an hour to Palm Springs to visit his
best paying client, a rich old man with an impeccable white wig and an
endless bank account. The Palm Springs palace is perhaps the biggest of
all the lavish homes he's been in to date. He stays for three hours each
time—one for sex and two for company—and leaves with significantly
more money than he came with.

Louis Labella is a world-renowned, pompously persnickety,
extremely private fashion designer. He is typically only ever seen sitting
front row at the fashion weeks— New York, Paris, and Milan—or in a
reserved box seat at the occasional concert for one of the pianists or
violinists he fancies. He is otherwise a self-imposed homebody.

Lou is a loud dresser, never without flounce, jewels, bright colors,
or patent leather platforms, even though he rarely leaves his personal
compound. He has a penchant for coattails, pastels, and different colored
diamonds. He doesn't consume alcohol, cuts almost everything from his
diet besides fresh organic produce, and takes supplements by the handful.
Self-preservation is the key, though Austin doesn't know who or what
exactly he is preserving himself for. He has no kids, no family that he's
close to. Many fawners, but no friends. The only numbers in his speed dial
are his plastic surgeon and Ms. Hunter. He has no life. His assistants do all
his grocery shopping, his chef does all his cooking, and Lou runs his
empire from bed, speaking to his servants via walkie-talkie only when he
needs something or when they need reprimanding.

He sought out Ms. Hunter's services because he said it was too
hard to find a decent boyfriend these days. But Austin knows it's really
because he can't keep a man. Lou is obsessive to a pathological degree,

particular about every aspect of his life, and very much set in his ways. He wants company but doesn't share space well. He has trust issues. He has control issues. He is a maddening perfectionist. And for as flamboyantly confident as he dresses and presents himself, for as unapologetically demanding as he is of his employees and those under him in the fashion industry, for as prevalent as his designs have been for the last four decades and will continue to be, for what a timeless figure he has become, he is an *extremely* self-conscious man. All of the above attributes have the very easy ability to drive others away. Unless, of course, they are paid to stay.

Like many other fashion elites, Lou has a rap for putting those below him in their place. He talks down and is lifted up. He can turn assuredness to meekness with one swift verbal lashing. His admirers fear him, as do many of his peers. It is also a very well-known fact that the designer hates most people.

But Lou has a soft spot for him.

Just like with all the high-class, high maintenance, highly difficult women he had serviced before this man, Austin has a knack for making the frigid melt. He'd heard that those who like to wield power in their professional life like to relinquish it in their private life, that those who love having complete control also love completely losing it in the right scenario. Such is the case here.

Austin is almost always on top when he's with Lou. Austin prefers it this way; at least he thinks he does, because in his mind it seems ever so slightly less homosexual penetrating a man as opposed to being penetrated by a man. Of course, there are the other things Lou likes that he has to do, and those services combined with the billionaire's salmon pink satin sheets—silk rubbing against his bare skin—makes it difficult to shake the whole gay element.

To shake the denial.

Austin is re-dressing after sex, tucking his shirt into the pinstripe pants Lou personally designed and gifted him with on one of his previous visits. He buckles the Hermes belt another client bought him, and slips his feet into the Corthay shoes he bought himself with part of his last paycheck. As he's rolling his sleeves up to reveal the sparkling Baume & Mercier Maggie surprised him with last week, his eyes spot Lou's extensive jewelry box sitting open on the white marble dresser.

"Where'd you get that gold roped chain with the big green gem?" Austin asks.

"Why do you ask?" Lou inquires from his spot on the bed, wrapped up in his white linen robe and vaping on his e-cig that's filled with high-grade liquid THC that he says is supposed to help with his OCD.

"My girl, Hermosa, she's really into turquoise and emerald right now. The blue greens. Those colors look real good on her, too. Most of her jewelry is the fake costume stuff. I mean I can't really tell the difference and she's fine with it, but I wanna get her somethin' real. I know she'd appreciate somethin' real."

"Aw Aussie, you know I don't like to think of you with someone else, much less *a woman.* Ugh. Now I'll be stuck with this heinous image of you straddling some Hispanic hussy. You know what a hard time I have shaking vulgar depictions from my mind. It takes *days* sometimes. Honestly, I don't know why you do this to me."

He catches the look Austin gives him.

"I'm sorry, honey," Lou quickly says. "Please forgive my imprudence. I know she's your lady. I most certainly should not have called her a hussy. Or a Hispanic. Although I do believe that's the proper term these days. It's just…it's hard for me, baby. I know what our roles are. I'm not living in a pixel-ly multicolored animated fantasy world, though I wish I were. I'm aware that this is merely a monetarily fueled arrangement for you, but for me it's a love affair for the ages. So take pity on me for this unfortunate plight of fervent jealousy I suffer so severely from, and grant me a pass for my ill spoken words." The older man looks up at him adoringly, batting his milky blue eyes. "Don't make me beg. I will."

"It's fine," Austin tells him, grabbing the money off the nightstand and stuffing it down into his pocket.

"Oh you're such a merciful, compassionate, beautifully brawny, gorgeously guileless young man. I simply don't know what I've done right in the world for God to bless me with a little angel like you, if only for three hours a week and thirty-thousand dollars a month. It's worth every minute and penny."

Austin musters a small, polite smile for his client.

"Why don't you take the necklace for your girlfriend," Lou offers.

"I'd prefer to buy her somethin' myself. I wouldn't feel right re-giftin' somethin' you gave me to her," Austin says, then, upon seeing Lou's hurt expression, quickly adds, "I appreciate your generosity, really I do, but I'd rather just know where I could get one like it."

"Well this is a rare treasure I got in Morocco during a trip I took back in the eighties. You'll never be able to find another one like it," Lou tells him. "But I did spy a women's necklace with a green gemstone at Tiffany's when one of my old associates dragged me out there the other week to look at her new collection. I prefer to have my jewels imported over the border and brought to me. The necklace is probably still at the store, it wasn't anything special."

"Ok cool," Austin says. "Thanks, Lou."

"You're welcome, doll baby. Anything for my boy."

Austin sees Paula Wilmington on Wednesdays. She had placed a call to Maggie a couple of months ago. He has been going over to her place once a week ever since, taking her on the occasional Saturday night date as well. Paula is a nice person, a divorced, forty-something dermatologist.

She'd sought out Ms. Hunter's services because dating after her divorce hadn't worked. Left mildly traumatized from the experience, she decided she'd rather pay for the companionship she desired than to be made into a fool again. Austin gets the feeling she hasn't known too many nice men in her life, so he tries his best to make her feel well-cherished and comfortable when he's with her. On this Wednesday, she lets him know just how appreciative she is of this.

"Do any of them look bad?" Austin asks her.

He's lying on his stomach on her bed, face resting on a pillow and arms folded up underneath his chin as she strokes his bare back. They spent the last hour having sex, and he's decided to linger afterwards because he knows she likes for him to, even though she rarely asks. For this, he doesn't tell Maggie or charge extra.

"Nope, all your moles look regular," she replies, flopping back down next to him on the bed with a contented smile.

"Cool," he says, staring into her eyes and smiling back.

She giggles to herself as she starts to run her fingers through his hair.

"What?" He asks lowly, lips quirking at the corners.

"I was just thinking how crazy it is that I'm having the best sex of my life at forty-three. Of course, I got married while I was still in medical school to a very vanilla, un-creative man. And even though he cheated on me rampantly, I never once slept with someone else the twenty years we were married. So I suppose I didn't allot myself much of a chance at good sex till now."

"Your ex-husband sounds like an ass," Austin comments.

"He was a cold workaholic whose favorite stress relievers were putting me down and screwing younger women. But he was nothing compared to the guy I dated after him." Paula's face looks pained just to think about it, and she looks away shaking her head. "That was just…a whole other level of shame."

"Who was he?"

"A twenty-something in ripped jeans and a biker jacket, with swarthy stubble and tattoos, who came on to me in front of the vending machine on the floor of the building my office is in. I never expected a younger guy to be into me, and he was *so* into me. And I had just got out of a bad twenty-year marriage. And I resented my ex for all his younger women. And I wanted to have the fun that he'd been having. Vincent—that's his name—told me he was a model. He had a motorcycle. He said philosophical things that sounded deep, and gave me public displays of affection my husband never did, and wrote me bad poetry, and made me feel wanted. He had such a way of making me feel wanted."

"What happened?"

"Turns out I wasn't what he really wanted," Paula says with a hint of sadness. "What he really wanted was my script pad."

Austin gives her a confused look.

"He was an addict. An opiate addict," she explains. "Oh he was such a good actor, though, I've never seen a strung out person play clean so well. Such a gentleman. Always saying the right things. Always putting on a good show. I thought he was simply perfect. I was totally smitten." She sighs deeply. "Meanwhile he's writing himself prescriptions for OxyContin and Percocet and Opana shots." She lets out a dry laugh. "I never even knew people injected Opana recreationally. I guess it's like heroine. Which he also does," she adds, shaking her head remorsefully. "Oh yeah, I rebounded real good."

"Everybody makes a bad dating decision at least once," Austin says supportively.

"Here I am, a forty-year-old woman with a PhD, an MD, multiple degrees, getting duped by a twenty-seven-year-old druggie. What must I have looked like to all my peers, and my family members, and my friends? I'll tell you what, an idiot. I looked like an idiot. I *was* an idiot."

"You weren't an idiot. You're not an idiot," Austin tells her ardently. "You were just…vulnerable. And he was a bad guy who took advantage of you when you was down. He's the idiot. Cause you're a great person."

Paula blushes and looks away. "Oh you're just saying that."

"No, really," Austin says honestly. "You're always nice to me. Not all of my clients are always nice to me. And some of my clients…well…I think they pay me cause they honestly don't have the personality for anybody else to want them."

The last part makes her chuckle, and he smiles.

"But you could get somebody," he continues. "Somebody good and decent. You're polite, and pretty, and independent. I know my boss probably wouldn't like me tellin' you all this, but you could have a real relationship with someone. Don't think that you couldn't. You've had some awful men, but not all men are awful."

"I know. You're right," Paula says, still looking down. "I just…I think I want to practice a little more before I take myself off the bench and return to the real game." She glances back up at him then. "If we can do that."

"We can do whatever you want," Austin tells her. "Are you sayin you want to…practice…some more right now?"

She bites her lip and nods.

He grins and rolls back on top of her.

On Thursdays Austin sees Demetrius Marshall, a wide receiver for the Oakland Raiders who lives in LA on his off-season.

Demetrius is a popular player, frequently seen in nightclubs with rappers in Miami and throwing hundreds at strip clubs in Atlanta on his down time, if not just to keep up the image the world has of him. These outings often produced snapshots that circulate social media of scantily clad females pushing up on him with the hopes of making him their baby daddy, having read about his twenty-million-dollar contract and multiple endorsements. Unfortunately, and unbeknownst to his groupies, they would never convince him to take the condom off, because they would never make it up to the bedroom, because Demetrius Marshall is entirely gay.

And completely and convincingly in the closet.

Demetrius is closer in age to Austin than Mr. Labella, only a couple of years separating them, which make the situation a bit less awkward.

However, Demetrius likes being on top, which means Austin has to be the bottom when they are together. Demetrius is a very well-endowed man, bigger than Calvin. It isn't always ideal, sometimes painful, but when Demetrius asks him if it's okay, he says yes and takes it. Sometimes it is okay; sometimes he is even almost into it. While Dee presents himself to the world as tough, and while in the bedroom he does like to do it a little rough, Austin knows him to be soft-spoken and somewhat feminine in demeanor. Some days Dee wants one thing and one thing only, but other days he isn't in any rush to get Austin out of the house, and after they've had sex he'll start a conversation or invite him to stay from some food. And Austin will linger awhile, listening to him talk and watching him in his habitat.

"What type of workout regimen you on?" Dee asks him casually this Thursday following their weekly romp. The football player has returned a pair of grey Nike sweatpants to his body, resting low on his hips as he moves about his high-end contemporary kitchen. There are chicken cutlets grilling on a small George Forman and vegetables sizzling on the stovetop in a pan as Dee expertly adds spices and seasoning to a bowl of sauce he's preparing.

"I do high intensity training twice a week," Austin replies from his seat at the marble island, fully dressed again, minus his shoes. "Try to do weight training at least five out of seven days, switch off between arms and legs. I don't really like the anaerobic stuff, but the Pilates really chisels out my abs, so I force myself to devote like thirty minutes a day to it. Oh, and I do run every morning. Five miles."

"I knew you had to take it pretty seriously," Dee comments idly. He opens the fridge, takes out a Britta pitcher, and fills two glasses with water. "Your body is bangin." He smirks impishly when he says it, briefly glancing at Austin out of the corner of his eye as he sits the glasses down on the island.

Austin chuckles bashfully, made self-conscious by the male-paid compliment, still unsure after six months how to take them. "My workouts are probably nothin' compared to what you gotta do."

"Yeah, coach and my PT put me through my paces."

And Austin's sure that's true. The professional athlete before him is ripped from head to toe, muscles rippling under his dark skin without flexing, not an ounce of unused fat.

"You ever play any sports?" Demetrius asks with his back to him. He's light on his feet, moving almost like a dancer as he flits with ease between the grill and the stove. He turns the chickens over, pressing down on them to sear, then flips the vegetables in the skillet with an elegant flick of his wrist.

"Yup," Austin replies, taking a sip of his water. "Did it all in elementary and middle school; baseball, football, basketball, soccer. In high school I narrowed it down to just baseball and football. But I got my scholarship for baseball. Ohio State."

"Hey, Ohio State got a pretty dope sports program," Dee comments, impressed. He dips a basting brush into his bowl and then slathers sauce onto the two chicken breasts. "What happened with that?"

Austin takes another drink. "Flunked out after the first semester."

"Oh," is all Demetrius says.

They fall into an awkward silence as Dee finishes cooking the food. He plates it artistically, and is wearing a proud grin when he brings it over to the island.

"Well this meal right here won't throw you off your diet," he says to Austin, sitting a plate down in front of him. "All lean meat, protein, and veggies. I sautéed the medley in low fat olive oil. And the sauce for the chicken has both cayenne powder and minced jalapeño in it, which will jumpstart your metabolism."

"Nice," Austin replies. He picks up his knife and fork and cuts into the cutlet. He takes a bite and nods his head. "That sauce is good. What else is in it?"

Dee smiles. "Can't tell. Secret recipe." He picks up a vegetable with his fork, glances over at Austin, and winks. "You know I'm Fort Knox with my secrets."

Austin smiles slightly and focuses on his food. They continue in silence as they eat.

He goes to the office when he leaves, promptly showers, changes, and then does some of that Pilates he talked about. Austin sort of likes hanging out at the office, the gym is there and he can often work off whatever's stressing him on the treadmill or in some of the meditative yoga maneuvers he's started doing in tandem with his other anaerobic exercises. The other guys are rarely there, and with the entire 57th floor to himself he soaks up the quiet time. Walking back into the main area he catches sight of the clock. Being that it's only eight, he decides he will go down the street to the bar for a burger and a beer. Hermosa has night class on Thursday evenings and won't be out till after ten, and if he's being honest with himself, he'd rather go hang out while Calvin works than go back to his empty apartment. A little quiet time is good, but too much and he's lonely.

As soon as he walks through the door he sees that AJ is already there, slumped over the bar on his stool, hands encircling a glass of bourbon. Austin can't help but wonder what number he's on. Calvin comes out of the back and meets Austin's eyes; he knowingly follows his gaze to AJ, and then subtly holds up four fingers. Austin shakes his head and continues on to the bar. Calvin starts mixing a drink for another patron.

"What's goin' on, man?" Austin says, pulling up the stool next to his coworker and sitting down gingerly. He waits a second for him to respond, and then gives him a slap on the back to get his attention. "Earth to AJ."

AJ startles like he had slipped into some kind of wakeful daze. When he turns his head and sees it's just Austin he relaxes again, smiling ever so slightly. "Oh. Hey. Here for the party?" His words are dismissive and dry. His eyes are bloodshot, and he looks exceptionally tired as he raises the glass to his lips and drinks with need. The ice clinks as he lowers it back to the counter and grimaces.

"Just how long has the party been goin on?" Austin amuses him.

"I've been here like one…maybe two hours," AJ replies hazily. He glances down at the glittering gold Rolex on his wrist, squints at the face for a second, then looks back away with a headshake. "I forget the damn thing isn't really set."

"Then why do you wear it?"

AJ grins then. "Because I can."

Austin rolls his eyes and then waves across the bar. "Hey, Cal, can I get a Budlight and a bacon burger fully dressed?"

"A bacon burger?" Calvin replies, fighting a smile as he sits down the glass he was drying and comes over to stand in front of them. "What are you trying to do, lose your figure?"

Austin gives him an implicitly playful look. "You know I burn them calories."

Calvin smirks. "Alright," he says, grabbing a tall glass and holding it under the Budlight tap. "I guess I'll let you indulge yourself."

"You want something?" Austin asks AJ.

"I'll take another bourbon on the rocks."

"I meant to eat," Austin clarifies. "A little sustenance to soak up some of that brown liquor you've been drinkin'."

AJ makes a queasy face like the thought of food disgusts him. "No, I'm good. These here peanuts will do just fine." He reaches in to the aluminum can, grabs one, cracks the shell, and plops it into his mouth with a showy smile. "See? *All* I need."

"I'll give the cook your order, give it about fifteen," Calvin says softly to him.

Austin smiles. "Thanks."

Calvin disappears into the kitchen. AJ reaches back into the can and grabs a couple more peanuts. Austin takes a sip of his beer.

"You're sleeping with him aren't you?" AJ suddenly says out of the blue.

Austin almost chokes. "What?"

AJ glances over at him and smirks. "Relax," he says, popping another peanut. "Maggie told me you've been taking male clients."

"She did what?" He's mentally trying to control his physical reactions to being found out, but he can feel his face getting hot with embarrassment against his will. And he knows he'll never be able to play it off with the contradicting rosy-cheeked confirmation he's displaying.

"It actually kind of slipped," AJ explains so he doesn't think their boss outed him, flicking a peanut shell across the counter nonchalantly. "I heard her say you had a date a with a mister something or other and I kind of put two and two together."

Austin can't look at his friend or form a response right at the moment, so he trains his eyes elsewhere, focusing on the condensation trickling down his glass. AJ drains his glass and immediately gets the female bartender's attention, motioning for her to refill it. She gladly does, because he's not acting as drunk as he should be, and he thanks her. Calvin is back on the floor, but at the opposite end of the bar. Austin continues to stare off into space.

"He's not my client," he says quietly after a moment.

"I know," AJ replies. "You look at him like...well..." He takes a drink and shrugs. "You *look* at him."

"I'm in love with Hermosa," Austin states, and there's no self-convincing or doubt to the statement, still he pauses. "But I also...I have feelings for him also. And I don't know what that means." His hand is unconsciously toying with the edge of the damp napkin sticking out from under his beer, and he's still staring straight ahead, refusing to meet eyes. "I don't know if that makes me bisexual or gay or straight or what. I don't know who or what I am anymore."

"You're just sexually fluent," AJ replies simply, like there's nothing to it.

Austin finally turns his head to look at him. "Sexually fluent?"

"That's the term all the kids are using these days," he says, which sounds odd since they are both still very much young. Nonetheless there's still quite a gap between the age they actually are and they age that they unfortunately feel. "We live in LA," AJ continues after taking an extended swig of bourbon. "Girls are sleeping with girls, guys are sleeping with guys, surgeons are turning penises into vaginas, and vaginas into penises. It's all kosher here. Everybody's going every which way and nobody cares." He holds his glass back to his lips and gives Austin a reassuring grin. "Labels are *so* last season."

Austin smiles to himself and picks his beer back up. "You don't think it's weird?" He asks self-consciously after a few seconds.

"I mean…it's not for me. But if it's for you, that's cool. Not weird at all," AJ replies, raising his glass in a show of respect. "More power to you for being proficient in both penis and vagina."

Austin laughs, glad that his friend doesn't think any differently of him. He feels a bit better about himself having talked about it and been so well received. But the situation he's gotten himself into is still confusing, and he can't help but to pose another question to AJ as he skims a finger up the side of his glass absently.

"Do you think you can have strong feelings for two people at the same time?"

AJ leans back a bit and blows air through his lips. "I don't know. I suppose. But I'd say one of those feelings has to be stronger than the other, and if you don't choose one over the other you're going to end up hurting both."

Calvin is conversing with some college girls on the other side of the bar, leaned over the counter in his well-fitted vest and deep burgundy shirt, smiling as he listens diligently to whatever drama they want to share. He's preoccupied and Austin can stare, which he doesn't allow himself to do very often.

"Not that you're going to hurt either of them more than you'll hurt yourself," AJ continues somberly, pessimistically. "Because let's face it, we as species of the human race are self-annihilators when armed with the weapon of love." He drains his glass with a gulp and grimaces. "Only fools wish for that shit."

Austin is staring at AJ now, giving him a look. "Are you okay?"

"Well I could really go for an Ambien right about now, but other than that I'm cool," AJ replies flippantly, smiling even though it's forced. He jostles the melting cube at the bottom of his empty glass. "Haven't had a decent night of sleep in…hell…I don't know when."

Austin takes a sip of beer and swallows. "Maybe you should lay off the coke."

"What the hell are you talking about?" AJ deflects with a confused chuckle like he has no idea where Austin pulled that bit of information. He goes to pick up his glass, before remembering it's empty.

"I may not have the largest vocabulary, or a college degree, or the most ambitious dreams. And I may sound like I'm from where I'm really from instead of somewhere more prestigious, and you may think all of that makes me stupid, but it don't," Austin tells him with a neutral smile. "I still got eyes that see and a mind that can put two and two together. Just like you."

"I don't think you're stupid," AJ says as he absently peels the shell off a peanut. He doesn't eat it, but after a moment he looks up. "It's recreational, not habitual. It's fun to do, helps me write, but I don't need it to function. It's not serious."

"Are you sure?" Austin asks to be sure, looking him in his eyes.

"Positive," AJ replies assuredly, affirmation in his eyes.

Austin nods as he turns back around, picking his beer back up. "Well don't let Maggie catch that shit in your piss. She'll have a cow."

"Please, she hasn't given a test in months," AJ replies, finally plunking the peanut in his mouth. "She's too busy screwing silver-foxes out in South Beach that she met on dating service apps. She doesn't care what's in my piss."

Calvin brings Austin his burger with a side of fries. They flirt for a moment before Calvin has to get back to work, and when Austin looks back over he sees that AJ has gotten the female bartender to give him his sixth refill.

He wants to believe him when he says it's not serious, but he's not stupid.

Chapter 22

Some days AJ just wants to be alone. Some days he drives out to the valley, holes up in his house, and doesn't tell anybody when he goes or when he'll be back. He rarely visits his Reseda home anymore, maybe once a month at most. He used to try to get out there any chance he could when he was with Anjanae. He used to enjoy playing video games with Toby and talking literature with Rebecca. He used to enjoy going on walks around the neighborhood, running into Fred and Nancy and shooting the breeze. He used to enjoy hanging out with Jesse or going over to the Farley's for dinner. But now all he wants from his short stays there is solitude and silence. So he turns his phone off, puts his car in the garage, and pulls all the blinds.

Some days he doesn't leave his bedroom.

In all honesty he should probably sell the house. He bought it back when he was living in a false reality. Back when he thought neighbors and a backyard and a glider swing would normalize him. Back when he was still holding on to the dream of having kids with another man's wife. He bought it for escapism. But now he has other things to help him escape.

He chops it up with a maxed-out credit card, scoots it and shifts it till it's all in one long perfect line across the middle of his study's desk. He's got a couple ones and a single hundred in his wallet. Of course he chooses Benjamin Franklin. He doesn't come up for air till he gets it all sucked up. He's dizzy when he raises his head, and the postnasal drip is undesirable. He curses himself for not making two smaller lines instead of one big one, he knows better, and now he's lost half of it down his throat. Oh well. He pours a little more out onto the table, and then shifts the mouse of his desktop Mac to wake it up. Now he's staring at the comments of a picture of the two of them Kadence posted on her Instagram a few days ago.

Some days he's a masochist.

AJ usually tries to stay off social media, resist the urge to Google himself, and not look at what the faceless commentators of the Internet are saying about him and his relationship. But some days he looks. And when he looks, he can't stop.

She can do so much better than him, one of Kadence's stupid little followers had typed. Probably some miserable, loveless loser from

Minnesota. Or Indiana. Or some other place that doesn't matter and makes one wish that they did.

I still don't know what her dude does though? Like who are you and how did you get Kadence Jane? I mean he's cute...buuut, another idiotic Internet troll who thinks she needs to know more than she does.

I wish she was still with that actor guy Jackson. I think he really luvd her. I bet they end up getting back together, just watch, says some basic little bitch who could never get Jackson Taylor or any of Kay's other former flings but thinks she has the right to prophesize on the subject.

Kay needs to stop messing with these LA boys and get her a Tennessee man, proclaims some unaware nitwit who doesn't know that he *is* a Tennessee man.

Yeah I don't think he does anything. He's probably after them coins #alimony

Don't worry. Kay's 2 smart to marry this loser. She's just having fun.

She's still with this guy? Why?

Is it just me or did he use to be more better lookin than this? He's slippin lol.

My fave needs a new boo. Someone more her equal.

He's getting too skinny. Kay needs a manly man.

I bet she's still getting the D from Darren.

AJ rolls his eyes and switches tabs to Twitter. The most trending post that includes his girlfriend this week is a #ThrowbackThursday tweet from one of her former boyfriends. A curly headed boy band member. The picture is of them together on some red carpet back when she had long hair. Captioned: *Me and this beaut at the Music Video Awards two years ago #Takemeback #TwoTalentedMFers #Winners #WantThatOldThingBack #Kidding #Maybe #WinkWink*

Fuck that bastard.

The next most trending post including his girlfriend is from an Internet famous bodybuilder from Texas who made Kadence his #WomanCrushWednesday. The overly tan, redneck juicehead captioned the pic he pulled from an image search with: *My crush every day. Would give up me left kidney, beer for life, and all the protein powder in the world to meet her. A true country sweetheart and perfect example of how a lady should be. #WCW #Perfection #OneOfAKind*

Little do you know, buddy. Little do you know.

He makes two short side-by-side lines this time. As he does so, he looks around. There's a half finished script he started seven or eight months ago that he never finished sitting in a box next to his desk, mocking him of his waste of talent. He really needs to throw it in the trash. There's a bookshelf overflowing with novels and memoirs and textbooks and encyclopedias across the room from him. He really needs to get rid of them, because he's not going to read them again. There's a framed picture of him and his mom staring at him. He really needs to turn it down.

He snorts the first one, takes a breath, switches nostrils, and then puts the bill back down on the next one. As he's inhaling, he hears the door separating his bedroom from his study creak open.

"Hey, I saw you pull in the driveway an hour or so ago. I thought I'd stop by and see if I could borrow your copy of *Call of the Wi...*" the young voice cracks and stutters to a stop as she takes in the image before her.

He spins around in his chair. "Rebecca, what the hell are you doing here?" His voice comes out higher pitched than he planned, one hand vigorously wiping at his nose and the other trying to cover up what's on his desk with a piece of paper.

Her eyes are wide and her mouth just hangs open as she stands there in her cropped jeans and pink converse and rock band t-shirt. Shocked beyond words.

"Listen, Rebecca," he starts in a tone that he hopes sounds calm and even. "This isn't what it looks like." He knows that's the most generic thing he could have possibly said, and he knows she's much too smart to ever believe that it's not exactly what it looks like. But he had to say something.

"*Call of The Wild*," she utters quietly, finding her voice. "We're about to start reading it in class...and I wanted to get ahead...and I knew you had a copy because I'd seen it before," she rambles nervously in mystified manner. "But you're never home anymore...and then I saw you today...I knocked downstairs but nobody answered. I shouldn't have just walked in." She's shaking her head ardently now and backing out of the room. "I don't know what I was thinking. I'm going to go."

"Wait," he says quickly, making a move to stand but then the room spins.

"I'm sorry," she says again. And she sounds scared. And he never meant to scare her. He would never want her to be scared, especially not of him. And it makes him sick. And so does what he's about to ask of her.

"Just...let's just keep this incident between you and me, okay?" He's looking her in her eyes and she's looking back. "Don't tell your parents that you came over here. Can you do that? Can you promise me that you won't?"

She's nodding her head quickly. "I promise I won't tell anybody."

"Okay," he exhales, sinking back into his chair. "Okay, well you can grab the book and keep it as long as you need. I think it's over there on the second shel–"

"I'll just get it at the library," she says, voice squeaky and threatening to break as she turns around and heads for the hall. "I'm just going to go home."

"Okay," he replies quietly, looking at the floor as she leaves.

He hears the stairs creak as she quickly races down them, then the opening and closing of the front a door a few moments later.

"Fuck," he says to himself, getting up and pacing into the bedroom. He runs his hands through his hair, closes his eyes, and forces a breath through his lips. When he re-opens his eyes they land on that fucking painting. The one Anjanae made him. The one hanging above his bed mocking him of all the fucking mistakes he's made. "Fuck!" He yells. And then he lunges, jumping onto the bed, yanking the framed mural off the wall, and smashing it down on the floor. Glass shatters, the frame breaks. He pulls at the thick paper until it rips down the middle, and then he wads up the two separate pieces and throws them in the wastebasket on his way back out of the room.

When he turns his phone back on and sees that Kadence has texted him to come to the studio he drives all the way back out to the city. Because being alone with his thoughts…his thoughts and his drugs…had been a horrible idea. And had produced an image in his head he won't soon be able to shake. The young girl's wide eyes and astonished expression that turned to horrified as she stared at a person she thought she knew. A person she once looked up to. A person she once thought was good. He had ruined that picture of himself for her forever. And then he'd asked for her to lie for him. To be quiet. Pretend that she never saw anything. It made his stomach turn. He makes his stomach turn.

He pushes his way into the recording room. She's sitting at the console with her Mac in her lap. She doesn't look up.

"Hey," he says, pulling up a chair and sighing. "The most awful thing happened today," he starts to vent to her, because it's too close to the surface not to come out, and because she's supposed to be his other half, and because she's right there. "I was at my house in Reseda this afternoon, by myself, and I was doing a little blow and…out of nowhere…Rebecca walks in. It was a total deer in the headlights moment. I didn't know how to act or what to say…it was horrible. I thought I had the doors locked, but obviously I didn't. I can't believe I let that happen. I should have never been doing that there. I should have never made it possible for that situation to occur. Gosh, I just…I can't imagine what she must be thinking. I really need to sit down and have a talk with her, but she's probably never going to want to speak to me again. She probably thinks I'm a crack-headed criminal. I mean, why wouldn't she? I'm sure that's what it looked like. I feel just terrible."

Kadence looks up. "Do you think I give a fuck about the little neighbor girl in your low-income cul-de-sac? I've got bigger fish to fry today, and *you?* You've got some *serious* explaining to do."

AJ leans back and gives her a hard look. "What the hell are you talking about?"

She turns her computer screen towards him. "Why does HotNewHipHop say Michael Easton is about to drop a new single entitled *Interrupted?*" She asks him accusatorily. "And why the hell does the snippet sound exactly like *Interrupted (deceptive)?*"

He gets up guilty and starts pacing the floor. "You didn't like it. I thought–"

"So you're saying it's true?" She asks rhetorically, slamming her laptop shut. "You're saying you gave one of my all time favorite songs that *I* wanted for *my* album…to *another* artist."

"I didn't *give* him anything. I sold it."

"For how much."

"Five thousand dollars."

"Oh my Gooodd," she drones dramatically, leaning back in the swivel chair with her hands over her eyes. "You are soo ridiculously dumb." She removes her hands and stares straight at him. "It was worth way more than that."

"Well you sure didn't act like it," AJ retorts dryly.

"What…did you need the money to put up your nose?" She asks pettily, getting up to pace the floor now also. "To buy new clothes? Did you do it just to spite me, AJ?"

"I sold it to him months ago," he explains. "I took the *deceptive* off of the title and changed a few of the words so it wouldn't have the whole cadence connection that would tie it to what we're doing. And you yourself haven't so much as mentioned that song in months, since the night you told me you hated it."

"I didn't tell you I hated it and I damn sure didn't give you permission to pass it along."

"You didn't write it so, with all due respect, *dear,* your permission wasn't needed. Plus, it's not my fault you aren't always in the most lucid state when making decisions about the album," he retaliates just as pettily. "Maybe if you wouldn't be so fucking fickle and if you could stay…I don't know…halfway sober some of the time, we could get on the same page about things."

"I am sober and I was sober when I told you I wanted to keep the song."

"What about when you told me you hated the song? Where you sober then?"

"I never told you I hated the song," she says one last time in a definitive tone, turning her back to him and walking towards the bar cart. "You're out of your fucking mind."

"You specifically said–"

"I didn't say shit!" She seethes as she spins around.

And then the back of her hand is flying across his face. He doesn't have time think; he sees the flash of skin, hears the slap, feels the sting. Something hard catches him on his temple, one of her rings. He stumbles back half a step.

He can't believe she just did that. He instinctively touches his hand to the right side of his face, then pulls his palm away to examine it. There's no blood, but rage billows inside him nonetheless. Rage he has to force himself to swallow down before he strangles her, all the while staring at her incredulously. She looks momentarily shocked by her actions. However, that look doesn't last long. She's quickly crossing her arms and sneering once more.

"Get out," she says. "You've ruined my day, you've ruined the album, and I'm so pissed I can't even look at you. So just get out."

AJ hesitates, giving her the evil eye for a second more, and then he turns and walks out the door.

He can't sleep. It's seven at night and he's been awake since seven in the morning three mornings ago. His face hurts from where Kay backhanded him with her brass knuckles the day before. And he has no cocaine to numb it. He did the last little bit he had back in Reseda. His head throbs from a lack sleep, probably improper hydration, and more than likely a myriad of other things. He's come down from yesterday's high already, but yesterday's lows still have his mind dwelling and his skin crawling. He used up all the Xanax he took from Mrs. Tevenot within the first seventy-two hours he had them. And now he has nothing. But then he has a thought. He picks up his phone and calls Jae, praying he's across the hall and not out in the food truck.

"What's up, playa?" Jae answers in his usual jovial manner.

"Hey," AJ says, trying to sound regular and pleasant. "Do you still happen to have any OxyContin left from when you got your wisdom teeth taken out last month?"

"Um…yeah. I only took one. It made me feel super weird and then I puked. Twice. I said no thank you, put them things right back in the cabinet."

"Good. You didn't throw them out. Look, I've got a headache from hell and have nothing to take. I've been trying to wait it out, but it's not going away."

"Oh. Well I've got some Advil if you–"

"No. Advil won't do it. This is like…a next level headache."

Jae hesitates, but then accedes. "Ok. I'll be over in a second."

"Thanks, man. You're a lifesaver." AJ hangs up the phone. He doesn't particularly care for pain pills all that much. He had done them a couple of times with Kay. It was okay. They are euphoric but didn't give him the buzz and creative clarity that cocaine does. And he'd much rather have a Xanax or a Valium to calm himself down after a binge or a stressful night, but he had to make do with what he had readily available.

He sits there on the couch, perfectly still so as not to throw himself more off balance, and listening to the blood rush in his ears as his palm sweats. He stares at the wall because the television isn't on, his apartment so quiet he can hear the Rolex on his wrist ticking. So quiet he can hear Jae's door open and close across the hall. He gets up too quickly and stumbles off-kilter, but catches himself, and gets to the door before Jae can even knock.

"Hey," Jae says tentatively.

"What's up?" AJ asks cordially, friendly for the sake of being friendly. He sees the translucent orange bottle in his friend's left hand.

"Nothing much. Just making my pharmaceutical runs," Jae kids as he enters the apartment and AJ closes the door. "You think one will do it?" He asks as he unscrews the cap off the bottle.

"Better make it two just to be safe," AJ says, holding out his hand. Jae does as he's told and shakes out two.

"Does your face look a little puffy?" Jae asks.

"No," AJ replies, walking into the kitchen with his hand closed around the pills. He drops them onto the counter and pulls a wine cork looking object out of the drawer, and then starts to crush them up on the hard surface. Jae watches rapt from the doorway as AJ forms the pulverized pills into a little line, then bends down and snorts them up like he does it every day.

"You couldn't have just swallowed them like a normal person?" Jae asks him.

"Hits you faster this way."

"Might as well put it on a spoon, suck it into a syringe, and shoot it on up if that's the case," Jae mumbles under his breath.

AJ rubs his nose and looks up. "You act like I have a problem," he says accusatorily, locking eyes with his best friend. "When have you ever seen me take anything for anything? You know I don't even drink like that. You know me well enough to know better. I'm not that type of person. I just have a headache."

"I know. No, you're right," Jae quickly backtracks. "I didn't mean it like that. I just...well...you've been acting kind of weird lately."

AJ's face softens; he hadn't meant to raise his voice at Jae. "I've just been stressed, man, that's all." He goes over to the fridge and opens it. He considers grabbing a beer, but rethinks it and takes out a bottled water instead. "Got a lot going on. Trying to finish this album for Kay by fall. Cranking out like six songs a week." He twists the cap off and takes a long swig. "Been taking on extra clients for Miss Hunter since Theo and Nique left us high and dry." He does half a headshake and rolls his eyes. "Every new guy she's brought on couldn't find a clit with a navigational kit. I think she lost her niche for picking them."

Jae just stares at him for a second. "You think maybe you might be spreading yourself a little thin?"

AJ chuckles like he finds the question amusing. He takes another swig of water and leans back against the counter. "Of course not," he says sarcastically.

"Be serious," Jae tells him.

He sighs. "And what would you suggest I do if I think I am?"

"Quit working for Maggie," he says simply.

AJ smirks to himself and shakes his head. "Can't do that."

"Why not?" Jae inquires honestly. "I mean...don't you make enough writing songs now that you don't really *need* her money."

"Everybody needs her money," AJ says with a glib smile, looking over at Jae out of the corner of his eye. "Her money is always on time.

Always guaranteed. Always plentiful." He takes a sip and swallows. "I'm not giving that up. I'm not stupid. This song writing shit could end for me tomorrow. Plus, I'm thinking about breaking up with Kay. And if I do that she's probably going to go off and slander my name all over town because that's just the kind of person she is, and then no one in the music business is going to want to work with me anymore anyway. So I'm sticking with Maggie. They say if you got something good don't mess with it."

"I don't know that what you have is good," Jae says quietly.

"I made ten thousand dollars last week, you don't think that's good?" AJ asks with a jesting grin, leaving out the part about how he only has a thousand of it left.

Jae decides to admit defeat. He's not being heard. "I don't know," he says in a reserved tone, looking down at the floor and kicking the carpet with the toe of his shoe. "I am glad that you're thinking of ending things with Kadence though. Truth be told, I never really did like her."

AJ smiles as he lifts the bottle to his lips again. "I know." He swallows and screws the lid back on. "I told you I take what you think seriously. You're my best friend."

Jae looks up.

"And I'm flattered that you're concerned about me," AJ adds. "But you shouldn't be. I'm the most mentally stable person I know. Well. Besides you."

Jae smirks. "Perhaps therein lies the problem, compadre."

"Funny, funny."

"Alright. I better get goin. Takin Britt to dinner in the hills tonight."

"You're a good man, Jae," AJ says, raising his water bottle in a droll show of respect and admiration.

Jae smiles slightly. "I try," he says, opening the door. "I'll see ya later."

"See ya."

The door closes. AJ tosses the bottle of water in the trash and goes back to the fridge to get a beer. As the cold air seeps out and he stares blankly at the bare necessities of nourishment that he keeps, he slowly realizes that there is only two Heinekens left. He'll have to go to the store soon. He hates going to the store. He closes the fridge and opens the freezer door above it. He spots a gallon of the vile vodka Kay likes, shoved in the back. She must have left it. There's only about a quarter of a gallon left. He hates the stuff, but when he remembers the spat they had yesterday he figures he will drink it just to spite her. Not making any sense out of what he's doing or comprehending the fact that she could buy five thousand more bottles of Grey Goose and still have enough money for five billion more. He grabs the cold glass bottle by the neck and heads to the couch. He can feel the pills starting to kick in. Everything's a little fuzzy around the corners, pain slowly alleviating and being replaced with dulled pleasure. The vodka will be a nice little additive to the numb feeling he's going for. He falls back against the soft cushions and flips on the television.

~

They make up two days later like they always do. A little cocaine, rough sex, and a hot shower, like they always do. That was last night. They don't go to sleep till the dawn of the next day, sleeping on opposite sides of her humungous bed, like they always do. They don't get up till midafternoon.

Now they're on the rooftop terrace having a very late breakfast that consists mainly of champagne and orange juice. She's laid back on one of the lawn chairs wearing an Oscar de la Renta caftan cover-up. Her oversized, sparkly Dior sunglasses are pulled down and she's sporting a floppy sunhat on her head to shade her pristinely pale skin from accidently catching a tan. She's got her drink in one hand and a magazine in the other. Bridget had dropped off the newest issue of *Vogue*, hot off the press, with none other than the star herself splayed across the cover in couture. He watches her stare at herself for many minutes, clearly infatuated, before flipping to the middle where her cover story will be. He's been through this before; she'll be engrossed for hours.

AJ walks to the edge with his mimosa, staring out at his perfectly manicured surroundings, high above it all. He fantasizes about jumping off her roof often. Sure, there are easier ways to do in oneself. He could purchase a pistol off the black market and blow his brains out in his apartment, or take all the pills he can get his hands on, wash them down with a glass of bourbon, and get into a hot bath while he waits on the reaper. But none of those ways would forge her name after the salutation on the letter that wouldn't be left. She'd be linked to him regardless because of their relationship; however, doing it so dramatically and at her house would be more fulfilling than the life he'd be losing in the process. It would serve her right in the worst of ways. My what a media frenzy that would be. The damage control she'd have to do, the statements she'd have to make. The things the media would say and the bloggers would write and the fans would think. *What secrets and lies must have been hidden under those happy smiles*, they'll all speculate. And the dark cloud of his death would forever be over her head and present in every endeavor that she'd attempt to accomplish.

But knowing his luck he'd catch a gust of wind on the way down and get blown into the pool and live. Of course the water would only shave a few seconds off his landing speed, and he'd still probably hit the bottom of the pool hard enough to sever his spinal cord and then he'd be spending the rest of his days as a paraplegic in a wheelchair. Because he probably couldn't even kill himself right.

"What are you thinking about?" He hears her ask idly.

"Nothing."

Of course, his wonderful girlfriend wasn't the only person he could charge with the crime of making him hate his existence. He wasn't doing himself any favors, nor was he doing anything to extricate himself from negativity. And the only other person he could place blame on—aside from the two aforementioned—was completely immune from the burden of guilt, so there'd be no fun or point in trying to make her feel what she couldn't. Kadence still had a little bit of conscious left to go before she got to that level. Maybe. She did just ask him what he was thinking; that was mildly thoughtful.

"Do you love me?" He asks, turning around to look at her.

"Of course." She doesn't look up, stop reading her magazine, or put any inflication in her response. But she doesn't hesitate either.

He leaves the edge and walks over to her, sitting down on the adjacent lawn chair. When she doesn't acknowledge him, he gently lowers the magazine from her line of vision. She looks at him now, albeit perturbed.

"What is it, AJ?" She asks, lifting her shades.

"I was thinking…I don't know…what do you think about getting out of LA for a while? Going to Turks and Caicos or St. Tropez or somewhere for a week or something."

She pulls her shades back down and turns back to the magazine. "I've got to finish this album. I don't have time to be taking an island vacay with my bae. I have work to do. You know that."

"Right."

He submits this time. He doesn't bring up that she makes time to sit on the roof and drink, time to bask in the sun and the bright lights of her own glory, time to throw slumber parties with her idiotic girlfriends, time to go shopping if not just to shut down an entire street and make the paparazzi scramble, time to attend every fashion show, award show, or televised event that offers her a front row seat.

"Well," she says after a beat, lofty acquiescence in her voice. "I suppose I could spare two days if we go somewhere close in the Caribbean."

His phone is suddenly vibrating in his pocket. He moves it far enough out to see the first two letters of the caller's name, and then mutes it.

"No. You were right," he says, standing. "We should focus on work. Get done what needs to be done."

"That's all I was saying," she replies, flipping the page and draining her glass.

"Want me to go make another pitcher?" He asks nicely.

"Thanks, babe. That'd be great."

He heads downstairs, taking out his phone and calling Maggie back just as soon as he's out of earshot.

Chapter 23

Friday is the night to pick up strangers.

Austin has found it's much easier to pick up rich men for one-night-stands than it is women. Austin was always leery to proposition random women, fearful that they'd take offense when they found out that he was an escort they'd have to pay. Men are much more receptive to the idea of paying for sex, and the assumptions you make of them while on the prowl are rarely an issue. It basically comes down to this: they have a need, and they could care less how it gets met or what you think of them for it. For these non-regulars, Maggie had set a rule to charge by the act and not by the hour, because with men not much time was needed, and they would never make any money if the toll didn't start running till the sixty-minute mark. On one hand, Austin likes dealing with men better than women. A few quick minutes in a hotel bathroom or the backseat of their luxury vehicles and he has his money and is on his way. He doesn't have to feign interest for an extended period of time while working in earnest to get them off like he does women. It's easy. On the other hand, servicing men has the tendency to feel demeaning at times. Sure, some of his female clients could be short with him, telling him what they want of him, getting it, and then promptly excusing him. But most of his women are sweet and personable, exchanging kind words with him in the interims and caressing him with care when he's inside them. Not zipper down, get it done, zipper up, nary a please or a thank you like a lot of men.

But he takes this Friday off to spend with Hermosa.

He hasn't told her about the men. She has no idea. The women were a hard enough pill for her to swallow, and that's with him wrapping the truth in something better and slipping it to her in small doses. He sugarcoats his job, plays it down. He tells her most of his clients just want a date to dinner, and that he only sleeps with a few and only on occasions. He told her that he had a conversation with Maggie where he expressed that he wanted to be more of an event escort and less of a high-priced hooker, and he told her that Maggie respected his wishes. That she lowered his amount of second tier folder clients dramatically. Of course, this is the exact opposite of what's really happening. Austin doesn't want to lie to Hermosa, but he doesn't want to hurt her either. And she'd be devastated if she knew the truth. So he chooses what in his mind is the lesser of two evils, hoping she believes him.

He's been saving money. He wants to buy her a house. He wants better for her than the cramped little apartment she's been living in. He wants to buy her a nice house in a nice neighborhood and give her everything she could possibly want or need. But he knows she won't let him, she doesn't want to be kept. So he's been thinking about proposing the idea that they get a house *together*. But if they get a house together he'll have to stop seeing Calvin. And if they get a house together it will more than likely force her to finally define the relationship, and if she defines the relationship he will probably have to go back to working at the airport, and then he'll no longer be able to afford the house. So it won't matter.

But he still wants to make her smile. He still wants to give her the world.

She knocks on his door a little after five, and he opens it within the second.

"Hey, babe," he grins.

She doesn't call him babe back, but she kisses him square on the lips, and he can instantly feel her familiar smile against his mouth. When they separate with a pop, he steps back a few feet to stare at her, smiling uncontrollably.

"I got somethin' for you," he says, walking over to the kitchen table and grabbing the little pale blue box. "I was on Rodeo the other day and decided to stop at Tiffany's."

"Oh Dios mio," she whines dramatically. "It's not a ring is it?"

He pauses a few feet from her. "If it was, would say you yes?"

She smirks cutely at him. "No."

"Then it's not a ring," he smirks back, closing the distance and handing her the box. "Just somethin' pretty for my pretty."

She fights her grin and tries to act disgusted by his sentiments as she slowly pulls off the lid, but once she sees what's inside, her eyes light up in a way she can't hide. It's a necklace. A simple gold strand with a small, but real, emerald pendant hanging from it. She lifts it out of the box to admire it.

"Thank you," she tells him softly. "It's beautiful." She puts it back in the box when she's had her fill of its exquisiteness. And then she looks at him seriously. "You know you do not have to spoil me like this though, right?" She sits the box back down and gives him a small smile. "I am not with you for your mucho pesos," she kids.

He doesn't miss the fact that she just said "with you." She's *with* him.

"I know," he says innocently. "That's why I'm pairin' the present with an affordable, totally non-fancy dinin' experience this evening." He cocks his head at her secretively. "Guess what's in Santa Monica tonight?"

"Don't tease me if it's not true…"

"It is true," he tells her. "I subscribed to text alerts. And guess what's on the menu?"

"If you say tacos I'm going to freak out…"

"Well go on and freak out, baby," he says, grin breaking out on his face. "Because we're having tacos on a Friday night!"

"What? I thought I was going to have to wait till Tuesday!" She exclaims excitedly. "What kind of Korean infused Mexican magic is Jae trying to put on us?"

"I know, right? Our stars must have been aligned right or something over here, I tell you what." He laces his arm in hers. "Come on, let's go."

They sit on a picnic table facing the ocean after they get their food from Jae's food truck. Her bare right shoulder is showing in the sundress she has on, and he has to lean over and kiss it. She smirks back at him and continues eating her taco, not stopping him from showing her affection this evening.

"How is everything?" Jae asks as he makes his way over to them, having left the business in Brittany's care after the line died down.

"Amazin' as always, man," Austin says, washing the last bite of his second taco down with a slurp of soda.

"You know I love your tacos, Jae," Hermosa tells him in a faux serious voice. "But when are you going to serve some El Salvadorian cuisine?"

"How you know I ain't already on it?" Jae jests back. "I've got customers all down Pico and Vermont. Hell, I park on 11th Street at least once a month. I know what they want, and Imma bring it to em. Coming soon."

"You are a true man of the people, Papi," Hermosa says with a grin. "I love it."

Jae laughs out loud at this.

"Hey…um," Austin starts to say unsurely, tone lowered and serious. "You seen AJ lately?"

Jae's face immediately graves a bit. "Yeah. Not often, though. You know he keeps a hectic schedule."

"He seem weird to you?" Austin asks.

"More like wired," Jae answers.

"Yeah," Austin agrees.

"I blame that girl," Jae says.

"Kadence?"

"Yup. That girl. And that woman."

"What woman?" Austin asks, momentarily lost.

Jae glances over at Hermosa who is preoccupied with peeling the foil off a burrito, and then he glances back to Austin and mouths *your boss.*

"Oh," Austin mouths back.

"Well...I better get back. Brittany doesn't like being left with the people too long. You two lovebirds have a good night."

They both wave him off, and then Hermosa turns to Austin.

"Does AJ have a drug problem?" She asks.

"I don't know," he answers honestly. "Maybe."

Chapter 24

He cuts his car lights. He's parked on Sunset, down the street from a popular Hollywood nightclub. The album is finally done and will be releasing in two weeks after the North American Music Awards. Kay's nominated for five NAMA's and will be performing a brand new song live for the first time. The award show should wrap around eleven, and at midnight her album will magically appear on iTunes, and the morning after physical copies will be in every department store, music shop, and coffee house worldwide. But all of that is still very much a secret. However, tonight Kadence is having a private listening party where she will play her album in its entirety for a select privileged few. He can already see the line wrapping around the front of the venue in his rear-view mirror. The paparazzi are still acting fairly tame, so he assumes she hasn't arrived yet. He hasn't seen her in a few days, so he doesn't know her plan, but he's sure it will be a grand entrance. It always is.

AJ grabs a little baggie out of his console and makes a white line on his dashboard. He briefly glances to his right and to his left before rolling up a fifty and putting it to his right nostril. It doesn't take him long to snort it all up. His phone dings in his lap. It's Jae telling him he's already inside. Kay actually told him he could invite a few people, so naturally he invited Jae and Brittany. He knows Jae will be out of his element around a bunch of snooty industry people. So AJ quickly wipes his nose, pulls on his jacket, and gets out of the car.

"AJ!" The paparazzi yell as he gets to the front of the building. "How does the new album sound? Give us something to go on, buddy! What's the name of the song she's going to do next week at the NAMA'S? When's Kay arriving tonight, AJ? Who all's going to be in the party? Is this album her best? Are you proud of your girl?"

He ignores them as the doorman grants him access to the invite-only soiree without having to ask who he is, opening the door for him. And then he's inside.

The tables are covered in white lace with gold urns of pink peonies and clear vases of gummy bears serving as centerpieces. Matte pink balloons are floating from the ceiling. Bottles of pink champagne and Grey Goose with sparklers in them are being brought out of the back. Waiters holding trays containing Sprinkles cupcakes, assorted fruit sticks, and glasses of Pinot stand in each corner. The lights are low and the air is sweetly scented. It's all very Kadence centric.

"AJ!" Her girlfriends call to him from the prime table upfront.

He smiles politely at them and waves.

"AJ!" A thankfully familiar voice yells this time.

He turns to see Jae waving at him from a table in the roped off VIP section of the club. His best friend is dressed a little too fancily in a black tux and bow tie. Brittany is dressed a little too scantily in a short and sheer white spaghetti strap dress, hot pink bra and orange tan on full display. They both wear big smiles.

"What up, guys," AJ smiles back, taking a seat at the table with them where his nametag is placed. "How you like the high life?"

"They seated us in VIP!" Brittany exclaims excitedly, leaning over Jae to talk to him directly over the loud music playing. A piece of her stringy bleach blonde hair gets stuck in her pink lip-gloss and she has to pick it off. "I feel like a movie star!"

"Yeah," AJ chuckles dryly. "Kay has a way of making people who don't know her feel special." He smiles to cover up the shadiness of his comment.

"It sure is nice, but we don't seem to have many drink options," Jae comments, looking between the full bottle of Rosé and the full bottle of Grey Goose that has been placed on their table, both of which have firecrackers shooting out of them. "Can a chingu get a beer or a glass of brown?"

"It's only pink, white, or clear tonight, baby," AJ replies dismissively, dismantling the two bottles and then pouring himself a glass of champagne. "And if you're looking for an orange or yellow bear," he adds, dipping his hand in the vase and plunking a red gummy in his mouth with a leer. "You won't find one here."

"The red and green ones are the best anyway," Brittany says, reaching across the table, grabbing a handful, and stuffing all of them in her mouth at once.

"I suppose I can drink the fancy stuff for one night," Jae consents, grabbing the champagne bottle and pouring a glass for him and a glass for Brittany.

"Thanks, babe," she says, kissing his cheek while still chewing.

"You're welcome, darling," Jae replies with a fake accent and a genuine smile, giving her cheek a kiss back.

"Oh my gosh!" Brittany shrieks suddenly. "AJ, you're bleeding!"

Jae turns around to look at him, his eyes going wide like his girlfriend's.

"What?" AJ says, sitting back up straight and setting his glass down. He looks down at his lap, and then at his hands. "Where?"

"Your nose," Jae informs him dryly.

AJ holds his hand to his nose, and sure enough it's wet. He removes his hand and sees a bright red smear on it. He mentally chastises himself for not doing that last line in the car through his left nostril. He forgot he'd already used the right nostril for the line he did before he left the house.

"Here," Brittany says, reaching into her purse. "I've got some tissues." She pulls a couple Kleenex from a travel packet and passes them to him.

"I'll be ok," AJ assures them, dabbing his nose with tissue. "Been battling a bad cold all week. Must have blown my nose raw. Damn allergies."

Jae is giving him a serious side eye, and is about to open his mouth to say something when the music stops. The microphone crackles. Everyone looks to the stage where the DJ has come on to undoubtedly announce Kadence's arrival.

AJ wads the bloody Kleenex up and stuffs it in his pocket.

She appears out of a cloud of smoke, as she always seems to do when enough people are around to witness. If there's a stage, there will be fog. It's so trite and basic. But the people are still screaming at the top of their lungs like they've never seen pyrotechnics or a pop star before. His eardrums feel like they're going to bust for the fiftieth time since he met her. He throws back his champagne and refills the glass with vodka. She's wearing some Goth looking getup that looks utterly ridiculous on her. It's like looking at Little Bunny Foo Foo in Medieval ware; black lace and lipstick with her pale skin and hair, dark mesh melding with her squeaky clean persona. He knows it's meant to reflect her new more somber sound, but when you're in all black and everything else in the room is pink and white (or blush and cream as she so eloquently likes to call it) you clash in a very counterfeit way. But the more he stares at her, the more it suits her. For the first time, maybe ever, her exterior reflects her interior. For the first time she doesn't look like a wolf wearing impeccably well-tailored sheep shearing's. Of course, to everyone else in the room looking up at her and smiling, she's still very much Mary's Little Lamb.

He's only vaguely aware that she's thanking everyone for coming out and thanking everyone who worked on her album and made it all possible; naming no one by name because no one's name is as important as hers. With that, Eddie presses a button on his laptop and the album that is every bit his as it is hers starts, and everyone begins to mingle and sway as the music plays.

As much as he hates it, that expensive vodka of hers goes down smoothly.

"Did you invite Austin?" Jae asks him, taking a teensy sip of his champagne.

"Yup," AJ says, taking a big gulp of his booze. "But seeing as I'm off tonight he had to…" He glances over at Brittany, sees she's busy rubbernecking to get a look at all the stars in the room, then looks back to Jae and does a subtle pelvic-thrust. "*Work.*"

"Right, right," Jae replies.

"Oh my gosh," Brittany exclaims in a high-pitched whisper, grabbing Jae's arm in excitement. "There's Fryderyka. She's like…my fashion inspiration. I absolutely love her. She's my all-time favorite model."

"You should introduce yourself to her," AJ tells her. "She's cool."

"Seriously?" She asks, blue eyes going big at the prospect.

"Sure. Go say hi. Tell her your AJ's friend."

"Ok. Ok," Brittany says to herself in a mystified voice. She runs her hands over her hair and then looks at her boyfriend. "Do I look alright?"

"You're the most beautiful woman in the room," Jae tells her.

AJ knows that's a damn lie, focusing his smirking face elsewhere so as not to give what he's thinking away.

"Aww. Thanks, babe." She gives Jae a peck on the cheek as she stands. "Ok. Here I go." She pulls her bra up and then walks off in the supermodel's direction.

Nobody is really trying to visit their table. After all, he's not famous for anything other than fucking someone famous, so AJ zones out a bit as he drinks. Jae sees Dominique approaching their section before he does, nudging him. AJ is surprised to see him there, because he sure as hell didn't invite him. But he forgets Nique is famous now. Famous enough for Kay to have invited herself. And he looks famous in his designer threads, bopping about the club, dapping and getting dapped, practically glowing with the glee of newfound stardom. It's almost nauseating, really. AJ watches as the familiar dimple-ended, white-toothed grin breaks out across his former co-worker's face.

"My motherfuckin' dog!" Dominique exclaims.

AJ stands up and puts on a smile. "Nique The Freak."

Their hands interlock and their shoulders lean in to touch.

"It's been a minute, bruh," Dominique says when they separate, still smiling.

"You've been busy blowing up," AJ replies tepidly, still fake smiling.

"I know, bruh. Shit's crazy. I mean look at us. I got two hit singles out. My debut album is dropping next month. And you…" He gives him naughty look, hits his arm, and then says in a lowered voice, "Breaking off the biggest songstress in the country. My man."

"Well you know how I get down, Nique," AJ says with a cool eeriness, picking up his glass of vodka off the table and taking a sip. "Songstresses, heiresses, millionaires, billionaires, directors' wives, housewives, dentists, and judges."

Dominique looks shocked that he just said that out loud, despite the loud music muffling their conversation and Jae being the only one within earshot to hear them.

"Actually…you might not have known about that last one," AJ adds with chuckle. "But shit, you do now." He takes another gulp and swallows. "Point being, pussy is pussy and I've probably had enough to be just a little bit jaded."

"Yeah," Dominique says tentatively. "But all that's in the past."

"Speak for yourself, brother," AJ replies curtly, raising his glass to his lips yet again. "I still got bills to pay."

Someone hollers Dominique's name. He glances over his shoulder to see a guy waving him over to a group of people chatting by the bar. He looks back.

"Hey, it was nice seein' you, AJ," he says cordially, still clearly taken aback by his old friend's odd behavior. "I gotta go holla at my peoples over there. Let's link up sometime though, okay?"

"Mmhm," AJ mutters, immediately sitting back down, wordlessly dismissing him.

Dominique slowly turns around and makes his way back into the crowd.

"You were kind of short with him," Jae says after a beat.

"Was I?" AJ asks, refilling his glass to the brim.

"I mean…yeah."

"He's a sellout. He takes whatever songs they offer him. His new singles sound like everything else on the radio, bubble gum hip-hop hits.

Dude could have been the next Marvin Gaye but he chose to be the next Trey Songz. They're marketing him as a sex symbol and he's letting them. Taking his shirt off five minutes into every set, prancing around on the stage like the little gigolo he still is deep down inside. Don't get me wrong, I'll always have love for the guy, but he's weak-minded as hell for letting the man talk him out his talent for a better check."

Jae is giving him a look that he'd be able to read if he wasn't so inebriated.

"What?" AJ asks him.

"Nothing," Jae covers quickly, looking away as he picks up his glass of champagne and takes a little sip. After a few seconds he looks back to his friend. "So, there's something I wanted to run by you. Before Britt gets back."

AJ leans back and crosses his legs. "Go on."

"I was thinking…I am thinking…" He takes a deep breath. "I think I want to pop the question."

"What question?" AJ asks, quirking a brow and pulling a face. "Are we talkin *the* question?"

"I want to ask Brittany to marry me," Jae confirms.

"Oh man," AJ replies, grimacing comically. "Now why do you want to go and do that? You're young. You're successful. You're a catch." He finishes off his drink and pours some more. "Pace yourself. Life isn't a race to the altar."

Jae smiles bashfully. "You know I'm not a player like that. Not that there's anything wrong with testing the waters, as they say, it's just not in me. I want a good career, a decent house, a wife and some kids." He takes another sip. "I'm on the right path with my career. I've saved money; I've got my life together. Now I'm ready to start a family. And Brittany…she's…she's got my heart, dude."

"You sure it's your heart?"

"Seriously, AJ."

"I'm just saying…are you sure she's the one? I mean, no offense, but you haven't dated that much. And she's…well…I just want to make sure you're sure."

"We've been together a little over seven months. I know it's a little soon. But I don't want to waste anymore time. I know what I want."

"Then…hell…go for it, man."

They're silent for a moment, and then Jae looks over at him again. "Can I ask you a question?"

"I love you, Jae. But I can't marry you," AJ jokes with a tipsy hiccup stuck in his chest.

"What ever happened to you breaking up with Kadence?"

"Aw man," AJ replies with a sigh. "I don't know. We fight, and fuck shit up, and sometimes I do hate her. But what can I say, she's my soul mate."

"Really?" Jae asks skeptically.

"Hell no. Anjanae is."

Jae just stares at him.

"I'm kidding, I'm kidding," AJ laughs enthusiastically. "I don't have a soul. I'm still kidding. Don't give me that sad look. Loosen up, brother. Have some more champagne. Let's toast to us, two ridiculously good looking young men living it up."

Brittany comes back as they're clinking glasses.

"What are we toasting to?" She asks with a big smile, sliding back in next to Jae and immediately sliding her arm around his shoulder.

"Um…I really couldn't tell you," Jae replies, turning his head to give her a little smile. She kisses him.

When their lips separate, her eyes are on AJ. "I can't thank you enough for inviting me and Jae here tonight. It's been freakin amazing. Fryderyka was amazing. She introduced me to some other models. And we danced! I danced with supermodels! And Kadence's album is awesome. Make sure you tell her that. Tonight was the best. You're the best. Isn't he the best, babe?"

"He's…he's a special one all right," Jae replies.

"It was no problem," AJ tells her. "I'm glad you all enjoyed yourself."

Thirty minutes or so later Jae and Brittany leave. He can tell Brittany doesn't want to leave, but Jae has a catering gig early the next morning, so she ends the night early for him because she's a halfway decent girlfriend. Unlike AJ's girlfriend, who made one stop to his table the entire night, more to flaunt her fabulousness in front of his friends than to see him. Now that Jae and Brittany are gone, AJ is alone at his table. The music is still playing—they might have restarted the album, he doesn't know—and the party is still going strong. He could get up and go hob-knob like everyone else, but he's not in the mood to brown nose or play pretend tonight. Dominique hasn't left yet and Kadence is currently chatting him up on the other side of the room. Probably telling him how much she loves his mixtape, and his music, and him. He watches her throw her arms around him, and of course Dominique hugs her back. AJ rolls his eyes, gets up, and heads for the door.

As soon as he's outside he takes a cigarette from the carton he's taken to keeping on him, and lights it. He takes a long first drag and walks around the corner of the building. He can hear someone talking, and when he gets to the back alley, he sees Sailor pacing the tight expanse between the back of the club and the parking garage next door, phone pressed to her ear. She seems to be having an argument with whoever is on the other line; a boyfriend, a manger, whoever, it really doesn't concern him or make a shit lick of difference. He leans up against the back of the building by the trashcans, propping one foot on the brick wall behind him as he puffs away. She's too busy hurling obscenities to notice him standing there, too caught up in her own life like Kadence and all her other cohorts. But there they are, sandwiched between two buildings together at two o'clock in the morning. When she does finally end the call and take inventory of her surroundings, she spots him the twenty or so feet away that he is. Rather, he assumes she spots him; he's purposefully not looking in her general direction now, playing impassive. He hears her heels on the pavement closing the distance.

"You got another one?" she asks him. "I've had a shit ass night."

He coolly tosses his Marlboro to the ground, takes his right foot off the wall and smashes it down onto the discarded cigarette to make sure that it's put out. He then turns, grabs her by the biker jacket she has on over her sultry little dress, and pulls her flush against him. His lips land on hers and he wastes no time getting his tongue into her mouth. She kisses him back thirty, maybe forty seconds, and then she's pulling away and feigning shock like her persona tells her to do. Of course, he's well versed by this point at separating personas from the actual two-faced people who hide behind them.

"What are you doing?" She asks breathlessly, like she doesn't know, looking up at him with lust all in her eyes that she can't hide.

"You like me, don't you?" He asks almost innocently with a knowing smile.

Sailor looks over her shoulder, glancing around to make sure that no one is around, her own troublesome smile giving her away. She faces forward again, grabbing his face with both hands and pulling him into a tongue-filled kiss. She's sloppy with the way she slobbers all over his face and neck like she wants to devour him alive. She's messy in the way that she's about to fuck her so-called best friend's boyfriend in an alley outside the building where she's currently having a party. But in the moment, AJ loves her lack of morals. He gropes her breasts through her dress, slipping another hand up the back to squeeze her ass harshly. She growls in his ear; he hears the sound of his zipper being pulled down. *Did she already get his belt undone? When did that happen?* He doesn't care. It doesn't matter.

"What about Kay?" She asks him huskily.

It's certainly an audacious and odd thing to ask when she's got her hand wrapped around his erection, stroking it with purpose.

He smirks. "It'll be our little secret," he says, pulling the chintzy scrap of material that she considers underwear to the side.

Her grip on him suddenly loosens and a long string of moans sound out in the alley as he pushes her past the last remnants of propriety with the heel of his hand. He works her over a few more moments with his fingers, then retrieves a condom from the enduring stash in his wallet. He quickly rolls it on, and then turns her around so her face is pressed up against the brick wall.

Fifteen minutes later they rejoin the party. He makes her run a hand through her hair and wipe the smeared lipstick off her face, because she's too dense to realize she should do it on her own. She walks in first, he counts to ten, then follows. He watches as Sailor immediately gets pulled back into the swath of Kadence worshipers who think they're her friends. She's not with them, though; he doesn't know where she is. Sailor grabs two multicolored shots from the tray they're passing around and double fists them, falling right back in to the giggling and dancing like nothing happened. AJ makes a lap around the bar, eyes darting around dizzily at all the drunk, smiling faces. He spots her on the other side of the venue. A popular British DJ who makes EDM and Dancehall crossovers is chatting her up. She's leaning into him and laughing, one hand going to his shoulder and lingering a little too long before she takes it back off. AJ can't hear what they're saying over the loud music and all the giggling girls and the pounding in his head from the Grey Goose he's perhaps been downing too fast. He comes up behind her and wraps his arms around her possessively.

"Hey, baby," he says, kissing her neck.

Her hand comes up to stroke his jaw in faux adoration. "Hey, babe," she replies back, annoyance that only he can decipher seeping through her practiced voice. "This is DJ Eric Deezy. He has the song–"

"I know who he is," he cuts her off, still placing sporadic kisses to her cheek and earlobe in a show just for the DJ with the dumb name, the tie-dyed shirt, and the tacky sixteen seasons ago Ray Bans with the stripes who's still staring at his girlfriend. At least AJ thinks he's staring, though he's sure it's hard for the idiot to see anything with those idiotic sunglasses on.

"Nice to meet you, mate. I was just telling Kay I would love to write with you. I'm working on a new album now. We should get in the studio sometime, yes?"

The fact that he feels like he can call her *Kay* rubs him the wrong way, but he tells himself to keep it under control. "Yeah maybe," he replies with coolness that borders on cold. "We'll see."

"Ok," Eric replies, clearly taken aback by AJ's aloofness. "You let me know then."

"Well it was so great catching up with you, Eric," Kadence says in an overly polite voice, unlacing her arm from around AJ's neck to momentarily put her hand back on Eric's shoulder. "Best of luck with your show tomorrow. And send Eddie that song you were talking about, I'd love to take a listen and add a verse. Okay?"

"Alright, love," Eric smiles. "Take care."

She gives the DJ a final smile for good measure, and then she's turning to leave, placing her hand on the small of his back and ushering him along with her.

"*Alright, love. Take care*," AJ mocks as they walk away.

"Why do you have to embarrass me in public like that?" She seethes under her breath, still smiling for all the spectators and acquaintances standing around.

"I don't know," he retorts. "Why do you have to give every guy the smoldering eye?"

"The *smoldering* eye? Are you serious right now?" She's got him cowered in a quiet corner away from everybody now. "He DJ'd for me at the London, Brussels, and Copenhagen stops of my last European tour. And he wanted to work with me back when I was just a regular star, before I was a superstar."

"The guy is a cornball. He's basically a hype man who can make beats. Silly beats that all sound the same for rage-goers rolling on E in Amsterdam and New Jersey to dance to. You don't need him, he needs you."

She crosses her arms and stares at him. "He has two songs in the top twenty right now, one his and one for another artist."

"And how many do you have?" He asks, lifting an eyebrow at her.

She looks down. "Four of my own and two with other artists," she says quietly.

"Exactly," he says, seeing that she's softening under his coded compliments. "And one of those is from your *last* album. You're a superstar now and he's still regular as hell."

"Ok. Fine," she relents after a second. "You're right." She looks up then and meets his green eyes with her baby blue ones. "Let's not fight tonight, okay?"

"I don't want to fight," he says in a voice that sounds sincere, shaking his head.

"Ok." She smiles, reaching for his hand and lacing their fingers together. "Let's rejoin the party, shall we?"

He returns her smile. "Lets."

They make their way back to VIP hand-in-hand like the happy couple they're not. Her ten terribly drunk besties welcome her back into the fold with a loud and slurred "Kaaayyy!"

She calls them her bitches in the most endearing way possible, even going as far as to kiss and hug some of them like she really missed them in the hour or so that they had been partying and she had been schmoozing. A new tray of pretty pink shots is delivered to the table and all the girls immediately grab them up.

"You want a shot, babe?" She asks him, kissing him lovingly on the cheek.

"Of course," he replies. And she hands him one.

"What happened to your face, Sail?" Kay asks her bff who is across the table from her. She dips her hand into the centerpiece that is filled with her favorite candy, and drops a handful of gummy bears into her mouth. "It looks like you got rug burn on your left cheek," she comments as she chews.

More like brick burn, AJ thinks to himself, throwing back his shot and motioning for another one. He listens as Sailor tells her about how she comically fell on the pavement when she went outside for a smoke, and then as Kay laughs hysterically about it and calls Sail a drunken klutz instead of the drunken slut it would have been had the story actually been true.

But there's never any truth, therefore there's never any bad blood. Five minutes later the two girls excuse themselves from the table, stumbling arm and arm together to the bathroom to put their noses on the back of a toilet like the class acts they are.

Chapter 25

Maggie is sitting at her office desk, searching layover-less plane tickets to Miami on her Mac. *This weekend feels like a South Beach weekend*, she thinks to herself with a smile. Ever since she got her timeshare a few months ago, she'd been making the trip almost every other weekend. Ever since her last real relationship tanked tremendously in a courtroom, she's been meeting men online. She's gotten rather good at it, if she's being honest. There are currently two handsome men in the Miami-Fort Lauderdale area who are thoroughly smitten with her. One thinks her name is Victoria, the other thinks it's Jaclyn. One thinks she lives in Philadelphia, the other thinks she lives in Seattle.

It's great.

Complete and total anonymity is great.

Having separate cities for business and pleasure is great.

Not having to worry is great.

The white phone rings before she can press buy on the tickets. She doesn't recognize the number, but that doesn't stop her from answering.

"Hello?"

"What's poppin'?"

"Who's this?" Maggie asks in her removed voice.

Dominique sighs on the other end. "You're soundin' more and more like the black man you think you are every day. *Who dis*. Who the fuck you think it is? Dominique Davis. I used to dick down housewives for you? Ring a bell?"

"Vaguely," she replies. "What do you want?"

"Damn. I can't get a 'how you been' or a 'congratulations on all your success'?"

"I don't inflate egos, Dominique," she tells her former employee flatly. "Get to the point of the call."

"Fine," Dominique relents. "I was just callin' to ask if AJ was alright. I saw him the other night at his girl's listening party and he ain't seem like himself at all."

"Andrew is fine."

"I don't know," Dominique says. "The boy was lookin' pretty wild eyed and wicked."

"It's the facial hair," Maggie placates.

"Nah," Dominique says. "I think it's the dilated pupils and scabbed over nostrils."

Maggie doesn't think his brass, albeit somewhat accurate, assessment of her employee warrants a response. So she lets her silence speak for her.

"Look," Dominique says after a beat, taking a more somber tone. "That's my guy and I just wanted to make sure he was cool. That's all. He seemed really different."

"I don't know, Dominique," Maggie says then. "Things are different. But you wouldn't know, because you haven't been here. You quit, Theo quit. We've got new employees, new clients, people have new girlfriends. Me, though? I haven't changed. I'm still here. And you know I make sure everyone is taken care of. So please don't take any time out of your highly successful, R&B singing, club appearance making schedule to check in on one of my workers. I've got AJ. He's fine."

"Man whatever. You're so full of—"

She ends the call while he's still midsentence.

Maggie doesn't return to her airline tickets. She sits and stares down at her desk. It was close to two years ago when she called a blonde boy named Caleb into her office and told him that he was fired. He too had blown pupils and blood-stained nostrils. In the weeks leading up to his termination he had been acting recklessly and erratically, and his clients had been complaining.

AJ's clients don't complain. AJ's clients only sing his praises.

It's hard to find good talent like that.

AJ is special. And if this is just something he wants to do recreationally, hell, she can overlook that. She understands he's a creative, and creatives are inclined to seek a little extra mental stimulation every now and then. And he does keep late hours with clients. And he does have to turn out songs on very little sleep. There's a lot being expected of him. He's a busy guy. He's an in-demand guy. She understands if he needs the occasional jolt. It's all very understandable.

If you're rationalizing, which she thinks she might be.

But fuck it; everyone is entitled to a vice.

As long as it's not negatively inferring with work. As long as it's not habitual. As long as he hides it from her, she can hide that she knows. That she's known for a while.

The ding of the elevator brings her out of it. She looks up and sees Austin stepping off. His cheeks are rosy and his dress shirt is crinkled, evidence of what he's been doing. He wordlessly hands her thirty thousand dollars in all hundreds, and immediately heads for the bathroom to brush his teeth and take a shower.

"Do you think AJ's drug use is daily or sporadic?" She asks out of the blue.

Austin pauses. After a moment he looks over at her. "I think you should talk to him."

Maggie nods silently. Austin continues down the hallway.

Maybe next week.

Chapter 26

AJ knows he's wrong for doing this. For doing her. But he doesn't care.

He's felt her eyes on him before, and he's sensed for a while now that she's needed a little something more than what she's been getting. And his natural inclination to please makes him want to give it to her. And his overwhelming need to feed his ego makes him want to hear her scream. Despite it being so completely wrong. Despite her not even being his type.

He's starting to think he doesn't have a compass or a type.

Who's he kidding? He's not thinking. Preferences and morals are irrelevant.

He'd heard her cheap heels in the hallway. He'd been drinking off his most recent binge, feeling rather good. He'd opened the door and told her that he wasn't home.

Now he's got her bent over his kitchen table and a handful of her blonde hair. To call it a kitchen table is a bit of an overstatement, because he doesn't really have a kitchen. He has one room that serves as everything; she can take in the ambiance of his entire place from her vantage point across the unvarnished oak of one of his few pieces of furniture. The table isn't even clean. There's at least six empty beer bottles sitting atop it, and an overflowing ashtray full of discarded cigarette buds and debris, last Sunday's coffee-stained *New York Times*, a napkin with a ketchup smear (on second thought it could be blood), a few stale french fries from the last time he felt like eating, a hardened yellow gummy bear, and probably some cocaine residue.

It wasn't a penthouse balcony view, but she doesn't seem bothered by it.

His view on the other hand is optimal. Her ass doesn't have any tan lines, letting him know she indulges in her vice nude. He gives it a smack and watches it shake. She lets out a sound that's somewhere between a scream and a growl. His right hand had been massaging her breasts before, but he knows it's time to slip it between her legs. She's pressing back against him; he's pressing firm circles to her clit. Her arms flail, a glass shatters. He thinks he hears something else in the background, but he can't bring himself to care. He knows she's about to come, fractured moans of *more* and clenching walls. His thrusts become harder and deeper, making the whole table rock. But when she turns her head to throw him the classic over-the-shoulder-look, her eyes catch something he can't see.

She freezes, dear in the headlights. AJ wants to turn her head back around, push it down, and continue to fuck her. But something about the panic imprinting itself across her face makes him want to look behind him, too.

And he does.

And there stands Jae.

Suddenly Brittany is pushing him off and out of her. She pulls her panties back on and immediately starts searching for the rest of her clothes, covering her bare chest in shame as she does so.

"Baby...baby, I messed up. I'm so sorry," she starts to ramble remorsefully, her valley girl voice all weak and shaky. "I promise...I promise it won't happen again." She gets her skimpy denim shorts buttoned, bypasses the bra, and grabs her t-shirt off the floor, which ironically has Jae's food truck's name plastered across the chest. "I promise...I promise I can explain. Please, just...lets just go across the hall and talk," she pleads. "Okay?"

Jae just stands there, in shock.

AJ pulls up his boxers and jeans nonchalantly, not even making an attempt at an apology or an explanation.

She wrestles to get her shirt over her head quickly. "I made a mistake. I was...and he was...but I love you," she continues to stumble over her words as she tugs her top down. "I love you, Jae. I love you so much."

"Did you pay him?" Jae finally speaks, his voice mystified and ungrasping.

"What? No." She's confused by the question, but then she gets her shoes back on and is walking straight towards him. "Please say you'll forgive me. I'll never do it again. I swear. I want to be with you. I want us to be us."

She reaches out to touch his face, but he pushes her hand away.

"Go," is all he says, diverting his eyes away from her.

"Please," she whines, begs. "Please, please don't do this."

"I didn't do this, you did." He shakes his head solemnly, briefly looking at her and then back away. "Just...go. Go. I don't want to look at you. I can't look at you."

"Jae..." she pleads, tears streaming down her face making her mascara run.

"Seriously, Brittany," Jae tells her, taking a stern tone now. "Get out."

She grabs her purse off the floor where it had been thrown upon her arrival, full out crying now, and walks back out the open door. The sound of her heels and sobs slowly fade as she disappears down the hall and into the stairwell, leaving the room silent in the aftermath. Jae stares at the floor for a long while, but then his eyes slowly start to rise to his still shirtless best friend.

"Look, Jae," AJ starts unremorsefully. "It was just a spur of the moment, one-time thing. It was just sex. It meant nothing. It's really not a big deal."

"Not a big deal?" Jae snaps in disbelief. "She was my girlfriend. I told you I was thinking about asking her to *marry* me."

AJ shrugs simply. "At least now you know what kind of girl she really is."

"No," Jae retorts without hesitation, holding up a hand. "At least now I know what kind of person *you* really are."

AJ snorts derisively and shakes his head once, brushing it all off as he picks his shirt up and starts to put it back on.

"I'll be moving out of the building just as soon as I find a new place," Jae says as he heads for the door.

"You're being dramatic," AJ tells him.

"I'd rather be dramatic than to be living across the hall from you," Jae replies simply, meeting his former friend's eyes. "So have a nice life. Live it up with Kadence, tell each other lies, make millions with your penis and lose it all through your nose. I don't care. I don't care if you catch everything that there is to catch and go out face down in a pile of coke. It is what it is, and you'll do what you do. Good luck and goodbye."

Jae walks out the door, slamming it shut behind him.

AJ snorts like he finds it funny, shakes his head once more, and then goes to the fridge for a beer.

~

The next few days leading up to North American Music Awards weekend and the subsequent release of *Progression in C* are filled with press. Kadence makes talk show appearances and AJ sits backstage and broods. It kills him that everyone knows what to put in her room. Grey Goose and gummy bears. Cashews and cranberries. Cupcakes and cookies from A-list bakeries drizzled in pretty pink icing. Fiji water and pineapple juice. Gift bags filled with expensive free shit that she'll probably never use and could easily buy for herself. Throw in a little top-grade cocaine and it would've been a scene from her dreams. He wonders if other guests get treated with such care, or if America's Sweetheart's ass gets kissed the best. She doesn't deserve any of it.

He doesn't deserve to be dragged around to all these promotional stops, but God forbid they not save face, God forbid she not have a man supporting her ungrateful ass from the sidelines. Thankfully all the appearances are in Los Angeles, so he didn't have to get on a plane for her. After all, he does still have clients to do in his downtime.

He had seen both Mrs. Tevenot and Mrs. Elliot earlier in the week, and had taken ten pills from each of their stashes. No longer caring if they notice what he's doing, no longer caring about taking a sensibly discreet amount anymore.

He's rather proud of himself when Thursday night rolls around and he still has all twenty pills in his possession. It wasn't an easy feat; he wanted to start popping them at multiple points in the week. The more time he had to spend with an extra-charged Kadence and her high-strung team of people running around like chickens with their heads cut off, the closer they get to awards night and the album drop, the more he wanted to slip into a half-asleep daze until the hectic week passed. But he continues to hold loosely onto what little restraint he has left.

As they exit the last promotional stop of the week, she tells him she'll see him Saturday, and he revels in the fact that he'll be free from her for the next forty-eight hours. If that's not a cause for celebration he doesn't know what is. He does a line in his car before he ever leaves the television studio lot, and then decides he'll go hit up Maggie and see if she can get him a desperate old lady to do last minute for a little extra cash.

However, on the ride to the office he finds himself getting more and more irritated the more he thinks about Maggie. Spurned by a little powdered courage, he decides he's going to address the issue of his inadequate workload with his boss. He feels like his client list has been dwindling, all the while everyone else's has been growing. He feels like she has purposefully been withholding new women from him, giving them to the new guys or to Austin. It couldn't be because they were a better lay than him. Could it be because he wasn't willing to take it up the ass like Austin? Were the new guys doing that, too? That shouldn't matter. He was willing to do anything with a woman, and Maggie was barely giving him two a week. A couple of months ago he was taking five or six down in a seven-day period. Did she forget all the overtime he did when Theo and Nique quit? When Garrett got sent to jail and Rafael got deported? Did she forget he saved her ass making a client out of Judge Rosemary Esque? Did she forget all the bitches he's brought in? Sure, he may ask for time off a lot, because unlike Austin he actually has other commitments, unlike the others he actually has a life. But that is no reason for her to space his regulars so far out, even giving a few away. He is going to find out what the problem is. He is going to ask her what her damn deal is.

He shifts back and forth restlessly on the balls of his feet as the elevator slowly ascends to the 57th floor. He shoots out as soon as the doors open, wound tight. It's quiet, too quiet, and he immediately knows no one is there. But then he rounds the corner, and there's Hermosa. She's on the couch, feet up on the cushions, painting her toes and thumbing through a magazine. Her head lifts when she senses his presence, a bright smile on her pretty mouth. But it quickly evaporates.

"Oh," she says, face returning to normal. "I thought you were Austin."

"Definitely not," he replies dryly.

He briefly glances at Maggie's glass-enclosed office, taking in the fact that she's not there, and then his eyes return to the girl on the couch. She's gone back to reading her magazine, and he takes a second to visually objectify her. She's wearing white shorts that accentuate her naturally tan skin, and a black tank top that shows off her toned arms and shoulders. Her long dark hair lays straight, going past her perky breasts that the fabric of her top hugs delectably. If she stood up it would probably go all the way down her back to her ass, which he imagines is firm and fine as can be. Her sandals are on the floor and she's barefoot, looking more at home than she should. She's always at the office and he doesn't know why. AJ has to wonder if she's secretly an aspiring madam, if she's trying to pick up all the nuances of the trade so she can overthrow Maggie one day and take over. Or was she merely patiently waiting for the day Maggie decides to drop the feminist charade and start pimping pussy? He smirks to himself. It is probably the later. She isn't cunning enough to be a boss. But she certainly looks like she'd be a damn good worker.

"You know if you keep hanging around like this Ms. Hunter's going to have to put you on payroll," he tells her as he walks over to the bar cart. He pours himself a tumbler of vodka, realizing after the fact that he is now willfully choosing the shit over bourbon, brandy, and gin.

"Yeah," she replies, not bothering to look up. "I'm not interested in being on Miss Hunter's payroll."

He always did think her little accent was cute. It was doing something to him. He'd never been with a Hispanic girl before. At least he doesn't think he has.

"I was kidding," he tells her collectedly, coming to sit on the opposite end of the couch. "You're too pretty to stoop as low as we go. You're too good to be any less than something special to someone special. Austin's a lucky guy." He takes a swig and cringes. "He's lucky to have you."

"I know."

AJ laughs. "I know you know," he says, taking another drink, her unabashed confidence turning him on even more. "I know you're fully aware of just how unbelievably sexy you are." He stares at her a long while as she finishes up her toes. "Actually," he adds. "I don't know that even Austin is worthy of you. Your presence. Your body. I think you might be too good for a simple country bumpkin like him."

"You better watch how you talk about him," she tells him sternly, eyes briefly rising. "Austin is a wonderful boyfriend."

"Come on, Hermosa," he chuckles. "He told me that you don't even like to call him a boyfriend. It can't be all sunshine and rainbows if you don't even want to claim the guy."

"I'm happy," she says simply, screwing the lid back on the polish and continuing to read her magazine.

"Are you?" He asks rhetorically, patronizingly. "Or are you just using him to scratch an inch that, in reality, someone else could scratch *way* better?" He drains his glass, puts it down, scoots closer.

"What are you doing?" She asks cautiously, finally looking up.

"What do you want me to do?" He asks with a lecherous leer.

"You know you need to chill," she tells him, giving him a scolding glare before turning the page and looking away from his undressing gaze. "Austin is on his way over here right now."

He scoots another inch closer. "I promise I can make you come in under five minutes."

"Stop," she says firmly, throwing her magazine down now and screwing her face up at him. "What the hell is wrong with you?" She asks him, highly perturbed. "He's your friend."

"I'd rather you be my friend," he says lowly. And then he puts his hand on her bare thigh.

She jumps off the couch. "Touch me again and I will slap the shit out of you," she seethes through clenched teeth.

"Relax," he says with an air of ridicule, leaning back against the couch. "If you don't want me, I don't want you. Your loss, though. There are plenty of women willing to pay for what I was offering you for free. See if you get the chance again."

"God you're fucking unbelievable!" She yells at him, quickly grabbing her purse and shoes off the floor. "Usted es tan vil."

"Mm. I'm sure that was a nasty statement, but it still sounded sexy," he says, standing and staggering over to the bar cart.

Hermosa rushes out of the room with her bag and shoes in hand, fumes of anger practically rolling off of her. The elevator dings and Austin steps off.

"Hey babe, are you ready to go to dinn– whoa, Mo, what's wrong?" He asks when he almost runs right into her. He instinctively puts both hands on her arms, and steps back to look at her. "Are you alright?"

"AJ just tried to get me to have sex with him," she spits out in a nerve-wrecked voice. "He was saying distasteful stuff and trying to seduce me and I told him stop and then he touched my leg–"

Austin's head spins around to stare at his coworker, who is currently leaned up against the bar cart drinking straight out of the bottle. AJ gives a nonchalant, jesting little shrug. Austin blinks a couple of times. And then he lunges across the room and punches AJ square in the face, landing his fist in his eye and knocking him to the ground in a single swing. The bottle he was holding hits the floor and shatters, sending glass and vodka everywhere. The elevator dings again and the doors open.

"What the hell is going on?" Maggie asks as soon as she can survey her surroundings, rushing past Hermosa who is standing perfectly still with her hand over mouth, and then stopping in her tracks when she sees all the glass on the floor.

AJ slowly moves into a sitting position, bracing his hands on the floor and then grimacing when a shard penetrates his skin. He pulls it out and flicks it aside.

"He's lost his fucking mind," Austin fumes breathlessly. "He just came on to Hermosa...got her all rattled...he ought to be glad I only hit him once."

Maggie stands rooted in the spot, looking from Austin with his fists still clenched, to AJ who is rolling his eyes, still on the floor, to a speechless Hermosa, and then back to Austin. Trying to wrap her mind around it all.

"He's a fucking fiend," Austin continues angrily. And then he turns his cold eyes on AJ. "You're a fucking fiend, you know that right?

You need rehab. Before you kill yourself or someone kills you. Because you're actin' and lookin' like a real mess right about now."

"Yeah. Well," AJ says coolly, cocking his head to the side and giving Austin a smug smirk. "At least I haven't let our boss convince me to suck dick for a better check yet."

Austin's face goes red and his eyes go wide.

"Wh…what?" Hermosa utters in disbelief, turning to look at Austin. "What is…what does he mean by that?"

"Oh he didn't tell you that?" AJ asks rhetorically, pleased grin taking over his face. "Imagine that. I guess he didn't' tell you that he's got a boyfriend either, huh? Or that he's a bunch of rich men's little bottom bitch?"

Hermosa is shaking her head, tears filling her eyes.

"Austin…" Maggie says, trying to sound calming as she takes a tentative step towards him. "Austin, let's not–"

But it's too late.

Austin jumps on top of AJ and starts pummeling him, holding him down by the throat with one hand and repeatedly slamming his other fist down into his face.

Hermosa shrieks.

"Stop!" Maggie yells, running towards them. "Austin, stop!" She's grabbing him by the shoulders, trying to pull him off AJ. "Stop, you're going to kill him!"

With a final grunt and one last punch Austin finally stops hitting him. He shrugs Maggie off, stands back up, and wipes the sweat off his forehead.

"Fuck," AJ mutters, somehow still conscious. However, he doesn't make a move to peel himself off the floor where he's plastered, face covered in blood.

"Oh my God," Maggie murmurs to herself, hand on her own forehead.

The sound of the elevator dinging again breaks the moment.

Austin spins around to see Hermosa's mascara stained face right before the doors close and she disappears. The floor is silent, save for AJ's pained groans. His eyes are closed and he cups his nose that very well might be broken. Maggie helps him to sit up.

"Fire him or I quit," Austin tells her, causing her to meet his eyes. "I swear."

With that he turns away and walks to the elevator, leaving Maggie on the floor knelt next to AJ, surrounded by broken glass, spilled blood, and the fragments of what used to be a friendship.

Chapter 27

It's Saturday afternoon, and the beginning of what he's sure will be an extremely long night. AJ is parked outside the Downtown LA hotel where Kadence is getting ready for the NAMAs. He's got his brand new suit in a bag in the backseat, and a dwindling bag of cocaine in the console. He takes it out and pulls down his visor mirror. He looks like he's been run over by a dump truck. Two black eyes, a busted lip, a slightly bent nose, and a lot of swelling everywhere.

Fuck Austin and fuck Maggie and fuck Hermosa.

On the plus side, Kadence hasn't seen him yet, and he knows the second she does it's going to send her into an instant tizzy. And also, his nose is already so grotesque looking, what he's about to do couldn't make it much worse.

However, he still takes care, putting a little bit on his pinky nail and then sticking his finger directly into his right nostril. It's a tighter space than it usually is; dried blood caked around the outside. He presses on the other nostril and grimaces, sniffing through the pain. He switches sides and does it again, hoping for numbness.

He rides the elevator up to the penthouse and is granted access by Mike and Bill into her room. The hotel room has been transformed into a high-end beauty salon. The smell of excessive hairspray and perfume is enough to give him an instant headache. Kadence sits perched like a princess upon her throne while one women works on her hair and another on her face. She's wrapped in a white robe, glass of pineapple and vodka within reaching distant; for her nerves is what he's sure she's told her hired help. Her makeup artist finishes applying a coat of mascara. His girlfriend blinks it into place, and then looks over to where he stands. Her entire demeanor shifts into horrified.

"Oh. My. God," she breathes out while glaring at him like she could kill. "You've got to be kidding. What in the ever loving hell happened to your fucking face?"

"I got into a fight," AJ says simply.

"Right before the NAMAs?" She asks, her voice verging on hysterical. Her help keeps right on powdering her face and straightening her hair, and she keeps right on unraveling. "Right before my big night you decide to be a brawler? Really?"

"Yup," AJ says, plopping down in a chair. "Been plannin' it for months."

"You are *so* inconsiderate. So reckless. So...*weak*." She scoffs condescendingly then. "You look like you got gang jumped. Did you even get a single punch in on the other guy?" She doesn't wait for him to respond before she's silencing him with her hand. "Never mind. I don't care. We've gotta get you into makeup. Catharine, can you do something?"

Catharine stops working on her and looks at him. "Can I call backup?"

"Yes," Kadence replies instantly. "Call every trustworthy and competent makeup artist in the city. Call a plastic surgeon. Order a skin graph. Borrow a mask from the props department. I don't care. Just fix his face."

"I'm on it," Catharine says assuredly, her fingers moving quickly over the screen of her phone. "I'm sending out a mass text to the rest of my team to get here STAT."

"Oh my goodness," Kay sighs dramatically. "Thank you so much. I love you. You're a lifesaver."

"No problem," Catharine tells her, and then looks over at him. "You ready to get started, AJ?"

"I'm a blank canvas, Cath," AJ tells the makeup artist with a troublesome smile. "Paint a pretty picture, will you?"

Kadence cuts her eyes at him. "You better be glad I've got people who can make you presentable."

"I've got two loose teeth, too, baby," AJ says with a pleased leer as he sits back in the chair and Catharine gets to work. "Your ass better pray they don't fall out on the red carpet. I'd sure hate to embarrass you."

She just glares at him. "Can we get a shot for the swelling?" She says over her shoulder, not breaking her heated stare. He won't break it either. When there's no response she finally flips her head around. "Shelly, can you not tell that I'm a little busy right now? Call my doctor and tell him to have a damn cortisone injection ran over!"

"Yes, ma'am. Kadence. Kay," Shelly's nervous voice comes from the other room. "I'll get right on that."

~

Two hours later and you can barely tell anything had happened to him. He's got on an all black tux. She's got on a black gown. Her back is out and the long fastener to the 3.1 million-dollar diamond necklace she has on hangs down her spine. He holds the limousine door open for her like a gentleman, and off they go.

"Do you know it was exactly nine months to the day that I first laid eyes on you?" Kadence says out of the blue a mile later, breaking the silence. "At an awards show, ironically enough."

AJ turns to face her. He had previously been staring out the window at all the traffic, but now he's staring at her. Because he doesn't know what she's talking about.

She's smiling at him dreamily now. "The Oscars," she says simply. "You were there with an older blonde woman. Your agent, I think. I don't know if you saw me, but I saw you." She reaches out and touches his face, rubs a finger across his jawline. "And the second I did…I knew I had to have you."

He's speechless. The affectionate gesture is random at best, and he no longer knows how to take her when she's acting docile. *Acting* being the operative word. He also doesn't know how to take what she's just told him. He never knew she saw him that night at the Oscars nine months ago. He met her A&R that night, and always assumed he'd given her his name. That's still probably how it went down, but once she found out that the handsome nobody she was ogling from a distance could write lyrics, well, she had to have him. At first, he'd thought she wanted a collaborator. A little later, a lover. But now he can see that what she really wanted, what she always wanted, what she was looking for in all those other guys before him that she couldn't find, was a whipping post.

Her hand on his face gets a bit firmer. "Don't make me regret pursuing you, getting you, and making you my boyfriend," she tells him seriously.

And then she scoots back to her side of the limo.

While she's admiring herself in her compact, he pops the first pill of the night.

The red carpet is blurry. Not that anybody is asking him anything. He is merely there to prop her up, be her arm candy, not unlike all his fake dates. The red carpet is bustling, and he feels detached from it all. He's alone in a sea of people. He doesn't mean a thing to a single one of them. And nothing means anything to him.

At some point they make it inside and the show starts.

He's sitting in one of the best seats in the house, fucked himself right into it, and if he could sell it to the highest bidder he would. His proximity to the stage is bittersweet, because the purposed "artists" who grace it lack the ingenuity he has but nobody sees.

She wins six awards for songs that he wrote word for word that she didn't contribute a single syllable to. She doesn't ask him to come on stage with her, and he doesn't offer. She doesn't thank him in even one of the six speeches.

Dominique is nominated for best new artist and best urban contemporary song. He loses to white people, but AJ doubts he would have thanked him for writing that whole fucking mixtape that got him in the damn door in the first place.

People are so ungrateful.

Use, use, use.

He shouldn't do anything for anybody anymore.

He'd pop another pill if the fucking cameras weren't on him. The cameras are always on him because he's always with her and she's the star of every show.

Kadence closes the show in a dress that for all intents and purpose is see-thru. Her boobs, ass, and crotch are covered in black panels, but the rest is as sheer as can be. As long as it's America's Sweetheart wearing something like that, it's viewed as artistic and elegant, and he already knows she'll be on every best-dressed list in the morning for both of her ugly dresses. He watches from his seat as she prances, and gyrates, and sings her cold little heart out. Everyone is on their feet but him. He knows they wish they knew the words, but it's a world premiere, and they didn't write the damn thing. The light show makes him feel like he could have a seizure. The crowd is going ape shit.

And then it's over. But it's never over.

It's only eleven-thirty and the album doesn't drop till midnight and there are after parties to attend. There are always after parties to attend. She reverts back to her girly, country-pop days, changing into a pink, frilly party dress. Once in the venue, he goes straight to the bar and she goes straight to the throng of people who were all waiting for her to arrive.

Sailor, the models, and the Beverley Hills girls are all there. Shelly, Susie, and the actresses are all there. Eddie, Salar, and all the other producers are there. Half of the awards show is there. Half of Hollywood is there. Actors she may or may not have fucked. Everyone is hugging her, congratulating her, gushing all over her. He couldn't get her alone for a minute if he wanted to, which he doesn't. He bets she wishes she could get a minute alone so she could–

That's when he gets an idea.

He takes a walk down the back hall, and finds Bill stationed near the bathrooms.

"Hey, Kay wants her clutch," AJ says to the tall man in all black, keeping his voice neutral and his face convincing.

Bill doesn't say anything. Bill never says much. Though AJ's sure he's heard it all; their loud and rough sex, their line snorting, and bottle breaking, and screaming matches where they call each other every name in the book. Bill considers him for a moment, stoic as ever. And then he relents, pulling it out of his deep pocket, and passing it discreetly to AJ. All of this time has obviously led the old washed-up bodyguard turned contraband guardian to trust him. He shouldn't.

"Thanks, man," AJ says with a smile.

Bill just nods. He'll be fired by dawn.

AJ exits back out into the main party, carrying the clutch low and out of view. He walks right past all the dancing celebrities. He walks right past all the drunken cohorts who wish they were celebrities. He walks right past all the happy and hopeless celebrators. He walks right past her where she's hob-knobbing in the center of the room with two of her gold trophies under her arms and a big fake smile plastered on her face. She never looks up at him, and he keeps right on walking. Right out the door.

He doesn't want to stay with her, and he knows all the hotels Downtown will be booked. So he takes a taxi down the road to Hollywood, and uses the credit card he finds in the clutch to check into a top floor suite.

He doesn't bother to turn on the lights or the television. He kicks off his shoes, shrugs off his suit jacket, and un-tucks his dress shirt from his pants. He pulls the string of the lamp that sits on the desk, which gives him just enough light to see what's behind the cabinet doors. None of the little bottles in the mini bar are big enough to fill the type of void he has. So he immediately calls room service and orders a bottle of bourbon that costs him three times what it would have cost had he bought it at a store. He doesn't care. It arrives ten minutes later with a bucket of ice and a glass tumbler. He tips the attendant and immediately pours his first glass. He made sure to grab the Advil bottle with the ten Xanax and ten Valium inside before he left his apartment earlier in the day. So far he's only used one. He pulls it out of his pocket now and shakes all the pills out on the table. He then takes the bag of coke he knew he'd find out of Kadence's clutch, and dumps all of the powder out onto the table next to the pills. He double checks the deadbolt on the door, and then pulls up a chair.

An hour later and three lines in, he pops two Xanax and washes them down with the brown liquid. It's almost five in the morning and he's wired tight and flying high. It's almost five and he wonders if Kadence is still out. The album has been out for five hours. He wonders if it's doing well. He wonders if his bank account is rising. He wonders how much more money that bitch is making off it than he is. He wonders what his mother would think if she saw him like this. He wonders what Anjanae would think if she saw him like this. He wonders if Julius Collins would take pity on him and remove his name off whatever Hollywood no-hire list he put it on if he could see him like this. He wonders if his clients would still want to fuck him if they could see him like this. He wonders why he's still wondering about any of this. He clearly hasn't done enough.

He's drinking straight out of the bottle now and it's half empty. The coke and the pills must have cancelled each other out because he feels neither alive nor calm. He feels stuck, stuck in quicksand and going down at a rapid rate. He gets up and stumbles across the room to the mini bar, choosing the miniature bottle of Grey Goose and cracking it open. Craving the taste he hates, craving pain while wishing for relief. He takes a gulp and half of it sloshes out of his mouth. It's awkward to drink out of something so small, and he's long lost his coordination. He throws the bottle across the room and watches as it hits the wall but doesn't break, the rest of the disgusting liquid left in it spilling all over the hotel floor. He ambles back across the room, tripping and knocking over the desk chair. He curses from the spot where he's fallen, but slides into a kneeling position nonetheless and arranges another line on the table. It's hard to get it straight when everything is spinning, and he ends up licking up what he can't get snorted. Using the pad of his finger to get the last little bit, then holding it to his nose and sniffing. After a while he gets up and goes to sit on the bed. He wrings his hands and rubs his skin as the seconds tick by, Cartier timepiece ticking on his wrist. The sun is rising over the Hollywood sign in the distance outside his window. He gets up and closes the blinds, shutting out the light, and then he takes a Valium.

He should probably wash it down with water. He should probably drink some water. He staggers to the bathroom and grabs one of the empty glasses off the vanity, flipping on the sink. It runs for a long while before he remembers what he's supposed to be doing. He realizes he's gripping the neck of the bourbon bottle; he must have picked it up again somewhere along the way. Fuck the water, he thinks. He's already swallowed the pill; it went down just fine without out. But he's hot. He's *so* hot. He turns the faucet back off and takes a good look at himself in the mirror. His face is covered in sweat. The makeup they put on him earlier has been sweated off, the shot more than likely wearing off. His face looks bruised and swollen. Not that he can feel his face, or anything for that matter. But he can see, and he can see that he looks like shit. Sallow skin, bags under his eyes, dried blood caked around his nostrils. A wave of repulsive rage comes over him and then he's swinging the bottom of the bottle at the mirror. It shatters in the middle, splintering outward in jagged lines. It drops out of his hand. He's got sticky bourbon all over him now. He knows he probably reeks of alcohol, but he can't smell. Something about broken mirrors and bad luck briefly flits though his mind as he goes back out into the room. He falls again on his way to the bed and this time stays down. The room is moving as he lays perfectly still, willing it to stop. He blinks his eyes a few times as the bottom of the bed goes in and out of focus, and then everything fades to black.

There's a sound. A thud. Either blood rushing in his ears or somebody at the door.

Thud, thud, thud. Rapid sound. Too loud.

He thinks about where he's at without opening his eyes, scared of the spinning scenery he'll see. He remembers the awards. He remembers coming to a hotel. He remembers a lot of drugs. He thinks he's on the floor, but he's not for sure.

Thud, thud, thud.

It was probably housekeeping.

"Go away!" He yells muffled into the carpet. *Carpet.* What his face is on feels like carpet. He *is* on the floor.
Thud, thud, thud, thud, thud.
He very slowly raises himself up and opens his eyes. Everything is blurry and he has to sit there for a while before trying to stand, combating the hot water rushing in his mouth, the intense urge to vomit up everything inside of him. All the while the person on the other side continues to bang on the door. He stands on unstable legs and wobbles to the door, unlocking and opening it without checking the peephole, fully prepared to cuss a maid out.

And there stands Kadence. She's in her incognito getup, wearing a hoodie that swallows her whole, a baseball cap, leggings, and sneakers. Her pupils are the size of saucers and he knows instantly that she's as high as a kite. She's got that wild look on her face and he can tell right away that they are about to fight.

"You look like a drug addict," she says, pushing past him into the room.

"You are a drug addict," he tells her, closing the door and turning around to look at her. "How the hell did you find me and who gave you my room number? Somebody at the front desk is getting fired."

"I'm Kadence Jane," she says simply, as if that's the answer to everything. Which it is. She grabs a bottle of Belvedere out of the open mini bar, breaks the seal, and takes a long swig. Her lips come off the bottle with a pop, and she momentarily holds a hand to her mouth as she grimaces the liquid down. "I've been calling you for eighteen hours straight and you ain't picked up once. What the fuck am I supposed to think? Am I not supposed to go investigate?" She itches her nose frantically for a second, then sniffs. "You ain't got a whore stashed in the bathroom, do you?" She slurs sloppily. "I'm not going to have to beat a bitch, am I?"

"You haven't been calling me for eighteen hours," he says, choosing to ignore her other comments. "I was just with you a few hours ago."

"It's eight o'clock at night, idiot," she tells him, taking another long gulp.

AJ is totally thrown by this, going silent as he attempts to absorb it into his fog filled, dopamine-depleted mind. And sure enough, when she walks over to the window and opens the blinds, the sun is burning low in the sky about to set.

"God, look at this shit," she says when she catches sight of the desk with the empty baggie, coke dust, and pills all over it. "Were you trying to stop your heart?"

"Maybe."

"You stole my coke," she says, more observation than question.

"Well you obviously found more," he replies cattily, sitting down at the desk and starting to form all of the left-over residue into a line.

"What are you doing?" She asks in her highly annoying, shrill voice.

"I need to get woke up," he says simply, picking up his discarded dollar, rolling it back up, and holding it to a nostril. "It's a new day."

"Stop!" She yells, smacking the dollar out of his hand. "It's mine you can't have anymore," she tells him pettily, messing up his line with her other hand.

"You've already done some today!" He yells back, smacking her hand away. "I haven't done any since last night. You're fine. You don't need to do anymore." Once she walks away he starts re-forming his line. "Have you even been to sleep?"

"Nope," she says, walking back over to the mini bar and grabbing a travel size Patron this time. "It's been a party!' She takes a drink. "And you missed it. You missed the entire thing. All our hard work...all the long hours in the studio...and when the album finally comes out you're not there to celebrate." She circles clumsily around the room. "You made me look like I picked a real winner. Everybody wanted to know where the hell you were and I had no idea what to tell them."

"Sorry," he says unapologetically, and then snorts up the rest of the coke.

She shakes her head. "I'm about to be done with you."

"Well I am done with you," he replies, wiping his nose and then standing back up. "Tell all your girlfriend's the going rate is five comma nine, nine, nine a night and to have their money ready at the door."

"You sound like a conceited ass lunatic," she tells him absently as she removes her cap and fluffs her hair one-handedly. "You're not making any sense."

"And when the hell do you make sense?" He asks, grabbing the little bottle of tequila out of her hand. "You're loaded ninety-eight percent of the time." He takes a swig. "And if there ain't a damn teleprompter in front of your face or a handler holdin' your hand you don't even know what the fuck to say."

"You do realize if we break up you aren't going to have shit, right?" She asks him, glaring as she steals the bottle back, sending liquid flying with her vigor. "You will *never* have an opportunity like this again." She takes a sip and swallows. "How are you going to survive without me, AJ?" She cocks her head to the side and gives him the condescending smirk. "How are you going to afford your *lifestyle* habits without me? How are you going to make money without me?"

"Was one of my prior sentences too complex for you to comprehend?" He asks, throwing her pettiness right back at her as he walks away. "Do I need to annunciate slower, take the unnecessary words out, do it how they did it on the Hooked On Phonics videos you probably had to watch as a kid?" He turns around to look at her then, reaching back

into the mini bar without looking and grabbing a random bottle.
"Don't feel bad, I bet a lot of things go over a lot of the kids' heads that
grew up in that poor ass backwoods town you're secretly from."

She drains her bottle and tosses it across the room. "You think
you're a *fucking* genius. But you ain't *shit*, AJ."

He takes a gulp of what he thinks is whiskey and grimaces.
"Newsflash. You *aren't* shit either, *Caroline*."

She crosses her arms. "Well the world sure seems to think I am."

"That's because that world don't know the real you." He leans
back against the dresser with a disconcerting smile and looks her dead in
her eyes. "The world only knows Kadence Jane. They don't know the
hateful, cruel, conniving, socially ignorant, morally deficient,
unsympathetic, self-centered, *nasty* little bitch that I know. What if the
world could hear some of the things you say behind closed doors? What if
they could see the way your team tirelessly throws themselves into
crafting your facades for you? What if they could see you slipping in and
out of consciousness after one too many recreational sleeping pills? What
if they could see you drinking straight out of the bottle? What if they could
see you snorting coke through their money?" His voice drops an octave.
"What if they could see you on your knees? What if they could see some
of the positions that I—and probably many others—have put you in? Have
had you in."

She just glares at him.

"Well the world would be just heartbroken, Caroline," he says
simply, holding the bottle back up to his lips. "The world would want a
fucking refund."

"I'm leaving." She secures her cap back on her head and looks
away. "This hotel. You. We're over." She swipes her hand over the
dresser and picks up the keys she placed there earlier with her fingers.
That's when, for the first time since she arrived, he realizes they are his
car keys.

"Are those my keys?"

"I don't know," she says dismissively, walking on towards the
door.

"I know you did not drive *my* car over here fucked up," he teems.

"You shouldn't have left it at *my* hotel if you didn't want me to
drive it."

"You don't even know how to drive a clutch, you probably fucked
it all up. That's a vintage 1969 mint condition Pontiac GTO. Do you know
that? Do you know what you just did?"

"Ohh a GTO!" She exclaims theatrically. "Gotdamn." She turns around just to roll her eyes at him. "I drive Bentleys and Porsches, get real. And I know how to drive a fucking stick. I got here, didn't I?"

"Well you're sure as hell not driving it back," he tells her matter-of-factly, starting to walk towards her with a menacing slowness. "You're drunk. And high."

"So are you." She undoes the deadbolt on the door behind her back

"I fuckin' slept it off, I'm fine." He's closing in on her.

"No you're not and I'm not giving them back," she heckles, easing the door open with her foot and not breaking eye contact with him as she does so.

"Give me the fuckin' keys, Kadence," he says between clenched teeth, his fists unconsciously clenching at his sides.

She smiles then. "If you want them back you're going to have to take them from me." Suddenly she's seizing the top half of the shattered bourbon bottle at her feet and hurling it at him. He ducks fast to avoid being hit with broken glass, and she dodges, slipping out the door at a dead run.

He chases after her down the hallway, leaving the trashed hotel room behind. She's stepping into the first elevator. The doors are closing. He jams his hand in the small space to stop it from closing. Her hand juts out to push his hand out of the way. They fight each other's limbs, and then he feels something sharp—a piece of broken bottle she managed to hang on to, perhaps the pointy part of his keys—slicing one of his fingers. It's enough to make him pull back just for a second, and that's all it takes

"Catch a fucking cab," he hears her sneer as the doors close in his face.

"Dammit," he curses. He frantically pushes the down button on the adjacent elevator as fast as he can, sucking the blood off his cut finger as he waits. It arrives quickly and he jumps on, pressing L for the lobby.

His elevator gets to bottom floor a second after hers does and he races out the second he spots her. She's zipped her jacket up and pulled the hood down over her head on the ride down. He comes up behind her and grabs her arm. She aggressively yanks it away.

"Please don't make me make a scene in this lobby because I promise you I will," he seethes in her ear.

"I'm about two seconds away from hitting you," she retorts under her breath.

"See if I don't hit you back this time."

"I'll call the police."

"Go ahead," he says as he follows her out into the parking garage. "When they get here I'll make sure to ask them to breathalyze you."

"Oh yeah cause you wouldn't fail that either."

"Then we'll both go to jail I guess." He spots his car and rushes over to it, getting to the driver's side before she can and standing in front of the door, blocking her from being able to get in. "You're not going anywhere give them back."

"No."

He roughly grabs her wrist, prying her fingers apart with his other hand.

"Get the fuck off of me!" She yells.

"Shut up." He gets them from her and starts undoing the lock.

The moment he gets the door open she's shoving him with more force than someone her weight should have, scrambling into the car like an un-caged animal.

"Kadence! Get the fuck out of my car!"

"No!" She pants back breathlessly.

He grabs her waist and starts trying to forcibly pull her out of the car. She kicks him in the crotch and he stumbles back. He takes a deep breath, scoffs, and then gives her a big shove onto the passenger side.

"Fuck it," he mutters, getting behind the wheel, slamming the door shut, and putting the keys in the ignition. The doors lock and the engine comes to life.

"Oh now you're going to take me hostage?" She assesses angrily.

"You had your chance to get out," he tells her with an unnerving calmness, harshly throwing the car into reverse. He backs out and then peels off, making the tires squeal as they lay down black marks on the cement floors.

"You're fucking crazy. Wait till I tell my manager about this." She's turning around in her seat, reaching behind her to root around in the backseat.

"What are you doing?" He asks hastily. He makes it to the end of the parking garage and swipes the card he finds on the inside of his windshield. As soon as the bar rises he guns it. The quick motion sends her flying back forward as he jets out in front of a line of cars coming down Hollywood Boulevard.

"What are you doing, idiot, trying to give me whiplash?" She snaps.

"Should have been facing forward," he replies with aplomb, speedometer ticking upwards. The streetlights are just starting to come on in the city. He wonders briefly if he's turned his headlights on, but then the concern is gone.

"And you should have let me drive." She's turned around again.

"I *said* what are you doing," he fumes at her, turning around to see for himself and swerving in the process. A car honks. He gets it back between the lines.

"I told you I'm calling my manager." She's grabbing her purse off the floor of the backseat, pulling her phone out of the side pocket.

"I'm taking you back to your fucking hotel, you don't need to call anyone." His foot presses harder on the gas. "Do you really think I want you in my car?" He crosses three lanes of traffic at once. Another car honks. He holds his middle finger up to the window.

"I'll call whoever the fuck I want to call," she smarts off, and he sees her pressing buttons out of the corner of his eyes.

"No you won't." He reaches over and snatches her phone out of her hands.

"Oh you jackass." She gets out of her seat and leans over, grabbing at the hand he's got the phone in. He attempts to control the car with the other hand while she obscures his vision with her flailing body.

"I know you don't, but act like you've got some damn sense and get back in your own seat!" He yells at her.

"Not until you give me back my phone!" She yells back. In her fit of rage she grips the wheel for leverage and ends up jerking it, almost causing them to hit a taxi in the next lane.

"God dammit, Kadence!" He curses, jerking it back. "Get your fucking hands off my wheel!"

"Fuck you!" She sears, slapping him hard.

He takes his free hand and pushes her out of his face, palm on her face. She bites him and he flings her back to her side of the car.

She lets out a noise that sounds like a growl.

He can see her moving in his peripheral.

He can see her coming back at him and he instinctively jerks the wheel in the opposite direction of what he thinks she's going to take it. But she doesn't grab the wheel this time. And he ends up crossing into the other lane in front of a truck. The driver sounds his horn. AJ jerks it out of the way at the last minute, but ends up overcorrecting. They hit the median going no less than ninety. He hears her scream. He feels the wheels leave the ground. As they flip through the air he catches the glimmer of headlights coming the other way. He braces himself for impact.

And then they collide.

With a crash.

To be continued...